Praise for
DARK DELICACIES®

"The alliterative title hints at something unsettling: *Dark
Delicacies*, a new anthology that can be described only as
horrifying." —*Los Angeles Times*

"Howison and Gelb have plundered their Rolodexes to re-
cruit a formidable lineup of horror's top creative talents."
—*Publishers Weekly*

"Howison was clearly successful in delivering his goal: a
diverse assortment focused solely on 'total horror.' To illus-
trate the variety he chose to bookend the anthology with
two vastly different luminaries—Ray Bradbury and Clive
Barker." —*Fangoria*

"[A] dark gem . . . The original stories commissioned especially for this collection revel in the macabre."
—*Library Journal*

"A good anthology, with impressive highs." —*Locus*

"Vampires, zombies, werewolves, necromancers all get
their due." —*Kirkus Reviews*

"Like any good anthology, *Dark Delicacies* weaves all over—and through—the world of horror. Here you will find everything from ghosts, zombies, maniac killers, vampires, and more . . . The primary mission for Del and Jeff with their horror anthology is to make it genuinely horrifying. Several of the writers within push themselves to the task admirably . . . If you want variety in your horror anthology, then this is the book for you."

—*Feo Amante's Horror Thriller*

"Del and Jeff did a great job compiling the kind of work that is indicative of its author, while at the same time giving some new voices a chance to shine among the big boys. There should be no hesitation on your part as to whether or not to pick this up, but just in case there is, I'll tell you now: Do it. Who knows how long it'll take for another collection of this caliber to be put together."   —DreadCentral.com

"An impressive lineup of authors."   —*Emerald City*

"Using top-notch names in the horror field, you should take notice . . . stories so sinister that it nudges *Dark Delicacies* into must-have territory."   —*Bookgasm*

DARK DELICACIES®

EDITED BY

DEL HOWISON AND JEFF GELB

ACE BOOKS, NEW YORK

THE BERKLEY PUBLISHING GROUP
Published by the Penguin Group
Penguin Group (USA) Inc.
375 Hudson Street, New York, New York 10014, USA
Penguin Group (Canada), 90 Eglinton Avenue East, Suite 700, Toronto, Ontario M4P 2Y3, Canada
(a division of Pearson Penguin Canada Inc.)
Penguin Books Ltd., 80 Strand, London WC2R 0RL, England
Penguin Group Ireland, 25 St. Stephen's Green, Dublin 2, Ireland (a division of Penguin Books Ltd.)
Penguin Group (Australia), 250 Camberwell Road, Camberwell, Victoria 3124, Australia
(a division of Pearson Australia Group Pty. Ltd.)
Penguin Books India Pvt. Ltd., 11 Community Centre, Panchsheel Park, New Delhi—110 017, India
Penguin Group (NZ), 67 Apollo Drive, Rosedale, North Shore 0745, Auckland, New Zealand
(a division of Pearson New Zealand Ltd.)
Penguin Books (South Africa) (Pty.) Ltd., 24 Sturdee Avenue, Rosebank, Johannesburg 2196,
South Africa

Penguin Books Ltd., Registered Offices: 80 Strand, London WC2R 0RL, England

This is a work of fiction. Names, characters, places, and incidents either are the product of the authors' imaginations or are used fictitiously, and any resemblance to actual persons, living or dead, business establishments, events, or locales is entirely coincidental. The publisher does not have any control over and does not assume any responsibility for author or third-party websites or their content.

DARK DELICACIES®

An Ace Book / published by arrangement with Carroll & Graf Publishers, an imprint of Avalon Publishing Group, Inc.

PRINTING HISTORY
Carroll & Graf edition / 2005
Ace mass-market edition / September 2007

A complete list of copyrights can be found on page 349.
DARK DELICACIES® is a registered trademark of Dark Delicacies.
Cover photograph of Stone Wall with Iron Gates by Luciana Frigerio/Images.com.
Cover photograph of Girl Holding Axe by Andrey Armyagov/Shutterstock.com.
Cover design by Annette Fiore.

ISBN: 978-0-441-01530-6

ACE
Ace Books are published by The Berkley Publishing Group,
a division of Penguin Group (USA) Inc.,
375 Hudson Street, New York, New York 10014.
ACE and the "A" design are trademarks belonging to Penguin Group (USA) Inc.

PRINTED IN THE UNITED STATES OF AMERICA

10 9 8 7 6 5 4 3 2

To my wife, Sue, partner, and more importantly, friend;
and to my three families—the one I inherited through blood,
the one I chose through marriage, and the one I found in friendship.
This could never have happened without you.
—Del Howison

For my wife and son, who always encourage me
to grow from strength to strength.
—Jeff Gelb

CONTENTS

FOREWORD, BACKWARD, UPSIDE DOWNWARD

RICHARD MATHESON

WHEN DEL FIRST invited me to a book signing at his store, Dark Delicacies, my probable reaction was: Okay, another signing, another bookstore.

I was right about the first part—a pleasant experience meeting some of my readers, gratification at being praised by them—plus, to be crass, some additional royalty money.

I was completely wrong about my second guesstimation. Dark Delicacies is most definitely not just "another bookstore." It is the most unique bookstore of its kind I have ever seen, a treasure trove of all those books whose dark delicacy makes them good-to-great-to-superb reading.

Plus hundreds of additional items that create within its walls a magical, mystical, provocative, and totally evocative environment—posters, photographs, objets noir-d'art, and gifts of all variety that possess a definitely, darkly, delicate fascination.

Not forgetting the thousands of volumes from the most current publication to classic fiction and nonfiction.

In brief, a delightful location wherein to amble, peruse, and enjoy. My God, even the bathroom has intriguing artwork on the walls!

Signing my books at Del's store has always been rewarding. How he lets it be known that I—and all the other writers, artists, and filmmakers—will be present, pen (or Marks-O-Lot) in hand, I have no idea.

I do know that making a bookstore of such a limited nature succeed is damnably difficult, incredibly demanding. Del and his hardworking wife, Sue, have done it though and continue to do it, a decade from its inception.

In the past two years, I have been unable to appear at Dark Delicacies because of a back problem. Del has generously brought me books to sign and, on occasion, has even driven me from my home and, later, back to it so I can attend an occasional signing at their store.

All this remarkable dedication and skill has permeated this *Dark Delicacies* anthology. Buy it, read it, enjoy it, keep it, and cherish it. I know I will.

Richard Matheson
June 2005

DARK DELICACIES

AN INTRODUCTION

JEFF GELB

I'VE SPENT A fair amount of time around children; first with my own son, and more recently, with two nieces. One thing I've always noticed is that kids love to be scared. The caveat, of course, is that they want to laugh shortly thereafter! It appears that the instinct toward fear is genetic, but so is the instinct toward safety, which prompts the laughter later.

The question is obvious: What makes us crave a good fright? Surely life is full of enough things to frighten us, especially in a post-9/11 world. In fact, as a horror anthology editor for nearly twenty years now, I have wondered more than once since 9/11 whether there was still a place for horror stories in this twisted world. But writers have been as responsive as ever to requests for submissions to my books. The Hot Blood anthologies, edited with lifelong pal Michael Garrett, are still selling to a coterie of dedicated fans (thank you very much). And certainly the success at the movies of everything from *The Ring* to *The Grudge*, from *Dawn of the Dead* to *White Noise*, and a laundry list of others, proves that people do indeed crave being scared. That is, so long as they can then step back into broad daylight and be reassured that the world is no worse than the one they left behind when they stepped into the theater.

In fact, it appears to me that therein lies the secret of horror stories: they allow us to experience a certain sort of mental orgasm, if you will; an opportunity for a release of some of the tension and stress that life pushes at us daily. In a good horror story, whether it's on the printed page, in a movie theater, or on a TV screen, we can let loose the worst nightmares imaginable, follow them to the most horrifying extremes, and still come out safe on the other side. And whether in the story the good guys won or not, the viewer or reader wins by finishing the story, setting aside the entertainment, and then diving back into the world at large, relieved of some pressure he may not have even known was eating away at his insides.

As the coeditor of the Hot Blood series, I've often done book signings for Del Howison, who, along with his lovely wife, Sue, runs America's only all-horror bookstore. For that matter, it may be the only all-horror bookstore in the world. One thing's certain: It's one of the coolest places in the planet for any fan of horror in its myriad media, from movies to comics to books to toys, and with tons in between. During one fateful signing, Del told me that he had the idea to brand Dark Delicacies in a whole new way, as a series of anthologies by many of the writers he'd hosted throughout the store's decade-long existence. It sure made a world of sense to me. Who wouldn't want to write a story for the fine folks who'd helped them sell so many books to so many fans over the years? And why not an anthology series named after the store, whose name defines horror to its dedicated clients and fans? Now, this sounded great!

I've had a ball compiling the Hot Blood books with Michael Garrett. But the opportunity to stretch my editorial wings with an anthology whose only theme was "write the best damn scary story you can think of" was of particular appeal to me. And our writers have done just that. Del and I are still unabashed horror fans, and I know I speak for him when I look at our list of writers and just have to say, "Wow!" From the grand master himself, Ray Bradbury, to Richard Matheson, from Clive Barker to the very last horror story by the much-missed Richard Laymon—and not slighting anyone in between—we think this may well be the most significant horror anthology in the past twenty-five years (and that includes my own books!). These stellar authors were asked to write a story that defined modern horror for them, and they came through like troupers.

One promise Del and I made was to pepper the "names" in *Dark Delicacies* with young writers, who make the pilgrimage to Del's mecca regularly, buying printed inspirations and then spending evenings and weekends studying those works and honing their own dark craft. I'm confident that we have found folks whose names are destined to become as legendary as the people they share pages with.

All of this talent under one cover may lead you to wonder, "Who's in volume two?" To which we just have to say slyly, "Come back in a year or two and you'll find out!" Del and I have many friends in the horror field and we'll be knocking on many more doors.

This is an anthology whose time has come. *Dark Delicacies* presents horror for a new generation, for the world in which we now live. And unlike that crazy world around us, *Dark Delicacies* gives you the opportunity to be scared and then to put the book down and feel better afterward!

We're confident that you'll enjoy *Dark Delicacies,* and invite you to contact us with your impressions. We hope you will watch for news of future volumes because we're in this for the long haul. For, as long as kids love to be scared by playing boo, or teens flock to horror flicks, or older folks (like Del!) get a delicious shudder by the power of the word on a printed page, there's room in this world for *Dark Delicacies.*

So why not indulge in a real treat that's obviously also good for you: an all-new horror anthology from the very best in today's horror authors, who have been invited to bring you into their nightmares.

Welcome aboard and come on along for the ride. We promise it'll be scary, but we also promise you'll be smiling when you close the book. Now honestly, can real life make a better offer?

DARK DELICACIES®

THE REINCARNATE

RAY BRADBURY

AFTER A WHILE you will get over being afraid. There's nothing you can do, just be careful to walk at night. The sun is terrible; summer nights are no help. You must wait for cold weather. The first six months are your prime. In the seventh month the water will seep through with dissolution. In the eighth month your usefulness will fade. By the tenth month you'll lie weeping the sorrow without tears, and you will know then that you will never move again.

But before that happens there is so much to be finished. Many likes and dislikes must be turned in your mind before your mind melts.

It is new to you. You are reborn. And your birthplace is silk-lined and smelling of tuberoses and linens, and there is no sound before your birth except the beating of the earth's billion insect hearts. This place is wood and metal and satin, offering no sustenance, but only an implacable slot of close air, a pocket within the earth. There is only one way you can live, now. There must be an anger to slap you awake, to make you move. A desire, a want, a need. Then you quiver and rise to strike your head against satin-lined wood. Life calls you. You grow with it. You claw upward, slowly, and find ways to displace earth an inch at a time, and one night you crumble the darkness, the exit is complete, and you burst forth to see the stars.

Now you stand, letting the emotion burn you. You take a step, like a child, stagger, clutch for support—and find a marble slab. Beneath your fingers the carved story of your life is briefly told: Born—Died.

You are a stick of wood, trying to walk. You go outward from the land of monuments, into twilight streets, alone on the pale sidewalks.

You feel something is left undone. Some flower yet unseen somewhere you must see, some lake waiting for you to swim, some wine untouched. You are going somewhere, to finish whatever stays undone.

The streets have grown strange. You walk in a town you have never seen, a dream on the rim of a lake. You grow more certain of your walking, you go quite swiftly. Memory returns.

You know every lawn of this street, every place where asphalt bubbled from cement cracks in the oven weather. You know where the horses were tethered, sweating in the green spring at these iron waterfonts so long ago it is a fading mist in your brain. This cross street, where a light hangs like a bright spider spinning light across darkness. You escape its web into sycamore shadows. A picket fence sounds under your fingers. Here, as a child, you rushed by with a stick raising a machine-gun racket, laughing.

These houses, with the people and memories in them. The lemon odor of old Mrs. Hanlon who lived here, a lady with withered hands who gave you a withered lecture on trampling her petunias. Now she is completely withered like an ancient paper burned.

The street is quiet except for the sound of someone

walking. You turn a corner and unexpectedly collide with a stranger.

You both stand back. For a moment, examining one another, you understand something about one another.

The stranger's eyes are deep-seated fires. He is tall, thin, and wears a dark suit. There is a fiery whiteness in his cheekbones. He smiles. "You're a new one," he says.

You know then *what* he is. He is walking and "different," like yourself.

"Where are you going in such a hurry?" he asks.

"I have no time," you say. "I am going *somewhere*. Step aside."

He holds your elbow firmly. "Do you know *what* I am?" He bends close. "Do you not realize we are the same? We are as brothers."

"I—I have no time."

"No," he agrees, "nor have I, to waste."

You brush past, but he walks with you. "I know where you're going."

"Yes?"

"Yes," he says. "To some childhood place. Some river. Some house. Some memory. Some woman, perhaps. To some old friend's bed. Oh, I know, I know everything about our kind. I know." He nods at the passing light and dark.

"Do you?"

"That is always why we lost one's walk. Strange, when you consider all the books written about ghosts and lost walkers, and never once did the authors of those worthy volumes touch the true secret of why we walk. But it's always for—a memory, a friend, a woman, a house, a drink of wine, everything and anything connected with life and—LIVING!" He made a fist to hold the words tight. "Living! REAL living!"

Wordless, you increase your stride, but his whisper follows:

"You must join me later, friend. We will meet with the

others, tonight, tomorrow, and all the nights until at last, we win!"

"Who are the others?"

"The dead. We join against"—a pause—"intolerance."

"Intolerance?"

"We newly dead and newly interred are a minority, a persecuted minority. They make laws against us!"

You stop walking. "Minority?"

"Yes." He grasps your arm. "Are we wanted? No! Feared! Driven like sheep into a quarry, screamed at, stoned, like the Jews. Wrong, I tell you, unfair!" He lifts his hands in a fury and strikes down. "Fair, fair, is it fair? Fair that we melt in our graves while the rest of the world sings, laughs, dances? Fair, is it fair, they love while we lie cold, that they touch while our hands become stone? No! I say down with them, down! Why should we die? Why not the others?"

"Maybe . . ."

"They slam the earth in our faces and carve a stone to weigh us, and shove flowers in an old tin and bury it. Once a year! Sometimes not that! Oh, how I hate the living. The fools. The damn fools! Dancing all night and loving, while we are abandoned. Is that right?"

"I hadn't thought."

"Well," he cries, "we'll fix them."

"How?"

"There are thousands of us tonight in the Elysian grove. I lead. We will kill! They have neglected us too long. If we can't live, then they won't! And you will come, friend? I have spoken with many. Join us. The graveyards will open tonight and the Lost Ones will pour out to drown the unbelievers. You will come?"

"Yes. Perhaps. But I must go. I must find some place ahead. I will join you."

"Good," he says. You walk off, leaving him in shadow. "Good, good, good!"

✧

Up the hill now, quickly. Thank God the night is cold.

You gasp. There, glowing in the night, but with simple magnificence, the house where Grandma fed her boarders. Where you as a child sat on the porch watching skyrockets climb in fire, the pinwheels sputtering, the gunpowder drumming at your ears from the brass cannon your uncle Bion fired with his hand-rolled cigarette.

Now, trembling with memory, you know why the dead walk. To see nights like this. Here, when dew littered the grass and you crushed the damp lawn, wrestling, and you knew the sweetness of now, now, tomorrow is gone, yesterday is done, tonight lives!

Inside that grand tall house, Saturday feasts happen!

And here, here, remember? This is Kim's house. That yellow light around the back, that's her room.

You bang the gate wide and hurry up the walk.

You approach her window and feel your breath falling upon the cold glass. As the fog vanishes the shape of her room emerges: Things spread on the little soft bed, the cherrywood floor brightly waxed, and throw rugs like heavily furred dogs sleeping there.

She enters the room. She looks tired, but she sits and begins to comb her hair.

Breathlessly, you listen against the cold pane, and as from a deep sea, you hear her sing so softly it is already an echo before it is sung.

You tap on the windowpane.

She goes on, combing her hair gently.

You tap again, anxiously.

This time she puts down the comb and brush and rises to come to the window. At first she sees nothing; you are in shadow. Then she looks more closely. She sees a dim figure beyond the light.

"Kim!" You cannot help yourself. "It's me! Kim!"

You push your face forward into the light. Her face pales. She does not cry out; only her eyes are wide and her mouth opens as if somewhere a terrific lightning bolt in a sudden storm had hit the earth. She pulls back slightly.

"Kim!" you cry. "Kim."

She says your name, but you can't hear it. She wants to run, but instead she moves the window up and, sobbing, stands back as you climb in and into the light.

You close the window and stand, swaying there, only to find her far across the room, her face half-turned away.

You try to think of something to say, but cannot, and then you hear her crying.

At last she is able to speak.

"Six months," she says. "You've been gone that long. When you went away I cried. I never cried so much in my life. But now you can't be here."

"I am!"

"But why? I don't understand," she said. "Why did you come?"

"I was lost. It was very dark and I started to dream; I don't know how. And there in the dream you were and I don't know how, but I had to find my way back."

"You can't stay."

"Until sunrise. I still love you."

"Don't say that. You mustn't, anymore. I belong here and you belong there, and right now I'm terribly afraid. A long time ago we had a lot of things to love, a lot of things we did together. The things we did, the things we joked and laughed about, those things I still love, but—"

"I still think those thoughts. I think them over and over, Kim. Please try to understand."

"You don't want pity, do you?"

"Pity?" You half-turn away. "No, I don't want that. Kim, listen to me. I could come visit every night; we could talk just like we used to. It would be like a year ago. Maybe if we kept talking you would understand and you'd let me take you on long walks, or at least be a little bit closer."

"It's no use," she said. "We can't be closer."

"Kim, one hour every evening, or half an hour, anytime you say. Five minutes. Just to see you. That's all, that's all."

You try to take her hands. She pulls away.

She closes her eyes tightly and says, simply, "I'm afraid."

"Why?"

"I've been taught to be afraid."

"Is that it?"

"Yes, I guess that's it."

"But I want to talk."

"Talking won't help."

Her trembling gradually passes and she becomes more calm and relaxed. She sinks down on the edge of the bed, and her voice is very old in a young throat.

"Perhaps"—a pause—"maybe. I suppose a few minutes each night and maybe I'd get used to you and maybe I wouldn't be afraid."

"Anything you say. Tomorrow night, then? You won't be afraid?"

"I'll try not." She has trouble breathing. "I won't be afraid. I'll meet you outside the house in a few minutes. Let me get myself together and we can say good-night. Go to the window, step out, and look back."

"Kim, there's only one thing to remember: I love you."

And now you're outside and she shuts the window.

Standing there in the dark, you weep with something deeper than sorrow.

You walk away from the house.

Across the street a man walks alone and you recall he's the one that talked to you earlier that night. He is lost and walking like you, alone, in a world that he hardly knows. He moves on along the street as if in search of something.

And suddenly Kim is beside you.

"It's all right," she says. "I'm better now. I don't think I'm afraid."

She turns you in at an ice-cream parlor and you sit at the counter and order ice cream.

You sit and look down at the sundae and think how wonderful, it's been so long.

You pick up your spoon; then you put some of the ice cream in your mouth and then pause and feel the light in your face go out. You sit back.

"Something wrong?" the soda clerk behind the fountain says.

"Nothing."

"Ice cream taste funny?"

"No, it's fine."

"You ain't eating," he says.

"No."

You push the ice cream away from you and feel a terrible loneliness move in your body.

"I'm not hungry."

You sit very straight, staring at nothing. How can you tell her that you can't swallow, can't eat? How can you explain that your whole body seems to become solid and that nothing moves, nothing can be tasted.

Pushing back, you rise and wait for Kim to pay for the sundaes and then you swing wide the door and walk out into the night.

"Kim—"

"That's all right," she says.

You walk down toward the park. You feel her hand on your arm, a long way off, but the feeling is so soft that it is hardly there. Beneath your feet the sidewalk loses its solid tread. You move without shock or bump in something like a dream.

Kim says, "Isn't that great? Smell. Lilac."

You touch the air but there is nothing. Panicked, you try again, but no lilac.

Two people pass in the dark. They drift by, smiling to Kim. As they move away one of them says, fading, "Smell that? Something rotten in Denmark."

"What?"

"I don't see—"

"No!" Kim cries. And suddenly, at the sound of those voices, she bursts away and runs.

You catch her arm. Silently you struggle. She beats at you. You can hardly feel her fists.

"Kim!" you cry. "Don't. Don't be afraid."

"Let go!" she cries. "Let go."

"I can't."

Again the word was "can't." She weakens and hangs, lightly sobbing against you. At your touch she trembles.

You hold her close, shivering. "Kim, don't leave me. I have such plans. Travel, anywhere, just travel. Listen to me. Think. To have the best food, to see the best places, to drink the best wine."

Kim interrupts. You see her mouth move. You tilt your head. "What?"

She speaks again. "Louder?" you ask. "I can't hear."

She speaks, her mouth moves, but you hear absolutely nothing.

And then, as from behind a wall, a voice says, "It's no use. You see?"

You let her go.

"I wanted to see the light, flowers, trees, anything. I wanted to be able to touch you but, oh God, first, there, with the ice cream I tasted, it was all gone. And now I feel like I can't move. I can hardly hear your voice, Kim. A wind passed by in the night, but you hardly feel it."

"Listen," she said. "This isn't the way. It takes more than wanting things to have them. If we can't talk or hear or feel or even taste, what is there left for you or for me?"

"I can still see you, and I remember the way you were."

"That's not enough, there's got to be more than that."

"It's unfair. God, I want to live!"

"You will, I promise that, but not like this. You've been gone six months and I'll be going to the hospital soon."

You stop. You turn very cold. Holding to her wrist you stare into her moving face.

"What?!"

"Yes. The hospital. *Our* child. You see, you didn't have to come back, you're always with me, you'll always be alive. Now turn around and go back. Believe me, everything will work out. Let me have a better memory than this terrible night with you. Go back where you came from."

In this moment you cannot even weep; your eyes are dry. You hold her wrists tightly and then suddenly, without a sign, she sinks slowly to the ground.

You hear her whisper, "The hospital. Yes, I think the hospital. Quick."

You carry her down the street. A fog fills your left eye and you realize that soon you will be blind. It's all so unfair.

"Hurry," she whispers. "Hurry."

You begin to run, stumbling.

A car passes and you shout. The car stops and a moment later you and Kim are in the car with a stranger, roaring silently through the night.

And in the wild traveling you hear her repeat that she believes in the future and that you must leave soon.

At last you arrive, but by then you're almost completely blind and Kim has gone; the hospital attendant rushed her away without a good-bye.

You stand outside the hospital, helpless, then turn and try to walk away. The world blurs.

Then you walk, finally, in half-darkness, trying to see people, trying to smell any lilacs that still might be out there.

You find yourself moving down a ravine past the park. The walkers are there, the nightwalkers that gather. Remember what that man said? All those lost ones, all those lonely ones are forming tonight to move over the earth and destroy those who do not understand them.

The ravine path rushes under you. You fall, pick yourself up, and fall again.

The stranger, the walker, stands before you as you walk toward the silent creek. You look and there is no one else anywhere in the dark.

The strange leader cries out angrily, "They did not come! Not one of those walkers, not one! Just you. Oh, the cowards, damn them, the damn cowards!"

"Good." Your breath, or the illusion of breath, slows. "I'm glad they didn't listen. There must be some reason. Perhaps—perhaps something happened to them that we can't understand."

The leader shakes his head. "I had plans. But I am alone. Even if all the lonely ones should rise, they are not strong. One blow and they fall. We grow tired. *I* am tired—"

You leave him behind. His whispers die. The pulse beats in your head. You walk from the ravine and into the graveyard.

Your name is on the gravestone. The raw earth awaits you. You slide down the small tunnel into satin and wood, no longer afraid or excited. You lie suspended in warm darkness. You can actually shift your feet. You relax.

You are overwhelmed by a luxury of warm sustenance, like a great yeast, being washed away by a whispering tide.

You breathe quietly, not hungry, not worried. You are deeply loved. You are secure. This place where you are dreaming shifts, moves.

Drowsy. Your body is melting, it is small, compact, weightless. Drowsy. Slow. Quiet. Quiet.

Who are you trying to remember? A name moves out to sea. You run to fetch; the waves take it away. Someone beautiful. Someone. A time, a place. Sleepy. Darkness, warmth. Soundless earth. Dim tide. Quiet.

A dark river bears you faster and yet faster.

You break into the open. You are suspended in hot yellow light.

The world is immense as a snow mountain. The sun blazes and a huge red hand seizes your feet as another hand strikes your back to force a cry from you.

A woman lies near. Wetness beads her face, and there is a wild singing and a sharp wonder to this room and this world. You cry out, upside down, and are swung right side up, cuddled and nursed.

In your small hunger, you forget talking; you forget all things. Her voice, above, whispers:

"Dear baby. I will name you for him. For him . . ."

These words are nothing. Once you feared something terrifying and black, but now it is forgotten in this warmth and feeding content. A name forms in your mouth, you try to say it, not knowing what it means, only able to cry it happily. The word vanishes, fades, an erased ghost of laughter in your head.

"Kim! Kim! Oh, Kim!"

BLACK MILL COVE

LISA MORTON

IT WAS STILL dark, forcing Jim to pick his way through the treacherous thistles and spiderwebs by the narrow beam of his flashlight. He stumbled once, his boot caught in an overgrown rut, and then he found the dirt track that ran along the shoreline. Even though the season had just opened and this morning was one of the lowest tides of the year, he realized he was completely alone on the path, and he thought, *Maybe Maren was right—maybe this isn't such a good idea.*

He'd left his wife in the warm bunk back in the camper, but he knew she was only pretending to sleep; they'd argued the night before, and now she was giving him the well-honed Maren Silent Treatment. She'd read an article in the paper last week about two divers who had been attacked by a shark while abalone hunting. One man's arm had been ripped off, and he'd bled to death in the boat before they'd made it back to shore.

"It says this happened about twenty minutes from Fort Ross, north of San Francisco," Maren had told him. "It's where *we* go, Jim."

"Honey, you know I don't dive," he'd tried patiently to remind her.

"You wear a wet suit."

"You've been with me, Maren. We go at low tide and shore-pick. I've never been in water deep enough for a shark."

"But you always go alone, Jim. It's not safe."

Maren had already decided that she didn't want him to go, though, and the argument had ended very badly. She'd come with him on the winding three-hour drive from San Jose, but he knew she wouldn't make the two-mile hike down to the cove in the predawn chill, and he hadn't asked her to. He just hoped that when he returned to the campground with a full limit of the rare shellfish, when they'd been cleaned and it was her turn, the sweet scent of the delicacy frying in butter would cause her to forget the argument. It'd happened before. Too many times.

When they'd married, he'd made it clear that he was a hunter. Sure, he had a job, family, friends, other interests—but his life was about that oldest and most sacred of sports. Nothing made him feel so connected, so *pure,* as putting meat on the table, meat he'd taken with his own hands. The hunt was usually difficult, sometimes even tedious, but that always made the final victory that much more satisfying. In fact, Jim could have said that when he was out in the field, in pursuit of his prey, was the only time he really felt alive.

Maren had endured his hunting trips, but she never actually picked up a gun or fishing pole or catch bag. He supposed it was just the difference between men and women; men were by nature the hunters, women the gatherers. Still, he was constantly left mystified by her desires. Maybe a child . . . but when he'd suggested that, she'd told him she wasn't ready. He didn't understand what she was ready for. After five years of marriage, he still didn't understand.

He tried to stop thinking about Maren and their failing marriage as he hiked another mile along the thin dirt lane

worn between the weeds. The sound of the surf was somewhere off to his left, and its quiet, without the pounding of
an incoming tide, soothed him. The path veered to the
right, but Jim spotted the fallen gray tree limbs that he used
as a signpost. He left the trail behind, once again picking
his way through nettles and dying grass. He knew from experience that he would walk about two minutes before he
came to the cliff, and he moved slower now, swinging the
flashlight beam until he spotted the edge.

That was another thing Maren had argued with him
about—the difficulty of reaching Black Mill Cove. After a
three-hour drive on hairpin curves along the frightening
Highway 1, the cove was still another forty-minute trek
from the campground. It was bounded by steep cliffs on
three sides and open sea on the fourth; only one narrow
ravine, half hidden by brush, offered a way down that
didn't involve actual climbing. Jim liked to hunt alone;
what if he got hurt down there, couldn't get back up? He'd
tried to tell her, of course, that the cove's isolation was
what made it ideal. In the three years since he'd found
Black Mill Cove, he'd seen only one other hunter working
it, and he'd been scuba diving. He knew he could always
get his limit of the elusive abalone in the small cove.

By the time he pulled up at the cliff top above the sea,
all thoughts of Maren had fled his mind, as he focused on
the task before him. First he had to make his way cautiously along the edge until he spotted the patch of shrub
that he knew marked the ravine. He stepped carefully
around the brush, and lowered himself down onto a boulder three feet below it. He was in the ravine now, and he
knew he'd have to find the rest of the way down by touch
alone. He put the flashlight into his belt, and started down.

The ravine was choked with boulders that formed a natural, although steep stairway down, and he made it to the
bottom without incident. The pungent smells of salt and
exposed seaweeds and the volume of the surf noise, ampli-

fied here by the cliff walls, hit him as soon as he left the ravine, and he pulled the flashlight out again. By its light he saw the tide pools a few feet ahead of him, black water surrounded by encrusted rocks and gleaming, slippery kelp. He felt the thrill of the hunt gathering in him as he quickly lowered the backpack onto a hip-high flat rock, took off his outer hiking boots, checked his catch bag and iron, and, lastly, turned off his flashlight.

There was just the faintest hint of gray in the sky as he began picking his way over the slimy rocks and slick kelp. He heard tiny scuttlings around his feet, and the occasional sharp *pop* as he stepped on a floater bulb in the exposed seaweed. His eyes were already beginning to sting from the salt spray, so he lowered his mask, ignoring the snorkel. He walked until he thought he was about forty feet from shore and could just make out the darker shade of a large pool to his left. He lowered himself into the water until it was up to his waist, then began feeling under the rocks.

His gloved fingers brushed past spiny urchins and sucking anemones, and within minutes he was rewarded with the feel of a large shell. The creature was wedged several feet under the water, and to reach it with the iron he'd have to either hold his breath or use the snorkel. He decided to try the former, took a gulp of air, got a good heft on the iron, and ducked beneath the water.

He chipped the abalone's shell getting the iron under it, but finally jammed it under and began to pry. The abalone was strong and the position precarious, and his lungs were about to burst before he felt the strong shellfish foot give way. The abalone fell into his waiting hand, and he threw his head up out of the water.

It turned out to be only a medium-sized abalone, but it didn't pass through the gauge, and he knew it was a keeper. With a feeling of satisfaction he placed the creature into his catch bag, and then continued hunting.

The first pool revealed no more treasures, and so he clambered to the next. This one was separated from the ocean by only a thin wedge of rock and weed, and it was a large, promising pool. He entered it, and began feeling under the outcroppings, keeping one hand on the exposed rock near his head. He didn't flinch when a crab as big as a salad plate sidled across his fingers.

He had found nothing under the first rock, and now turned to the next. This one had a long underwater slope away from him, and the water was up to his chin as he struggled to reach the back. He was working his way left to right when he felt something that was long, thick, with jointed shreds on one end.

It felt, in fact, like a bony human arm.

He jerked back as if bitten, his breath catching. He'd felt what he'd sworn were wristbones, then fingers, with some flesh still attached.

That was ridiculous. A severed arm in a tide pool? It had to be a strange weed, or driftwood branch, trapped there at the last high tide. Or it could be (*shark*)—

He looked around, panicked for a moment, suddenly wishing he'd waited until sunup to come down here. No, he'd wanted to be hunting while the tide was still going out, before it began its mad rush back to land. He'd had to come down here in the pre-dawn salty blackness. Alone.

It was just light enough now so that he could make out his own fingers, if he held them up close before him. He pulled the mask away, squinted painfully until tears welled and washed the brine from his eyes, then he forced himself to reach back under the rock.

He found the thing again, got a good grip around it, and pulled. After a brief struggle it came free, and he brought it up out of the water, held it up before his eyes.

It was, without question, a human arm.

He cried out involuntarily and dropped the thing. It was

mostly bones, just a few tatters of skin or tendon still attached. The fingers seemed to be complete, and it ended about where the elbow would have started.

He backed frantically out of the pool, and up onto the rocks, his heart pounding, eyes tearing. He tried to scramble back more and fell flat as his feet slid on the kelp. The impact with the crusty rock, the pain as his gloves tore on the sharp facets of limpets and barnacles, jarred him enough to make him stop and consider the situation.

What the hell . . . how did . . . that get here?!

It had to be Maren's shark, right? He suddenly looked around and realized he was on the ocean side of the tide pool, peering out into barely seen, gently sluicing waves. Seaweed and driftwood bobbed here and there in the surf, sometimes breaking the surface like a head coming up out of the water. Or a fin.

He scrabbled backward on all fours and into the pool again. The *plosh* of his own body hitting the water startled him, and with fresh panic he realized the arm was in this pool—wasn't that it brushing against his ankle? He cried out, throwing himself at the nearest rock and hauling himself up over the edge of it, then turning to the shore and crawling toward it.

He crawled a few feet before he was calm enough to think again, then he stopped to catch his breath (*fuck, I'm about to pass out!*), and think.

Okay, obviously I've gotta get back to the camper, wake Maren up, and drive to the campground offices. They'd tried their cell phones before from the campground, but there was no signal out here. Then, he supposed, he'd have to come back here and show the authorities where he'd found the arm. Of course the tide would be in by then, and they'd probably have to send out their own divers.

He hoped they had shark protection.

He had a plan; he knew what he had to do. He realized he'd somehow gotten to the far left edge of the cove, and from here the easiest way back to shore would be to simply wade through several large pools.

Several large pools that could hold more pieces.

He knew instantly he couldn't do it. What if the next pool held something worse than an arm—like a head, a half-skeletal head with a terrible grin . . .

He forced himself to think again. By the dreary light he could just barely pick out a path back to where he'd left his backpack—and the flashlight. He told himself to move slowly and cautiously, but he was shaking and it was harder to keep his balance—

His foot slipped and one leg went down into a pool.

Even though it was only up to his ankle, he snatched his foot back up as if it'd been thrust into liquid fire. He found himself peering into the water, then at the rocks around him. Any of those lengths of stripped, whitened wood could have been bone instead, those broken shells, bits of nail, or teeth . . .

He tried to stop shaking, but couldn't. Instead, he reached for a large driftwood branch (*too big to be anything human!*), which would serve as a walking stick. Using his newly acquired staff, he thrust into tricky patches of kelp or rock before setting foot there, and so finally came to the bottom of the ravine.

He let himself fall onto the flat rock as he threw the makeshift staff away. For a moment he just lay there, feeling relieved, feeling safe and alive. After a moment, he stopped shaking. He was away from the tide pools and the terrible secrets he'd found there. He only had to climb the ravine, and he'd be safe.

He sat up, quickly opened the backpack long enough to get a towel to wipe his agonized eyes with, and was briefly surprised to see a black patch on the white towel; he was bleeding badly from a cut in his hand. He wrapped the towel around his palm, then pulled on his hiking boots, thrust his arms through the backpack straps, and started up the ravine.

It was light enough overhead now to see the top of the cliff as he clambered up over the rocks. He stopped occasionally to orient himself, then went on to the next rock. He was almost to the top when something blocked the light overhead. He looked up—

—and saw the shadow of a man standing there.

He started to call out, grateful for the presence of another (*living*) human being, but then something froze the shout in his throat, and he just stared instead.

The man overhead was carrying something, something big. It was black, and Jim thought it was probably a forty-gallon plastic trash bag, the kind Maren used as a liner at home. Except this bag was stuffed, bulging with something.

What the hell, is this guy dumping his goddamn trash out here?!

The man hefted the bag, and Jim saw that it was obviously very heavy.

And then he knew.

Oh my God. Oh Jesus fuck, fucking hell—

The bag was full of body parts.

And the man was stepping down into the ravine with it.

Jim didn't know if the man knew he was there; he thought he didn't, yet. Jim's ascent had been quiet, and he was in the shadow of the ravine, in a black wet suit. But if the man hadn't seen him yet, he would certainly discover him in the narrow ravine—

—because he was coming down now, and was only five feet above Jim.

Jim instinctively began scrambling down backward. There was no place to hide in the ravine, but maybe if he could get to the cove, to a boulder or a tide pool . . .

At least maybe he could reach the thick branch of driftwood he'd thrown aside, the one that had made a nice staff . . . or club.

The man above him was moving slowly, trying not to rip the overfilled bag, and that gave Jim a slight advantage, even though he was moving in reverse. He reached the big, flat rock where he'd rested only moments before, dropped beside it in a crouch, and felt around until his fingers closed on the reassuring bulk of the branch. Then he started working his way to the left, pressed against the rocky slope of the cliff.

He heard a small rattling of pebbles and jerked to a stop, his stomach in his throat, until he realized the sound had come from the other man, losing his footing and tearing a few pebbles loose from the wall of the ravine. He heard the man curse under his breath, then saw him emerge from the ravine, stepping onto the large, flat rock and setting the bag down there to rest.

Jim's heart was pounding in his ears as he dropped to a crouch, although there was no boulder to hide him. He could see the man because he was outlined by the sky, and because the man had now removed his own small penlight from a pocket. If the man turned the penlight in Jim's direction . . .

He didn't. He turned the ray on the tide pools before him, hefted the bag, and stepped off the rock, evidently intent on his task.

Jim knew he had two options now; the classic dilemma of fight or flight. He could try to wallop the man with his branch, but if the guy heard him and was armed, Jim would be dead. Or he could try to make it up the ravine before he was discovered; he knew that if he waited much longer, the lightening sky would point him out like a spotlight. He had to choose quickly.

He decided to opt for the latter, but thought he should wait until the man was as far away from the ravine as possible. Jim was young, and could probably outrace the man even if he were discovered, but again—if the man were armed . . . It was the only real choice. Jim slid out of the cumbersome backpack, since it would slow him down. Then he waited, kneeling beside the cliff wall, his eyes riveted to the man with the bag as he picked his way down to the first large tide pool. Once there, he set the bag down, reached in, pulled something out—

(*oh Jesus it's a leg, it's a fucking leg*)

—and put it carefully down into the tide pool. Once he'd placed it there, he reached behind him, and Jim guessed he was finding another rock to use as a weight, to hold the limb down under the water. Where it would be when the tide came again, bringing with it the sea creatures that would quickly and efficiently dispose of the evidence, leaving only a few bones that would probably never be found in this isolated cove . . .

Jim suddenly sprang to his feet and ran for the ravine.

It was a bad, clumsy run, and he knew it, knew it with the same certainty that told him he was about to die. Still, he had a chance, clumsy didn't matter if he was just quiet—

He slipped sideways and banged against a rock. The forgotten abalone dying in his catch bag rattled loudly, so loudly.

As Jim scrambled desperately to his feet, the penlight beam flickered across him.

For a moment he was paralyzed, and the only thought in his head (*deer in the headlights!*) was ridiculous. Then he realized the man was turning toward him, trying to run across the unstable tide pools. The man was also reaching into a pocket, and the penlight flickered across—not the barrel of a gun, but a knife blade.

Of course he has a knife. You don't carve people up with a gun.

Jim started to run, but saw he'd never make the ravine in time. So he stopped and hefted his club up in both hands—

—and the man advancing on him stopped.

Jim had only one brief second of surprise before the man seemed to reevaluate him, and started forward again. Suddenly the penlight beam stabbed into his eyes, blinding him. He nearly reached up to block the light, but instead swung the branch blindly.

And felt it hit something solid. He heard a grunt of painfully exhaled air from the other man, and a clatter as the man went down. But when he heard the man curse ("Fuck!"), he knew he hadn't knocked him out, and the man would be on him in a second, with that knife.

Jim backed away—toward the tide pools, since the other man had fallen between him and the ravine—and raised the branch again.

The other man turned off the penlight now and tossed it aside, and Jim realized there was enough light now that he could make out some of the man's features. He was slightly older than Jim, but not much, and was wearing dark sweats and sneakers. His most noticeable feature, of course, was the knife in his hand.

Suddenly he jumped forward, and Jim stepped aside, the knife slicing the air where Jim's body had just been. Jim tried to swat at the man with the branch, but he missed and was thrown off balance. He caught himself just as the other man came down above him, and Jim tried to roll aside but wasn't fast enough. The knife caught him in the shoulder.

The pain was immense, but not paralyzing, and Jim swung the branch at the other man's feet. The branch connected and the man was thrown sideways. He went down in a jumble of rocks, and groaned. Jim got to his own feet, teeth clenched against the pain in his torn shoulder, and he staggered backward. Then his boots caught on something and he went down—

—into the plastic bag.

He cried out as the bag burst around him, releasing an acrid stew of gore and limbs. He batted and kicked and clawed his way back from the gruesome mess, and this time was grateful when he fell into a tide pool of cleansing salt water. He splashed up out of the pool as he saw the other man rise. He wasn't sure, but he thought there was something black on the man's head that might have been blood.

He started to heft the branch, and realized, with fresh horror, that it had cracked somewhere along the line and was nothing but a useless foot-long piece of lightweight driftwood. He tossed it aside and frantically looked around for something else he could use—another branch, a boulder, even a sharp piece of shell . . .

And then the other man was on him.

Jim caught his arm as he swung it down with the knife, and they both went down on the rocks, Jim's back colliding painfully with a grapefruit-sized boulder. Their elbows slipped on a length of kelp, and the knife blade drew sparks as it ground along an outcropping. Jim found enough strength to throw the other man off, and his hand found a weight at his side, a weapon he'd forgotten about: the abalone iron. When his opponent regained his feet, Jim was waiting. He brought the iron down on the man's head as he rushed Jim. There was an especially gratifying *crack!*, and the man went down.

This time he didn't groan or move, and Jim knew that, at the very least, his blow had knocked the man out, maybe killed him.

He didn't wait to find out.

He took off for the ravine, regardless of how many times his feet slipped or stumbled. He reached the ravine and forgot about his backpack or his wounded hand and shoulder. He hauled himself up out of the ravine, and before he knew what had happened he was running down the dirt track toward the camper, out of breath but aware that he'd made it.

He paused long enough to turn, to be sure the man wasn't behind him. His lungs were burning, and when he saw that there was no pursuit, he stopped, doubled over to catch his breath. And before he knew or understood, he was laughing. He laughed at the sheer sense of relief, of victory. This time he'd been the hunted, and he'd escaped. He'd confronted death and lived to tell Maren about it.

Maren . . . wait until he told her. He turned and started running for the camper again, a smile still creasing his face.

Maybe I'll be a hero. Maybe there's a reward. Won't Maren love that, when her friends see my picture in the paper . . . ?!

He finally turned and ran unthinkingly through the brush, heedless this time of stinging nettles and grasping roots. He saw the campground in the dawn light, his camper truck the lone resident.

"Maren!" he started calling, even though he knew he was still too far for her to hear.

"Maren!" he called again, as he jogged up to the truck and around the driver's side to where the camper door was.

And then he staggered and stopped.

The camper door was hanging open, creaking slightly in the morning breeze, and there was blood. Lots of it, great gouts around the door and the step-down and the pavement. A thick swath of it led off a few feet and then disappeared. After that there were only a few bloody footprints leading off into the brush, footprints made by a pair of men's sneakers.

Jim couldn't bring himself to look inside. It wouldn't do any good, because he knew Maren wasn't in there—at least, not most of her. He knew where she was, and what had happened to her.

And as he realized just how badly he'd lost, he began to scream in the chill morning air.

KADDISH

WHITLEY STRIEBER

THE MORNING SKY was dull orange, the air sharp with the smell of the refineries that crowded banks of the Houston Ship Channel. On summer mornings when the sea breeze swept up from the Gulf of Mexico, you could smell them even this far north. Maybe all the way to Arkansas. The smell of prosperity.

Hal had been out on the back porch with his Bible, preparing for his day as he always did, by letting the book fall open in his hands. God's hand was there in the chance of it, he felt sure. He looked down—and this time was truly amazed at the verse he saw. "Thank you, Lord," he murmured, "for caring for this unworthy servant."

After he finished, he closed the book with the Great Seal of the State of Texas on its cover and went inside. Maddie was just laying out breakfast, and the kitchen smelled of bacon and coffee. Morning sun slanted in the windows, past the yellow-checked curtains they'd put up together when they bought the house. The air was cool from the air conditioning, the house filled with the quiet energy of morning. Upstairs, showers hissed and there were faint thuds as the kids hurried to be ready at the required time.

"James spoke," he said. "Spoke just to me when I opened the Good Book. Listen, Maddie. 'Consider it pure joy, my brothers, whenever you face trials of many kinds, because you know that the testing of your faith develops perseverance. Perseverance must finish its work so that you may be mature and complete, not lacking anything.' "

"Husband, that is a blessing, truly."

A glance at the kitchen clock told him that they had only a few seconds alone. He went to her and took her in his arms. He kissed her forehead. "We are blessed, Wife," he said. Then she had to break away, take the handbell from its place at the end of the kitchen pass-through counter, and ring it.

As the familiar sound pealed through the house, the children came downstairs in line, eldest first. Paul was fourteen, correctly dressed and neatly groomed for his day as a high school freshman. The other children, all younger, wore the regulation uniforms of Texas public school students; Ruth and Mary in blue jumpers and white oxfords, Mark in his khakis with his ROTC cap folded neatly in his belt.

Hal had reason to be proud of this family of his. For one thing, his children wanted to be as they were. They were not like the children of liberals and heretics, dressing the part just so they could receive a state-sponsored education, then going home to learn ridiculous lies like evolution from their Christ-hating parents.

They'd be most welcome in the Russell Unit, all of them.

He took his place at the head of the table. The children stood behind their chairs. He said grace, then took his seat. The boys followed him to their seats while the girls helped their mother serve him and his sons.

When all the plates were ready, the women took their seats. Bacon and eggs and strawberry Toaster Strudel. Cof-

fee for himself and Maddie, milk for the kids. "Maddie,"
he said, "girls, thanks for this food and service, praise be."

"Praise be, Father," Ruth replied.

"Thanks," Paul and Mark both murmured. "Praise be."

After the meal, Hal asked, "Has anyone anything to ask,
or any announcements?"

The children sat silent, heads bowed. Mary giggled.
Maddie shook her head, short and sharp.

"No, I know what everybody's burning to ask. Go
ahead, love," he said to Mary. "It's very much allowed."

"Daddy, will you really talk to Vice President Duke today?"

"Yes, Mary, the vice president is scheduled to telephone
me at the unit at ten-twenty."

All eyes were on him. Wide, expectant. He could not
conceal his delight. So much for the gravity of the Christian father. "What will you say?" Mark asked.

"We do not interrogate our father," Maddie cautioned
him.

"No, my dear, we do not. Your mother is entirely correct. And I cannot tell you what I will say because I will answer his questions. If he should by the grace of God see fit
to encourage me, I will thank him for it."

"David King says you're in danger."

The word hung there. It was true enough, in this strange,
fallen world of ours, that there could be danger to him on
this day. "That's in God's hands," he said to his oldest boy.
He'd heard the fear trembling in Paul's voice. "But the
state protects us pretty well out at the Russell, so I don't
expect that any trouble will develop."

"He said that Sweden is going to file a charge against
you in the International Criminal Court. What's the International Criminal Court?"

"An illegal organization in a faraway country that has
nothing to do with us." He did not add that it meant that
their planned vacation to see the churches of Spain next

summer would have to be canceled. He did not add that, because of the duty he would perform this day, he would become a wanted man across most of the world. "Any more questions or comments?"

"Husband, our meal is concluded."

The children rose.

"Very well, then, as you know, God has graciously given me a trial to face today. Will you pray with me now?" He stood, also, then bowed his head and closed his eyes, and asked God to bless his efforts this day in support of the will of the legislature and governor of the State of Texas.

"God," Ruth said, "please do your will on our daddy today."

"God bless you all," he said. "Ruthie, thank you for that special help."

The children came in line, and each kissed him good-bye. At the kitchen door, Maddie embraced him in her comfortable arms. "God be with you," she said.

"And with you," he replied. He looked at Mark, gave him a wink.

Mark smiled.

"Jesus protect the Luther Middle School football team," Hal said, "and give the tight end the ball when it counts."

"Thank you, Father. Praise Jesus."

"Dad," Paul said, "Coach says we aren't supposed to pray to win. Coach says that Jesus will favor us according to His will."

"Coach is right," Hal said, "but here at home, among ourselves, there's no reason not to give Jesus a little hint."

"Dad," Mark asked, "why the tight end?"

"Aren't you the tight end?"

"I'm tailback."

"Ah. Then, Lord, I revise my prayer. Give the ball to the tailback when it counts."

He straightened his tie in the hall mirror and put on his jacket. It was a hot February day, so there was no need for his old overcoat. He put his hat on, though. Nowadays, he felt naked without his hat. He remembered the times before, when men had strolled around in open T-shirts, gone to work without ties, let alone hats.

He got in his Buick and headed off toward the highway. His sons had been hinting of late that the family might stop by the dealership and look at the new Roadmaster, but he didn't consider a car bought in 2003 any sort of a candidate for trade-in. Still, he had to admit that 118,000 miles was a fair amount, and, in fact, since the company had forced the old dealer to sell to a Christian, he might at least go in and take a look.

As he passed the Wal-Mart, he saw a new banner, "Now Certified All Christian, Praise the Lord." He could not resist calling out "Praise Jesus"—it made him feel so wonderful to see that.

The Religion in Life Act of 2010 was having a very good effect on America, and those who had struggled for its passage had reason to be proud. Companies had gone through a great deal of trouble Christianizing, given all the antidiscrimination lawsuits by liberals and heretics.

He pulled out into traffic and turned on NPR for the morning sermon. It was the Reverend Gates Hughes out of Atlanta, his subject, "Suffer the heretic to burn." Hal listened with half an ear. He knew who had inspired the sermon: He had. What he would do today had the whole nation talking. Most were raising their voices in praise and thanks, of course, but the liberals and heretics were still out there. They weren't open about it anymore, of course, but if you looked at the Internet on some unfiltered search engine from abroad, you'd find plenty of disagreement.

He would see plenty of that today. Normally, it was illegal for members of the press even to speak to state officials, let alone question them. Of course, the rules were bent for friendly American press. As far as unfriendly press from abroad was concerned, they were strictly enforced. More than one reporter from Mexico or England or some other heretic nation had done time for questioning state officials. Deservedly so. He'd like to have one end up on his unit, to see how *real* prisoners were treated. The pasty bastard would find out what punishment really meant, then.

He sighed. The press could not be kept out, by order of the State Supreme Court. If the execution was to be public, as the legislature had mandated, then he was going to have to answer questions. Of course, the U.S. reporters would be fine. The whole media, from radio to television to newspapers to the Internet—all of it—was united behind the government. America had been blessed by God that he had not been in Washington on Obliteration Day.

He had brought his strong heart, his loving kindness, and his brilliance to the job of acting president, and for the last eleven years, he had never failed in the exercise of loving firmness and Christian principle. In his deepest heart, even a thirty-second call from the president would have meant more to Hal than the allotted six minutes with Vice President Duke. The vice president was a fine man, of course, but the president was the savior of the nation.

"Lord, forgive me my selfishness," Hal said aloud. He should be grateful for the incredible honor of a call from the vice president. "I thank you and I praise your name," he said.

He thought about that business of the International Criminal Court. He'd been indicted last week, along with three thousand other federal and state officials, for all manner of crimes against humanity. Crimes against secular humanism, more like. Of course, he could tell his family nothing about that. That was all classified. You had to be able to reach Web sites outside of the country to find that out. His indictment had been an ugly one: 7,110 counts of murder, one for every prisoner executed at the Russell Unit under retroactive laws.

The EU had sent commandos to Mississippi to get Wade Cole, the head of the Federal New Towns Program that was relocating the Negroes. Wade Cole was in jail in Norway or somewhere. It was the foreigners that were the problem. They were a bunch of zoo animals, in his opinion, humble before God. Frogs, Wogs, Eyties, Russkies, Polacks, Micks, Brits, Canucks, you name it. Their reporters would be there today, all of them would be there screaming out their rat-shit questions.

"God be with me," he said, "may it please you for me to represent the State of Texas in a manner satisfactory to you."

Traffic on the 55 was unusually heavy. His car was stifling, the air conditioning broken and Freon embargoed. Thanks again, EU.

He switched to the all-news feed off the satellite. "Over four thousand registered heretics in New York City were banned from use of the Internet for illegal surfing of extra-U.S. Web sites," NPR reporter Gareth Harrington intoned. Hal would like to get them in the unit, too. They'd learn something pretty darned serious about being a heretic in a godly country.

Finally, the traffic report: "Police activity on the 55 North has slowed traffic to a crawl . . ."

He said aloud, "Phone. Office." An instant later the car responded, "Office ringing."

"Jenny," he said, "it's me. Yes, praise His name. I'm on the slow side of an arrest on the 55. I'm going to be about fifteen minutes late. No, don't back up anything, and the call is still on, of course. If you have to patch it through to the car, be ready to do that. And get Elaine to start that scout troop on its tour and I'll catch up with them if I can. And listen, I want a meeting with that structural engineer, Williams—what's his name? That guy. I am looking at full three-foot cells in the new wing. I think we've got that human confinement study, it was saying, I think, twenty-eight inches would work on width. That's gonna give us a nice increase in density. I want it redrawn—you tell him that. Redrawn before he sees the board of governors. Yeah, and tell him to thank me for saving his job, Jesus be praised."

As traffic began to pick up, he told the phone to hang up. Over his six years at the Russell Unit, they had gone from 18,000 prisoners to 41,000. This new wing would take them up to 62,000 and an extension into Sam Houston County was already being eminent domained. Unfortunately, every darned farmer in the county was a certified Christian more than five years faithful with church records to prove it, so the land had to be paid for.

He passed the scene of the arrest. A Mex was being hauled up. Of course, who else? The police had put an official "Shot for Running" sign on the guy, who bled and kicked while a blood-covered woman screamed into a cell phone and tried to raise him on her shoulders. She was no dummy. She knew a less-than-healthy man would suffocate during a dangle.

The law required that felons who ran be suspended to immobilize them. Until a doctor declared him unfit for this procedure, he would remain there. And the county ambulance that contained the doctor was unlikely to be in a hurry. Why should Texas pay to keep some foreigner behind bars? Mexican speeders, no U.S. ID, no rights. Oldest story in the book. Probably had a car full of liquor.

The traffic cleared out on the far side of the dangle, and he got back up to seventy. The rest of the journey to the unit went just fine. Soon he was turning onto Freedom Road, the way into the unit from the 55. Lining it were foreigners, each holding a protest sign and an open passport. They were really Americans, every traitorous one of them, who escaped to the EU and came back as European citizens under diplomatic protection. Hal knew that the secret Compulsory Renationalization Act was just about to be signed into law by the president. As soon as that happened, all of this scum would get renationalized and charged with treason. He was driving past hate-filled faces that would, he knew, in a few months be looking at him just a bit differently in the execution chamber.

As he pulled up to the gate, the warning bell jangled and the siren gave the three short bursts that meant the warden was arriving. Guards saluted as he drove in. Prisoners in their orange uniforms turned, stood at attention, and bowed their shaved heads.

Russell was a small unit in a state with a prison population of over a million. The new Sandler Huntsville Prison Extension was the largest single unit, with 81,000 serving mostly light sentences. Ten-to-twenty-year felons, Internet violators ranging from arrogant liberals who'd bypassed federal filters and gone on illegal offshore Web sites, to people whose computers had turned up in automated porn sweeps. S-H inmates had it easy compared to Hal's charges. They got phone privileges and access to their own lawyers if they had the money for such. There was a prison hospital.

Russell was 80 percent lifers and 20 percent death-row prisoners. With the new twelve-week appeal rule now in force, that group was finally turning over at a reasonable speed. Gone were the days when a man could live to a ripe old age on death row. The scum and their scum lawyers who'd kicked America in the teeth with their traitorous appeals were learning a fine lesson just now.

If a jury of your peers says you have to die, that ought to be it. DNA tests, all of that mumbo jumbo—that junk should not be given validity over the opinion of sworn American Christians. And fortunately, the Supreme Court had finally agreed. God said, "Thou shalt not suffer a sorcerer to live," and that went for all of them, the whole damn "scientific community," as they called themselves, and all their ideas and junk discoveries and all that garbage. DNA was a Satanist plot and they were all heretics, atheists, and Marxists, every one of them. The

Word was clear, the Holy Bible was the law . . . or would be, as soon as the president, the Congress, and the state legislatures finished the work of the Lord.

He went into the blessed cool of the administration building and down the long tiled hall to his office. Except for administrative areas, the state prison system had required that all air conditioning be permanently discontinued in order to comply with cost-per-prisoner legislated mandates. The only exception was prison hospitals when the interior temperature reached 93 degrees. As Russell had only an infirmary for work-related injuries, that was not an issue here.

"Good morning, sweetheart," he said to Jenny as he walked in. He paused, smiled slightly at her, then sailed his hat toward the hat rack. It soared in an arc, rose a little, then dropped as softly as a leaf on the rack.

"Praise Jesus," she cried.

Hal laughed. He knew that there was a monthly pool on his hits or misses, and he knew that Jenny was on the "hits outnumber misses 2-1" line, which was currently at 18-1 odds.

Wise place to be, even so. Nobody realized that he could control his tosses perfectly. He'd gone close to the line for the express purpose of juicing her chances. He was an efficient tennis player and as good a golfer as old President Bush, with whom he had been privileged to play one day three years ago, at the Houston Country Club. Along with the other five big unit wardens, he had been the invited guest of Senator DeLay.

Jenny came in with the day's con, as his schedule was called.

"You have the vice president in eight minutes, then the press for ten minutes, then the execution, then lunch with Minister Apple—"

"When did that come up?"

"He called just now. Your wife told him you were free."

What in the world would Clay Apple want with lunch in the middle of the week? "I'm obviously not free, not right after this execution."

"Then a two o'clock with the Sam Houston County planning commission, then an intake meeting on fifteen c.m.s, then that Red Cross thing has come back."

"Scratch that."

"I, uh, are you sure? He's in the prison."

"He's here? Now? Where?"

"We're not supposed to escort him."

"I'm not going to be talking to the Red Cross. What goes on in this prison is not the business of the Red Cross. No matter *what* he thinks he's found."

"Well, sir, the governor's office wants—um—wants you to."

The governor knew that he was running the unit according to regulations. So why would he be sending this legally protected felon here on a harassment mission? "The governor's office," he said. "Fine."

Suddenly a weariness overtook him. As she left he said, "Close my door." He leaned back in his chair. Last night, very late, he had taken his old telescope out in the backyard. In times past, there had been stars from horizon to horizon. He'd stood there last night in the thick air and seen not one. Not one single star. The weather report had said it was clear and 68 degrees. Well, they hadn't mentioned the haze, had they? And it hadn't been any 68 at his house. At four minutes past midnight on February 20, his thermometer had read 82 degrees. Of course, the official records were changed and that was what the weatherman had to go by.

You didn't want environmentalists with treason in their eyes to make a stink about "record heat" in the foreign press. "Pollution means work," the president had said, "and American work is the work of God." Therefore, he did not need to add, pollution is a holy thing.

His phone rang. He looked at it. Jenny cracked the door and gestured wildly.

Hal's heart was fluttering like a moth when he picked up the phone. Immediately, he heard the vice president's resonant but warm accent, gentle with the music of the South. "Good morning, Warden," he said.

"Mr. Vice President, this is an honor for myself and for all of us here at the Russell."

"It's truly an honor to be talking to the man who will carry out the first public execution in this country since 1936. Did you know that, Warden Michaels?"

The vice president was known for the depth and accuracy of his historical knowledge. Hal did indeed know, but he remained silent. Not for a mere prison warden to step in the way of something the vice president of the United States cared to say.

"Well, it was in Kentucky. They charged admission. Is the state of Texas charging admission?"

"Yes, sir, a donation of one thousand dollars or more is being required for auditorium admission. And the state is getting eleven million dollars from Fox, of course. That's been in the press."

The vice president chuckled. "The *London Times* claims more like fifty million."

"Well, sir, I don't have access to the foreign press, but I do believe that the governor said eleven million was the correct figure."

There was a silence. "Perhaps so," the vice president finally said. "Perhaps so. Again, accept my congratulations and my support, and my personal assurances that the EU extradition on you will not be honored."

Hal waited for the dial tone, but it did not come. "Sir?"

"Ah, Warden. We have a little, uh, pool up here. You know, an office pool?"

"Yes, sir."

"I just thought you might be aware that the president is in at seventeen minutes. And, uh, if that was a good bet?"

No wonder the White House had requested the medicals on the private run. The man had suffocated for fourteen minutes, and he had a bad heart. "I think, given the condemned man's age and state of health, that seventeen minutes is a reasonable bet."

"Because, it would be—you know—if the president won . . ."

"Yes, sir." He could see to it that the thing would end after seventeen minutes. The network contract called for fifteen minutes guaranteed, to make certain of adequate commercial time. Anything over that would be considered gravy, anyway.

With that, the vice president hung up. Hal stared at the phone. He was absolutely stunned, and not about the office pool at the White House. The execution was a sensational bet in Las Vegas, in Atlantic City, you name it.

No, the betting had not concerned him, what had concerned him was the way the vice president put it when discussing the indictment. Until this moment, it had seemed distant—fictional, even. The president had declared that the United States would never honor extradition of Christians to stand trial in the courts of secular countries, but the Arab Confederation, a bunch of EU toadies, had threatened an oil cutoff if the demanded extraditions did not take place.

The administration was going to give in, Hal thought. "God help us," he murmured, "praise thy name."

At that moment, Jenny rushed in and grabbed his cheeks and shook them. "You were wonderful, you brilliant man! Oh, let's call Maddie, let's play it for her!"

"Play it? You recorded it?"

"Darned right I did, and you are saving it for your grandchildren, mister, or both of your wives are gonna whup your cute little bottom!" She giggled. She was ten years Maddie's senior, but she still seemed so wonderfully girlish.

Seeing as his children with Jenny were grown, it was Hal's duty to live with Maddie and his younger family. Jenny chose to stay in their old house in Gladewater, where it was quiet. But the two of them still took every other weekend for themselves, and she "Aunt Jennie'd" the new gang of kids with truest mother love.

Holidays, the whole clan got together, both wives, all nine kids, assorted dogs, cats, gerbils, birds, and fish, and he and Jenny and Maddie celebrated a night of conjugal enjoyment together, with each woman taking her turn beside him, separated only by the marriage sheet with its neatly hemmed hole.

When he was a boy, multiple marriage had been banned in the United States, but the Reconstruction Congress had allowed it for those declared righteous by national churches, according to the legally established definition of the term. This definition included a minimum of ten years' documented church membership and attendance, involvement in Christian charity, tithing according to established standards, a spotless arrest record, active proselytization of the Christian faith, and, of course, ownership of property. In other words, except for the ten-year requirement, the same criteria that had to be met before a church would certify a parishioner to become a voter.

Hal fulfilled all of the requirements, and had been declared among the righteous by old Pastor Williams, God rest his soul, on the day the Separation of the Righteous Act became the law of the land.

And why should it not be? Abraham had two wives and Jacob four, and the Lord spoke of loyalty in marriage and the sanctity of the bond, not of the number of wives. In his humble opinion, the Christianization of marriage in the United States had resulted in a vast increase of human happiness.

It was then, as Jenny was turning to leave the office, that he noticed Henry Clair standing in the doorway. He stood up. "Henry"—he crossed his office—"welcome." He took Henry's hand in both of his own and pumped it. "Come on over here," he said. "Just sit right down."

Instead, Henry backed away from him. His face, usually so genial, was gleaming with perspiration. His heavy eyes glowered. "Hal," he said, and then he held out a thick document.

Hal looked down at it, perhaps two hundred pages spiral bound. The cover was blue with a red cross at the top. Beneath it, in black typed letters, "Report for the International Red Cross Committee on State of Texas Prison Russell Unit Number One, Hellman, Texas."

"I guess we didn't pass."

Henry said nothing.

Hal took the report from him. "Should I read this, buddy?"

"I got into the Disciplinary Center," he said, his voice flat and dull.

The tone was surprising, although it should not have been, of course. Henry and his Red Cross team were an irritant. The government was about to withdraw from the International Red Cross, and none too soon, in Hal's humble opinion.

"Well, that's part of the prison," Hal said. Henry had a right to do just that, acting under treaties signed before the destruction of Washington, treaties that had been confirmed in the years after the bomb, when the country was helpless and in chaos.

"Hal, I saw an organized system of torture."

"You saw a system that imposes effective discipline on difficult prisoners."

"I saw a human finger, Hal, that I was unable to trace. A human finger in a garbage can, wrapped in plastic wrap. Nobody would explain that to me."

"An accident." He knew exactly what happened in that program. He'd designed it himself. The control of so many prisoners with so few guards required a copious flow of information. The removal of a finger was an effective inducement.

"Hal, I think if you look at page 121, you'll see that we were able to disinter the body of a man who died while in your disciplinary area."

It felt as if the world had shattered around him, shattered like a pretty glass ornament fallen from a Christmas tree. "That's impossible."

"The family approved the disinterment."

"What family?" They were liable to criminal prosecution, no question. There had to be some law.

"They're now in Canada, Hal, out of your reach forever. You can read the autopsy report. In fact, I'd be very pleased if you could figure out how to explain that the needles the man swallowed were an accident."

"It must've been suicide."

Now he drew something else out of his briefcase. A black DVD holder. "This was taken in one of your interrogation rooms. It shows a man called William George Samuels being forced to swallow needles, among other things. I have your own approval, signed by you, as an appendix to the report itself." He paused. "Now, if you'll just sign for this copy. I need a confirmation that this has been tendered to you as per paragraph 141.2 of the treaty protocol."

"I refuse to sign."

"So noted. You taking the wives out after the execution?"

"No, I hadn't planned—"

"It's such a great day for you, Hal, I thought you'd be out celebrating."

"It's a man's death."

"Cause for celebration, considering that he aborted a hundred and sixteen fetuses."

"Murdered a hundred and sixteen human beings."

A hardness came into Henry's eyes. "He carried out these abortions when it was still legal to do so in the United States."

"The man murdered babies and the law states that it's retroactive to the first abortion performed in this country post–*Roe v. Wade*. Henry, hey, I'm just carrying out the law, here. I'm not a bad man." And he wasn't, he was a good and holy man, a Christian to the depths of his merciful heart. "It's a blessing on the guilty that they be punished in this life, that they may be free in the next."

Without another word, Henry turned and left.

Jenny said over the intercom, "The scouts are in your conference room, baby."

Hal stayed where he was. His chest hurt. He took deep breaths, one, another, trying to calm down. "Jesus," he whispered, "help me here. Help me with this, Lord."

That Red Cross report was supposed to remain confidential, but it would not; the sleazy European government would leak the damned thing far and wide.

He went over to his desk and poured himself a glass of ice water from the engraved silver pitcher his first son had given him. Roy, beloved Roy, dead of radiation poisoning. Did Henry know what that was like? How it felt to see the skin fall off your beautiful twenty-two-year-old boy, to listen to him begging God for death? Did Henry know how it felt to try to comfort the mother of such a son—Jenny out there—who had held Roy in her arms while he died?

The boy had walked all the way from his congressman's apartment in Alexandra, Virginia, to Atlanta. All the way in the horrible days after, when the smoke from Washington blew all the hell over the place, contaminating everything from Richmond to Boston, dear God, and breaking the United States, breaking the greatest country in the world with a bomb built in Iran, yes, out of Russian parts, for sure, and brought here in an Indonesian oil tanker, black ship up the Potomac, oh God.

And now they were going to burn him in the world press and make him the Butcher of the Russell Unit, you see if they didn't, in *Le Monde* and the *London Times* and the *Frankfurter Allegemeine Zeitung*—oh, he knew them all— the heathen papers of the heretic countries, the countries that harbored to this day the very same America haters who had blasted Washington to radioactive smoke and memories, and Roy, dear Roy, with his laughing eyes and his curls and how Jenny had cried at the barbershop that first day, and his voice on the phone every evening, "Hi, Dad, guess what happened today?"

O America, you of the dead sons and daughters and the lost road, the freedom road we had to step off just for a few years as the president said, God love his strength and his humanity, just a few years off the freedom road while we recover, and we make this the Christian nation that the pilgrims intended from day one, and then when we are Christian and pure and good in heart and deed, we will be free again before God and man, free again.

He got up, threw back the rest of the water, told his heart to either stop hurting or stop beating, and went in to see the scouts.

His big table that was normally surrounded by the business types who kept the massive factory that was the Russell Unit humming was surrounded on this morning by a spit-and-polish troop of Texas Ranger Scouts in their handsome black uniforms and gold sashes. They were fresh of face, their eyes pure and full of boyish excitement, their cheeks glowing. How beautiful they were, good Christian children, each with his cross and his Lone Star on his starched collar.

"Well, boys, I hope you have good seats for the program today."

Their captain rose. "Sir, we're in the front row."

"In front of all the cameras—that's good. Don't you boys turn around, now, or your face is gonna be plastered all over some foreign news program."

"Yes, sir, Colonel Watts told us. Sir, why is the foreign press allowed in our country?"

"I think you boys might be able to answer that yourselves. What would happen if we kicked them out?"

"We'd be free to make America Christian faster."

"So true. But they would also kick our reporters out of their countries. So we would no longer get news from the heretic world. And if that happened, something might sneak up on us, something we wouldn't like."

He continued his give-and-take with the boys as long as he could. Five minutes. The execution was scheduled for noon, and he wanted it to start on the dot. He sent them out to the auditorium with Fred Watts, and told Jenny to let the death house know that he was in motion.

"The prisoner is in prep," she called after him. "They had to give him Zofran—he was puking all over the place."

"Figures." The man was one of three dozen condemned abortion doctors on the unit. He was fifty-two and a real coward. Not a Christian, had had to have spiritual advice enforced.

The man had killed one hundred and sixteen human beings and you would think he was some kind of saint or martyr for all the howling that was going on abroad. The U.S. press was uniform in its praise of the action, and of the decision to go back to the Bible and execute these people in a way that fit the horror of the crime.

What would be just about a man who had murdered a whole damn nursery full of babies getting put to sleep like a beloved old hound? That was not right, which was obvious, which anybody who thought for one single second about it had to see.

And yet here he was indicted and he couldn't even show his kids the darned churches of Spain without risking jail. What in God's good name was just about that?

He knew that he had that press conference, but he was running late and he could not allow that to get in the way.

The U.S. reporters all had his printed Q&A; they'd use that. The foreigners could stuff that Red Cross report down each other's throats.

The death house was stifling. He went along the Row, past the silent cells. There was no talking allowed on death row, so the men inside did not make a sound. They'd learned the rules, some of them the hard way.

When this was built, each cell had been intended to confine a single prisoner. There were six to a cell now, and death row had only post-appeals prisoners, people who were certain to die. The rest of the condemned, those still on appeal, were held in the general population, which was a bomb waiting to explode, which he had told the governor time and again.

He turned the corner into the ready room, and there was good old Sol Goldberg, Jesus love him, sitting there in his orange prison-issue underpants, shackled and gagged, listening to the Reverend T. Holden Stanley read from the Book of Job.

"The gag is new."

"Reciting illegal prayers," Dr. Karen Unger said. "Jew stuff."

"You look real pretty, Karen," he told her. She did, too, all made up with a new hairdo and all.

"The TV people did it," she said, her voice bubbling. "They say we're gonna have a worldwide audience of more than two billion, Hal; can you imagine that?"

He tried to chuckle. The reverend finished and closed his book. "You hear that, Sol? Karen says you've got a kind of a biggish audience."

Sol stared at him in silence.

He and Karen went down the short corridor together to the stage. In the center was a steel chair with leather manacles. Lights went up, cameras turned on. Hal waved a hand, and the shadows again descended. It wasn't time for that.

"Sir, what about the press conference?"

"Varden? Ve haf kestion!"

"Then learn to speak English. Karen, this looks just fine. Real fine." He lowered his voice. "Duke let me in on a little secret. The president's at seventeen minutes in the White House pool."

She smiled softly. "I think you better be at seventeen minutes, too, then, Hal."

"You can control it that well? An absolute flatline at exactly seventeen minutes?"

"You bet, fella."

Back in prep, the prisoner was being given an enema.

"Is that gonna be enough? We don't want him letting go out there."

She indicated a thick black plug in a silver dish. "That'll keep him dry, no matter how much peristalsis we get."

"Three minutes, sir," a guard said. Hal winked at the scouts, who were scuffling and laughing, typical boys. He hoped they'd be properly respectful of the state when the execution was in progress.

He watched the guards get Sol into close restraint. They took off his gag. He would be allowed to speak during the performance. The Pavulon in a 300 microgram drip would make quick work of his ability to do so, but he didn't know that. No doubt he had some speech prepared dumping on the country or some such thing. Well, it would not be delivered—got news for you, mister.

Makeup came and dusted Hal's face and blushed his lips. "See there," he said, "you've made me look twenty years younger just like that."

Karen said to Sol, "Can you come with me, please, Sol? Are you able to walk?"

He was back in his shorts, sitting hunched on the holding bench. He let out a long belch, a typical response from a frightened man. "I'm sorry," he said.

"No, no, it's natural. Here, come on, now."

Sol got to his feet, then abruptly sat back down. "It feels like that thing's gonna fall out," he said.

"No, that's fine."

"Billy, George," Hal said, "please carry the prisoner out."

The two powerful guards took Sol out onto the stage. This time, the lights flared like the face of the sun, flooding everything in white glare.

"Boy, is it ever quiet," Karen said as she and Hal watched them strapping Sol in the chair.

"You okay?"

"Let's do it, Chief." She put on the surgical mask that would preserve her anonymity.

The two of them walked out onto the stage together. It felt like the inside of a cathedral, vibrant with silent life. Hal went to the podium. "Good morning ladies and gentlemen," he began.

Suddenly, from behind him, there came a loud voice; *"Yisgadal v'yiskadash shimay rabo!"*

It was Sol, yelling some Jew prayer. Perfectly legal to do that in a home or synagogue, but not on state property.

"Ladies and gentlemen," he repeated, raising his voice, "acting upon warrant duly executed upon the prisoner Solomon Samuel Goldberg—"

"May He give reign to His kingship in your lifetimes and in your days," shouted a voice from the audience.

"Now," Hal said, "we will have order here."

"—and in the lifetimes of the entire Family of Israel," Sol cried out.

"It's set," Karen said. "It's set!"

"—I hereby execute—"

"O say shalom bim . . . romov . . ."

His voice grew softer and softer, until only his lips moved. It seemed then that half or more than half of the audience took up the prayer, and the ancient words sang through the room, to the rafters.

"May His great name be blessed forever and ever."

It was not just foreigners, it was Americans, too, and they were all committing a crime and they would all be punished.

"This is a criminal act! This is not a Christian prayer, here," he shouted. Then, to Karen, "Get that drip going."

"It's going—should I do it faster?"

"Hell, no! We obey the law in this unit!"

And so they executed him with suffering that had been ordained by law, this man who had taken one hundred and sixteen lives, and as the drug gradually suffocated him, his voice that had been raised in Kaddish dropped from a murmur to the softest of whispers, and his lips turned blue and finally he forgot his prayer and probably every darned thing, even his name, and he gave the performance that he had been brought here to give.

He thrashed from side to side and bared his teeth, and white foam came out of his mouth, and sweat poured off him, and when he became erect, Karen covered his midriff with the olive-colored prison towel that she had brought for that purpose.

After a time, his head fell forward and his hands, which had been grasping and fidgeting, stopped grasping and fidgeting.

"Sir," Karen said, "this prisoner has expired."

"Thank you, Doctor. This execution is concluded."

As the curtains closed, he looked at his watch. Seventeen minutes exactly, and here he'd forgotten to put his money in the darned jailhouse pool! Heaven only knew how much the president must have won at the White House.

If he had any guts, he'd call up there and ask the old man for a nice little cut of his winnings. It would be only fair.

Another execution was scheduled in twenty minutes. Not public—nobody was interested in a Negro car thief.

They'd do him in the basement quick enough, so nobody need be late for lunch.

As he walked off the stage, though, he did not feel well at all. His chest was hurting again, deep inside, an ache of the heart. He wondered if this was a heart attack. The way he ran, it could be, God knew, at the age of fifty-four.

Jenny was there waiting for him, and he was glad to see her. "Let's go, buster," she said. "You look like you need a little mama-san."

That was the truth, and he went with her back to his office.

"Here," she said, handing him a form. A death certificate for Albert A. Taylor, Jr.

"I've gotta get down there."

"Sign it."

"He's not dead yet."

"He will be. Now sign it, and you go in there and lie down."

"I can't. That's not—"

"The law states that you sign on confirmation of death. It does not require that you attend. Only the regs require that, and you're the person who enforces them."

She thrust the pen into his hand. He signed. "I thought this man's offense was car theft. Is that a capital crime now?"

"Three times down, it doesn't matter what the crime was. He's on his third conviction, and that's curtains."

"I wonder what he did the other two times."

She held out a pill—a Valium—and water. "Who cares? The important thing that he's off the streets and not costing you and me a dime after today. Take this."

"I've got an afternoon. The—uh—Planning Board, was it?"

"I've cleared your calendar."

"You're an angel."

"Not yet, Husband. But I'm working in that direction, God willing."

He knocked back the pill and went to his daybed, and she rubbed his forehead while he fell asleep.

He dreamed that he and Jesus were walking through the Woodlands Mall together, and he was feeling just so wonderfully loved, and was hand in hand with his Lord—and then a little girl was watching them, and he realized that Jesus was naked. "Oh, Jesus," he said in his dream, "you can't do this, it's a life sentence if she tells."

He woke up suddenly. It was very quiet, no sound but the air conditioning hissing softly. Dull sunlight shafted across the floor. He sat up, then went to his desk and poured himself some water.

"Jenny?"

They'd all gone, and he went, too, hurrying down the long hall with his briefcase in his hand.

Outside the administration area, the air seemed to clutch at his throat, to challenge him to breathe at all. The sky was yellow, the sun deep orange, just setting behind the north tower, rendering it black against the blood-streaked sky.

On the way home, he listened to the news. The NPR story was that the execution had been performed flawlessly, that the criminal had suffered appropriately for his crime, and that all had ended well. Nothing about those idiotic outbursts. He reminded himself to have security look at the surveillance video of the audience. Every person who said Kaddish would be punished, the foreigners deported, the Americans charged under appropriate statutes.

It was late when he got home, already dark this past hour. There was a scent of pot roast coming from the kitchen, the sound of the girls practicing in the basement. "Blessed be the ties that bind . . . "

Maddie came and kissed him.

"Did you see?" he asked.

She nodded.

"The kids?"

"At school. But they saw. Everybody saw."

Softly, from below, rose the song of the daughters of music, ". . . our hearts in Christian love; the fellowship of kindred minds, is like that to that above. . . ."

"What did they think?" He was disappointed, frankly, in the lack of celebration in this house. This had been a day of accomplishment for a member of the family.

"The boys are out on the deck with the telescope."

He went out, looked up into the dim sky, glowing tan, starless.

"What're you looking for?" he asked.

"Daddy," his youngest said, "you said you could see the stars from here when you were a boy. Where are they now, Daddy?"

He felt as if a great blanket was descending from the sky, a blanket of dense prison air and the cries of the dying. He heard Sol's Kaddish as it had been at the last, faintly, faintly, a ghost made of breath.

"The stars are gone," he said.

"Why, Dad?"

He went in to get some pot roast. Maddie watched him dish it out for himself. "Why are you crying?" she asked.

"I'm not crying."

"Hal, you are." She reached up, touched his cheek with the tips of two fingers, wiping away the cool of his tears.

"I'm not crying," he repeated. "I'm just a little tired today. I don't know why."

He wanted to bury himself in her shoulder, to cry his eyes out, to let the shadow of the starless night slip out of him, to hide himself away in her kind and gentle heart.

". . . and perfect love and friendship reign . . ." came the voices from below. Then they died. The song was done.

"Well then," she said, "eat your dinner. *CSI*'s on in ten minutes; you hate to miss the start."

THE SEER

ROBERT STEVEN RHINE

DANIEL PULLED UP his black nylon socks and slipped on his polished wingtips with a tarnished brass shoehorn. He loathed the Macabees' Christmas party, hearing all the petty stories about mundane jobs and spoiled children. Lives so painfully predictable. It's not that Daniel's was so special. It was quite ordinary, actually. A watchmaker born in Pittsville, New Hampshire, he hadn't achieved his goals of *National Geographic* explorer or paleontologist as he had dreamed when he was a boy. He gave them up long ago when he saw he had no chance of ever realizing them. Daniel had learned to live with life's setbacks. If only others could.

He knotted his bow tie, something he had mastered without looking in the mirror. Then, he carefully wound his wristwatch stem, forward and gently back, forward and gently back. It was a 1927 Bulova with a black dial, gold train, and sixteen-jewel movement in a Curvex-style case. It was his grandfather's and had been passed down to him by his father in his will. The watch was in dire condition when he received it, but he had lovingly restored it and now it ran admirably. He had done such a fine job that his neighbor had him repair hers, which led to a few more timepieces, and before Daniel could blink, he was trapped in the back of his watch shop, his eye glued to a magnifying loupe.

He put his ear to the quad-beveled crystal and listened to his life ticking away. He was forty-nine. His father and grandfather had each lived to fifty-three. That left 1,825 days, 43,800 minutes, and 2,628,000 seconds. . . . tick . . . tick . . . tick . . .

Daniel's wife Mindy had told him to stop counting that way or risk a self-fulfilling prophecy. That made Daniel smile.

He combed his thinning hair, with his back to the mirror, then stared at the wispy remnants in the comb's teeth. He noticed his reflection in a hand mirror lying on the vanity.

"Honey, we're going to be late. What's taking you so long?!" hollered Mindy, his tarnished trophy wife, glancing at her vintage pink gold Lady Elgin bracelet watch on her skeletal wrist as she entered the bathroom. There was a crunch of glass beneath her Prada heels. With a knowing sigh, she stared down at her fractured image in the puzzle pieces. It had been such a beautiful mirror, with a tortoise-shell frame.

"Darn it, Daniel! That was my mother's!"

As she grabbed a dustpan and swept up the shattered shards, she muttered, "Do you have to break every mirror in the house?! Just what we need—another seven years' bad luck!"

Actually, three, Daniel predicted silently.

They drove in their Buick LeSabre in a deafening void. The roads were icy and Daniel drove extra cautiously. *Maybe the party will be over before we get there,* he wished secretly.

"You're driving like a turtle!" Mindy nagged. "Do you want to miss the party?!"

Daniel leaned his wingtip on the gas, accelerating to

fifty . . . sixty-five . . . seventy. Mindy didn't care if he crashed the car. Actually, she would have preferred it to driving in an eight-year-old Buick. But the watch-repair business had slowed in Pittsville, while Mindy's shopping had soared.

Mindy hadn't exactly acquired the life or husband she'd dreamed of. Before Daniel, she had courted a wealthy podiatrist and had been engaged until he ran off with a prettier pair of feet. Life was full of compromises. You could see it etched in the frown lines between her tweezed eyebrows. At least before the Botox.

The Buick skidded to a stop on the ice in front of the Macabees' four-column Colonial house. The modest estate was illuminated with Christmas lights like a supernova. But the facade hid a dark secret. DeeDee Macabee had wanted children, but too few eggs and anemic sperm don't a baby make. They could have adopted, but that would have admitted their failure to conceive, and in Pittsville, gossip spread like toxic fallout.

Daniel's wife Mindy, on the other hand, was fertile as a rabbit. But Daniel had vowed to end his family's legacy, and Mindy had two abortions to punctuate it.

Daniel squinted, sensing a migraine, as he trudged toward the Macabees' overly decorated front door.

"Stand up straight, you're slouching," ordered Mindy, shoving her wrist into his spine as she rang the bell. Bing bong!

She dusted the dandruff off Daniel's lapel as the door opened.

"Mindy and Daniel! What a pleasure!" gushed Deedee Macabee, acting surprised to see them, as she had rehearsed. "I didn't think you were coming."

"We RSVP'd." Daniel slouched. "What'd ya expect?"

"Well," DeeDee wheedled, grimacing like a stroke victim. "It sounds like someone needs some eggnog."

Daniel stumbled over the entryway mumbling, "Eggnog . . . a warm vat of holiday phlegm."

The living room was decorated with tinsel and forced cheer. There were thirty or so guests bumping together like billiard balls in front of the fake Yuletide log.

They all stared at Daniel and Mindy as they entered—the last to arrive. Daniel spotted the Flanders's overweight, pimpled teenage son Jason wolfing microwave pigs in blankets; Burt and Frank, two curmudgeon neighbors in their seventies who stood all day like lawn jockeys complaining about their cataracts; Holly Weaver, a perky bottle-dyed redhead with rock-hard breast implants, who chaired the Pittsville PTA; Chester Sosnowski, the old town barber, who had a standing appointment every Tuesday to trim Daniel's goatee; and Phyllis and Mark Burnside, in their crisp New Hampshire Police uniforms, hanging a tin ornament of a squad car on the overdecorated Christmas tree.

Daniel, head down, made a beeline for the drink cart. It was one of those brass-and-glass numbers with a bottle of store-brand vodka, gin, whiskey, and a plastic jug of Diet Coke. Daniel reached for the whiskey.

"You promised!" Mindy whined.

Daniel gripped the bottle, momentarily glancing at his reflection in the mirrored cart, and hissed through his veneers, "I'm not going to make it, with 'these people,' if I don't have *something*."

Mindy sighed like the air going out of a tractor tire.

Daniel poured himself a tumbler of whiskey and took a calming slug. As his esophagus warmed, he peered at his rippling face in the amber liquor. But then, another image appeared in the whiskey. It was Daniel, and he was oddly missing his jawbone.

"Daniel!" a voice chirped, like someone had found a missing sock. It was Florence Lipkin, principal of Pittsville Elementary. A shriveled woman with a glass eye, Florence had recently brought Daniel a beautiful early twentieth-century, 18K rose-gold Hamilton, with diamond numerals, eight-day lever, and blue steel overcoil hairspring. He admired the restored watch on her wrist as she cradled Prince Valiant, her shivering shih tzu.

Florence had lost her eye in a freak shuffleboard accident six months earlier, but she still kept the cloudy temp marble gripped in the moist socket. Everyone in town gossiped about how cheap Florence was and that she stole bottled water from the school cafeteria. But only Daniel knew that she'd inherited a cool million when her husband expired eight months earlier. Daniel knew it long before she did. But he didn't tell anyone, including his wife. He contemplated the possibilities of how that kind of money might change his life. He could finally leave Pittsville and see the world. If only she would make him the beneficiary in her will.

"How's my favorite watchmaker?" Florence prattled to Daniel, as she personalized her greetings to everyone, like: "How's my favorite mailman?" or "How's my favorite butcher?" or "How's my favorite eye doctor?" Daniel wondered how long before Florence would have a "favorite mortician."

"Not bad." Daniel forced a smile while eyeing the drink cart.

They stood uncomfortably for several moments, just the occasional click of ice in Daniel's tumbler.

Suddenly Daniel was struck on the back so hard his teeth chomped together.

"Daniel, me boy . . . heh . . . heh," a voice boomed like a leprechaun on steroids.

He warily peeked over his shoulder and saw his muscular insurance man, Mike Johnson—all five-foot-four of him.

"Have I told you, Danny, about our new whole-life triple-premium policy? Your principal triples every nine years!"

"Yeah, you have," Daniel flatly replied.

Mike (or Mick as his friends called him) threw a second pitch; "Well then, why haven't we signed ya up?!"

"I won't be needing it."

The ex–star linebacker of the Pittsville High football team, who was too short for a college scholarship, grinned smugly. "What are you, psychic?"

"Well . . ."

Mindy whirled Daniel around. "Honey, look who I just found!" she giddily squirted in her nylons.

Daniel had no idea who the handsome towhead in his late twenties was, though Mindy waited impatiently several moments for his jubilant recognition. The Adonis tried helping out, spreading a cocksure smile and raising his trademark eyebrow.

"Uh," Daniel shrugged, "do I know you?"

"It's Jack Conroy!" Mindy squealed.

Jack nodded with kind understanding at Daniel as if he had a learning disability. "Happens all the time. Everyone thinks I'm an old friend from school or someone they know from work."

Daniel, dumbfounded, stared blankly at the man he had never seen before, or even had the vaguest idea of who he might be . . . or care.

Mindy jumped in desperately, "He's Dr. Randy Marshall . . . from *The End of Our Lives*!"

Jack gave a reassuring wink and clamped Daniel's hemophiliac palm in his meaty paw. "That's all right, Danny—people act kinda funny around 'celebrities.' "

"Don't I have to know who you are for you to be a celebrity?" wondered Daniel aloud.

Jack threw back his head, bleached teeth unhinged in a forced guffaw.

Mindy elbowed Daniel in the ribs, a little too hard.

"What are you doing in Pittsville, Jack?" Daniel edged toward the drink cart. "We don't get many 'celebs' here."

"Just winged in for the holidays. My buddy Lance was born here, and I thought it would be fun to see how the country folk live. I'm a city boy, born in Manhattan. Now, that's a city. Ever been there, Danny boy?"

"No." Daniel paused. "Never will."

"Why not?" spit Jack, munching an imitation crab puff, then plucking the cartilage from his front teeth. "It's only a couple hours from here."

"I just know . . . I'll never go."

"How do you know?" Jack scoffed, "I mean . . . that's how everyone feels about New York before they actually go there. But soon they're singing . . . Newww York! . . . Newwwww . . . !"

Several guests glanced up from their tuna empanadas as Jack's Juilliard-trained voice rang out, ". . . Yorrrrrrrk . . ."

"Hey, I've got that CD!" exclaimed Stuart Macabee, Florence's "favorite gynecologist," as he dashed over, turned off *Wayne Newton's Rockin' Christmas,* and popped in Sinatra.

Jack sang along, booming over "Ol' Blue Eyes."

"Stop singing the bluueess . . . I'm lucky todayyyy, I want to taste a slice of it . . . New Yorrrk, Neww Yorrrrrk . . ."

Florence muttered, "Those aren't the lyrics."

"Who cares? He's gorgeous!" Mindy swooned.

Jack stepped left, found his spotlight, and kicked out his feet for the big finale like the Rockettes. "Look up at meeeee . . . Newwww Yorrrrrrk . . . NeeeEWWwwww . . ."

Daniel took another gulp of whiskey and observed Mindy, entranced by the handsome crooner.

". . . YORRRRRRRRRrrrrrrKKK. . . !"

The last part drifted off key.

Huge ovation.

Mindy hugged Jack as if he had just dismantled a nuclear bomb. Daniel couldn't help noticing the discreet pat on Mindy's flank.

"So, Danny, what do you do?" Jack inquired, inexplicably out of breath.

"I'm a watchmaker."

Mindy studied her out-of-date pumps.

"They still got those?" chortled Jack.

"Yes, I think so," Daniel deadpanned.

"Any money in it?" Jack was eyeing Mindy like a pork chop.

"No, not really," said Daniel. "Acting?"

"You kidding me? I made over six hundred Gs last year. 'F.U.' money, we call it in Hollywood. How many watches you got to repair for that?"

Rather than responding, "All the watches in the Northern Hemisphere," Daniel sullenly slurped his scotch.

Mindy, Jack's newest publicist, chimed in, "Did you hear? Jack did a movie!"

Jack corrected modestly, "Well, Mindy, actually we haven't started shooting yet—but they have half the financing."

"That right?" asked Daniel, "What about the soap?"

"I'm not going to be stuck on a soap the rest of my life," Jack scoffed. "I'm taking an 'out' in my contract to do this movie. Then after a few films, I'll start directing."

Mindy gazed at Jack like a puppy in a Keane painting.

Daniel rolled the ice cube around his glass, round and round, faster and faster until it put him into a trance, and when it stopped . . . he saw his reflection.

And a lot more.

As Jack turned away to smile at Holly, the flushed redhead in the corner, Daniel garbled under his breath . . .

"Not exactly."

"Excuse me. What did you say?" Jack's cocked eyebrow twitched.

"Not exactly," Daniel quietly reiterated.

"What are you talking about?" Jack was growing irritated.

"You sure you want to know?" Daniel made eye contact for the first time that evening.

"Sure, I'm sure!"

Mindy gave Daniel a "don't-you-dare!" glare, which only encouraged him.

"Okay," Daniel began softly. "Though you've left the

soap for the movie gig, the film will lose Canadian financing at the last moment—actually, two weeks from Monday. Your agent, Marty, will wait until you don't pick up your phone to leave the message. Meanwhile, you're out paying cash for that jade green convertible Jag you've been eyeing in the window. But what you don't know, because you haven't heard your agent's message, is that they've already written your character off the soap. He overdoses on morphine, by the way, which he steals at Central Hospital. Stay tuned for the upcoming irony. Anyhow, the producers are so annoyed that you've abandoned your role that they write your character overdosing and crashing off a cliff as you're driving to meet your blind mistress. Your character's face is tragically—and conveniently—burned beyond recognition. Only a face transplant can save you.

"Anyhow, one day you try to drive onto the lot at CBS in your new Jag, but the security guard tells you your pass has expired. 'Screw them!' you say as you screech a U-turn off the lot. 'Who needs 'em!' you snort, trying to convince yourself that this is the best thing that could have happened. Meanwhile, your role of Dr. Randy Marshall, as now played by heartthrob Matt Starling, earns him a Daytime Emmy. For several months you sit at humiliating cattle calls with dozens of younger and better-looking men, but you just can't land a gig. There's a few callbacks but your acting is too wooden, too soap, or so the casting agents say after you've left the room. Then, after a year of ego-crushing auditions, they stop calling altogether. Your agent Marty drops you and signs Matt Starling. You crawl on your hands and knees back to the producers you snubbed on the soap and now beg to get back on. 'What if my character has a brother?!' you implore the producer when you finally get her to take your call. But she tells you that Matt Starling is getting a much higher TVQ and the fan letters are flowing. Ratings are up two points since your unfortunate accident. Over the next four years, your gleaming smile yellows and your mane of blond hair turns gray and recedes toward your back. The gorgeous women who used to eye you now look past you as you circle ever-seedier downtown bars, being sucked toward the drain. Finally, you turn to drugs—methamphetamine specifically—and, here's your irony Jacko, when you run out of rent, you start selling to a few close friends. Actually, this is the closest to a film set as you're ever going to come. You are invited to a few 'C' parties but only if you bring the 'stuff.' Never one to acknowledge your bisexuality, the drugs finally free you to take a lover—your old buddy Lance, another skin popper with whom you occasionally share needles."

Daniel paused, "Shall I go on?"

Jack's mouth was slung open, while Mindy's eyes brimmed with tears.

Daniel stumbled into the powder room and splashed cold water on his face. He dried off on the embroidered pink hand towels—the ones just for display.

When he looked up, Daniel saw the future in the bathroom mirror.

Horrendous things: Jack Conroy whiffing amyl nitrate while having anal sex with Mindy; Florence taking out her glass eye, popping it in her mouth, bathing it with saliva and choking to death; Phyllis Burnside, wearing her NHPD uniform, answering a call to 7-Eleven only to be shot in the head by a fleeing robber—the Flanders's acne-crusted son Jason; The redhead, Holly Weaver, happily on her honeymoon in the Bahamas with Officer Mark Burnside, unaware of her oozing breast implants slowly killing her . . .

Daniel tried to avert his searing eyes away from the horror in the mirror, his heart thumping in his chest, a migraine drilling a hole between his eyes, but he was compelled to stare, as he saw more flashing images: Burt grabbing his chest on his front lawn and collapsing with the sprinklers running; Matt Starling, at the Academy Awards holding up his Oscar and thanking Jack Conroy

for giving him the role that launched his career (as a di-
sheveled police mug shot of Jack provides a comedic
backdrop); Deedee Macabee in her bathroom, gazing into
a blood-filled toilet at her stillborn, tears glistening down
her cheeks; Mindy, at Dr. Macabee's office, reacting to
some news regarding an HIV test; and, finally, Daniel saw
himself sitting in his Buick, wrapping his lips around the
chrome barrel of a Glock 9mm and . . . Blam! Blam! . . .
blood splattered onto an image of Jesus, Daniel's jaw
missing. . . .

A shattering of glass.

Daniel stepped out of the bathroom, clenched knuckles
dripping blood, as Bing Crosby crooned "White Christmas."

Deedee Macabee spotted a droplet of blood on the carpet and shrieked, "Not on the new Berber!"

❖

Daniel reclined on the tufted settee, facing a bookshelf
lined with such book titles as *Neurology, Pathology, Anxiety, Sobriety, Obsessive-Compulsive, Depression, Addiction, Bipolar, Dependency, Dysfunction*—like a run-on
sentence. Daniel noted there were no books on suicide.

He could hear his Bulova ticking, pure precision. *Who
would hear its last tick?* he wondered.

"So, Daniel, are we still having problems with mirrors?"

Sheila Merryman rocked back in her ergonomically designed recliner, her blood red fingernails steepled under
her chin, balancing her head like the scales of sanity.

"When did *you* start having trouble with mirrors?"
Daniel retorted, mocking the plurality of her query.

Sheila didn't give an inch. "Do you think *I* have trouble
with mirrors?"

Daniel hated how therapists bent everything back into a
question mark. It made you feel crazy, even if you weren't.
For two hundred dollars an hour, you'd think they'd answer
a flippin' question.

Nevertheless, Daniel continued their cerebral tango, only this time he asked her a question that she couldn't answer with a question. "Are we really what we see in the mirror, or is our reflection only what we want to see?"

Sheila was silent. Check. Then . . . "What do you think?"

Daniel sighed, "A mirror's just a piece of glass with a silver backing. Our reflection's merely what our eyes see, which our brain interprets."

"So, if we're blind, we have no reflection?"

"What do you think?" Daniel parried.

Checkmate. Or, so he thought.

"Do you want to talk about what happened at the party?" she volleyed back.

"No, I want you to answer my question."

"Fine," Sheila replied calmly. "What you're saying is, if a mirror is in the forest and there's no one to look at it, then there's no reflection?"

"That's what I'm asking *you*," Daniel realized that she had weaseled another question.

"We'll never really know that, now will we, Daniel?"

"Yes, we will. Because, I've seen the forest . . . in the mirror."

Sheila had a befuddled expression.

Daniel continued their philosophical tug-of-war. "It's not the same for you," he explained. "I see the future in reflections. So, if I see myself in the mirror with a gun in my mouth, how do I know if I'm seeing myself in the future, or the present?"

"Have you been having suicidal thoughts, Daniel?"

Yet another question.

Daniel knew exactly when he was going to die because it would be exactly like his father and grandfather, who each put a revolver in his mouth at age fifty-three and blew off the top of his skull when he could no longer deal with his "abilities."

The pain of knowing how and when you're going to kill

yourself is torturous, especially when you see it as clearly as the shine on your wingtips or the reflection in the mirror.

"*You* control your own destiny, Daniel, not the mirror."

"You're missing the point. What I see in the mirror *is* destiny," Daniel articulated, growing frustrated. "And it's never wrong."

Sheila nodded methodically, her face a knot of concerned doubt. "But if you've seen yourself committing suicide in the mirror, yet you're here talking with me about it now, isn't that proof that you can't truly predict what will happen?"

Daniel knew she doubted him; they always did until he told them their own destiny. Most of his ex-therapists couldn't handle that. That's when they released him as a patient, or retired, or went crazy themselves. It's hard to live with your future laid out before you like a losing poker hand. The marriages, the children, divorces, accidents, financial hardships, illnesses, and death. And no matter how hard you tried to alter your course, you couldn't. If Daniel told you that your wife was going to cheat, you might try so hard to stop it that you'd push her into her lover's arms. Or, if Daniel revealed that you were going to die in a crash, you would avoid airplanes only to die in a car wreck.

But still they'd always ask. . . .

"So, tell me, Daniel, do you see what will happen to me?"

❖

Daniel drove home from his psychiatrist's office.

Sheila hadn't taken the news well. But Daniel knew she would delay nine days before the nagging seed that Daniel had planted in her brain would start affecting her sleep. She would finally schedule an appointment with her doctor, reassuring herself that it was a "routine checkup." She wasn't about to give in to her delusional patient, suffering from clinical narcissism coupled with paranoia. She even laughed about it with her gynecologist, Stuart Macabee, breathing a sigh of relief when he found nothing abnormal.

But, seven months later, a blood test would prove Daniel prophetic. Sheila had ovarian cancer.

It didn't make Daniel feel better to be right.

The truth doesn't always set you free. Sometimes it sets you adrift.

Daniel didn't return Sheila's frantic calls on his answering machine, desperately wanting to know if she would survive chemotherapy? What her odds were? How long she had to live?

Daniel felt it best not to answer any more questions.

✿

Three years had passed.

Mindy had since run off with Jack Conroy, Florence had died and left all her money to her diabetic shih tzu, Jason Flanders was back in prison (this time for carjacking), Holly Weaver was featured on TV's Extreme Makeovers and received new double-D breast implants, and Mike Johnson died of a brain tumor less than a week before his triple-premium policy was funded.

A Buick LeSabre was parked at the edge of the Pittsville scenic-view overlook. Water reflected off Lake Winnipesaukee, which glimmered beneath the cliff. So inviting. A perfect spring day.

But Daniel wasn't interested in the view.

Mindy had left Daniel the Buick in the divorce and little else, besides the dusty watches in his meager shop. He wound his Bulova gently, put it to his ear, and listened to his fifty-third birthday ticking down the steep side of the tracks like a death coaster.

He reached into the glove compartment and lifted out his Glock 9mm, which he had bought at the local sporting goods store that morning. The salesman, Mark Burnside, had suggested the used model. It had been Officer Burnside's trusty sidearm before he retired. He had never drawn it on duty, but Daniel saw something in the chrome barrel and knew that the gun was going to commit murder, someday.

"How's Holly doing?" Daniel had inquired, making small talk with the ex-cop as he weighed the weapon.

"Oh, you know," replied Mark, avoiding Daniel's psychic gaze.

Word had gotten around about Daniel's supernatural talents and he had become a pariah in Pittsville. It was as if Daniel was causing afflictions, not predicting them.

If only he could have 911'd his psychiatrist, Sheila. But she had expired, on schedule, eight months earlier from ovarian cancer.

Daniel opened the glove compartment.

He lifted out the loaded 9mm. It felt cold in his trembling hand as he studied his knuckles, scarred by years of broken mirrors.

He couldn't live another second, let alone another year with the excruciating gnawing of knowing how and when he would die.

He slid the gun barrel between his lips and stared at the cross dangling from his rearview mirror as he breathed through his nostrils.

A fishing skiff cut across the mirrored lake and Daniel spotted Frank, trolling for bites, a radio in his boat for company where Burt used to sit.

Daniel suddenly began sobbing, his sputum dribbling down the chrome barrel. He pulled the gun from his mouth and dropped it in his coat pocket. He would no longer be guided by his visions. He would take destiny into his own hands.

He started the car's engine, revved it several times, and simply drove off the cliff . . . as he stared at himself in the rearview mirror.

✿

The Buick was momentarily slowed by a jack pine growing from the rocks. The car nevertheless created a huge wave on impact, rocking Frank out of his boat to dive after the sinking car. It took three attempts, but Frank finally pulled Daniel from the partially submerged car and swam him to the tree-lined shore. He pumped the water from Daniel's lungs and performed CPR.

But irreparable brain damage had occurred.

✿

Daniel had lain in a vegetative state for eleven months when Mindy finally came to the convalescent home to visit.

Her emaciated body sat by the window, sunlight illuminating the purple Kaposi's sarcoma sores around her neck and mouth. She held a single blue balloon that read: "Happy 53rd." Her hand loosened on the string, releasing the balloon out the window. She watched it slowly drift skyward until it became a tiny dot, swallowed by the clouds.

Then she calmly opened her purse and took out Daniel's Glock 9mm.

It felt cold and heavy.

She placed the gun in Daniel's hand, curled his stiff fingers around the grip, and raised it beneath his chin.

"Till death do us part."

She pulled the trigger and blew Daniel's brains all over the cross on the wall.

Then she blew out hers.

Just as Daniel had seen in the mirror.

THE FALL

D. LYNN SMITH

"They created a contemptible spirit in order to adulterate souls
through this spirit."
—THE SECRET BOOK OF JOHN

RYAN IS AFRAID of the dark. He is afraid of the thunder that rumbles outside like the stomach of some hungry beast. He is afraid of the lightning that gives glimpses of things hiding in the dark. In one flash he sees the dark maw of the kitchen arch. FLASH, he sees the refrigerator door with an angel magnet, its wings spread to protect the picture of him, his mom and dad, and the twins. FLASH, he sees his father sitting at the kitchen table, head hanging as if he slept sitting up.

Then the darkness returns and he sees only afterimages of those glimpses swimming before his eyes.

"Dad?"

"Go back to bed, Ryan," his father says.

"When's Mom coming home?"

"Soon."

Thunder growls.

"I'm afraid," Ryan says.

"So am I."

But Ryan knows it isn't true. His father is a fireman. He

saves people's lives while risking his own. Lightning pours into the room. His father hasn't moved. Ryan turns away.

The hall is dark, but a little light pours through a doorway at the far end. He walks past the twins' room. The door is shut so he can't see inside. Sometimes he wished he could close a door in his head so he didn't have to see inside it, either.

He moves down the hall and into the light spilling from his aquarium. Five discus swim over to the glass to greet him. His mother didn't want him to get discus. The petshop guy said they weren't good for kids. They're skittish. They don't like vibrations like those from kids jumping around. But Ryan convinced his mom that at twelve years old he was no longer a kid.

These are red turquoise discus. They have red-brown stripes and are blue around the outside of their bodies. Each one has a name. Sally, Jack, Alice, Sam, and Bill.

Jack is a little bit smaller than the rest, but he acts like he's the biggest fish in the tank. He eats first and nobody gives him any grief. Ryan likes that. It makes Jack his favorite.

The twins had always wanted to come in to see the fish. But they would tap on the glass, so Ryan had kept them out. He wishes now he had played with them more.

Ryan didn't realize he had fallen asleep until a deafening crash of thunder makes him jump awake. There are voices in the kitchen, so he creeps down the dark hall and stands beside the refrigerator.

FLASH. His father stands facing Ryan's mother. She's beautiful. Her skin is white and smooth, her brown hair short and sort of wild looking. She wears the T-shirt Ryan gave her that says, "World's Greatest Mom."

DARKNESS.

"Jess," Ryan's mother says. "Let's not fight. I love you."

Ryan hears his father murmur something, but thunder rumbles and he can't make out the words. FLASH. His mother embraces his father and, for a moment, Ryan thinks that maybe everything is going to be okay. Maybe his mother is back for good and they are going to be a family again.

DARKNESS. Ryan hears the muffled sound of the gun. A wail cuts through the night and the thunder crashes in unison. FLASH. The T-shirt blossoms with blood in the "a" of "greatest." His mother's mouth twists and her fangs descend. DARKNESS. Ryan covers his ears against the terrible wail filling the kitchen. FLASH. His dad raises the gun to his mother's forehead. DARKNESS. The crack and flash of the gun is worse than that of the thunder and lightning. The sulfurous stink of the gunpowder hurts his nose.

FLASH. His father picks up a machete and raises it above his head. "I love you, too," he says. Then he brings the machete down. DARKNESS. Ryan knows his mother is no more.

The keening that should have stopped when his mother's head separated from her body continues. Ryan realizes it's coming from his own throat. FLASH. His father drops the machete and turns. His face is a reflection of the grief that Ryan feels ripping through his body. DARKNESS. Ryan runs to his dad and holds on. He cries. But it's okay, because his dad cries, too.

✧

Southern Florida is crisscrossed with a network of roads where developers have run out of money and abandoned their housing developments. Palmettos grow where bedrooms should be. Street signs used for target practice are riddled with holes. Rusted-out refrigerators and stained mattresses are the only lawn art here. These are lonely, desolate places.

If you follow one of these roads back into one of the subdivisions, you'll find an old trailer set on cinder blocks. It looks like it's been deserted for years, but close inspection shows fresh tire prints in the soft dirt and flattened grass where a jeep has passed.

Ryan's bike bumps along this grassy track as he races toward the trailer. The air is thick and heavy. His shirt sticks to him. Sweat runs down to sting his eyes.

He bikes past three white crosses. In front of one is a rectangle of freshly turned earth.

He stops when he reaches his father's jeep. Then he lets his bike fall and runs toward the trailer.

A deep-throated rumble stops him in his tracks. His eyes dart around. A shadow moves beneath the trailer. There's a hissing and a growl that crawls inside his stomach and curls up into a hard knot.

A twelve-foot bull alligator has taken refuge from the sun underneath the trailer. When Ryan was six years old, a neighbor took him out to show him the alligator that lived in the lake behind her house. The neighbor was going to feed it a chicken breast. It ate her arm instead.

Ryan screws up his nerve and slowly makes his way toward the trailer's steps, keeping a wary eye on the alligator. Having issued his warning, the gator goes back to napping.

Inside the trailer a man stands spread-eagle, his arms suspended from the ceiling with chains, his legs similarly spread and chained.

Ryan's father sits on a stool in front of the man. "I told you to go straight home after school," he says.

Ryan's mouth is dry as the man's head swivels toward him. No, not a man. A creature that *almost* looks like a man. Except its nose is kind of flat and its eyes are round and black like marbles.

The creature's mouth spreads into a wide smile when it sees Ryan. There are only four pointed teeth, two on the top and two on the bottom. Pink gums glisten through the lips.

"My boy." Its voice sounds a lot like the hissing of the alligator.

Ryan forgets to avoid looking into the creature's eyes and he falls into a jumble of disjointed memories. The death smell of swamp in the twins' room. The thump of a body hitting the floor. A tongue licking blood from pale lips. The sharp smell of pee. A little girl's whimper.

A stinging slap brings Ryan back to the present. There are tears in his eyes.

The creature's laugh fills the room with the smell of rotting swamp.

Ryan's father grabs him by the shoulders, jerking him away. "Go home," he says.

Ryan's tears begin to spill down his face. "I didn't help them," he says. "He killed them and I just stood there."

Ryan's father shakes him. "You couldn't help them. That thing enthralled you. That's why you can't look into its eyes."

Ryan stares into his father's eyes, wanting to believe, wanting to be enthralled so he can forget. "I want to kill it," he says. "I have to kill it."

His father's eyes are hard. Ryan hopes he doesn't see how afraid he is.

"Food animals don't kill," hisses the creature. "They die."

Ryan's father takes a deep breath. "It's late," he says. "Come back tomorrow. I'll show you what I know."

"Aren't you coming home?"

"I can't leave him alone. Will you be all right?"

Ryan feels a flash of fear, but he also feels a flash of pride that his father trusts him to stay home alone. "Yeah," he answers. "I'll make peanut butter and jelly."

"Bring me one tomorrow, okay? Extra jelly."

❖

When Ryan returns the next day, his father is deep into experimenting on the creature. "This thing isn't like what your mom became," says Ryan's father.

"She was excrement," hisses the creature.

Ryan's father raises a cattle prod and touches it to the center of the creature's bare chest. Its scream sounds like the scream of the neighborhood cat Ryan saw hit by a car. Chessie was dead, lying on her side, and yet her body kept twisting and jumping two feet into the air as that death scream oozed out of her.

Ryan's father continues to hold the cattle prod to the creature's skin, not seeming to notice the screaming. "This thing has never been human. The only weakness I've found so far is to electric shock. Look at its chest."

Ryan watches as the creature's skin blackens in a round circle around the end of the cattle prod.

"Electricity burns it." His father takes the prod away and the screaming fades into a hiss. "It heals quickly."

The blackened skin sloughs off and healthy, pink skin appears beneath.

"His arms look funny," says Ryan.

"That's because they're not just arms. Come, look at this." Ryan's father was flushed with the excitement of discovery. It had been a long time since Ryan had seen him like this. Not since that time in Zion National Park when he had found a real Indian arrowhead.

"The elbows don't bend like ours do. They bend kind of sideways and back." He reaches up and grabs the creature's arm, bending it back. The creature turns and hisses at him, his face a mask of terror and rage. Yellow spittle flies from its mouth and drips down its chin.

Ryan steps back but his father puts a hand on his shoulder. "He can't hurt you now," he says.

He pulls at the membrane that runs along the creature's arm and down its side to its feet. "It's a wing, Ryan. Like a bat. That's how he got out of the twins' room so quick. He jumped out the window, then flew away."

"Your young make good food," hissed the creature. "So easy to take, so succulent. It's why I came back for the mother."

Ryan feels the barb hit his heart. *I was enthralled,* he reminded himself. *It wasn't my fault.*

"Can I shock him, Dad?" he asks.

His father's eyes have gone dead as he stares at the creature. He hands the cattle prod to Ryan. Ryan lifts it to a small pink nipple on the creature's chest. The creature's scream is that of many dying cats. Ryan feels satisfaction.

✧

Ryan's father stays with the creature each night for a week. Ryan calls in sick for him. Then he microwaves frozen macaroni and cheese or makes peanut butter sandwiches. He takes some to his dad, but his dad doesn't eat much. He doesn't bathe. He doesn't put on the clean clothes Ryan brings him.

He smells bad. His face is dark with whiskers and each time he hugs Ryan they scratch his cheek and hurt.

But the creature doesn't die. His dad has strangled it, stabbed it, and shot it. Each time the skin heals and the creature laughs, its rotting breath chasing away even the smell of his father.

Ryan knows how to kill it. He'll do it tomorrow. Then his dad will come home.

At home, Ryan goes into his room, and the discus swim to the glass to greet him. He takes some flake food and drops it in—only what he knows they can eat in five minutes so leftover food doesn't soil the water. Jack darts around catching the biggest of the drifting flakes. He is greedy. Ryan wonders if the others get enough to eat. Maybe Jack is eating their share.

Ryan taps on the tank. All five fish dart away as if they were hit by an invisible bat. Then they go after the food again. Jack is first. Ryan taps the glass again. The fish dart away.

The creature had called the twins "food." "Good food," it said.

Ryan taps the glass.

Before it had drained them, the creature had smelled them.

Tap.

It put its face down by their necks and breathed in their little-kid smell.

Tap.

Then it bit them and Ryan watched the life run out of their eyes a little at a time. He didn't look into the creature's eyes. He wasn't enthralled. He was afraid. And in his fear he'd peed his pants.

The aquarium glass breaks and Ryan's hand has a deep slice from which blood runs. The discus slide out on a waterfall and land on the floor. They flop up and down like a dead cat, their mouths gaping, their eyes bulging. Ryan stands and watches as blood mixes with water around the tortured bodies. Jack is the last to die.

✧

Ryan goes to church. He tells them his father is sick. They offer to bring communion to the house, but Ryan tells them he can't eat anything. Not even communion.

They ask about Ryan's injured hand. They want to peek under the gauze he has wrapped around it. The blood has started to seep through. Has he seen a doctor? He needs a tetanus shot. They'll take him to the hospital since his dad can't.

No, he tells them. It's not bad. Just a scratch from working on his bike.

Ryan takes communion. He watches the priest bless the sacrament, then, when it's his turn, he walks to the front and kneels.

On the wall above the altar is a stained-glass window with the image of Christ, broken and bleeding on the cross. An angel hovers above his head, a look of sorrow on its face. Ryan wonders why the angel doesn't rescue the son of God.

The priest dips the wafer, the body of Christ, into the wine, the blood of Christ, and places the dripping wafer into Ryan's mouth. The blood will cleanse him of his sins and allow him to enter the kingdom of heaven. His mother used to take communion. The twins had been too young.

Ryan leaves the church and rides his bike back to the trailer. The bull alligator is still there. It hisses and rumbles at Ryan, but Ryan doesn't even notice.

Inside the trailer, the creature is starving. Its hair is falling out in clumps. Its bones show beneath sallow skin. Its wrists and ankles are raw and swollen. It pants and whimpers.

His father is down on his hands and knees, examining the claws on its feet. He has a pair of pliers on one claw. He pulls. The creature whimpers again as the claw comes free and a bloody hole is left on its foot.

Ryan's father looks up as Ryan enters. He doesn't look much better than the beast. "It cuts glass," he says. "Watch."

He leads Ryan over to a window where there are several slices. He uses the claw to slice the last side of a square. Then he gently taps on the glass and the square falls out into the weeds. "Just like a diamond," he says.

He sees Ryan's backpack with the handle sticking out. "What's that?" he asks.

Ryan pulls out the machete. His father stares first at it, then at Ryan.

"I'm going to chop off its head," says Ryan. "I'm going to kill it."

The look in his father's eyes fills Ryan with doubt. It looks like panic. "Don't you want to kill it?" he asks.

"It hasn't paid enough."

"I want you to come home."

His father notices the bandage. He takes Ryan's hand in his and says, "What happened?"

Ryan shrugs. His father begins to unwrap the bloody gauze. The creature stirs.

"This looks bad." The cut is still oozing blood. The skin around it is red and angry-looking. "You need stitches."

The hand hurts, but Ryan doesn't care.

The creature raises its head. Ryan meets its eyes. Nothing. No memories. No enthrallment. Ryan sneers at it. Only it's not looking at him. It's looking at his hand. It begins to whine.

Ryan's father turns. He takes the bloody bandage and waves it in front of the creature. The whining grows louder. Yellow drool drips from its chin.

"Is this what you want? My son's blood? My blood?" He holds the bandage closer, just out of reach as the creature strains to take it into its mouth. "You will not have it," says his father.

The creature convulses so violently that the trailer trembles. Ryan and his father are knocked against the wall.

The metal roof screams as a second convulsion hits the creature. One of the shackles breaks free from the buckling roof. The arm falls to the creature's side as if made of lead.

Ryan's father dives for the cattle prod, but the trailer shakes like a giant metal dog and the prod is knocked away. The second shackle breaks. The creature falls onto his face on the floor.

Ryan watches as its body begins to change, the bones shifting beneath the skin with hideous snaps and pops. The creature flips onto its back and its back arches. It opens its mouth and a darkness issues out like a swarm of gnats.

Right there before them the creature transforms. Its skin becomes translucent. From its back sprout wings of white feathers. All its wounds heal. Its face transforms to one so beautiful Ryan cannot bear to look at it.

The trailer stops its metallic screams. The silence is

filled with the angel's harsh breathing as it struggles to its knees, then to its feet.

Ryan's father is between Ryan and the angel. He is on his knees, his face in his hands, supplicant to the being before him.

The angel moves to kneel in front of his father. It reaches out and pulls his hands away.

"Do not kneel before me, for I am the source of your anguish," says the angel, its voice like the chiming of church bells.

Ryan's father looks up into the angel's eyes. "I tortured you," he says, his voice cracking.

Shame washes over Ryan as he realizes that his father is crying.

"You released me," said the angel. "Our jealousy of man blinded us. Tasting man's blood made us forget who we were. Man's blood bound us to the evil we had become. In denying me that blood, you have allowed me to be reborn."

Ryan remembers standing in the twins' room, watching as they died one at a time.

"We can end this, you and I," says that musical voice. "We can find my brethren and help them regain their natures."

Ryan remembers the blood on the front of his mother's shirt. He remembers her fangs. He remembers the creature calling her "excrement."

"Mankind will be free of us, and perhaps we can regain heaven," the angel sang.

"Yes," says Ryan's father. That one word cuts through Ryan like a butcher knife. He picks up the machete.

"Yes," his father repeats. "Let's end this."

"Let's end this," repeats Ryan. His father and the angel look at him as if they'd forgotten he was there. He sees understanding in both their eyes the instant before he swings the machete.

"No!" his father screams.

But the blade swings true and the angel's head hits the

trailer floor with a satisfying thunk. The body takes longer to fall. When it does, all the white feathers are covered in red blood. The same color blood as the twins' and his mother's.

Ryan's father jumps to his feet and pushes Ryan away. "What have you done?" he screams. His hands are balled into tight fists; his face is red, the veins in his neck are pulsing. "You murdered an angel."

"He wasn't an angel," yells Ryan, his anger raging to the surface. "He was the monster that killed the twins and made Mom into that thing."

"He was an angel!"

"You were enthralled," says Ryan.

"You saw him. He changed. He wanted to help us."

"The blood of Christ is for us, not him. He doesn't get forgiveness. He doesn't get to go to heaven."

Ryan's father lunges for him. Ryan doesn't think. He reacts. And it's not until his father's eyes widen in surprise that he realizes he defended himself with the machete.

"Ryan . . ."

"You were going to let him go."

"Ryan, I love you. . . ."

"He killed them and you were going to let him go." Ryan pulls the machete from his father's stomach. A torrent of blood comes with it.

"I'm going to find them all and make them pay." He raises the machete. "I'm not afraid anymore."

Ryan brings the machete down and another head hits the floor with a satisfying thunk.

PART OF THE GAME

F. PAUL WILSON

"**Y**OU HAVE BEEN brought to attention of a most illustrious one," Jiang Zhifu said.

The Chinaman wore long black cotton pajamas with a high collar and onyx-buttoned front. He'd woven his hair into a braid that snaked out from beneath a traditional black skullcap. His eyes were as shiny and black as his onyx buttons and, typical of his kind, gave nothing away.

Detective Sergeant Hank Sorenson smiled. "I guess the Mandarin heard about my little show at Wang's pai gow parlor last night."

Jiang's mug remained typically inscrutable. "I not mention such a one."

"Didn't have to. Tell him I want to meet him."

Jiang blinked. Got him! Direct speech always set these Chinks back on their heels.

Hank let his cup of tea cool on the small table between them. He'd pretend to take a sip or two but not a drop would pass his lips. He doubted anyone down here would make a move against a bull, but you could never be sure where the Mandarin was concerned.

He tried to get a bead on this coolie. A call in the night from someone saying he was Jiang Zhifu, a "representa- tive"—these coolies made him laugh—of an important man in Chinatown. He didn't have to say who. Hank knew. The Chink said they must meet to discuss important mat- ters of mutual interest. At the Jade Moon. Ten A.M.

Hank knew the place—next to a Plum Street joss house—and he'd arrived early. First thing he'd done was check out the alley behind the place. All clear. Inside he'd chosen a corner table near the rear door and seated himself with his back to the wall.

The Jade Moon wasn't exactly high end as Chinkytown restaurants went: dirty floors, smudged tumblers, chipped lacquer on the doors and trim, ratty-looking paper lanterns dangling from the exposed beams.

Not the kind of place he'd expect to meet a minion of the mysterious and powerful and ever-elusive Mandarin.

The Mandarin didn't run Chinatown's rackets. He had a better deal: He skimmed them. Never got his hands dirty except with the money that was pressed into them. Dope, prostitution, gambling . . . the Mandarin took a cut of everything.

How he'd pulled that off was a bigger mystery than his identity. Hank had dealt with the tongs down here—tough mugs one and all. Not the sort you'd figure to hand over part of their earnings without a fight. But they did.

Well, maybe there'd been a dust up and they lost. But if that was what had happened, it must have been fought out of sight, because he hadn't heard a word about it.

Hank had been running the no-tickee-no-shirtee beat for SFPD since 1935 and had yet to find anyone who'd ever seen the Mandarin. And they weren't just *saying* they'd never seen them—they meant it. If three years down here had taught him anything, it was that you never ask a Chink a direct question. You couldn't treat them like regular people. You had to approach everything on an angle. They were devious, crafty, always dodging and weaving, always ducking the question and avoiding an answer.

He'd developed a nose for their lies, but had never caught a whiff of deceit when he'd asked about the Mandarin. Even when he'd played rough with a character or two, they didn't know who he was, where he was, or what he looked like.

It had taken Hank a while to reach the astonishing conclusion that they didn't *want* to know. And that had taken him aback. Chinks were gossipmongers—yak-yak-yak in their singsong voices, trading rumors and tidbits like a bunch of old biddies. For them to avoid talking about someone meant they were afraid.

Even the little people were afraid. That said something for the Mandarin's reach.

Hank had to admit he was impressed, but hardly afraid. He wasn't a Chink.

Jiang had arrived exactly at ten, kowtowing before seating himself.

"Even if I knew of such a one," the Chinaman said, "I am sure he not meet with you. He send emissary, just as my master send me."

Hank smiled. These Chinks . . .

"Okay, if that's the way we're going to play it, you tell your master that I want a piece of his pie."

Jiang frowned. "Pie?"

"His cream. His skim. His payoff from all the opium and dolla-dolla girls and gambling down here."

"Ah so." Jiang nodded. "My master realize that such arrangement is part of everyday business, but one such as he not sully hands with such. He suggest you contact various sources of activities that interest you and make own arrangements with those establishments."

Hank leaned forward and put on his best snarl.

"Listen, you yellow-faced lug, I don't have time to go around bracing every penny-ante operation down here. I know your boss gets a cut from all of them, so I want a cut from *him*! Clear?"

"I'm afraid that quite impossible."

"*Nothing* is impossible!" He leaned back. "But I'm a reasonable man. I don't want it all. I don't even want half of it all. I'll settle for an even split of his gambling take."

Jiang smiled. "This a jest, yes?"

"I'm serious. Dead serious. He can keep everything from the dope and the heifer dens. I want half of the Mandarin's gambling take."

Hank knew that was where the money was in China- town. Opium was big down here, but gambling . . . these coolies gambled on anything and everything. They had their games, sure—parlors for fan-tan, mah-jongg, pai gow, sic bo, pak kop piu, and others—but they didn't stop there. Numbers had a huge take. He'd seen slips collected day and night on street corners all over the quarter. Write down three numbers, hand them in with your money, and pray the last three Dow Jones numbers matched yours at the end of trading.

They'd bet on just about any damn thing, even the weather.

They didn't bother to hide their games either. They'd post the hours of operation on their doors, and some even had touts standing outside urging people inside. Gambling was in their blood, and gambling was where the money was, so gambling was where Hank wanted to be.

No, make that *would* be.

Jiang shook his head and began to rise. "So sorry, De- tective Sorenson, but—"

Hank sprang from his chair and grabbed the front of Jiang's black top.

"Listen, Chink-boy! This is not negotiable! One way or

another I'm going to be part of the game down here. Get that? A big part. Or else there'll *be* no game. I'll bring in squad after squad and we'll collar every numbers coolie and shut down every lousy parlor in the quarter—mah-jongg, sic bo, you name it, it's history. And then what will your boss's take be? What's a hundred percent of nothing, huh?"

He jerked Jiang closer and backhanded him across the face, then shoved him against the wall.

"Tell him he either gets smart or he gets nothing!"

Hank might have said more, but the look of murderous rage in Jiang's eyes stalled the words in his throat.

"Dog!" the Chink whispered through clenched teeth. "You have made this one lose face before these people!"

Hank looked around the suddenly silent restaurant. Diners and waiters alike stood frozen, gawking at him. But Hank Sorenson wasn't about to be cowed by a bunch of coolies.

He jabbed a finger at Jiang. "Who do you think you are, calling me a—?"

Jiang made a slashing motion with his hand. "I am servant of one who would not wipe his sandals on your back. You make this one lose face, and that mean you make *him* lose face. Woe to you, Detective Sorenson."

Without warning, he let out a yelp and slammed the edge of his hand onto the table, then turned and walked away.

He was halfway to the door when the table fell apart.

Hank stood in shock, staring down at the pile of splintered wood. What the—?

Never mind that now. He gathered his wits and looked around. He wanted out of here, but didn't want to walk past all those staring eyes. They might see how he was shaking inside.

That table . . . If Jiang could do that to wood, what could he do to a neck?

Fending off that unsettling thought, he left by the back door. He took a deep breath of putrid back-alley air as he stepped outside. The late-morning sun hadn't risen high enough yet to break up the shadows here.

Well, he'd delivered his message. And the fact that Jiang had struck the table instead of him only reinforced what he already knew: no worry about bull busting down here. No Chink would dare lay a hand on a buzzer-carrying member of the SFPD. They knew what would happen in their neighborhoods if anyone ever did something like that.

He sighed as he walked toward the street. At least during his time in the restaurant he'd been thinking of something other than Luann. But now she came back to him. Her face, her form, her voice . . . oh, that voice.

Luann, Luann, Luann . . .

◐

"I should have killed the dog for his insult to you, Venerable," Jiang said as he knelt before the Mandarin and pressed his forehead against the stone floor.

Instead of his usual Cantonese, Jiang spoke in Mandarin—fittingly, the language the Mandarin preferred.

"No," the master said in his soft, sibilant voice. "You did well not to harm him. We must find a more indirect path to deal with such a one. Sit, Jiang."

"Thank you, Illustrious."

Jiang raised his head from the floor but remained kneeling, daring only a furtive peek at his master. Many times he had seen the one known throughout Chinatown as the Mandarin—not even Jiang knew his true name—but that did not lessen the wonder of his appearance.

A high-shouldered man standing tall and straight with his hands folded inside the sleeves of his embroidered emerald robe; a black skullcap covered the thin hair that fringed his high, domed forehead. Jiang marveled as ever at his light green eyes that seemed almost to glow.

He did not know if his master was a true mandarin, or merely called such because of the dialect he preferred. He did know the master spoke many languages. He'd heard him speak English, French, German, and even a low form of Hindi to the dacoits in his employ.

For all the wealth flowing through his coffers, the master lived frugally. Jiang had gathered that he was part of a larger organization, perhaps even its leader. He suspected that most of the money went back to the homeland for weapons to resist the invading Japanese curs who had ravaged Nanjing.

"So this miserable offspring of a maggot demands half the gambling tribute. Wishes to be—how did he put it?— 'part of the game?' "

"Yes, Magnificent."

The master closed his eyes. "Part of the game . . . part of the game. . . . By all means, we must grant his wish."

Jiang spent the ensuing moments of silence in a whirlpool of confusion. The master . . . giving in to the cockroach's demands? Unthinkable! And yet he'd said—

An upward glance showed the master's eyes open again and a hint of a smile curving his thin lips.

"Yes, that is it. We shall make him part of the game."

Jiang had seen that smile before. He knew what usually followed. It made him three-times glad that he was not Detective Sorenson.

☯

Hank held up his double-breasted tuxedo and inspected it, paying special attention to the wide satin lapels. No spots. Good. He could get a few more wears before sending it for cleaning.

As always, he was struck by the incongruity of a tux in his shabby two-room apartment. Well, it should look out of place. It had cost him a month's rent.

All for Luann.

That babe was costing him a fortune. Trouble was, he

didn't have a fortune. But then, the Chinatown games would fix that.

He shook his head. That kind of scheme would have been unthinkable back in the days when he was a fresh bull. And if not for Luann, it would still be unthinkable.

But a woman can change everything. A woman can turn you inside out and upside down.

Luann was one of those women.

He remembered the first time he'd seen her at the Serendipity Club. Like getting gut-punched. She wasn't just a choice piece of calico; she had the kind of looks that could put your conscience on hold. Then she'd stepped up to the mike and . . . a voice like an angel. When Hank heard her sing "I've Got You Under My Skin," that was it. He was gone. He'd heard Doris Lessing sing it a hundred times on the radio, but Luann . . . Luann made him feel like she was singing to him.

Hank had stayed on through the last show. When she finished he followed her—a flash of his buzzer got him past the geezer guarding the backstage door—and asked her out. A cop wasn't the usual stage-door Johnny and so she'd said okay.

Hank had gone all out to impress Luann, and they'd been on the town half a dozen times so far. She'd tapped him out without letting him get to first base. He knew he wasn't the only guy she dated—he'd spied her out with a couple of rich cake eaters—but Hank wasn't the sharing kind. Trouble was, to get an exclusive on her was going to take moolah. Lots of it.

And he was going to get lots of it. A steady stream . . .

He yawned. What with playing the bon vivant by night and the soft heel by day, he wasn't getting much sleep.

He dropped onto the bed, rolled onto his back, and closed his eyes. Luann didn't go on for another couple of hours, so a catnap would be just the ticket. He was slipping into that mellow, drowsy state just before dropping off to sleep when he felt a sharp pain in his left shoulder, like he'd been stabbed with an ice pick.

As he bolted out of bed, Hank felt something wriggling against his undershirt. He reached back and felt little legs—*lots* of little legs. Fighting a sick revulsion, Hank grabbed it and pulled. It writhed and twisted in his hand but held fast to his skin. Hank clenched his teeth and yanked.

As the thing came free, pain like he'd never known or imagined exploded in his shoulder, driving him to his knees. He dropped the wriggling thing and slapped a hand over the live coal embedded in his shoulder. Through tear-blurred vision he saw a scarlet millipede at least eight inches long scurrying away across the floor.

"What the—?"

He reached for something—anything—to use against it. He grabbed a shoe and smashed it down on the thing. The heel caught the back half of its body and Hank felt it squish with a crunch. The front half spasmed, reared up, then tore free and darted under the door and out into the hallway before he could get a second shot.

Hell with it! His shoulder was killing him.

He brought his hand away and found blood on his palm. Not much, but enough to shake him. He struggled to his feet and stepped into his tiny bathroom. The bright bulb over the speckled mirror picked up the beads of sweat on his brow.

He was shaking. What was that thing? He'd never seen anything like it. And how had it got in his room, in his *bed*, for Christ sake?

He half-turned and angled his shoulder toward the mirror. The size of the bite surprised him—only a couple of punctures within a small smear of blood. From the ferocity of the pain, he'd expected something like a .38 entry wound.

The burning started to subside. Thank God. He balled up some toilet tissue and dabbed at the wound. Looky there. Stopped bleeding already.

He went back to the front room and looked at the squashed remains of the thing. Damn. It looked like something you'd find in a jungle. Like the Amazon.

How'd it wind up in San Francisco?

Probably crawled off a boat.

Hank shuddered as he noticed a couple of the rearmost legs still twitching.

He kicked it into a corner.

☯

"The usual table, Detective?" Maurice said with a practiced smile.

Hank nodded and followed the Serendipity's maître d' to a second-level table for two just off the dance floor.

"Thank you, Maurice."

He passed him a fin he could barely afford as they shook hands. He ordered a scotch and water and started a tab. This was the last night he'd be able to do this until the Mandarin came across with some lucre.

He shook his head. All it takes is money. You don't have to be smart or even good looking, all you need is lots of do-re-mi and everybody wants to know you. Suddenly you're Mr. Popularity.

As Hank sipped his drink and waited for Luann to take the stage, he felt his shoulder start to burn. Damn. Not again. The pain had lasted only half an hour after the bite, and then his shoulder felt as good as new. But now the pain was back and growing stronger.

Heat spread from the bite, flowing through him, flushing his skin, breaking him out in a sweat. Suddenly he had no strength. His hands, his arms, his legs . . . all rubbery. The glass slipped from his fingers, spilling scotch down the pleated front of his shirt.

The room rocked and swayed as he tried to rise, but his legs wouldn't hold him. He felt himself falling, saw the curlicue pattern of the rug rushing at him.

Then nothing.

◑

Hank opened his eyes and found himself looking up at a woman in white. He looked down. More white. Sheets. He was in a bed.

"Where—?"

She looked about fifty. She flashed a reassuring smile. "You're in St. Luke's and you're going to be just fine. I'll let your doctor know you're awake."

Hank watched her bustle out the door. He felt dazed. The last thing he remembered—

That bite from the millipede—poison. Had to be.

The pain had tapered to a dull ache, but he still felt weak as a kitty.

A balding man with a graying mustache strode through the door and stepped up to the bed. He wore a white coat with half a dozen pens in the breast pocket and carried a clipboard under his arm.

"Detective Sorenson," he said, extending his hand, "I'm Dr. Cranston, and you've got quite a boil on your back."

"Boil?"

"Yes. A pocket of infection in your skin. You shouldn't let those things go. The infection can seep into your system and make you very ill. How long have you had it?"

Hank pulled the hospital gown off his shoulder and gaped at the golf-ball-size red swelling.

"That wasn't there when I put on my shirt tonight."

Dr. Cranston harrumphed. "Of course it was. These things don't reach that size in a matter of hours."

A flash of anger cut through Hank's fuzzy brain. "This

one did. I was bitten there by a giant bug around seven o'clock."

Cranston smoothed his mustache. "Really? What kind of bug?"

"Don't know. Never seen anything like it."

"Well, be that as it may, we'll open it up, clean out the infection, and you'll be on your way in no time."

Hank hoped so.

☯

Bared to the waist, Hank lay on his belly while the nurse swabbed his shoulder with some sort of antiseptic.

"You may feel a brief sting as I break the skin, but once we relieve the pressure from all that pus inside, it'll be like money from home."

Hank looked up and saw the scalpel in Cranston's hand. He turned away.

"Do it."

Cranston was half-right: Hank felt the sting, but no relief. He heard Cranston mutter, "Well, this is one for Ripley's."

Hank didn't like the sound of that.

"What's wrong?"

"Most odd. There's no pus in this, only serous fluid."

"What's serous fluid?"

"A clear amber fluid—just like you'd see seeping from a burn blister. Most odd, most odd." Cranston cleared his throat. "I believe we'll keep you overnight."

"But I can't—"

"You must. You're too weak to be sent home. And I want to look into this insect. What did it look like?"

"Send someone to my place and you'll find its back half."

"I believe I'll do just that."

☯

Two days cooped up in a hospital room hadn't made Hank any better. He had to get out to seal the deal with the Mandarin. But how? He was able to get up and walk—shuffle was more like it—but he still felt so weak. And the pounds were dropping off him like leaves from a tree.

The boil or whatever it was had gone from a lump to a big open sore that wept fluid all day.

He was sitting on the edge of the bed, looking out at the fogged-in city when Cranston trundled in. "Well, we've identified that millipede."

Here was the first good news since he'd been bitten.

"What is it?"

"The entomologists over at Berkley gave it a name as long as your arm. Other than that, they weren't much help. Said it was very, very rare, and that only a few have ever been seen. Couldn't imagine how it managed to travel from the rain forests of Borneo to your bed."

"Borneo," Hank said. Everybody had heard of the Wild Man from Borneo but . . . "Just where the hell is Borneo?"

"It's an island in the South China Sea."

"Did you say South *China* Sea?"

Cranston nodded. "Yes. Why? Is that important?"

Hank didn't answer. He couldn't. It was all clear now. Good Christ . . . China . . .

The Mandarin had sent his reply to Hank's demand.

"There's, um, something else you should know."

Cranston's tone snapped Hank's head up. The doctor looked uneasy. His gaze wandered to the window.

"You mean it gets worse?" Cranston's nod sent a sick, cold spike through Hank's gut. "Okay. Give it to me."

Cranston took a breath. "The millipede may or may not have injected you with venom, but that's not the problem." His voice trailed off.

Hank didn't know if he wanted to hear this.

"What *is* the problem then?"

"You remember when we did a scraping of the wound?"

"How could I forget?"

"Well, we did a microscopic examination and found what, um, appear to be eggs."

Hank's gut twisted into a knot.

"Eggs!"

"Yes."

"Did you get them all?"

"We don't know. They're quite tiny. But we'll go back in and do another scraping, deeper this time. But you should know—"

"Know what?"

Cranston's gaze remained fixed on the window.

"They're hatching."

◑

Next day, one of the green soft heels, a grade-one detective named Brannigan, stopped by to ask about Chinatown. He'd been assigned to look for a missing white girl last seen down there. He was asking about the Mandarin. Hank warned him away, even went so far as to show him the big, weeping ulcer on his shoulder.

Suddenly he was seized by a coughing fit, one that went on and on until he hacked up a big glob of bright red phlegm. The blood shocked him, but the sight of the little things wriggling in the gooey mass unnerved him.

"Oh, God!" he cried to Brannigan. "Call the doctor! Get the nurse in here! Hurry!"

The eggs had hatched and they were in his lungs! How had they gotten into his lungs?

Sick horror pushed a sob to his throat. He tried to hold it back until Brannigan was out the door. He didn't think he made it.

◑

Hank stared at the stranger in the bathroom mirror.

"It's not unprecedented," Cranston had said. "Larvae of

the ascaris roundworm, for instance, get into the circulation and migrate through the lung. But we've no experience with this species."

He saw sunken cheeks, glassy, feverish eyes, sallow, sweaty skin as pale as the sink, and knew he was looking at a dead man.

Why hadn't he just played it straight—or at least only a little bent—and taken a payoff here and there from the bigger gambling parlors? Why had he tried to go for the big score?

He was coughing up baby millipedes every day. That thing must have laid thousands, maybe tens of thousands of eggs in his shoulder. Her babies were sitting in his lungs, sucking off his blood as they passed through, eating him alive from the inside.

And nobody could do a damn thing about it.

He started to cry. He'd been doing that a lot lately. He couldn't help it. He felt so damn helpless.

The phone started to ring. Probably Hanrahan. The chief had been down to see him once and had never returned. Hank didn't blame him. Probably couldn't stand looking at the near-empty shell he'd become.

Hank shuffled to the bedside and picked up the receiver.

"Yeah."

"Ah, Detective Sorenson," said a voice he immediately recognized. "So glad you are still with us."

A curse leaped to his lips, but he bit it back. He didn't need any more bugs in his bed.

"No thanks to you."

"Ah, so. A most regrettable turn of events, but also most inevitable, given such circumstances."

"Did you call to gloat?"

"Ah, no. I call to offer you your wish."

Hank froze as a tremor of hope ran through his ravaged body. He was almost afraid to ask.

"You can cure me?"

"Come again to Jade Moon at three o'clock this day and your wish shall be granted."

The line went dead.

⟡

The cab stopped in front of the Jade Moon. Hank needed just about every ounce of strength to haul himself out of the rear seat.

The nurses had wailed, Dr. Cranston had blustered, but they couldn't keep him if he wanted to go. When they saw how serious he was, the nurses dug up a cane to help him walk.

He leaned on that cane now and looked around. The sidewalk in front of the restaurant was packed with Chinks, and every one of them staring at him. Not just staring— pointing and whispering too.

Couldn't blame them. He must be quite a sight in his wrinkled, oversized tux. Used to fit like tailor-made, but now it hung on him like a coat on a scarecrow. But he'd had no choice. This had been the only clothing in the closet of his hospital room.

He stepped up on the curb and stood swaying. For a few seconds he feared he might fall. The cane saved him.

He heard the singsong babble increase and noticed that the crowd was growing, with more Chinks pouring in from all directions, so many that they blocked the street. All staring, pointing, whispering.

Obviously Jiang had put out the word to come see the bad joss that befell anyone who went against the Mandarin.

Well, Hank thought as he began his shuffle toward the restaurant door, enjoy the show, you yellow bastards.

The crowd parted for him and watched as he struggled to open the door. No one stepped up to help. Someone inside pushed it open and pointed to the rear of the restaurant.

Hank saw Jiang sitting at the same table where they'd first met. Only this time Jiang's back was to the wall. He didn't kowtow, didn't even rise when Hank reached the table.

"Sit, Detective Sorenson," he said, indicating the other chair.

He looked exactly the same as last time: same black pajamas, same skullcap, same braid, same expressionless face.

Hank, on the other hand . . .

"I'll stand."

"Ah so, you not looking well. I must tell you that if you fall this one not help you up."

Hank knew if he went down he'd never be able to get up on his own. What then? Would all the Chinks outside be paraded past him for another look?

He dropped into the chair. That was when he noticed something like an ebony cigar box sitting before Jiang.

"What's that? Another bug?"

Jiang pushed it toward Hank.

"Ah no, very much opposite. This fight your infestation."

Hank closed his eyes and bit back a sob. A cure . . . was he really offering a cure? But he knew there had to be a catch.

"What do I have to do for it?"

"Must take three times a day."

Hank couldn't believe it.

"That's it? No strings?"

Jiang shook his head. "No, as you say, strings." He opened the box to reveal dozens of cigarette-size red paper cylinders. "Merely break one open three times a day and breathe fine powder within."

As much as Hank wanted to believe, his mind still balked at the possibility that this could be on the level.

"That's it? Three times a day and I'll be cured?"

"I not promise cure. I say it fight infestation."

"What's the difference? And what is this stuff?"

"Eggs of tiny parasite."

"A parasite!" Hank pushed the box away. "Not on your life!"

"This is true. Not on my life—on *your* life."

"I don't get it."

"There is order to universe, Detective Sorenson: Everything must feed. Something must die so that other may live. And it is so with these powdery parasite eggs. Humans do not interest them. They grow only in larvae that infest your lung. They devour host from inside and leave own eggs in carcass."

"Take a parasite to kill a parasite? That's crazy."

"Not crazy. It is poetry."

"How do I know it won't just make me sicker?"

Jiang smiled, the first time he'd changed his expression. "Sicker? How much more sick can Detective Sorenson be?"

"I don't get it. You half-kill me, then you offer to cure me. What's the deal? Your Mandarin wants a pet cop—is that it?"

"I know of no Mandarin. And once again, I not promise cure, only *chance* of cure."

Hank's hopes tripped but didn't fall.

"You mean it might not work?"

"It matter of balance, Detective. Have larvae gone too far for parasite to kill all in time? Or does Detective Sorenson still have strength enough left to survive? That is where fun come in."

"Fun? You call this *fun*?"

"Fun not for you or for this one. Fun for everyone else because my master decide grant wish you made."

"Wish? What wish?"

"To be part of game—your very words. Remember?"

Hank remembered, but . . .

"I'm not following you."

"All of Chinatown taking bet on you."

"On me?"

"Yes. Even money on whether live or die. And among those who believe you soon join ancestors, a lottery on when." Another smile. "You have your wish, Detective Sorenson. You now very much part of game. Ah so, you *are* game."

Hank wanted to scream, wanted to bolt from his chair and wipe the smirk off Jiang's rotten yellow face. But that was only a dream. The best he could do was sob and let the tears stream down his cheeks as he reached into the box for one of the paper cylinders.

THE BANDIT
OF SANITY

ROBERTA LANNES

DANIEL FREDERICKS SAT behind his glass and chrome desk in his Donghia chair and crossed his legs. He picked at a speck of dust on his wool gabardine Hugo Boss slacks and smiled at his handmade Italian shoes. He luxuriated in the sensation of just having worked out, showered and dressed his best, and eaten a spa-made breakfast at the Phoenix Health Club. Catching his reflection in the chrome picture frame of his infant son, he thought perhaps he could use another self-tanning session.

The light blinked over the door informing him his next client had arrived. She was twenty minutes early, as usual. He took her handwritten file from the cabinet behind his desk and set it in front of him.

Jeanette Samuelson. Age 34. Married with two children. Husband stockbroker. Original complaint: dysphoria with an anxiety axis.

Visit 1—10/9/02—General anxiety over being an adequate mother and good wife. Depressed over changes in her body after pregnancy. Breast-feeding two boys 7 mos and 1 1/2 yrs old.

Visit 2—10/16/02—Discussed marriage. Loneliness and obsessive concern for her children are connected. Her friends are all married with children of similar age. Mother and father live nearby and mother tends to interfere and criticize. Mother-in-law lives across the US, but phones daily for support, which patient more readily accepts. Bitch mother insists that daughter must not breast-feed, and puts daughter down. Patient received suggestion to disregard mother and tell her to eat shit and die.

Daniel's notes changed from one session to another, sometimes during a session, which disturbed him. The tone shifted and the handwriting changed. For the first few months, he went to doctors, expecting something neurological. After all, he was in top psychological form after ten years of analysis. The doctors tested and scanned and probed without finding a diagnosis to explain the aberrations in Daniel's motor and mental lapses. He began to notice his tennis game was off; setting up serves and wailing the ball at his opponents or spectators, then snapping back into form. Occasionally, his wife was complimentary about his sexual performance, which was unlike her. He was a rote lover, uninterested in innovation or in pleasing her. Daniel was further upset by the fact that when his wife commented on her grateful pleasure, he couldn't recall having had sex at all. One moment they were cuddled in bed, the next he was in the shower.

He worried that he might slip out of himself and hurt the son he so adored. Rory was nine months old, the image of himself at that age. He'd rather kill himself than hurt his angel boy. So far, the only sign he'd done anything odd was finding himself with Rory in the tub, suddenly aware they were naked, giggling over a game he could only vaguely remember playing. They both had erections, but that wasn't unusual. They were boys, weren't they? And he often bathed Rory to give his wife a break.

Then there were days he didn't care about how he dressed or what he said, too tired to keep the dark Daniel at bay. He fought with it, sure it was an obsessive reaction formation over his perfectionism and rigidity, working through it by ego splitting. He watched the two Daniels warring; one choosing a pressed handmade shirt, the other putting a tattered old Pendleton jacket over it. The one washing his hair and letting it dry flat, the other desperately combing and spraying to repair it.

Daniel's wife was suspicious, but she said nothing. He could tell by the way she stared at him, as if she was seeing someone else and wondering how he got there—where had Daniel gone? Even if she'd voiced her concern, it wouldn't have moved him to take action. He was his own man. A man who needed help and found it almost impossible to allow himself weakness.

Francine De Santos was the best psychoanalyst in California. Yet she struggled with his sudden changes, suggesting the unthinkable; that Daniel had developed a latent form of schizophrenia, which happened. Or worse, sudden-onset MPD, multiple-personality disorder, which was not only unusual, but unprecedented. Medications did nothing to affect the fluctuations in personae, nor relieve his anxiety over the changes. Talk therapy wasn't helping, either. It just reminded him he was not all right.

He opened the door to his office. The waiting room was big enough for a love seat and two chairs, a table on which he kept magazines on travel, wine, and food. Sitting in one of the chairs was Jeanette, a pale blanket over her chest and her suckling child.

"Jeanette, come on in." Daniel grinned, focusing on her face.

Jeanette was dark-haired, with a round face gone sunken from worry. Her large eyes seemed forever near tears. "I hope you don't mind, Dr. Fredericks, but they wouldn't take Kevin in day care. He's got a cold." The baby's breathing was mucusy and labored as he breast-fed.

"Not at all." He waited for her to gather her baby bag and child up and scurry into the office. She sat on the couch and settled into her motherly service.

"Let's start where we left off last week. You were saying that Ted felt threatened by all the time you were giving the children. What did he say or do to make you think that?"

As Jeanette spoke, the blanket edged off the baby, exposing her round breast with dark brown areola and nipple tucked firmly in the baby's mouth. Daniel's eyes flicked from Jeanette's face to her breast. He could feel the spark of sexual excitement and crossed his legs. He put his clipboard on his lap and hoped he wasn't blushing. The whoosh of blood in his face and ears made her voice seem far away. One hand slid beneath the clipboard to caress the head of his prick.

The next moment he was aware, he was on Jeanette Samuelson, shoving her child aside and suckling madly at her breast, one hand down inside her panties massaging her clit, while rubbing his groin against her leg and coming. The baby wailed, half in surprise at the sudden change of feeding schedule, half in terror at being discarded so roughly. Jeanette was not screaming. She was lying there, eyes nearly rolled back in her head, moaning softly with pleasure.

It was as if he had just been thrust physically, really, into a fantasy he'd entertained a couple of times as he treated Jeanette. The shock of it felt worse than falling into ice water. He scrabbled off of his client and onto the floor, uprighting himself to a standing position as gracefully as he could. He straightened his gabardines, now stained with cum, his hand smelling of her discharge. Pulling a handkerchief from his jacket pocket, he wiped furiously.

With his change of behavior, Jeanette curled up in shame. She reached over to her child and tugged at his foot, a kind of sadness in her. Then she rearranged her top and bra. She wouldn't look at Daniel, which was fine with him. He couldn't imagine that even though he was losing time and splitting in his mind, he could abuse a client.

Finally, Jeanette took her wailing baby into her arms. Daniel went to the refuge of his Donghia chair behind his desk and took his clipboard in hand. He began writing down meaningless blather about her, just to appear busy at his job. The wailing stopped. Daniel glanced furtively at Jeanette. She had little Kevin on her breast again; this time, it was her hand working inside her pants, her eyes shut. Daniel knew he shouldn't watch, but he did. Spent, he barely registered arousal, but he silently urged her orgasm. It arrived quietly and without Kevin's notice.

Daniel checked the clock. Time was up.

"Will I see you again next week, same time?" He kept his eyes on his clipboard.

She gathered up her bag, her child, and went to the door. Her voice was soft, almost sultry. "That would be nice."

"I'll mark my calendar." He waited for her to leave, for the door to click back into the jamb. Seconds went by and he was forced to glance up, fiddle with his hair over his ear. She was looking at him, imploring him to say something about what had just happened. He knew her well.

"Good-bye, Jeanette. See you next week." The dismissal worked. She left.

Daniel closed his eyes. When he sighed, a moan and tears came with it. What the hell was happening to him?

✧

Daniel began to log the lost time, the episodes of bizarre behavior, at least the ones he was aware of—when he snapped back into himself while it was going on. He photocopied his notes where the handwriting shifted along with his language and attitude. The file, which grew rapidly, he called The Sanity File. He'd keep it to make sure he was sane. After all, he figured, an insane person wouldn't keep records or know that he was nuts. Francine De Santos agreed with him.

"Even if only for legal reasons, it makes sense. You are aware that these behavioral aberrations occur as 'lost time,' that you have no deliberate intention to do harm or act in an illegal manner."

"Cover my ass? I don't think so, Francine. If someone broke into my office and found that file, I'd be brought up before the State Medical Quality Assurance Board and lose my license to practice in the least, and maybe my freedom. What's happening with my clients . . . that's the worst. On my own, on the street, at my club, at home . . . I can make excuses. Not at work. I—"

"You and I will work at this and figure it out. You've had every neurological workup I can think of, endocrine and otherwise. This is mental. It may simply be stress. You have a huge client load, Daniel. You could cut back."

Daniel stared out the window through the miniblinds to the trees in the yards of the Beverly Hills homes beyond. Everything was just as he'd planned it all along. He was capable, ready to handle his life. What was missing?

"I could . . . but not yet. Not now. I've lost a client, oddly enough not because of my behavior. She moved out of state. I won't fill her spot. I have a waiting list. . . ."

"Your ego is tied into this success of yours."

"Yes, understandably. I get a tremendous amount of gratification and sense of worth from what I do."

"Let's play 'what if?' You wake up tomorrow and you can't work as a psychologist. What are you doing for work, for pleasure?"

Daniel's skin went cold, his heart began racing. His vision tunneled. He was gone. When he returned, he was in his Mercedes going up the hill to his home, his shirt

THE BANDIT OF SANITY | 105

drenched with sweat. He smelled like sex. He grabbed his cell phone and called Francine. Her service answered and he asked, a little too frantically, for her to return his call, as quickly as possible. When he arrived at his home, he pulled into the garage and sat in the car, waiting for her call.

His wife, Rayla, rapped hard on the window, waking him. He panicked, began hunting for his cell phone, babbling. She opened the car door.

"Danny, it's 11:30! I was getting ready to call the police!"

The police. No, no police. "I fell asleep. I was waiting for a call and . . ." He shivered. His shirt had dried, wrinkled, with the smell of fear on it. Flop sweat.

"Come inside. Take a shower. Go to bed. But quietly, baby. Don't wake Rory. It was hard to get him to sleep."

Daniel peeled himself from the car. Thinking of Rory, of his beautiful, loving wife, he knew he couldn't keep this just between himself and Francine. Rayla embraced him, her much shorter, thin body meshing with his. He put his hands in her hair, bent and inhaled the warm, flowery scent of her conditioner. Then his cell phone bripped in his jacket pocket.

Rayla went inside. "Dr. Fredericks."

"Your service calling, Doctor. We have one of your patients, a Mrs. Samuelson on the line. She wishes to speak with you." Daniel marveled at how all the women at his answering service sounded the same.

"I am in the middle of handling another emergency. Send her message to my voice mail and tell her I will call her back as soon as I am out of this one."

"And if she . . . insists?"

"They all insist. They suck you dry then rip you to shreds and shit on the pieces. Tell her to go fuck herself. I'm busy." He snapped the phone shut. "It's time for *my* life." He growled as he slammed the Mercedes door shut.

✿

Daniel woke up at four in the morning. Rayla was tangled in his long legs. He unwound himself from her and went to pee. The dream he'd just had was strange, eerie. He hadn't thought of Justin Cook in ten years. Justin was one of his first few clients, a nineteen-year-old sociopath who had fooled Daniel for a year before he caught on. Justin told tales of ferocious parental abuse. It made his demonic behavior seem the likely outlet for all his rage. But when Daniel investigated, he learned Justin Cook came from an extraordinarily supportive home with a younger brother and sister who were terrified of him.

In the dream, Justin was in Daniel's old office; the room above an auto mechanic's garage that was quiet only at night. He was the shrink while Daniel lay on the grubby tweed couch. Justin was very bright, and had often attempted to play the psychologist in their real-life sessions. In the murky light, Justin asked Daniel if he liked having crazy sex.

"Crazy sex?"

"You're one of those guys who likes hopping on, getting your nut, then rolling off. It's different now. Maybe you're liking this crazy stuff. Fucking your wife up the ass. Fingering your breast-feeder while you dry-hump her. Making that whore real-estate lady take your ten inches until she choked on it. Letting that weird kid Leon lick your asshole while he beats off. You know what I mean."

Dream Daniel felt himself getting excited. He remembered some of the lust-driven stuff, and yes, he was liking it. He nodded at Justin.

"So you're loosening up, dude."

"Loosening up. Yes." Daniel began stroking himself, to Justin's delight.

"Go for it, Dan. Hey, you liking my take on your crazy patients? How about what I wrote about that dude who has a little too much of a fixation on his sister? Am I right, he's sexualizing her sweet understanding treatment of him? Oh, wait, I am the doctor. I am always right!"

Daniel was suddenly standing before his old desk, Justin grinning too wide for a human being, his teeth ten inches wide. Justin's head was open at the crown, blown open. Gore and bone straggled down his forehead and cheeks. His face was ashen.

"Are you dead, Justin?" He got no response. "Did you kill yourself?"

Justin nodded his head and brains fell out onto his lap.

Daniel felt his stomach lurch. "Why? Did I do something wrong?"

They were now standing in the park, or was it a graveyard? Lots of green, trees, benches. Justin knelt at a headstone. The inscription was a blur, yet he was tracing it with his fingers.

"They really loved me. Look at the nice things they said about me." Justin looked over his shoulder at Daniel. He seemed so young, not nineteen. Not after years of killing animals, assaulting older people, stealing money, and maiming kids in his neighborhood. Innocent, maybe eight or nine, though he looked as he had the last time Daniel had seen him.

"They did. They tried to love you so that you would heal, but they weren't able."

"That was your job, Daniel."

"You're the doctor. Not me."

"You were supposed to heal me. You really fucked that up."

"No. You're the doctor."

Justin opened the top drawer of Daniel's old faux oak desk. Dream Daniel felt nostalgic for his first few years of practice. Two or three patients a day. Time to peruse their files, do research, take their calls if need be. He was single then, dating two women, one in L.A., one in Dallas where his parents lived. He took classes in cooking and interior decorating, joined a health club to stay fit after college. Life was good then. Justin took his file from the desk and waved it in front of Daniel as if he was a magician and he had cards fanned out.

"Pick a page, any page." Justin threw the file up and papers flew like baby birds, swaying in the air and dropping to the floor and desk. "Your lies."

"What lies?" Daniel felt afraid. He remembered how dangerous Justin could be—not with him, but with everyone in his life outside the office. He had written the clinical truth. Always had.

"Where does it say here that you loved me?" He waited for a response from Daniel. "You *did* love me. You *showed* me how you loved me."

Daniel's dream stomach fell. Had he interfered with Justin in an inappropriate manner? He wasn't gay; why would the thought have even entered his mind?

"I never touched you."

Justin was beside him now. In the dream, Daniel could smell the young man. It was feral and clean, sweet and cloying, then rotting and putrid. He backed away.

"I wanted you to. That was all I wanted was for you to love me."

"You liked girls. I remember you telling me—"

"*Lies!* All of it. I expected you to be good enough to see through what I did. What I said. See my pain, my need."

Daniel was stunned. "I didn't know! I would never take advantage of you. I took an oath. I'm so sorry." And he was. Then Justin began to smother him with kisses, holding him, pressing against him. He didn't want it, yet it was arousing, and he had to urinate. Justin took his penis from inside his pants and the urge grew.

That's when he woke up. He found himself standing in front of the toilet, empty bladder, holding his flaccid penis, and wondering why he had such a vivid dream. Why he would dream of a client who stopped therapy and disappeared from his life so long ago?

✿

Rayla refused to speak to him when he came into his sleek brushed-aluminum and teak dining room for breakfast.

"What? Did I say something in my sleep? Are you angry because I came home so late last night?"

She shook her head. Rory was in the high chair, resisting strained peaches.

The phone rang. Daniel picked it up. It was his service. Four calls. One, Francine. Her message was curt: "Do not call; do not come back to my office; do not contact me again." Why was everyone around him bailing? What had he done? Was he splitting off so often he was no longer aware it had happened?

He grasped the cup of coffee in his cold hands. It felt real; he was real. So was this hell. He had to share it with Rayla, even if it meant she felt betrayed. He knew she would.

"Ray, I've got to tell you something. I hope you will stick by me through this. I'm terrified."

This stopped her. She turned to him. "Okay." She was tentative. "Talk."

He did. He told her as much as he could without his sanity file to remind him of all the various indiscretions, splits, each of the rabid acts of lovemaking she'd enjoyed that occurred without his knowledge. He inferred he'd acted inappropriately with clients, but said nothing about the sexual aspects. And he told her the dream.

"Do you think there is a connection between this dream and what's happening to you?" She was frowning, trying with difficulty to be supportive in the face of Daniel's massive mental lapses and illness.

"I don't know." He began to cry. Softly, like he had

when he was a boy and no one was around to see. "I just know I'm afraid. And I am hurting people. People I am sworn to protect and help."

Rayla continued to feed Rory. "I think you should find someone else to help you if Francine is out of the picture."

"Good advice. I'll do that. I . . . We can't live like this."

Rayla looked at him the same way a parent does a stupid child. Daniel finished his coffee, forced the rye toast down, and kissed his wife and child good-bye.

His first client on Fridays was Simon Harcourt, an actor in a drama on television. Daniel took out his file and flipped to the last entry.

> Visit 28—6/10/04—Simon spoke today about his sorrow over the loss of his sheltie dog Wayne. Wayne was 17 years old. Long attachment. Grief is appropriate. Mentioned his twin brother for only second time. Issues with his twin (fraternal) are behind much of his sense of impotence in the face of abusive behavior. Brother often impersonates Simon with women and behaves badly, humiliating Simon.
>
> Problems continue with Simon's roommates. They are messy and inconsiderate. Simon hates that he portrays a tough cop on TV and is a wimp with his personal relationships.
>
> I don't feel sorry for him. He wallows in his misery and deserves every bit of shit he gets. What the hell is wrong with this guy? He has everything, but he's obsessed with what he can't have. What he isn't. Pathetic loser.

Daniel shook his head. The voice of the "other" Daniel seemed familiar today. Who spoke like that? Who could be so without compassion?

The light went on signaling Daniel that Simon had arrived. He closed the file and stood. Justin. That's what the dream was all about. The 'other' Daniel was just like Justin!

Just knowing felt like power. Daniel stretched, exhaled. Whispered, "Justin, get the hell out of my head." Then he went to let Simon in.

The rest of the day, Daniel was himself. His notes were consistent. He was quick and concise with his patients. He called Rayla to tell her that their talk had helped. She didn't sound mollified. Between his 5:00 and 7:45 P.M. clients, he went through his old files to find Justin's. He got caught up reading some of the old files, enjoying his early earnest innocence, his drive. Justin's file was in the last box from his first year.

Visit 1—Justin Cook; age 18. Sent by California Youth Authority. In custody for numerous assaults. Parents chose me by referral (Mark Moore).

Justin is tall, well-built, with a face that might be handsome one day, but is now softly rounded. He wears a permanent scowl. Responded to questions with sarcasm, one-word responses, or silence. Asked him who he was angry at and he laughed. "Who am I NOT angry at! Everyone I ever dealt with. My parents, my family, my teachers, other kids. Everybody treats me like I'm nuts." I asked if he was "nuts." He laughed again. He appears to enjoy the thought that he is "getting" at me or has a secret I want that he isn't going to give up. I repeated the question. "No, I am fucked up." I pointed out that we all were. He asked about me, how I was fucked up, and I turned it onto him—how does he think I am fucked up. He was extraordinarily accurate! Issues with control, power, inadequacy. I smiled and told him that when a patient tells me how I am crazy, it reflects on his or her own issues. Justin seemed to want to tell me how he was different from my take on patients. He gave me the silent treatment for the next ten minutes. I must have looked bored because he shouted at me to give him my attention. I asked him to tell me about his childhood. He proceeded to tell me one dramatic tale of horrific abuse after another. I am skeptical. They have a staged sound to them. When asked if he was content to see me again, he looked at me for a moment and I saw the child in him, sensing someone cared, then it was gone. He replied, "I don't have a choice if I want to get out of CYA."

Daniel remembered. It all came back. The anger dotted with moments of fear, the lies peppered with truth. He never connected with Justin and decided the boy was a sociopath. When the mandated period of visits ended, Justin's parents asked Daniel to continue with him. To Daniel's surprise, Justin agreed.

He reread all the notes he could manage before his 7:45 P.M. client, then went back to them later. He searched for clues, not knowing what to look for. Was Justin gay? Was he acting out, fearing his homosexuality wouldn't be acceptable, so he created a wall of hostility? If so, how could he not see it? He found the parents' phone number and dialed. It was late. He hoped they would be awake.

Wrong number. They moved. It was nearly twenty years ago Justin stopped coming. Daniel called his friend Gil at LAPD and asked for help finding the parents, Esperanza and Frank Cook. He wouldn't hear anything until morning.

Justin's file was spread over his glass desk. Emotionally, it was hard to read. Justin's assaults, his harm to animals and children, were terrible. He reread the last visit.

Visit 221—Justin Cook 5/14

Justin seems listless, bored. I've seen him like this only a few times. He is less resistant. Great time for questions. I asked him about the baby-dropping incident at the mall. He grabbed a woman's baby when she told him off for talking to the salesgirl, keeping her from her duties. He ran to the second-floor mall railing and held the baby out. He screamed at the woman to apologize. She was in shock, capable only of wailing. Mall cops tried to intercede, so Justin dropped the baby. It landed in a planter below on a bed of mulch and was only bruised and scraped. Justin shrugged. "If people thought they could lose something valuable for being a bitch or an asshole, they'd wouldn't do half the shit they do. I was just letting her know her attitude earned her potential baby loss." I asked if he knew he was dropping the baby onto a softer surface. He smiled. My turn to guess. I said I knew he had figured it out. He just wanted to teach people and animals a lesson, make a point. He liked my hypothesis. I was fishing. I asked him why he never inflicted pain on himself, why only others. He found this question uncomfortable and squirmed! I finally touched a nerve. I asked him what he was feeling. He didn't know. Maybe hurting others was the only way for him to feel anything. He was so shut off inside. I praised him for the insight. Then he asked me what he should do to himself. Should he pay himself back for all the harm he'd done? I pointed out that it all comes back to us in other ways eventually. He'd paid in CYA custody for three and a half years. Missed high school, his prom. Maybe someday someone would do to him what he'd done to others. He changed then, turned ugly, vicious. "No one is going to do anything to me again. I won't let it happen." I asked him how he could assure himself of that kind of protection, that no one was immune from the "slings and arrows" of life, of other people. He looked away, ashen, as if a horrid thought had just occurred to him. Accountability? The session ended with that. I look forward to the next.

When Justin didn't show up the next week, Daniel had called his home. His parents told Daniel that Justin had run away and if he returned, they would make sure he came back for help. But they never called. And Daniel hadn't followed up. His practice was growing, and he was about to move into the first of several finer office spaces.

Rayla was asleep when he got home. He crawled in beside her and kissed her exposed shoulder. She stirred. He
whispered, "I love you." He smiled at her, hoping she'd
stay asleep. She rolled over and sighed, still deep asleep.
He laid back and stared up at the ceiling.

He was dreaming again. It seemed real, lucid, like the
night before. Dream Daniel stood in a filthy bathroom near
a beach. He could smell the salt air and wet sand besides
the stench of piss and shit. He was wearing beach shorts
and thongs, a towel over his bronzed shoulders. Real
Daniel would never wear thongs or expose his bony feet. In
the dream he grinned at this.

"Hey, Doc!" Daniel turned to the voice. Justin was
standing on a toilet seat, a noose around his neck. He was
nude, covered in sand and dirt, as if he'd fallen in it coming
out of the water. Sand on his eyelashes glinted in the harsh
exposed bulbs of the restroom.

"What are you doing to yourself, Justin?" Dream Daniel
spoke with benign resignation.

"Making sure nobody messes with me anymore. I'm *as-
suring* myself."

"I can teach you ways to deal with people that don't hurt
them and that protect you. Let me do that." Then, as an af-
terthought, "Why here?"

Justin's feet slipped off the wet toilet seat and he hanged
himself. His eyes bulged and his tongue jutted from his
mouth. Daniel watched without feeling, noting Justin wet-
ted and crapped himself, and his cock was hard as he died.

Daniel turned to go. Justin spoke in a rough voice. "Hey,
Doc! You sad fuck. You missed it all along. I loved you. I
wanted you to love me. You needed someone to love you as
much as I wanted to love you, but you couldn't see it." Daniel
looked back at Justin. His black tongue licked his pale lips.
Daniel shook, suddenly, overwhelmed with guilt and horror.

"Is this why you're stalking me?" He didn't know what
else to call it.

"Stalking? Noooo. Think of me as a permanent client, Doc. I'm riding along for the duration, as they say."

"I don't get it, Justin. I don't understand." Daniel was helpless; tears fell and he dropped to his knees in the filth. "Help me understand."

Justin tugged at the noose until it loosened and he dropped to the tile floor. He patted Daniel's head, cooing there now's. "Stand up, Doc, and give us a hug."

Daniel stood, allowed Justin to put his arms around him. He continued to weep. He was so sorry. Sorry for Justin, sorry for himself. If he missed this essential diagnosis in Justin, what else had he missed and in who?

"Poor Daniel . . . poor sad Daniel." Justin pressed his naked body to Daniel's. "See, this was all I wanted. You never asked me if the abuse my parents heaped on me was anything but violent or sexual. You assumed. Doc, they never touched me. Never looked at me. Maybe my mom touched me to diaper me when I was an infant, but I don't remember that. If I cut my knees playing rough, Mom put the antiseptic and bandages on the counter. 'You fix it,' she'd say. I had a fever, I had to put the thermometer in my mouth and take it out and read it myself. I had to feed myself as far back as I remember. I never felt loved, or cared about."

"They seemed like such nice people." Daniel tried defending them.

"Nice people can be neglectful and cold. You know that." Justin forced Daniel to look at him then, holding his cheeks in his hands. "That's you all the way. Ever hold your own son? Hold your wife's hand when you take a walk . . . ever take a walk with her?"

Daniel shook his head. The head he lived in. Had he ever touched a woman in a merely affectionate manner, without it being sexual? No.

"You'll wake up and probably forget this dream, but I'm here now. Stop fighting me. Love me. Let me be."

Rayla pushed at him. "Daniel, wake up!" He sat up with a start.

"What!?"

"You were crying and shouting 'No!' Are you having a nightmare?"

He wiped his face. It was wet. "I must have. God. What's wrong with me?"

✥

Gil left the phone number for Justin's parents on Daniel's voice mail. Before his first client, Daniel sat back in his Donghia chair, took his Cross pen in hand, put paper on his desk, and took a deep breath. Then he dialed. The number had an unfamiliar area code.

The woman who answered bore a trace of an accent, as Esperanza Cook had.

"This is Daniel Fredericks. I was Justin's therapist back in 1983. Do you recall that?" His heart was slamming in his chest. He hadn't considered what he was going to say. "It was when Justin was with—"

"California Youth Authority. I remember very well, Dr. Fredericks."

Was she upset? Angry? Her voice gave him nothing. "I was going through some of my old files and Justin's was so big. I started reading and realized he'd just stopped coming. It made me curious. I wondered how he was doing now."

"Now?" Her voice told him her mind was working hard to fathom what that meant. "Well, he's been gone almost twenty years."

"Gone. Moved out? Or is he incarcerated?"

"Gone. He's dead. He hanged himself. He wrote you a letter. I sent you a copy."

Sudden hysterical giggles spilled out of Daniel. They weren't his giggles. He struggled to speak. "I never . . . knew . . . I never got . . ."

Then his voice wasn't his. "Moms, I'm here. I finally got what I need from the doc. Hell, I'm *in* him. Ya!"

"What is this sick joke? How dare you call and say this to me! Do not call here again!" She hung up.

Daniel felt warmth rise up from his toes into his legs, his groin, his abdomen, like a blush. It was Justin on a cellular level, now—not just in his head—stealing his body and his mind.

"What did I ever do to you to deserve this?" He whimpered, frightened.

Justin's voice came into his head as clear as if he was thinking the words himself. The dream was waking now.

"You wouldn't just love me. Be close to me. Touch me."

"I'll get rid of you. I have a life to live." Daniel stood, angrily grabbing his head as if pulling his hair would pluck out Justin.

"Get used to me, Doc. I'm here for good. We're going to have more fun. Like what we did to your shrink. Only now you'll get to enjoy it while I'm at the wheel. And hey . . . you know how you couldn't stand how I wouldn't let you in? Well, now you'll know it all, every bit of it, just like I know every bit of you! That's a plus for you."

Daniel closed his eyes. He wondered about Justin's childhood, his early puberty. Years and images and thoughts washed through his head. Fascinated, he let it come. It rocked him and surprised him and awed him. Justin was so much more than he'd let on.

Justin broke in. "Hey, hey, man, slow down. We got a lot of time to play."

Daniel smiled. "Yes, we do." Justin had been the one that he could never crack, never help the way he wanted to. Now he could. And maybe he might one day be able to do what Justin longed for. Love him.

His cell went off in his pocket bringing him back to the moment. He checked caller ID. It was Rayla.

"Hi, Ray. What's up, baby?" Justin was there with him.

"Baby?" He could hear Rory crying and male voices. "Look, Danny, there are two detectives here. They'd like to speak to you about some complaints. And . . . about Francine."

Justin's voice was loud in his head. "We make a run for it now, Dan. Yeah, that's what we do. No way I want to spend the rest of your life in a cell as somebody's ho!"

"Francine. She filed a complaint?"

"No, Danny, she committed suicide. They said something about her note . . ."

"I'll be right home."

"Hurry, Danny. They're scaring me."

"Sure, baby. I'm on my way."

Daniel flipped the phone shut and dropped it into his gabardine trouser pocket. Justin wondered if the car had a full tank of gas. Daniel realized they would have to fill up on their way to wherever they were going now. Justin laughed. Daniel grinned.

"I just have to grab this one file of mine. . . ." Daniel went for The Sanity File in his locked cabinet. Justin waited inside, humming like a well-tuned car, ready for whatever came next.

MY THING FRIDAY

BRIAN LUMLEY

Voice Journal of Greg Griffiths,
3rd Engineer on the *Albert Einstein*
out of the Greater Mars Orbital Station

DAY ONE:

Probably the 24th Feb 2198 Earth Standard, but I can't
be sure. The ship's chronometer is bust—like everything
else except me—and I don't know how long I've been out
of it. Judging by the hair on my face, my hunger, the bump
on the back of my head, and the thick blood scab that's
covering it, it could have been two or three days. Anyway
and as far as I can tell it's now morning on whichever day,
which I'm going to call Day One. . . .

What I remember:

We passed through the fringes of an old nebula; a cloud
of gas that looked dead enough, but it seems there was
some energy left in it after all: weird energy that didn't
register on instrumentation. Then the drive started acting
up and quit entirely maybe four or five light-years later.

When we dropped back into normal space, I put on a suit, went out and for'ard to check the fuel ingestors. They were clogged with this gas that was almost liquid, and dust that stuck like glue; it couldn't be converted into fuel and had hardened to a solid in the scoops . . . weird as hell, like I said. Ship's Science Officer Scot Gentry said it could well be "protoplanetary slag"—whatever the hell that's supposed to be!—and a total pain in the backside. And down in engineering we scratched our heads and tried to figure out some way to shift this shit.

Then the sublight engines blew up and we saw that the dust was into everything. The antigravs were on the fritz but still working, however sporadically, and by some miracle of chance we were just a cough and a spit off a planet with water and an atmosphere: a couple trillion-to-one chance, according to Gentry. But by then, too, we knew we were way off course—light-years off course—because this protocrap had got into the astronavigator, too.

As for the planet: It had continents, oceans, but there was no radio coming up at us, no sign of cities or intelligent life-forms. Well, if there had been, it would have been a first. The universe has been looking like a pretty lonely place for a long time now. And to me, *right* now, it looks lonelier than ever.

Coming in to make landfall the antigravs gave up the ghost . . . so much for a soft landing. Six thousand tons of metal with nothing holding us up, we fell from maybe a hundred feet in the air. Higher than that and I probably wouldn't be recording this. I was in a sling in a gravity tube, trying to burn slag off the gyros, when this uncharted planet grabbed us; the sling's shock absorbers bounced me around but saved my life.

As for the other crew members, all fifteen of my shipmates, they weren't so lucky—

—Or maybe they were. It all depends on what this place has in store for me. But right now I have to fix my head,

eat, give myself shots, then get all the bodies off the ship or
the place won't ever be livable. . . .

DAY TWO (MORNING):

Yesterday was a very strange day . . . and by the way, I
think the days here are just an hour or two longer than
Earth Standard. I reckon I was right about coming to fairly
early in the morning, because it seemed like one hell of a
long strange day; but then again—considering what I was
doing—it would.

I had started to move the bodies out of the ship.

No easy task, that. And not only for the obvious reasons. I cried a lot, for the obvious reasons. But with the old
Albert E. lying at thirty degrees, and her (or his) once-
round hull split at all the major seams, buckled and now
oblate, and leaking all kinds of corrosives, lubricants and
like that . . . no, it was no easy task. Don't know why I
bothered, really, because I see now there's no way I can
live in the *Albert E.* Ship's a death trap!

Perhaps I should have left the bodies as they were,
sealed them in as best I could right there where they died;
the entire ship with all these bodies—my buddies—in it,
like some kind of big metal memorial. Rust in peace . . .

But it's way too late now, and anyway there's lots of stuff
I have to get out of there. Medicines and such; ship's rations;
a big old self-inflating habitat module from the emergency
survival store; tools; stuff like that. A regular Robinson Cru-
soe, I be—or maybe a marooned Ben Gunn, eh, Jim lad?
Oh, *Ha-harr!* But at least there's no sign of pirates.

I thank God for my sense of humor. Just a few days ago
on board the *Albert E.*, why, I would crack them up so
hard—they would laugh so hard—they'd tell me I'd be the
death of them! Well, boys, it wasn't me. Just a fucking big

cloud of weird gas and dust, that's all. But it cracked us up good and proper . . .

LATER:

I managed to get more than half of them out of there before the sun went down, and I'll get the rest tomorrow. But tonight will be the *last* night I'll spend on board ship. It's nightmarish on the *Albert E.* now. Tomorrow I'll fix up the habitat I unloaded, get a generator working, power some batteries, set up a defensive perimeter like the book says. And whatever those things are I hear moving around out there in the dark—probably the same guys who were watching me from the forest while I worked—fuck 'em! I do have a reliable sidearm. Shouldn't need to use it too much, though; once they've had a taste of the electric perimeter— that's assuming they're the overly curious kind—they won't be in too much of a hurry to come back for more.

As for tonight, I have to hope they're not much interested in carrion, that's all. . . .

DAY THREE (MIDDAY):

I feel a lot better in myself, not so knocked about, no longer down. Well, *down*, naturally, but not all the way. I mean, hell, I'm alive! And just looking at the old *Albert E.*, I really don't know how. But the air is very good here; you can really suck it in. It's fresh, sweet . . . unfiltered? Maybe it's just that the air on the ship, always stale, is already starting to stink.

I got a generator working; got my habitat set up, electric perimeter and all. Now I'll bring out all the ship's rations I can find, and while I'm at it I may come across the two bodies I haven't found yet. One of them is Daniel Geisler, a dear pal of mine. That will hit me hard. It's all hitting hard, but I'm alive and that's what matters. Where there's life there's hope, and all that shit. . . .

I've been finding out something about the locals who I was listening to last night. I was in a makeshift hammock that I'd fixed up in an airlock; left the airlock open a crack, letting some of this good air in. Partway into the night I could hear movement out in the darkness. After an hour or so it got quiet, so it seems they sleep, too. Could be that night and sleep are universally synonymous. That would make sense . . . I think.

But how best to describe them? Now me, I'm not what you'd call an exobiologist, Jim, lad, just a grease monkey; but I'll give it a try. From what I've seen so far, there appear to be three kinds of what is basically one and the same species. See what I mean about not being an exobiologist? Obviously they're *not* the same species; and yet there's this peculiar similarity about them that . . . well, they're very *odd*, that's all. . . .

Anyway, let me get on.

There's the flying kind: eight-foot wingspan, round-bodied and skinny-legged; like big, beakless, stupid-looking pale pink robins. They hang out in the topmost branches of the trees and eat what look like fist-sized yellow berries. Paradoxically and for all their size they appear to be pretty flimsy critters; no feathers, they're more like bats of maybe flying squirrels than birds, and they leap and soar rather than fly. And when they're floating between the sun and me, I see right through their wings. But they're not the only flying things. There are others of approximately the same size and design, but more properly birdlike. And this other species—very definitely a separate, different species—they stay high in the sky, circling like buzzards. I kept an eye on these high-flyers because of what I was doing. I mean, I was laying out my dead shipmates, and buzzards and vultures are carnivores. On Earth they are, anyway . . .

Then there's the landlubbers or earthbound variety. These are bipedal, anthropoid, perhaps even mammalian or this world's equivalent, though as yet I've seen no sign of tits or marriage tackle. Whatever, I reckon it's probably these manlike things—this world's intelligentsia?—that I heard bumping around in the darkness. But since they're the most interesting of the bunch I'll leave them till last, get back to them in a minute.

And finally there's the other land variety, the hogs. Well, I'll call them hogs for now, if only for want of a better name. They're some four or five feet long, pale pink like the soaring things and the bipeds, and they rustle about in the undergrowth at the fringes of the forest eating the golf-ball-sized seeds of the big yellow berries. But they, too, have their counterparts. Deeper in the woods, there are critters more properly like big, hairy black hogs that snort and keep well back in the shadows.

And there you have it. But the "Pinks"—as I've started to call all three varieties of these pale pink creatures: the quadrupeds, bipeds, and flyers—it's as if they were all cut from the same cloth. Despite the diversity of their design, there's a vague similarity about them; their drab, unappealing color, for one thing, and the same insubstantial sort of flimsiness or—I don't know, wobbliness? jellyness?—for another.

Fascinating really . . . *if* I was an exobiologist. But since I'm not they're just something I'll need to watch out for until I know for sure what's what. Actually, I don't feel intimidated by any of these critters. Not so far. Not by the Pinks, anyway.

More about the manlikes:

When I opened up the airlock this morning, there was a bunch of them, maybe thirteen or fourteen, sitting in a circle around the remains of my shipmates. I've been laying my ex-

friends out in their own little groups, their three main ship-
board cliques, but all of them pretty close together with their
feet in toward a common center. Ended up forming a sort of
three-leafed clover shape with four or five bodies to a leaf.

The aliens (yeah, it's a cliché, I know, but what are these
things if not aliens? They're alien to me, anyway—though
it's true that on this world I'm the only real alien—but anyway): the *locals* were sitting there nestling the heads of the
dead in their laps. And I thought what the hell, maybe
they'd spent the whole night like that! Well, whatever,
that's how it struck me.

So then, what were they doing? Wondering if these
dead creatures were edible, maybe? Or were they simply
trying to figure out what these things who fell from the sky
were; these vaguely familiar beings, whose like they'd
never known before? They did seem briefly, particularly,
almost childishly interested in the difference between the
Albert E.'s lone female crew member's genitalia and the
rest of the gang's tackle, but that didn't last. That was fine
because she—a disillusioned crew-cut exobiologist dyke
called Emma Schneider—wouldn't have much liked it.

Anyway, there they were, these guys, like a bunch of
solemn mourners with my old shipmates. . . .

After I tossed down a spade and lowered a rope ladder,
however, they stood up, backed off, and watched me from a
distance as I came down and began to dig graves in this
loamy soil. With so many holes to dig, even shallow ones, I
knew to pace myself, take breaks, get things done in easy
stages: a little preparatory digging, then search for usables
in the ship, more digging, fix up my habitat, make another
attempt at finding my two missing buddies, set up my
generator—and so on. And that's pretty much how it's
been working out. . . .

But as yet I haven't actually described the manlikes.

Well, Jim, lad, here's me recording this under my habitat's awning, and while I speak I'm watching the locals do

their peculiar thing. Or perhaps it's not so peculiar and they're not so very alien. Well, not as alien as I thought. Because it appears they understand death and revere the dead—even my dead—or so it would seem. But how can it be otherwise? I mean, how else to explain this?

They've brought these instruments from somewhere— "musical" instruments, if you can call them that—from wherever they dwell, I suppose. And if this isn't some kind of lament they're singing, some kind of dirge I'm hearing from their drums, bang-stones, rattle-pods, and bamboo flutes, then I really don't know what it is. And I think that the only thing that's keeping them at a respectable distance from my dead ones . . . is me.

I'm looking at them through binoculars. Can't tell the male of the species from the female; hell, I don't even know if they *have* sexes as such! Ameboid? I shouldn't think so; *that* wobbly they're not! But human*like*? They are. Emphasis on "like." They have two each of the things we have two of, er, with the exception of testicles, *if* they have males and if their balls aren't on the inside. Oh, and also with the exception of breasts—*if* and et cetera, as previously conjectured.

Their eyes are watery-looking; not fishy, no, but uninspiringly pale, limpid and uniformly gray, large in their faces and forming triangles with their noses. As for those noses: they're just paired black dots in approximately the right places. Their mouths are thin-lipped; their dull white teeth look fairly normal; their ears are ears; and their shining black hair falls on their thin shoulders. Their hair is the most attractive—maybe even the only attractive—thing about them. They're about five foot five inches tall, with slender, roughly pear-shaped bodies thick end down. They've got three fingers to a hand, three toes to a foot. But while their legs seem strong, giving them a flowing, gliding, maybe even graceful mobility, their arms are much too thin and look sort of boneless.

So then, that's them, and I'm guessing they're the dominant species. Certainly they're head and shoulders above the rest of the fauna. And while I'm on about the rest of them:

Today I've seen several pink hogs doing their thing in the shrubbery at the forest's edge. Totally harmless, I'd say, and I'm not at all worried by them. From back in the deeper undergrowth, however, I've heard the occasional snuffling, grunting, and growling of the pink hogs' cousins; their big, hairy black shapes trundling to and fro, but yet keeping a safe distance. Well good! And likewise the flying Pinks in the treetops: I've seen them looking down at me, but it doesn't bother me much. On the other hand *their* cousins, the actual high-flying buzzards—if that's what they are—well, there's something really ominous about their unending circling. But so far, since I haven't seen a one of them come down and land, I'm not too concerned.

Enough for now. I've had my break, eaten, brewed and drank a pot of coffee; now I'll go back into the *Albert E.*, see if I can find poor Daniel . . .

LATER (LATE AFTERNOON, EARLY EVENING):

This is really amazing! It's so hard to believe I'm not sure if even seeing is believing! It started when I was in the ship.

I'd found Scot Gentry's body in his lab, crushed flat under everything that wasn't tied down. Then, while I was digging him out, I thought to hear movement elsewhere in the vessel. I told myself it was just loose wreckage shifting, settling down. When it happened a second time, however, the short hairs on the back of my neck stood up straight! What the—? After all this time, three days or more, could it be that I wasn't the only survivor after all, that someone else had lived through the wreck of the *Albert E.*? But there was only one someone else: my buddy Daniel Geisler! What would Dan's condition be?

Hell, he could be dying even now!

The way I went scrambling then, I could have broken my neck a dozen and more times on those sloping, often buckled, crazily angled decks; skidding and sliding, shouting myself hoarse, and pausing every now and then to hold my breath and listen, see if I was being answered. Finally I did hear something, coming from the direction of the airlock that I was using.

It was four of the manlike Pinks. They must have followed me up the ladder I'd left dangling, and . . . and they'd found my good buddy Daniel. But he wasn't alive, not with his head stove in and his back bent all the wrong way. And there they were, in the airlock, these four guys, easing Daniel into the sling that I'd fixed up and preparing to lower him to the ground.

Oh, really? And after they got him down, what else did they have planned for him? Advancing on them, I glared at them where they stood blinking back at me, with their skinny arms dangling and, as far as I could tell, no expressions whatsoever on their pale pink faces.

"All right, you weird fucks!" I yelled, lunging at them and waving my sidearm. "I don't know what you're up to, but—"

But one of them was pointing one of three skinny fingers at his own eyes, then at mine, finally out the airlock and down at the ground. It was like he was saying, "See for yourself." They backed off as I came forward and looked out. And down there . . . well, even now it's difficult to believe. Or maybe not. I mean, alien they may be—hell, they *are*—but that doesn't mean they don't have humanlike emotions, routines, rituals, ceremonials. Like their cradling the dead, their dirges, and now this.

But now what—eh, Jim lad? *Now the shallow graves that the other Pinks were digging down there*, that's now what! The whole group, using my spade, scoops made from half-gourds, even their bare three-digit hands, to dig as neat a set of graves as you'd never wish to see right there in the soft, loose loam!

Well, what could I say or do after that? Nothing that they'd understand, for sure. So letting the four Pinks get on with it, I went back for Gentry's body. By the time I returned, the sling was back in position, and the four volunteers were out of there. They'd gone below and were working with the rest of the tribe, digging for all they were worth.

I might have liked to find a way to express my gratitude—to this quartet, at least—but couldn't see how to do it. These creatures looked so much of a muchness to me, there was no sure way to tell my four apart from the rest of them. Ah, well . . .

DAY FOUR (MIDDAY):

I slept well last night; I suppose I was sort of exhausted. But I was also easier in my mind after letting the manlikes finish off burying the dead . . . well, except for Scot and Daniel. They wouldn't bury those last two until they'd sat with them through the night, their heads in their laps. A kind of ritual—a wake of sorts, a vigil—that they go through with their dead. Also with mine, apparently. It isn't a job I would have cared to do. After four or more days dead, Scot and Dan weren't looking very pretty. They weren't smelling too good, either. Could be the manlike Pinks do it to keep the buzzards and hogs from scavenging, which is something else I don't much care to think about.

This morning, their yelping, rattling, and piping woke me up just as they were finishing with filling in the last two graves. As I put up my awning I saw—just outside my habitat, outside the electric perimeter—one of the Pinks sitting there watching me. Now I know I've said they don't have much in the way of facial expressions, but this one was cocking its head first one way and then the other, and if anything, looked curious as hell. I mean curious about me. He, she, or it kept watching me while I boiled water, shaved, made and drank coffee, and ate a ship's-rations facsimile homeworld breakfast.

I tossed the Pink a cookie that it sniffed at, then bit into carefully, then got up, went unsteadily to the side of the clearing, leaned on a tree, and threw up. Credit where credit's due for perseverance, though, if for nothing else, because when it was done throwing up it came right on back and sat down again, watching me like before but just a shade less pink. Then when I set out to have a look around, explore the place, damned if he, she, it didn't come gliding after, albeit at a discreet, respectful distance.

As for why I wanted to go walkabout: long before we discovered that the galaxy was a pretty empty place, someone wrote in the survival handbook that if you get stuck on a world and want to know if there are any higher civilizations, just take a walk along a coastline. Because if there *is* intelligent life, that's where you'll find its flotsam and jetsam. Doesn't say a hell of a lot for intelligence, now, does it? Anyway, ever since I clambered from the wreckage of the *Albert E.* I've been hearing this near-distant murmur. And no matter where you are, the sound of small waves breaking on a beach is unmistakable.

I followed a manlike track through the woods until I came across a freshwater stream, then followed the stream and track both for maybe a quarter mile . . . and there it was, this beautiful ocean: blue under an azure sky, turning turquoise where it lapped the white, sandy beach; gentle as a pond and smelling of salt and seaweed. All that was missing was the cry of seagulls. Well, no, that's not all that was missing; there was no flotsam and jetsam, either.

No ships on the horizon, no smoke rising in any direction, and no footprints in the sand except my own. But I did have my Man, Woman, Thing Friday, following dutifully behind me.

Sitting on a rock looking at all the emptiness, I told him, her, it: "You know something, you're sort of indecent? Well you *would* be, if you had a dick or tits or something!" There was no answer, just those huge limpid eyes watching me, and that small pink head cocked on one side, displaying—or so I thought—a certain willingness to at least try to understand what I'd said . . . maybe. And because of that, on impulse, I took off my shirt and put it on Friday, who just stood there and let me. The Pink being small, that big shirt would have covered its naughty bits easily—if there had been any to cover! Anyway, it made Friday look just that little bit more acceptable.

We walked perhaps half a mile along the beach, then turned and walked back. But as we approached the stream and the forest track, that was when I discovered that there was a fourth variety of Pinks. And as if to complement the others—the bipeds, the quadruped grubbers in the woods, and the soaring aerials in the treetops—this time it was the swimmers, where else but in the sea?

These two dolphinlike Pinks were hauling a third animal—for all the world a real dolphin, or this world's equivalent—up from the deeper water into the shallows. The "real" dolphin was in a bad way, in fact on its way out; something big and, I have to assume, highly unpleasant had taken a very large chunk out of it. Almost cut in half, its plump body was gaping open, leaving a long string of guts trailing in the water behind it. I suppose that no matter where you are, if you have oceans you have sharks or things much like them. It did away with an idea I'd been tossing around that maybe later I would go for a swim. Reality was closing in on me again, and it was all pretty sick-making.

I moved closer, and Friday, oddly excited, came with me.

The oceangoing Pinks didn't seem concerned about our nearness; preoccupied with pushing the "real" dolphin up out of the water, they more or less ignored us and I was able to get close up and take a good look at them. First the fishy dolphin:

Even as I watched it, the poor thing expired. It just lifted its bottle nose out of the water once, gave a choked little cry, and flopped over on its side. It was mammalian, a female, slate gray on its back, white on what was left of its belly. If I had seen it in a SeaWorld on homeworld I would have thought to myself: dolphin, probably of a rare species.

As for the sea-Pinks: if I had seen *them* in a SeaWorld I'd have thought to myself, weird! From the waist up they were much the same as the bipeds, even to the extent of having their thin rubbery arms. Maybe in their upper bodies they were more streamlined than the land-dwelling variety, but that seemed to be the only difference. Oh, wait; they also had blowholes, in the back of their necks. From their middles down, however, they were all dolphin, the pink merging into gray. And I could see just looking at them that they weren't stupid.

Meanwhile Friday had taken out a bamboo flute from a little bag on a string around his (let's for the moment say his) waist, and had begun tootling away in a high-pitched register that was almost painful. And before I knew it a half-dozen manlikes had come down the track to join us on the beach. Keeping their distance from me—almost ignoring me—they hurried to the water's edge and very carefully began to drag the dead dolphin creature up the beach into the shade at the rim of the forest. And while one of them sat cradling the dead thing's head the rest of them set to work scooping out a grave. Astonishing! But—

—Well, I thought, don't people have this special affinity with dolphins back on Earth? Sure they do. And as Friday

and I headed back along the forest track toward the *Albert E.*
and the clearing, already I could hear the mournful singing,
the rattling and banging of the Pink burial party on the
beach. What was more, back at the wreck, I saw that they'd
even been decorating the graves of my shipmates, putting
little markers on them with various identifying squiggles.

Damn, but these guys revere the dead!

LATER:

This afternoon I went back into the ship searching for
anything that might make my life here just that little bit
more comfortable, more familiar, and—what the hell—
homeworldly? I took a small stack of Daniel's girlie magazines that I'd been coveting for God knows how many
light-years, a photograph album with pictures of some ex-
girlfriends of mine, some busted radio components I might
try tinkering with, and various bits and pieces like that.
Friday climbed up there with me, then went exploring on
his own. . . .

LATER:

It's evening now and raining. Even though the stream
looks pure enough, I'm using my awning to collect the
rain. Friday appears pretty fixated with me. He's taken to
me like a stray dog. So I switched off the perimeter and let
him in out of the rain. He's sitting there in one corner, not
doing much of anything. When I ate, I didn't offer him
any; as we've seen, ship's rations don't much agree with
him.

Speaking of rations, what I didn't realize till now is that
most of the stuff I took from the *Albert E.*'s galley was dam-

aged in the crash. I've preserved what I could, but at least seventy-five percent of it is wasted. I'll burn it tomorrow.

Which means, of course, that sometime in the not-too-distant future I'll have to start eating local. Maybe I should keep an eye on the Pinks, see what they eat. Or maybe not. If Friday can't eat my stuff, it seems unlikely that I can eat his.

It's all very worrying. . . .

DAY FIVE (MIDMORNING):

When I woke up this morning I caught Friday going through Dan's soft-porn mags. My old photograph album was lying open, too, so it looks like Friday's curiosity knows no bounds! Alas, he also appears to be disrespectful of my personal property. Thoroughly PO'd with him without really knowing why (I suppose I was in a bad mood), I switched off the perimeter and shooed him the hell out of here, then went walkabout on my own. The last time I saw him, he looked sort of down in the mouth—about as far down as a Pink is able to look, from what I've seen of them so far—as he went drifting off in the general direction of the *Albert E.*

Something entirely different:

I've discovered that the manlikes go hunting, with spears. I saw a bunch keeping very low and quiet, sneaking off into the thick of the forest. There was a second bunch, too, with half a dozen members who were watching me just a little too closely as I moved around the clearing. It seemed to me they were interested in *my* interest in these graves I've been discovering. I can tell that these mounds in the forest's fringing undergrowth are graves because of the markers on them. But not all of them have markers, only the more recent ones, which are easily identified by the freshly turned earth. I don't know if that's of any real significance.

Anyway, this second party of hunters kept looking at me, at each other, and at their spears, as if wondering if they should—or if they dare—have a go at me! Maybe they didn't like me looking at the graves because I wasn't showing sufficient reverence or something; I don't know, can't say. But it was as I was examining the more recent graves that these hunter Pinks became especially disturbed. Then, as I knelt to examine a thick-stemmed cactus or succulent that was sprouting in a marked mound—a fleshy, sickly-looking green thing with a pinkish head, something like a bulbous great asparagus spear—that was when the hunters displayed the most anxiety, even to the extent of looking more than a little hostile.

However, whatever *might* have happened next was averted when the first party of hunters came bursting from the forest in hot pursuit of a hairy black hog that was also in pursuit of a small pink grubber. The big black was rampant, so I could only suppose that the small Pink was in heat; but however that might be, the hunters were interested only in the black. And again I *supposed* they'd been using the little Pink as bait. Well, right or wrong in that respect, at least I now knew what they had been hunting and could reasonably assume that this was what they ate—that it was one of their staples, anyway.

In the confusion, as the big horny hog tore round the clearing after the small scurrying Pink, I tried to make it back to my habitat. Bad idea. In rapid succession the hog took three or four long thin spears in his back and flanks, lost all interest in the small pink grubber, and went totally crazy! Squealing and trying to gore everything in sight, with both parties of hunter Pinks now getting in their best shots as they glided after him, he turned, saw me, came slavering and snorting straight at me!

Of course I shot him; my bolt stopped him dead, exploded in his skull, sent blood and brains flying. He immediately bit the dust, twitched once or twice, and lay still . . . following that there was total, motionless silence; so that even with the hunters all over the place, they'd become so frozen into immobility that the clearing looked like nothing so much as an alien still life!

And that's the way it stayed, with nobody moving so much as a muscle until I broke the spell, holstered my weapon, and made my way stiff-legged and head high right on back to my habitat.

Friday was already in there, sitting in his corner on a box of old clothes he'd rescued from the *Albert E.* Probably figured he was doing me a favor bringing stuff out of there. Anyway, I was glad to see he was still my pal, and maybe even my only pal in these parts now.

Looking out from under my awning, I watched the end of this business with the hog. Finding their mobility again, several of the hunters hoisted the dead tusker and carried their trophy in a circle round the clearing in an odd, paradoxically muted celebratory procession. At least I'm supposing that's what it was. But when they passed out of sight, that was the end of that and I haven't seen the hog since. But I imagine there'll be a merry old feast in the clearing tonight.

LATER:

Toward evening I ventured out again. There was no sign of festive preparations, no fires, nothing. Come to think of it, I've never yet seen a fire. Maybe they don't have fire. Me, I can't say I fancy raw hog!

Anyway, there was no sign of the spearsmen, and the handful of Pinks who were out and about seemed as bland and harmless as ever; they paid little or no attention to me.

But in any case I wasn't out too long before it started in to rain again, so that was the end of tonight's excursion.

Friday is already asleep (I think) on a layer of old clothing in his corner. Not a bad idea.

So it's good-night from me, Jim lad . . .

DAY SIX (MIDMORNING):

Didn't sleep too good and it's left me grumpy. Late last night the Pinks were at it again, howling, thumping, and rattling, and that includes Friday. I woke up (very briefly) to find him gone and my defensive perimeter switched off—the little pink nuisance! I got up long enough to switch it on again, then went back to sleep. But I *must* find a way to get through to him, warn him against doing that. It's either that or simply ban him from the habitat altogether.

Everything tastes lousy this morning, even the coffee. Must be the water: It's *too* clean, *too* sweet! My poor old taste buds are far more accustomed to the recycled H_2O aboard the *Albert E.* Maybe I should climb up there one last time and drain off whatever's left in the system. Also, I should look for a remote for my defensive perimeter switch; the habitat didn't have one.

Actually, there are several items in the handbook that the habitat doesn't have: inexcusable deficiencies! Some dumb QM's assistant storeman on the Greater Mars Orbital should have his ass kicked out of an airlock!

As for last night's ceremonial rowdyism:

There's a new grave under the low vegetation at the rim of the clearing. I reckon it's the hog. Having eaten the thing—or at least the parts they wanted—the Pinks must have buried whatever was left. So their rituals extend even to their prey. This is all conjecture, of course; but again, as with the dolphin, I can't find this practice altogether strange. I seem to remember reading somewhere that many primitive tribes of Earth had a similar attitude toward Ma Nature's creatures: an understanding, appreciation, and respect for the animals they relied upon for food and clothing.

LATER:

I've managed to fix up a remote from some of the electrical kit I took from the *Albert E.* Now I can switch on my defensive perimeter from outside. Not that the manlikes have been intrusive—well, except for my man Friday—but I like to think that my few personal possessions are secure, and that I'm retaining at least a semblance of privacy . . .

Today I went fishing with a bamboo pole and line I managed to fix up. Friday went with me, showed me the grubs in the sand that I could use as bait. I brought in an eight-inch crab-thing that Friday danced away from. It had an awful lot of legs and a nasty stinger, so I flipped it back into the sea. The fish that I caught were all small and eel-like, but they taste fine fried and make a welcome change from ship's rations. I offered one to Friday, which he didn't hesitate to accept and eat. So it seems these small fish are another Pink staple.

LATER (EVENING):

I had a sleep, woke up in the afternoon feeling much refreshed, and went walkabout with Friday. We chose to walk a forest trail I never used before; Friday seemed okay with it, so I assumed it was safe enough. When we passed a group of Pinks gathering root vegetables, I paused to point at a small pile of these purplish carrotlike things and raise a questioning eyebrow. Friday must have understood the look; he pointed to his mouth and made chewing motions.

Going to the pile, he even helped himself to three of the carrots. None of the gatherers seemed to mind. So I have to assume that these tubers are yet another Pink staple.

Then, because it was getting late, we headed for home. But, did I say home? I must be going native!

Back at the habitat, as we were about to enter, I witnessed something new. Or if not exactly new, different. First off, as I went to use the remote to cancel the electrical perimeter, I noticed Friday looking up into the sky above the clearing. And Friday wasn't the only one. As if suddenly aware of some imminent occurrence, all the other manlikes were sneaking back into the shadows to hide under the fringing foliage. Several of them had taken up spears from somewhere or other, and they were all peering up into the sky.

I went into the habitat with Friday, and we both looked out from under the awning. At first I couldn't see anything of interest. But then, on a level with the highest of the treetops, I saw a small shape drifting aimlessly to and fro. It was a young aerial Pink. (I immediately thought of it as a fledgling, which if it had any feathers I suppose it would have been.) Whatever, it was a pink flyer getting nowhere fast, looking all confused and lost up there.

Then, much higher overhead, I spotted something else. Spiraling down from the dusky indigo sky there came a black speck, faint at first but rapidly increasing in size. Its wings—real wings this time—gradually folded back, becoming streamlined, until in the last moment the hawk-buzzard-vulture dropped like a stone and swooped on its prey . . . and itself *became* the prey!

In the instant before it could make deadly contact with the young floater, a great flock of adult aerials launched themselves from the high canopy, converged on the buzzard, and slammed into it from all sides. Squawking its pain, winded and flapping a broken wing, the thing tumbled into the clearing. Even before it hit the ground there was a spear through its neck and it had stopped complaining. And up in the treetops, the aerial ambushers were already drifting back to their various roosts.

Now, if I hadn't witnessed this event with my own eyes, I'd *never* have believed that the adult flyers could move so fucking fast and with such deadly intent! Not only that, but to my mind the incident formed a perfect parallel with what had happened to the black hog: Both had been examples of deliberate entrapment. And I wasn't in the least surprised as night came on once again to hear the mournful ceremonial wailing, rattling, thumping, and piping of the manlikes. . . .

Another staple? Possibly. Another grave in the morning? I'd bet my shirt on it—if I hadn't already given it to Friday. . . .

DAY NINE (MIDDAY):

I'm getting a bit lax with this. But the less I have to do, the more I feel like doing nothing! The last two days I've spent my time on the beach fishing, dozing, getting myself a tan that my old shipmates would have killed for. It's alarming how pasty we used to get in space, keeping away from naked sun and starlight and all the gamma radiation. But this is a friendly sun and I'm protected by atmosphere. Friday's skin must be a lot more fragile than mine; he made himself a shelter from spiky palm fronds and spent most of his time in the shade.

Then again, he has been looking kind of droopy just lately, all shivery and sweaty. Since my human routines, activities, and such aren't naturally his, I think it's possible that Friday's been spending too much time in my company and that it's beginning to tell on him. I find I can't just shoo him off, though, because now it seems I've grown accustomed to his face. (Ugh!)

DAY TWELVE (EARLY TO MIDMORNING):

For breakfast I sliced and fried up some of the purple carrots that Friday has been bringing in for me. Wary at first, I took just a single small bite. Not at all bad, they taste something like a cross between chili peppers and green onions; but like an Indian curry, they do cause internal heat and lots of sweating. Maybe Friday has been eating too many of them, because he gets sweatier day by day! Then again, I've seen quite a few of the manlikes with the same condition: their skin glistens and moisture drips from their long-nailed fingers, especially when they cradle the dead before burial.

And speaking of the dead:

Just an hour or so ago, a hunting party of five Pinks went out into the forest. In a little while they were back, four of them carrying the fifth between them. He'd been torn up pretty badly—gutted in fact, I expect by a black hog—and he died right here in the clearing. His hunter buddies at once took up his body again, headed off down one of the tracks with it, and the regulation party of mourners and "musicians" went trooping after. So they obviously have a special burial place for their own kind somewhere in the woodland. . . .

LATER (TOWARD NOON):

Friday's veggies have given me bad indigestion. Maybe I should have left them alone, but I was trying to show my appreciation of his generosity. Anyway, since I know I'll have to start living on local stuff sooner or later, it probably makes sense to start eking out my dwindling stock of ship's rations right now with anything I can forage—or whatever Friday can forage for me.

LATER (MIDAFTERNOON):

Midday, after Friday went off on his own somewhere, I took the opportunity to sneak into the forest along the same track taken by the manlike burial party. This was after they had returned, because I didn't want them to get the idea that I was spying on them, which I was. Maybe a mile along the track I chanced upon their village and discovered something weird and wonderful!

For some time I had been wondering about biped society: did they have a communal place—I mean other than the clearing—where they lived and brought up their kids? . . . stuff like that. Because until now I hadn't seen any manlike children. Only now I had found just such a place. But it wasn't only manlike kids that I saw.

The track ended at a limestone cliff that went up sheer for perhaps eighty, ninety feet. And there were ladders, ledges, and even tottery-looking balconies fronting the hollowed-out caves. The cliff face was literally honeycombed with these troglodyte dwellings. And that was it; the biped Pinks were cave dwellers. But that wasn't what was so weird and wonderful.

I've told how these pink species seem to parallel the various types you might more reasonably expect to find on a burgeoning world: feathered birds, wild forest tuskers, even dolphins. Now I saw that there was something more to it than that, though exactly what I couldn't say. But the extensive cleared space at the foot of the cliffs was like a Pinks playground watched over by a handful of adults, and they weren't just looking after the manlike kids who were playing there. No, for there were little pink hogs running around, too, also being cared for. And on the lower ledges, and in the many creepers climbing the cliff face, that's where gatherings of infant pink floaters roosted. What's more, in a freshwater pool fed by a gentle waterfall, I thought I could even make out a young pink dolphin practicing "walking" on his tail! The whole place was a Pinks kindergarten, but for *all* pink species, not just manlikes! And hiding behind a tree, suddenly I knew my being there wasn't in order and my presence wouldn't be appreciated.

Then, hurrying back toward the clearing, I glimpsed hunters heading my way and moved quickly, quietly aside into the forest shade. The hunting party passed me by; but back there under the trees I had found another Pink graveyard—*the* Pink graveyard, the graveyard of the manlikes! All of the graves had the weird asparagus plants growing out of them; some with as many as four spears, each as thick as my forearm and from eighteen inches to two feet tall, with bulbous tips as big as a clenched fist. But there were also some with collapsed stems and bulbs with empty, shattered husks. And once again I experienced that sensation of trespassing, of feeling that I really shouldn't be there.

How did I know this was the biped graveyard? Because every plot was well tended and marked with unmistakable, stylized *pictures* of manlikes drawn on papery bark, that's how. And one of the graves—a mound *without* the weird plants—was brand-new and the soil still wet!

I would have left at once but the strangest thing happened. One of the fattest of several asparagus stems on an older grave had started quivering, and the leaves or petals on the big bulb at its tip were peeling back on themselves and leaking a gluey liquid. Not only that, but something was wriggling in there—something pink!

That was enough. I got the hell out of there.

Luck was with me; I got back to the clearing and my habitat without encountering any more Pinks, and Friday was waiting for me with a big bunch of those purple carrots. This time, though, I haven't accepted them. Actually, I've only just realized that I've been feeling a little sick and dizzy ever since breakfast.

DAY FOURTEEN (I THINK . . . OR MAYBE FIFTEEN?):

God, I'm not at all well. And what happened this morning hasn't much helped the way I feel.

I was dreaming. I was with this woman and it was just about to turn into a wetty. We were in bed and I was groping her: one hand on her backside, the other on her breasts, while the, er, best of me searched for the way in; but damned if I could find it! And even for a guy who has spent most of his time in space, that wasn't at all like me. I mean, it simply wasn't there! But anyway, as I went to kiss her, she breathed on me, causing me to recoil from her strange, sweet breath—and likewise from the dream.

I woke up—came startling awake—and saw these big limpid, alien eyes staring straight into mine! It was Friday, under the sheet with me, and both of us were sweaty as hell!

What the screaming fuck? He (shit, maybe I should have been calling Friday "she" all this time!) was holding my face in *its* wet, three-fingered hands, its body trembling with some kind of weird passion. I jerked back, kicked it out of there, and was on my feet before it could get up from the dirt floor. But finally it did, and there it stood in a padded bra, frilly panties, and a lacy chemise that could only have belonged to Emma Schneider. And I knew it was so because Friday's mouth was a ghastly crimson gash that was thickly layered with the *Albert E.*'s ex-exobiologist's fucking hideous lip gloss!

Jesus H. Christ!

And out he, she, *it* went; out of my habitat, out beyond the defensive security perimeter, and out of what's left of my life in this fucking place for good. And I hurled the February 2196 issue of *Lewd Lustin' Lovers* it had left lying open on my folding card table right out there into the clearing after it! But even after I'd washed myself top to toe, still I felt like I'd been dipped in dog dirt, and here it is noon and I still do. . . .

LATER (MIDAFTERNOON):

I went down to where a stream joins the ocean to swim in a pool there. I'm still not a hundred percent, crapping like a volcano blowing off, and throwing up purple, but at least my skin feels clean again.

When I was in the water, I thought I saw Friday lurking near the rocks where I left my pants, socks, and shoes, but he wasn't there when I came out and dried off. Back in the habitat when I went to switch on the perimeter, I couldn't find my remote . . . I could have sworn it was in my pants pocket. And that's not all; the perimeter's wiring had been yanked out of the generator's connection box. It's not impossible that Friday did it accidentally when I tossed him out of bed, but it's also possible he's been in here sabotaging stuff. When I'm felling better I'll fix things up again, try to knock together a new remote.

But that's for when I'm feeling better. Right now I'm feeling lousy, so I'm going to have to get my head down . . . rest and recuperation, Jim lad.

LATER (EARLY EVENING):

Went back to the old *Albert E.* I was going to climb the ladder, go looking for tools, electrical gear, and like that. No way, I was too weak. Made four rungs and had to come down again before I fell.

Down there under the ship's crumpled hull, it suddenly occurred to me maybe I should pay my respects to the crew, which I haven't been doing for a while now. And what do you know, these slimy shoots were gradually uncoiling, standing up out of their graves.

Dizzy and staggering about like I was falling-down drunk, I went to kick the things flat, crush, destroy, and . . .

and murder them? But a bunch of bipeds got hold of me, guiding and half-carrying me back to my habitat.

I thought I saw Friday standing there, just watching all of this—the little pink fairy! But hell, it could have been any one of them. No, I reckon it was him. And now I can't help wondering if maybe he's poisoned me—and if so, was it deliberate?

My temperature's way up . . . I'm sweaty and dizzy as all get-out . . . puking all over the place but bringing nothing up. What the hell? Is this the end of it?

✧

Don't know what day it is, but it feels like morning.

They've carried me out into the clearing, and I think it's Friday who's cradling my head. He doesn't seem to mind me talking to my personal log. He's seen me do it often enough before; probably thinks it's some kind of ritual, which in a way it is or has become. Well, and we all have our rituals—right, Jim lad?

I'm no longer sweating; in fact I feel sort of dry, almost brittle. But my mind is very clear now, and I think I've figured it out. Something of it, anyway. It's that thing called evolution. If I was an exobiologist like Emma Schneider, I might have worked it out earlier; but no, I'm just a grease monkey.

Evolution, yes. We human beings became the Earth's dominant species by evolving. We walked upon the dirt—the earth under our feet, terra firma—but wanted a whole lot more. What about the winds above the earth, and the vast waters that flowed over it? So we made machines, vessels to sail on the seas and in the skies; finally we even built spaceships, to journey beyond the skies. So you might say that in a way we achieved our dominance mechanically: that old opposing-thumb-theory-thing.

Well, the Pinks are also becoming dominant, on their

world as we did on Earth. Except so far, with them, it's all biological. For the time being, they don't have much need for machines; they're conquering the skies, seas, and forests without mechanical devices, by utilizing and changing the DNA of the various species that live in those environments and then by inhabiting them themselves.

On Earth we took out the predators, who were our competitors, by killing them off. Well, the Pinks are doing it, too—except they are doing it by *becoming* them! It explains why the vultures stay way high in the sky and why the black hogs stick mainly to the deeper woods— because having evolved alongside the Pinks, they're learning to keep their distance. As I should have kept mine . . .

✿

I must have passed out but now I'm back. Probably for the last time, Jim lad.

Friday is still cradling my head, but his sweating has become something else. The Pinks are unisexual, I'm pretty sure of that now. I can't any longer feel my body, my limbs . . . can only just speak or whisper, and I'm able to turn my head a few inches, but that's all. My eyes are still working, however, and from time to time as Friday relaxes his efforts (fuck it, I've gone and made him a "he" again!) I can see it's his time. What time? Well, see, he's not sweating anymore, he's ovulating!

I see these silvery droplets with their tadpole cores issuing drip by drip from beneath the steeply arched nails on his central digits, his ovipositors. And now he sticks his fingers deeply into my neck. I can barely feel it, for which I'm truly, truly glad, Jim lad.

Who knows, maybe me and my old *Albert E.* shipmates—or I should say our pink descendants somewhere down the line—maybe they'll get back out into space again. Because it surely has to follow that whatever issues from us will be a lot more manlike than these manlikes.

And that, I think, is all for now, probably forever. Uh-oh! Maybe we should make that definitely forever, because here come the musicians. . . .

OUT TWELVE-STEPPIN', SUMMER OF AA

(with apologies to Joe Lansdale hisownself)

NANCY HOLDER

THERE WERE SEVERAL times when the cliffhanger fade-to-blacks of the Chronicles of the Cannibal Cats seemed to indicate that Dwight, having secretly nursed innumerable resentments against Angelo, who was hipper, handsomer, and richer—initially, at least—would devour Angelo, thus freeing himself from his homoerotic codependence on his blood brother, and become his own person.

Alas.

When they had first arrived in Los Angeles, young and hopeful glam rockers, Dwight hadn't even been capable of dreaming of the fame and fortune that would befall them. Mansions, cars, chicks. They went platinum with each new offering, then double platinum. The movies they were in set new records.

The universe had blessed Angelo and him overly much, and who could say where the credit really lay? Dwight knew they were a team; he knew that he added something to the mix. He just wasn't sure what it was. So he let Angelo live.

At least, that was what he told himself. On other days, long ones, and longer nights, he knew that he loved Angelo and couldn't imagine life without him. Not that they were gay. They had never done anything like *that*, but Angelo had fed Dwight his little toe when, in his deep depression, he had stopped eating. In the old days, before all the metrosexual stuff, men could be close without people misunderstanding what it was all about.

So, the money was mind-bending and the fame was mind-blowing, except that success loaded a lot of pressure onto their cannibal lifestyle. Devouring people—okay, women, call them misogynistic for preferring the taste of women over that of men, maybe it was estrogen or some kind of fat content—was a lot harder to get away with when reporters routinely went through your trash.

Because sometimes your trash contained mandibles and patellas and stuff. They were always careful, but there was always a lot to clean up. Eating people wasn't like some chichi coke habit, for God's sake. You couldn't just flush your leftovers down the toilet.

"We have to stop," Angelo announced one night, after a tasty treat of a couple of untraceable groupies.

Dwight was completely caught off guard. Angelo's timing was majorly bizarre, because the night was beyond perfect. The girls were nobodies—the safest of victims—and they had succumbed to the drugs in their drinks very quickly. The boys had plenty of time—these were not girls who were going to be missed—so they washed them and dried them and told them good-bye in their own special ways. Slow heartbeat, clean, sweet flesh; it didn't get much better than that. Dwight had been weeping with contentment; being an artist, he was emotional. A therapist he'd seen at a few parties—he would never dare to actually see a therapist—had once told him that she thought people in the arts were defended deep feelers. Dwight liked the ring of that. He was a defended deep feeler.

So after devouring his girl, he had wept without shame.

His tears dried as Angelo sat cross-legged on the water bed beside him. Angelo had just showered and was wearing a fluffy white bathrobe. Though he was in his midfifties, Angelo Leone still had the goods. The chiseled jaw, the high cheekbones—though plastic surgeons maintained it, he had come by his sculptured profile naturally. Dwight Jones, not so much. Dwight was wearing a kimono one of their groupies had given him long ago. His bright red hair was brightened chemically. His blue eyes had faded. He was getting a tummy. He was starting to have boy boobs. Dr. Cohen was warning him that really, the best way to keep the liposuction and the Botox going was to get enough sleep and exercise. Dwight knew he should listen. This was the same guy who had surgically implanted stubs on his and Angelo's matching missing pinkie tips.

Angelo continued, "We need the best kind of help to help us stop." He looked hard at Dwight, whose mouth was hanging open while his tears dripped down the end of his nose. "You know I'm right, Dwight. This is going to catch up with us. Already has."

Dwight couldn't quite hear his heartbeat. He couldn't hear anything. Then the sound came back in slowly.

". . . give it a shot," Angelo said. "We've talked about quitting before, but we've never done it."

They talked about quitting, yes, they did. They *talked* about quitting. Usually when they had almost gotten caught. Once the danger died down, that conversation went away.

"We have to at least try," Angelo insisted. "That's all I ask." He reached out a hand. "If I don't quit, I'm going to die."

Dwight sighed at the drama, knowing he was already defeated. Whatever Angelo wanted, Dwight gave to him.

It was their way.

✧

"Drinking is just a metaphor," Angelo reminded Dwight, as they stepped onto the grounds of the United Methodist Church on Franklin in Los Angeles. They had dressed carefully for the occasion, Angelo in a black sweater and black leather pants, Dwight in, well, a black sweater and black leather pants, too. It was pretty much all they wore; except that when it was warm, they switched to black T-shirts. They had to dress like that. They were rock stars.

It was very early in the morning. Hollywood was not a late-night town, which was problematic for music people unless they were of the caliber of the Cannibal Cats, who made their own fun at private parties in private clubs. Sleepy pepper trees shaded bubbly, lead-lined glass windows like the Tiffany windows of Oyster Bay at the Met in New York. Dwight had never actually seen the Tiffany windows—that would be so gay—but a prop guy he knew had made copies of them for *Thunderstorm,* their first movie, and was very proud of showing them off.

A huge red AIDS ribbon was plastered against the bell tower, which assured Dwight and Angelo that although their destination was a traditional Christian edifice, the people who were running it were liberals. Dwight liked the tricked-out monastery look: The courtyard was quaint, with privet hedges and a fountain that trickled merrily, liquid nickel against a pewter sky. The church had been used as a location in many films including *Sister Act II.* A location manager would have to be blind to overlook it, set in the heart of Hollywood as it was.

Dwight was going soundless with anxiety again. His palms were wet. He shivered with goose bumps. He did not want to run into any of their fans. Anonymity be damned; you were gonna tell people if you ran into the Cannibal Cats at an AA meeting. He fretted about that as his boots clomped down concrete steps toward the basement. He felt them, couldn't hear them.

He fretted about going deaf. He fretted about going inside a basement. There weren't that many in L.A., because of the earthquakes. He and Angelo had been in L.A. during the Northridge quake of '94 —not in a basement, but in the Capitol Records building—and it had been terrifying. It was like that disaster movie; like a dozen movies. A chick they knew had watched her stove fly across the room and land upside down. Then her chimney collapsed. She moved to Florida.

Some people just have bad luck.

But here they were, staring into the basement, and Dwight couldn't hear a fucking thing. They stood together framed by double doors that opened into a large room bathed with gray light from a bank of more leaded glass windows. Dwight briefly pondered if he should have been a cinematographer, he was so interested in light.

There were folks seated away from him in rows of metal folding chairs facing a podium. Wow, the guy at the podium was something else: bald with one earring; really dark eyebrows and eyelashes, framing iridescent blue eyes. They were so blue he looked like some kind of exotic bird. His had never been so blue. Contacts, Dwight surmised. He wore a black T-shirt and he was *cut*.

He took one look at the Cannibal Cats, and he lost track of what he was saying.

That was okay, because Dwight couldn't hear him anyway.

The smell of coffee and cream cheese—scents of a million dressing rooms on the road—wafted toward Dwight, who looked to see where the food was. He saw some silver trays on a trio of wood-topped card tables. Bagels and orange slices. Coffee urns like in the churches back home in the Midwest. He wasn't hungry, but he sure could use some caffeine.

Podium Guy waved them in with his fingers. He looked like he was about to have an orgasm. Fifty heads or more turned in their direction, and he recognized at least eight of the attendees of this, their very first AA meeting—no, make that an even dozen attendees—four A-list actors, three directors, two producers, and three other rock stars, a couple of whom were almost as famous as the Cats, which was saying something.

The recognized grinned conspiratorially, as if to say, *No shit! You guys, too?*

Angelo murmured, "Showtime, Dwight."

Taking a deep breath in unison, they walked steadily toward the bank of chairs, passing movie-star flesh, film-producer flesh. The elite of Hollywood were like Kobe beef, massaged and beer-fed.

Only not this crew. No beer. At least, not anymore.

"It's so cool to be in a basement," Dwight babbled to Angelo. He was so nervous. "Not a lot of basements in town. Earthquakes."

"Ssh," Angelo snapped. "He's reading."

Dwight focused hard, tried to hear. Words were being very weird to him. *"We admitted we were powerless over alcohol, that our lives had become unmanageable . . ."*

"It's a metaphor," Angelo reminded him.

✧

The guy with the blue eyes was Bob V. People didn't share their last names. And now Bob V. was Angelo's sponsor.

It was obvious to Dwight that he was kissing up to Angelo because of who Angelo was, and not because he had ten years of sobriety and "needed to give something back." He simpered like a roadie chick, and Angelo just dug it. Angelo slung his fingers in his pockets and listened hard, took the literature, agreed to call him every day.

"At least once," Bob V. ordered him.

And twice.

And three times. And they didn't talk much about Angelo's life-or-death metaphorical need to stop drinking. They talked about Jimi Hendrix, who people said Angelo sounded like; and Eddie Van Halen, and all the new rockers. When Bob V. mentioned that he liked Ottmar Liebert, Angelo said, "Wow, me too!"

That was pure and utter bullshit.

Then one moody, cloudy night, the two Cats were sitting on the concrete railing of their fabulous Spanish Revival mansion up in the Hollywood Hills, each propped up against a column. The garden below was dotted with lush palms, illuminated with canny Art Deco lanterns that glimmered dazzling light in the swimming pool and hot tub. Dwight had wanted to go in the Jacuzzi, but Angelo demurred. Too cold, he said.

Dwight's sponsor was a B-list actor named Lou S. Lou S., who was about forty, with silvery hair and a long nose and thin lips, had been reduced to making training films for corporations because he had fucked everything up with his out-of-control drinking.

"Doesn't matter," Lou S. assured him. "I'm happier now than I have ever been in my life."

Then you're an idiot, Dwight informed him silently.

But Dwight had promised Angelo to give this whole stupid thing a fair trial. So he met with Lou and received his Big Book, which was the AA instruction manual, and promised to "work his steps."

The first time Dwight had gotten together with Lou in his weird little apartment in Woodland Hills, Lou had said, "Do you know what Al-Anon is? You might try them. Or there's a CoDA meeting on Wednesday nights. CoDA is a twelve-step program designed specifically for people with codependent issues. That's what their name means. Co-Dependents Anonymous."

Dwight was infuriated. Codependent issues? Did this no-name loser have any idea who he was fucking with?

But while Dwight seethed, Angelo thrived. He was working his steps, all right.

Work *this*.

Now, a month into their program, as Angelo set down their bottle of Jack Daniel's and unfolded another pamphlet, he said, "So what we say when we're alone is 'We admitted we were powerless over *cannibalism,* and that our lives had become unmanageable.' It is a disease of isms. That's what Bob told me." He skimmed the pamphlet.

"So, let me tell you about my addiction," he commanded, looking up and smiling at Dwight.

Dwight started to sigh, but Lou had told him the heavy sigh was the mating call of the codependent.

Lou had also told him that he, Dwight, would resent him, and that that was natural. Because the part of him that wanted to stay sick would fight tooth and nail—Lou had no idea of the irony there!—to keep his current sick thinking in charge of his actions.

"But it will kill you, Dwight," Lou had told him. "Untreated, unmanaged, your addiction will bring you down."

Angelo cleared his throat impatiently.

"Okay, Angelo, tell me how you are powerless over cannibalism," Dwight said dutifully, folding his hands around his knees.

Angelo got into character, sighing deeply. He could sigh deeply if he wanted to. His sponsor didn't give a rat's ass.

"If we don't stop, we're going to get caught. If we get caught, they'll probably give us lethal injections. I know that, but I still don't want to stop. That I guess makes me powerless over my addiction." Angelo was clearly thrilled.

Dwight pursed his lips and nodded somberly. "Yes," he said like a therapist. "I understand."

Angelo frowned. "What?"

Dwight was flustered. Isn't that what he was supposed to say? Then he blurted, "If you don't want to stop, why are we going to meetings and shit? I mean, if *you* don't want to stop, why are *you* going to meetings and—"

"I'm of two minds about it," Angelo said. He gestured

to his shoulders. "Angel." He touched his right shoulder. "Devil." He chuckled and pointed at Dwight. "Evil twin."

"Blood brother," Dwight amended, feeling the heat in his face.

"Yes." They had become blood brothers in high school, with blood, which tasted awesome. Then when Angelo had accidentally sliced off the tip of his pinkie and Dwight had popped it in his mouth and man oh man oh man, it was psychedelically delicious. (That was how they had talked back then.) Anyone who said it tasted like chicken was a total poser. Once you tasted human flesh, going back to chicken was like playing some low-rent lounge in Vegas once you've done the Universal Amphitheater.

Now on the lounge: They fired the manager who booked them that gig. As for the chicken thing, they eventually made a list of women they wanted to eat when they came to L.A. A couple of the names on the list had sunk into obscurity, then risen again to fame, in part from singing duets with the Cannibal Cats:

1. Tina Turner
2. Madonna
3. Cyndi Lauper
4. Janet Jackson
5. Annie Lennox

There would be way too many questions asked if any of those chicks disappeared, so they stuck to women no one would miss—well, except that hot *yakuza* babe—and there were even a few glitches with that. Angelo had eaten Dwight's girlfriend Alice, and Dwight had still never forgiven him for that. Dwight was looking forward to Angelo's amend on that one—which would come with step nine, where you made things right with people you had harmed.

"Okay, let's reframe this for our sponsors," Angelo said, lighting up a joint. He poured himself a whole hell of a lot more Jack Daniel's and handed the bottle to Dwight. "Because we are famous rock stars, we have to stop drinking so much. We're getting older and alcohol is affecting our performance."

"And our livers," Dwight said, taking a drink. "Add that. Because it's true. All this protein is messing with our systems. "

"Atkins is so full of it."

"We should eat him," Dwight chuckled.

"He's dead, dork." Angelo grinned.

"Hasn't always stopped us."

"He's a guy," Angelo said.

"He's a guy," Dwight agreed.

Dwight felt better. Reconnected. After chugalugging about a third of the bottle, Dwight traded the bottle for the joint. They smoked the best marijuana on the planet. He was getting pretty loaded. The air was swirling, the moonlight washing Angelo's dark ringlets with silver.

Angelo drank the Jack and tipped the bottle upside down. He said, "Dwight, go get another?" and Dwight slid off the railing, opened the sliding-glass door that led into their massive kitchen, and walked unsteadily around the breakfast bar.

About halfway to the booze cabinet, it occurred to him that, hey, Angelo had two good legs, too, so why was he, Dwight, the one who always went after everything?

The familiar tightening in his gut told him to lighten up. Back home, Angelo had been richer, cooler, and had not had a father who beat his mother to death. But that was then, and this was fast-forward to a life together of amazing accomplishments. A few slights, maybe, but then, Angelo had brought the money into the partnership. Money bought state-of-the-art guitars, costumes, lessons, and a few connections. Dwight had just brought a little talent and a lot of hope, and in Hollywood, every kid who got off the bus had some of that.

But he had parlayed his shot into the life he led now.

I am every bit as good as he is.

Even though he was already in the kitchen, he turned around and said, "Angelo, I think *you* should get a new bottle of Jack's."

Whatever Angelo was going to say in response remained unspoken, because Angelo's cell phone rang.

He whipped it out of his black leather pants and said, "Hello?" with no trace of slurring. He was remarkable that way, could hold his liquor and his dope better than any rock star around. "Oh. *Bob.*" He smiled big time and looked across the breezeway to Dwight.

Dwight murmured, "Shit!"

"A twelfth-step call?" Angelo asked brightly. "What's that? Oh. Okay. I'm here with Dwight—can he come, too? Cool. We'll show."

He pantomimed writing on paper; Dwight got the magnetized notepad on the Sub-Zero fridge, which they had bought for Maria del Carmen, their maid, which was headed HAY QUE COMPRAR, *To Buy.* They always needed a lot of trash bags and paper towels. And sponges and Formula 409.

She never asked why.

Dwight hurried back with the pad to Angelo, who wrote down an address and some directions. He said, "Yes, all right. Got it. Okay. Half an hour."

He hung up and said, "We're supposed to meet him at some guy's house. The dude is drunk and he's talking about killing himself."

"Then he isn't really going to do it," Dwight said authoritatively. Being rock stars, they had a lot of experience with people who talked about suicide. "If you talk about it, you don't do it."

"Well, addicts are different people," Angelo reminded him.

"We should sober up. Brush our teeth and use a lot of mouthwash," Dwight said. "He'll smell it on us."

"We should shower," Angelo replied. "Bob's cagey. And observant. We're going to have to be careful around him."

Dwight wondered why Angelo had picked a cagey, observant sponsor. And then he remembered that the whole point of AA was to help them with their addiction. Even though it was a metaphor.

✿

They wanted to get to their destination unseen—otherwise, paparazzi—so they took their little black Beemer. They had motorcycles and exotic cars like Lotuses and all that, but a Beemer was business as usual in Los Angeles.

Angelo drove. He always drove. They took the 5 North up past the Getty and the off-ramps for Sherman Oaks, heading toward Burbank. They had recently looped some songs for an animated feature up there. There was a cool horror bookstore, too, owned by a hot chick and a guy with white hair who looked like the folksinger Arlo Guthrie. They had the most massive collection of cannibal items Dwight had ever seen. In fact, now that he thought of it, the name of the store—Dark Delicacies—was a cannibal name, pretty much.

Maybe there are more cannibals in L.A. than we realize, Dwight thought. *Maybe if we made contact with a few, we could get some tips on how to be more discreet. We wouldn't have to give it up . . .*

And at the thought of giving it up—of never eating human flesh again—Dwight broke out in a cold sweat. His stomach cramped; his hands shook. For one crazy moment, he thought of jumping out of the car.

"Do we take the 134?" Angelo murmured, looking at the directions.

It started to rain. Dwight was startled. Angelo turned on

the windshield wipers and continued to mutter about the directions.

Dwight couldn't hear him. He couldn't hear the windshield wipers. He couldn't hear the rain.

I'm not going to do it, he realized. *I'm not going to stop eating people.*

A thrill of exhilaration surged through him. He glanced over at Angelo as if his blood brother could read his mind.

If I have to lie to him, I will, he thought. *But I'm not giving it up.*

He let the power of his decision propel him along for about six miles, which, when one is driving at sixty miles an hour, is about ten minutes. But Angelo was doing ninety.

Then dread washed over him, hard and cold. He sat breathless in his seat and watched the billboards and lit-up buildings flash past. He couldn't swallow past the constriction in his throat.

Your alcoholism will do anything it can to survive, Lou the Loser S. had told him. *It will make you lie, cheat, steal, and it will tell you that you aren't really an alcoholic. It will convince you that you can control your drinking.*

And then it will kill you.

Dwight shook his head as if he were actually conversing with Lou. *I don't care if I'm addicted to raw human flesh. I'm going to eat it no matter what.*

"Dude, are you tripping?" Angelo asked, cutting into his reverie.

Dwight said, "Just practicing in my head." They were going to do a concert at the Hollywood Bowl in six weeks.

Angelo nodded vaguely. He was checking the directions he'd written down. He swung a quick left—Hollywood Way—and muttered something. Part of what he was saying sounded like *mdfahdlajfhadll.* The other part sounded like "He said to follow the signs to the airport."

Dwight was dizzy. Like he was operating a video-game

character, he swiveled his head and squinted out the window. The rain was coming down so heavily he couldn't read the street sign. His stomach lurched. He took a slow, deep breath.

"Okay, we need Magnolia," Angelo went on.

Dwight wanted to turn to him and shout, "Shut the fuck up! Shut up now!" but that wasn't on the menu of operating instructions. What was on the menu was just maintaining. He stared at the rain.

Another flash of lightning ripped the sky; the rain came down and Angelo muttered some more. The car rolled to a stop and Angelo said, "We should have brought some fucking umbrellas," but the thing was, nobody in Los Angeles ever remembered umbrellas. What was important to Dwight was that he actually heard Angelo say the words. His momentary psychic break had passed.

We're in this thing together. We're okay.

I will die if I stop eating people.

Angelo got out of his side; Dwight did the same. The rain was plummeting like cold pebbles. Dwight was sad about their black leather jackets and black leather pants, but they were rich; they could buy more.

He paused, waiting for Angelo, who pointed down the street and said, "There they are!"

They? Dwight thought anxiously, as he followed Angelo, who began to trot along the sidewalk. He was not seeing whatever Angelo was seeing, and he began to worry that he was losing his vision. All he saw was gray rain and Angelo's black-and-gray hair, bobbing along slightly ahead of him like a disembodied head. He wanted to reach out and touch Angelo's shoulder to make sure the rest of him was there, but he knew that would be dorky.

Angelo said, "See, a twelfth-step call is when you go to help another alcoholic. It's the twelfth step, being of service."

Dwight processed that. He wanted to say, "But we're on

step one," but the syllables were scattering like so many droplets of mercury. He wondered why they hadn't discussed any of that while they were in the car.

"Hi, Bob!" Angelo called, moving ahead into the rain. Dwight broke into a run, then slowed. Running after Angelo was so codependent.

Getting out of the rain was not.

As he slogged forward, he saw a yellow light; it was a porch light. A lot of people around here—grips, gaffers, sound guys—lived in small homes, bungalows really. No fancy mansions in the shadow of the Warner Brothers water tower and the mountains behind the lot.

Dwight heard Angelo's voice and followed it toward the light. He was trotting up a walkway, then stepping onto a wooden porch. A screen door was open; Angelo disappeared into the house and Dwight followed after.

Warmth, light, and a man sitting on a plum-colored velveteen sofa, weeping. He was middle-aged, maybe Hispanic, maybe Middle Eastern; this was L.A., and everyone was melting into one color anyway. The air around him was a cloud of alcohol: whiskey, maybe, or scotch. Or tequila. Suddenly Dwight wasn't so sure about his sense of smell, either.

Bob V. was sitting on a green wooden chair across from the guy. He had a cup of coffee between his hands. When he saw Dwight, he said, "Hey, man. Glad you could make it."

"Hey." The words emanated from the mouth of Dwight's detached gamelike persona. The real Dwight was standing more deeply inside his body, watching Angelo embracing an extremely hot young woman, who was crying on his shoulder. She had on a pair of faded jeans and a turquoise sweater. Long, curly hair tumbled to the small of her back. Her dark eyes were enormous. She had big knockers, maybe fake.

Actress, Dwight thought, wishing he could smell her. Women smelled so good; it was like catching a whiff of the turkey on Thanksgiving, back when turkey had held his interest.

"I just can't stop," the guy on the couch moaned. "I just want to drink all the time. I swear, it's gotten worse since I joined the program!"

Bob held out the coffee, which the guy ignored. Dwight wanted it. He was standing there in soaking black leather and his balls were squishy.

"That's your self-will," Bob said. "It's running riot. It's doing whatever it can to keep its hold on you. It *wants* you to drink, Elario."

Elario. So, he was Hispanic. Across the room, Angelo held the beautiful girl as she reached toward Elario and said, "Daddy, Daddy, goddammit! He just lost another fucking job. . . ."

Elario lapsed into Spanish, probably trying to explain why the thought of not drinking alcohol sent him to a place of terrified silence. Angelo was gathering up the curls of the lovely young girl as he massaged her shoulders through her sweater. She was very lean, very fit. Stringy.

"Remember what we talked about," Bob said to Elario. "Think about the broken bridge. All blown up. The wreckage of your past. Body parts everywhere. You want to fix that bridge, but you can't. You can't fix it, Elario. You have to build a new bridge."

Body parts.

Angelo's fingertips brushed the girl's left tit as she sank back into his arms, crying silently again. Angelo took a long look at Dwight, then turned and walked her out of the room.

Leaving Dwight with Bob and Elario.

Elario was moaning like a Jehovah's Witness. Bob was silently watching him with the coffee cup between his hands. Dwight wondered if Bob had lost the power of speech, or if there was simply nothing to be said.

They made a little tableau, the three of them; Dwight standing in his steamy pants, watching Bob watching

Elario. He scanned the room and saw Angelo's jacket slung over the wooden chair. Of course he had taken it off. Angelo was a creature of comfort. Dwight had no idea why he hadn't done the same. Why he didn't do it now.

Then Bob said to him, "There's a can of soup by the stove. Can you heat that up?" Directly to him, Dwight. Bob didn't glance around in surprise, didn't ask where Angelo was. Or Elario's daughter.

And suddenly Dwight had the thought that this was a setup. This wasn't about twelfth-step work and all that shit. Bob V. had called Angelo because he had a hot chick for him to devour.

Wait a minute. He's supposed to help him stop drinking. Drinking, yeah. But not cannibalism . . .

"Um, Dwight?" Bob V. said.

"On it," Dwight assured him. "The soup."

He walked into the kitchen. There was a clean, empty pan on the stove, and a can opener and a can of chicken noodle soup on the pink Formica counter beside it. Chicken noodle soup was Dwight's favorite.

Maybe that's a sign.

Of what?

The stove was gas. He turned on the burner, and lifted up the pan. Turned on the faucet to run the water. The sound of the stream filled his ears. White noise.

Then he looked up and to the left, on top of the refrigerator.

Bottles. Most of them two-thirds to half-full. Tequila. Scotch. Gin. Glittering and shimmering in gauzy halos of light; as if behind gels and scrims and wide-angle lenses.

Beside the can of chicken noodle soup, a roll of paper towels.

He thought about how Bob had let Angelo walk right out of the room with someone to eat.

He thought about how much Angelo had said he wanted to stop eating people.

He thought about the broken bridge with all its body parts.

He thought about how handsome Bob was, and what a fucker he was.

Dwight's father had taught him a lot of things. How to swear. How to hit. How to drink.

"It's a dog-eat-dog world, son."

Wrong, Dad. So very wrong.

He got down the bottles, swigging a little out of each one.

"How's that soup coming?" Bob called jovially.

"Just fine," Dwight called back.

Dwight wadded the paper towels into the bottles. Then he found shit to make seals—pieces of plastic plates, other stuff. He got into it. It had been a long time. Some things you never forget. Bicycles, Molotov cocktails.

He was getting ready to light them when Bob walked into the kitchen. He was holding Angelo's jacket like it was Elvis's cape.

He said, "Everything okay in here?" His glance ticked toward the bottles, lined up in a row. "What are you doing?"

"Yes, Bob V., everything is okay," Dwight told him.

Then he picked up the soup pan and swung it at Bob like a baseball bat, catching him full in the face.

The man slammed hard against the wall. Blood spurted from his nose and he shouted, "Gah! Gah!" as he flailed at Dwight.

Dwight grabbed the tequila bottle, lit the paper towels wadded down in it, and thrust it at Bob, igniting his black T-shirt. It smoked. Bob screamed, so Dwight hit him with the pan again, in the face again. Once more, just for good luck, and Dwight dropped the bottle on the floor. He gathered four others against his chest, lit them quickly, and ran out of the kitchen.

Elario had stood up; he was staggering toward the kitchen, yelling in Spanish. Dwight charged him and knocked him over. Then he stomped on his face and started throwing the bottles at the walls. They exploded. Fire blazed everywhere.

He ran out of the room in the same direction where he had seen Angelo leave with the babe, shouting. "Angelo! Stop!"

Angelo burst out of a room at the end of the hall. He was naked and erect; he looked past Dwight to the smoke pouring out of the living room and yelled, "What's going on?"

The girl's face appeared under his arm; she screamed, "Daddy!" and pushed past Angelo, grabbing his wrist, letting go, rushing over to Dwight, pushing him backward. She ran into the blazing room, and Dwight did nothing to stop her.

"What the fuck did you do?" Angelo bellowed.

There was a roar from the fire, and a lot of agonized screaming. It was the chick.

Angelo grabbed Dwight's wrist and they raced out the back door of the house, out to the small backyard, where Angelo threw Dwight to the ground and covered him with his body.

And then the house exploded. It just went up, *whoosh!* Wooden boards and electrical wires and roof tiles and furniture and a bathtub; it just went up in a fireball, whirling and churning, dropping stuff everywhere like bombs.

Angelo said, "Come on!" and heaved Dwight to his feet. Then he dragged him along to their Beemer, which was still down the street at the curb, and they got in that sucker and drove off just as the very first neighbors started poking their heads out of their houses.

"What the hell happened?" Angelo demanded.

Dwight hung his head. He said, "I saved your life."

Angelo didn't appear to have heard him. "There must have been a fucking meth lab in that house," he said. He gestured to the backseat. "Get me a blanket, for Christ's sake."

They usually kept a blanket back there so they could

cover up a victim if they had to. Like when they pulled over and grabbed someone off the street.

As Dwight covered Angelo's chest and privates with the blanket, Angelo glanced over at him and said again, "What happened?"

Dwight sighed. Heavily. "I don't know. Bob got up to make Elario some soup, and the next thing I know, he's throwing flaming bottles of alcohol at me and they're just, like, exploding! He went crazy!" Dwight covered his face, wishing that Lou S. had half his acting talent. Just for Lou's sake. "I thought I was going to die. I fought him off—I got him good—but by then everything was on fire!"

"And you came to save me. Damn it, Dwight." Angelo welled up. "I'll bet we do some research, it turns out Bob had some grudge against us. Maybe we ate someone he knew. Maybe he thought we owed him royalties off some song he wrote that sounds like one of ours."

Maybe he just wanted to be your new best friend, the fucker.

"Screw it," Angelo said, waving his hand. He started laughing the laughter of a guy who had just nearly died. "Screw the metaphor. Let's go for the epiphany, dude! If life's going to be dangerous anyway, we might as well enjoy ourselves."

He grinned at his blood brother, his friend, his fellow cannibal. "Goddammit, Dwight, let's go out and find some hot young chick to eat. And if they catch us, I hear the drugs they use to kill you are fucking righteous."

Dwight said absolutely nothing. He was back in the zone, back in the silence.

But what he thought was, *I gotta get my butt to CoDA.*

I am too codependent by half.

•

BLOODY MARY MORNING

JOHN FARRIS

"**S**O YOU WERE in St. Bart's for four days," George Whitaker said to his wife Lisa, "and Lyle just happened to show up."

"Yes," Lisa said.

"Happened to show up."

"Yes."

Thunder shook their limousine, which wasn't moving in rush-hour traffic downtown. Lisa flinched slightly. She didn't like thunderstorms. She didn't like being cooped up with George anytime he was taking a certain tone with her. Rain pelted down.

George said idly in his soft Texas drawl, "Did you evah wondah what the fuck kinda name is *Lyle*?"

"No," Lisa mumbled, scrolling on her BlackBerry. Sitting as far away in the back of the limo from George as she could get. He occupied the corner where the bar was. Eight forty-two and he was having a Bloody Mary morning. "I don't know." Five seconds ticked by. She didn't look up. She knew what expression she'd see on his lean, handsome, sardonic face. "Scottish," she said. "Lyle is a Scot on his mother's side."

"Is he hung pretty good, Lise?"

Lisa breathed deeply enough for George to hear. Another point for him. She imagined which smile he was wearing. She wished the goddamned limo would *move.*

"I'm . . . not going to do this, George. I have . . . you know I have a presentation to make at ten o'clock. I have sweated my fanny off on this deal, and—"

"My little career gal."

"Just shut."

"Of whom I am so proud."

"The fuck up. I didn't *inherit* a company, George, I have worked—" More thunder jolted her. Lisa's lips drew back in a rictus. They moved a few feet. Stopped. There was a bus right on the limo's bumper.

"Jump out of your skin?"

"I hate—"

"Almost as fast as you can jump out of your clothes when ol' Lyle shows up."

Now she made herself look at George. Wanting him to see the hatred in her face.

George had one of those playful little smiles marinated in rattlesnake venom. Her expression didn't bother him a bit.

"Lyle, Lyle, crocodile. My guess is with a pussy name like that, he has to be haulin' big lumber to interest a connoisseur like yourself. How long did it take Lyle to get to you, ovah there in sunny St. Bart's?"

"Oh, God."

Lisa stowed away her BlackBerry, locked up her attaché case, and reached for an umbrella.

"I've always been generous in sharin' my little adventures with *you,* Lise. So I'm up in Washington getting my ass filleted at a RICO hearing . . . you didn't spend the night with him in our digs? That would've violated one of our rules. We only wake up in the mornin' with people we're married or uthuhwise related to."

"Oh, God."

"Hey, where're you going?"

"I'm *walking!* I mean, this time for good!"

"What do you mean? Walkin' out on *me*?"

"Yes, you asshole."

"Aw, c'mon, Lisa. Just tell me you didn't wake up in bed next to Lyle with the toucans chatterin' in the palm trees or whatevah the hell toucans do. And I'll leave the subject alone." His voice took on a familiar whine. "I had kind of a bad week, Lisa. Henry says I could go to Club Fed for ten years. Damn it, nobody is playin' *fair* with me."

He lunged in her direction, reached past her, and took hold of the door on Lisa's side just as she was opening it. He elbowed her back into her seat. Lisa grimaced.

"Hey, just sit still a minute. I got somethin' for you."

George picked up his own Hermès attaché, put it on his lap, undid gold locks while Lisa struggled to get her breath back from the cruel elbowing. She looked at him, lips apart. Not afraid. Just sick of him, and contemptuous.

"Asshole," she said again.

George nodded soberly, as if they had concluded a deal. He bit his lower lip momentarily, then took out a black steel Heckler & Koch .32 automatic and shot her in the forehead.

Her head rocked back on the leather seat. The look in her eyes was quick-frozen, a fish on ice. Then her head sagged forward. Her body remained upright, wedged into the corner.

George's vision was a little blurred. He blinked but couldn't clear the cloud obscuring the sight in his left eye. He took off his amber-tinted, steel-rimmed glasses and saw that a drop of her blood had spattered the lens. He didn't have anything handy with which to wipe it off. He put his glasses back on in spite of the annoying blood spot.

The limousine had been moving but stopped again.
George leaned forward, the automatic still in his right
hand, and knocked on the privacy panel with the butt.
When the black glass slid down the chauffeur looked
around at him. George held the .32 below seat level.

"Yes suh, Mr. George? I do apologize but the traffic
lights is all flummoxed this mornin'."

"Hey, don't give it another thought, Delano." George's
mouth was very dry but his voice was steady as she goes.
"Delano, I'm truly sorreh; you know I could kick myself."

The chauffeur looked puzzled. From his angle behind
the wheel he couldn't make out Lisa's still form back there.

"Excuse me, Mr. George?"

"I forgot to ask you: How are the wife and kids?"

"Oh, well, they be doin' just fine, suh." Delano blinked.
"Mr. George? Pardon me, but there's somethin' on one lens
of your—"

"I had a Bloody Mary on the way in. As is my mornin'
custom."

"Well, sure. Thass right."

"It must be the Tabasco, Delano. I wonder if you have a
tissue?"

"Surely do."

When Delano looked away from him and reached for the
box of tissues on the other seat, George raised the H & K
and shot his chauffeur over the right ear. When Delano's
foot left the brake pedal, the limo surged forward ten feet
and ran into the back of a double-parked UPS truck.
Stopped there.

George picked himself up off the floor. He reckoned,
peering through the heavy rain, that they were still two
blocks from his office.

When he was seated again he reopened his attaché case
and laid the pistol inside next to the Van Cleef & Arpels
box that contained a ruby bracelet he had designed for
Lisa. He looked at her. She looked back at him. The hole in

her forehead was oozing a little. Otherwise she looked okay, really. It wasn't a very large hole.

Blood dripped from the left lens of his glasses and fell on the Van Cleef & Arpels box. So the morning could have gone either way, George reflected. Pay or play. Lisa had played, and collected her payment.

"I may be an asshole," he said to his wife's corpse, which looked hazy through that smudge of her blood, "but you're fuckin' dead."

George opened the door on his side and stepped out into the slash of winter rain, attaché case in his left hand. With his other hand, he pulled up the collar of his Burberry. He strode toward the office through an obstacle course of potentially lethal umbrellas. Horns, horns, horns in the streets. The irritability level of his fellow citizens was reaching blow-off proportions. With cold rain in his face, George still felt calm, even jaunty. But the damned bloodstain wasn't washing off his glasses. He reached up and removed them. Then he was more than half-blind, but at a familiar corner.

He paused there, shuddering, and wiped the back of his free hand across his eyes and matted lashes. He was jostled and almost lost his balance.

For the rest of the short walk to the building where George's company occupied three high floors, he kept his head down and into the blowing rain, wiping and blinking. Barely able to see anything.

Then he was inside the huge marbled atrium with a hundred office workers or visitors headed for one bank of elevators or another. All the people were mere shadows to his eyes. Lightning, then thunder outside. The atrium lights dimmed momentarily.

George was drenched. Should've taken Lisa's umbrella. Other than that he wasn't thinking about what else he had left behind him in the stalled limo on the traffic-choked street.

Ten minutes upstairs in his private office suite, he reckoned. No more. That would be long enough to remove the
six million in bearer bonds from his safe along with mucho
cash, after he made one phone call. His Falcon Jet would
be fueled and ready for the two-hour flight to Panama.
From there he'd move on to a well-stocked hideaway, obtained on the basis of his father's experience and wisdom.

*George, always know when the exits are about to be
closed.*

Given the traffic pileup outside, call it thirty minutes before the cops got a peek inside the limo. By the time they
began seriously to desire a conversation with George
Whitaker, he'd be high over the Gulf of Mexico having another Bloody Mary.

Ole, motherfuckers.

Express elevators. Five people waiting. George joined
them. Their faces were indistinct. A mother with a little girl
who looked to be about eight years old. Black woman with
a large superstructure, carrying a purse the size of a sad-
dlebag. Young couple wearing school jackets who couldn't
get enough of nuzzling each other. George reached for the
glasses he'd stowed away. The inside pocket of his
Burberry felt sticky, as if someone had poured pancake
syrup in there. He winced and tried to get a grip on a temple bar of the glasses as he followed the others aboard the
newly arrived elevator.

The doors closed. The black woman sniffed and looked
around at everyone as if she smelled something dirty, or
ominous. The mother with the kid was by the control
panel, the girl calling out, "Your floors, please."

"Forty-four," George requested loudly.

The girl hit forty-seven by mistake.

"Damn it, I *said* forty-four!" George snapped, surprising everyone by his tone. The Teen Queen's husky
boyfriend glowered at him as George succeeded in freeing
his glasses from the stickiness in his coat pocket.

The other passengers reacted with varying degrees of shock and horror, instinctively pressing away from him.

"Mama!" the little girl said shrilly. "His hand's got blood on it!"

A small dog with a flat pugnacious face poked its head out of the black woman's tote and began excitedly to bark.

George stared at his incarnate hand and the soaked cuff of his trench coat, at the glasses he was holding. The spot of Lisa's blood that had left the limo with him was still there, round as a quarter on the lens it had spattered. Now it seemed to be producing blood of its own, drops at the rate of one every three seconds, without diminishing in size.

"Oh, my *God!*" the Teen Queen said. "You *are* bleeding!"

"No, I am not!" George snapped again, shoving the glasses behind his back. "It isn't me! I mean, I'm all right! It's not even blood!"

"Oh, yes, it is," the black woman said, stroking her manic little dog with one hand. "I was an ER nurse for seventeen years, and I *know* what fresh blood smell like! Mister, you done hurt yourself even if you don't recollect how it happened. You best get off the elevator right now and—shut up that yappin', Marquesa!" To the woman with the small girl, both of them looking petrified, she instructed, "Hit the 'mergency button if you please, because I also knows a 'mergency when I sees one."

"Don't anyone touch a damn thing!" George snarled. "I have to get to my office. I—I'm late for an important meeting! Just let me off and y'all go about your own business!"

He had no sooner finished speaking than the elevator jolted to a stop. The lights went out. The other passengers gasped and squealed. The dog went nuts.

"It's nothing!" George said. "The power has gone off. It's the storm outside. Don't be gettin' your panties in a bunch." He felt blood dripping off the hand that was holding the glasses behind his back. "We can't fall," he insisted. "We are perfectly safe."

"Yeah, everybody be cool," the high school jock advised.

"Oh, Johnny, I'm so scared!" the Teen Queen cried.

The little girl who had been playing elevator operator began to wail.

"Hush, hush, Charlotte!" her mother said, but her own voice had a quaver.

"I smell blood, too," the Teen Queen moaned. "I think I'm gonna puke."

"Everyone just stay still, now," George said. "I have a cigarette lightah with me." He spun the wheel. An inch of flame illuminated faces and the muzzle of the little dog as it tried to squirm free of the black woman's tote. The dog's bulging eyes had a mad cast in them from the flicker of light. "And madam: You must do something about your little dog. I nevah have cared for dogs. Or animals of any kind, for that matter. All animals make me nervous."

The woman glared at him. The dog went on barking hysterically.

"Johnny," George said to the high school jock, "would you be so good as to hold my lightah for me?"

The boy held out his free hand—his other arm cradled the cowering Teen Queen—and took the lighter from him.

George set his attaché case on the floor, put his dripping glasses on, and opened the case.

"Have any of you evah noticed," he said conversationally, "how one little thing goin' wrong can lead inexorably to anothah, and screw up what started out to be a promisin' day? Of course, there is no point in gettin' upset when the elements go against you: Now is there? And a little inconvenience like a stalled elevatah when you are in a hurry—why waste energy gettin' all fussed about that? These are mattahs ovah which we have no control. But a savage-actin' little barkin' dog that irritates the nerves"—George pulled the .32 automatic from his case—"*that* we can do somethin' about."

"Omigod!"

"He's got a gun!"

"Hey, man!"

George straightened up with the gun in his less-bloody hand. The droplets of blood from the red lens of his glasses had become a steady thin stream over his chin and down the length of his Burberry.

"We're all going to die!"

Shrieks of horror. George shook his head slightly and made a pacifying gesture.

"Nonsense. I don't wish to bring harm to any of you. I am just going to shoot this miserable yapping excuse for a—"

With that the black woman yanked her toy pooch free of the tote with an expression of outrage, clutched him to her bosom, stepped forward, and kneed George in the groin. She also slapped him with her other hand. Blood flew into her face and the dog's. As George tried to stay upright on the blood-slippery floor of the elevator the dog squirmed from the black woman's grasp, flew at George's face, and locked its small sharp teeth into his cheek.

George pushed the woman away from him and yanked at the fluffy tail of the dog hanging from his cheek. It weighed only eight or ten pounds, but it had the bite of a badger. The dog wouldn't let go. No use yanking any harder on its tail; he was likely to lose half his face. He stuck the automatic in the dog's belly and shot it. The dog jerked a couple of times—then went limp—but its jaws remained locked on George's cheek.

The lights in the elevator flickered, came on full strength. The elevator surged upward once more. George, gun in hand, the odor of dead dog entrails stifling him, looked around at the other passengers pressed against three of the four elevator walls.

Ten minutes in his private office suite. That was all he would need. The exits were closing, but they weren't all shut yet.

His glasses continued to drip blood. His cheek hurt like

hell. Maybe the dead dog would release him at sundown, like snapping turtles were supposed to do. George felt very tired. But he had calmed down. Calm was essential for straight thinking. Ten minutes. The jet gassed and ready to go. Panama. Paradise. No worries.

The elevator arrived on 44. At last.

"Madam," George said to the hysterical black woman as he backed off the elevator into the smartly appointed, carpeted reception area, "I very much would like to return your animal, for a proper burial I suppose, but for the life of me I can't figure out how." He waved the pistol at them. "Now you all go about your business, as I intend to go about mine, and let's not make too much of this."

The elevator doors closed. George turned around. The girl at the reception desk was Heather. A knockout, tall and poised. Usually. This morning she had the expression of someone who had just driven a Ferrari into a telephone pole.

"Mr. Whitaker—!"

"Not entirely my fault, Heather," George admonished her. "I was attacked by the little monster. I had no recourse but to protect myself."

"Should I—do you want me to call—"

George stood on the pearl gray carpet he was staining rapidly with Lisa's blood, looking around slowly at paintings of his predecessors as heads of the oft-beleaguered family firm. His father, of course. His great-uncle Tab, who had made a career of underestimating the IRS. His older brother Bailey, who never got it through his head that continually drawing to inside straights was a bad practice in business as well as poker.

There was space for his own portrait, which now he would never get around to posing for.

"I'll be in my office," George said. "Traffic bein' what it is today, kindly have a helicopter waitin' for me on the roof. I'll be catchin' a flight soon as I've tidied up. Oh, and Heather? Admit no one who might be inquiring of my whereabouts."

"Yes—sir."

He trudged down a hallway with the dead dog hanging from his cheek and his glasses bleeding profusely, almost a torrent now from that one little spot not much bigger than the pupil of Lisa's turquoise eyes. He accessed his private elevator and rose to his sanctuary, half a floor in size and kingly in its comforts. There he was alone. Or was he? He thought he heard his father's cheery tone.

They never caught a single one of us with our pants down. Did they, boy?

"Easy for you to say," George muttered, fingering the dead dog he wore like some sort of outlandish piercing.

"It's Whitakers who choose how and when. His uncle Tab reiterating his favorite philosophy.

Mind you don't miss that last exit.

"I took care of it already," George said defensively, but he knew it was time. He heaved a couple of sighs and got to his feet, walked slowly through a couple of cool silent rooms to the vault. The sight of it refreshed him. Hadn't been much of a day so far, but it was about to improve.

He dialed the combination with bloody fingers, gave the wheel a couple of hard turns. The thick steel door swung open and George walked into the vault.

The atmosphere inside was gloomy, stuffy. Old brick walls with mortar oozed between layers. Curved ceiling overhead. The floor dusty. He took off the bleeding glasses. But the troublesome spot of Lisa's blood seemed to be gone. He still had the dog hanging from his cheek but as he touched the furry corpse, it shriveled up and fell away. He rubbed the cheek the dog had bitten. No pain. No wound.

He heard voices from deeper inside the vault. One in particular made him smile.

Never caught us with our pants down.

Can't get up early enough to get ahead of a Whitaker.

And brother Bailey in high dudgeon exclaiming, *Goddamit, there's that eight I was needing!*

George walked through a short passage and down a flight of steps toward a candle's flame and there they were, gathered around some long-deceased Whitaker's stone bier, Tab shuffling the pasteboards with his skeletal hands, Daddy looking up with what seemed to be a twinkle in the glass eye that remained in his hairless skull, smiling toothily.

"Here he is!"

"What kept you?" Uncle Tab grumbled.

"I don't know," George said. "Some little inconvenience, I suppose." He looked around the family crypt with a glum smile. Lacking a woman's touch, it would take some getting used to.

Uncle Tab passed the shuffled shabby deck to Bailey, who looked up at his brother before he began flipping the cards around.

"Deal you in?"

"Might as well," George said.

◊

The homicide detective finished his scan of the back of the limousine, then yielded the scene to his CSI colleagues for a closer examination of the body and the weapon used. He walked back half a block to a sector car, one of several units on the scene along with a fire-department paramedic bus. The rain had nearly stopped but the street was still awash. Uniforms had the traffic moving again, slowly. One of the cops touched the bill of his cap and opened the rear door of the sector car. The detective took off his hat, shook rain from the brim, and got in.

"Mrs. Whitaker? I'm Lieutenant Peterson."

Lisa Whitaker looked up with grief-emptied eyes. Her hands were twisted tightly together in her lap. She had chewed most of her lipstick from her lower lip. Her lips parted as if she were going to speak, but then she simply shook her head in an anguished way.

"I know how rough this has been for you, Mrs. Whitaker."

"Rough," she repeated dryly.

"I'll be as brief as I can."

"Thank . . . you."

"Your chauffeur, Mr. Stokes, said he didn't hear or see anything. What can you tell me, Mrs. Whitaker?"

"Well . . . he shot himself. It was . . . so quick. And so awful. He had just handed me . . . this." Lisa showed Peterson the bracelet crumpled in her hands. "It's platinum. The stones are rubies."

"Birthday? Anniversary?"

"No." Words came slowly. "No particular reason for a gift." She smiled tautly. "Except George liked giving them." Lisa drew a great shuddering breath. "When I . . . looked up to thank him . . . the muzzle of the gun was against his temple. George was . . . smiling. I couldn't begin to describe—" She lowered her head, clenching the bracelet again. "Then he did it. I only had a second or two to react. It was that quick. No way . . . no way I could believe what he'd done."

"I understand your husband's father committed suicide after a string of business failures."

She looked at him again, blinking. As if she had cobwebs in her eyes. She wiped at the lashes. "It's like . . . a family curse. That aptitude for making huge sums of money, but then . . . just slips through their fingers. George's father, his brother, an uncle or two . . . they all took their lives rather than . . . you know. Jail. Humiliation. They gladly left the humiliation for . . . loved ones to endure." She looked as if she wanted to cry again, but there were no tears left. "I know George was in trouble. That federal investigation. But to do such a thing—in front of me—*monstrous.*"

"I have to ask you this. Were you and your husband getting along, Mrs. Whitaker?"

"Oh . . . we had our differences, like any married couple. Nothing we weren't mature enough to deal with." Lisa reached out suddenly and seized one of Peterson's wrists. "Lieutenant. I'll never forget what I saw! *Never.*"

"I'm so sorry, Mrs. Whitaker."

"There was something I noticed . . . in George's eyes, in that moment before he squeezed the trigger. They say when we're about to die, our entire lives flash through our minds. But could it be . . . for those who deserve it, there's something else they see? A vision of heaven, or . . . hell."

A uniform tapped on the window; Peterson turned his head and let the window down.

"Mrs. Whitaker's chauffeur is here with another car, to drive her home."

"Can I go?" Lisa asked anxiously.

"Yes. We'll need for you to sign a formal statement when you're up to it. By the way—was your husband familiar with guns?"

"This is Texas, Lieutenant Peterson. Aren't they all? It's a custom of their manhood."

"So he always had a pistol with him?"

"Yes. We also have an indoor range. He practiced three or four times a week. In fact, he was downstairs on the range before breakfast this morning."

"How about you? Handy with firearms?"

Lisa looked back at him as she was getting out of the car.

"Not at all. I just don't like them."

"Thank you, Mrs. Whitaker. My sympathies."

✧

Lisa rode in the front seat of the rented Town Car on the way home.

"Thank God that's over," she said as they left the city behind them.

"Yes, ma'am. Praise the good Lord."

"Sooner or later, he was going to do it anyway. It's in the family genes. We just helped George realize his destiny without the usual difficulties. The indictments. Handcuffed on the six-o'clock news."

"I know he been done a blessing, Mrs. Whitaker."

"And God knows I didn't feel like waiting around for *later*, FBI snoops all over, attachments on all our properties. My nerves couldn't take it. Just dispose of my gloves the way I told you, Delano."

"You can count on me."

"And don't go on a spree in Mo' Bay or wherever you decide to take up residence. Don't spend a lot of money conspicuously."

"I didn't fall off the back of no turnip truck yesterday, Mrs. Whitaker. Got me plenty of livin' left to do." Delano grinned broadly. "And like Mr. George always used to say, 'Life sure be a hard act to follow.' "

A GENTLEMAN OF THE OLD SCHOOL

A story of Saint-Germain

CHELSEA QUINN YARBRO

"**B**UT SURELY THE Count is willing to talk to the press? He's been very generous, and I would have thought he'd want to make sure people know about it." The reporter was a crisply attractive woman in her midtwenties, bristling with high fashion and ambition; she was hot on the scent of a story. She lingered in the door of the secluded house in an elegant section of Vancouver, a tape recorder in one hand, a small digital camera in the other. "And there is the problem of the murder, isn't there? The VPMNC audience wants to know."

The houseman—a lean, middle-aged man with sandy hair and faded blue eyes, roughly the same height as the reporter: about five-foot-seven—remained unfailingly polite. "I am sorry, but my employer has a pronounced dislike of all public attention, even if the intention is benign." He nodded to the young woman once. "I am sure there are many on the hospital board who will be delighted to give you all the information you seek. As to the murder, you should speak to the police—they will know about it."

"Everyone's talked to them, and there's nothing new to get out of them," the reporter complained. "Everyone's looking for a new angle on the case, and the Center was a good place to start. That led me to the Count, and I found out about the Count only through the Donations Administrator's secretary, and that was over a very expensive lunch." She frowned. "I was told that the Count visited the facilities only twice: shortly after construction began and just before it was opened: The Vancouver Center for the Diagnosis and Treatment of Blood Disorders. Ms. Saunders said the Count's donation covered more than seventy percent of the cost of building and equipping the facility, and that he provides an annual grant for ongoing research. That's got to be a lot of money. I was wondering if the Count would care to confirm the amount? Or discuss the body found on the roof of the Center two days ago?"

"Neither is the sort of matter my employer likes to talk about. He is not inclined to have his fortune bruited about, and the investigation of crime is not his area of expertise. He leaves such things to the police and their investigators." The houseman stepped back, preparing to close the door.

"Then he's talked to them?" the reporter pursued.

"A crime-scene technician named Fisk has asked for various samples from the Count, and he has provided them." The houseman started to swing the door shut.

"Fisk—the new tech?"

"That was his name. I have no idea if he is new or old to his position. If you will excuse me—" There was less than three inches of opening left.

"I'll just return, tonight or tomorrow, and I may have some of my colleagues with me: I am not the only one with questions." This last was a bluff: She was relishing the chance for an exclusive and was not about to give up her advantage to any competition.

"You will receive the same answer whenever you call, Ms. . . . is it Barradis? If you want useful information, I would consult the police, Ms. Barradis." The houseman lost none of his civility, but he made it clear that he would not change his mind.

"Barendis," she corrected. "Solange Barendis."

"Barendis," the houseman repeated, and closed the door firmly, setting the door-crossing bolt into its locked position before withdrawing from the large entry hall, bound for the parlor on the west side of the house that gave out on a deck that was added to the house some fifty years before. It had recently been enlarged to make the most of the glorious view afforded down the hill, colored now with the approaching fires of sunset.

The house had been built in 1924 in the Arts and Crafts style, with cedar wainscoting in most of the rooms, and stained glass in the upper panes of many of the windows, all in all, a glorious example of the style, for although it did not appear to be large from the outside, it had three stories, and thirteen rooms, all of generous proportions. The parlor, with its extensive bow and the deck beyond provided the appearance of an extension of the room through two wide French doors into the outside, making it one of Roger's favorite places in all the house. Here he lingered until a beautiful Victorian clock chimed five; then he started toward the stairs that led to the upper floors, to the room on the south side of the second floor, a good-sized chamber that once held a pool table, but was now devoted to books. He went along to the library and tapped on the door, opening it as soon as the occupant of the room called out, "Do come in, Roger."

Roger opened the door and paused on the threshold,

watching his employer, who was dressed in black woolen slacks and black cashmere turtleneck, up a rolling ladder where he busied himself shelving books at the tops of the cases. "The reporter was back." The French he spoke was a dialect that had not been heard for more than two centuries.

"Ms. Barendis?" the Count asked. "I'm not surprised to hear it. I'm a little puzzled that she hasn't brought more press with her, considering."

"She has threatened to do so. She said she was asking about the Center, but it—"

The Count sighed. "She had another topic in mind, I suspect."

"You mean the body they found?" Roger knew what the response would be.

"That, and her reporter's inclination to uncover information that appears to be hidden."

"Such as the size of your donation to the Blood Center; a legitimate story as well as a workable excuse to talk to you to find out about the murder victim," said Roger, a bit disgusted. "She asked about the money as well as about the body."

"I doubt she will pursue the money: it isn't scandalous enough. The murder is more intriguing than money, since it appears to be one of a series," said the Count drily. "Even the Canadians are fascinated by human predators, it would seem."

"And this young woman is stoking the furnace," said Roger.

"All the more reason for her to find more combustible fuel to consume—money hasn't the engrossing power of serial murders, especially such messy ones as this man commits—he is seeking as much gore as he can create," said the Count. "The murder is scary and exciting—large donations only spur a moment of greed, which is insufficient to hold the audience's attention."

"Whatever the public may find interesting, this reporter is proving as persistent as a burr." Roger came a few steps into the room and flipped on the light switch, banishing the thickening shadows with the gentle glow of wall sconces. "She says she'll be back tomorrow."

"I would not doubt it," said the Count, coming down the ladder. "So long as she confines her pursuit to the daytime, she will be nothing more than inconvenient. We have dealt with far worse than she." As he said the last, he put his foot on the floor.

"She may expand her inquiries," said Roger, sitting on an upholstered rosewood bench and giving his attention to the end table beside it; he picked up a small ivory carving of Ganesh riding his Rat and moved it to a less vulnerable place on the end table. "I recommended she speak to the police."

"If they lead her away from me, so much the better," said the Count, sitting down in a leather recliner. "You know, when we first came here in—was it '38?—well, after we left California, near the start of the war—I didn't appreciate what a handy place this would be, or how pleasant. Who could have foreseen the expansion of the Pacific Rim, especially then, as the war was getting under way? This has been a much better investment than the house in Winnipeg." He reached over and turned on a floor lamp with a frosted tulip motif, banishing the last of the gloom; the shining paneling, along with the array of spines, gave the place a cozy elegance.

"Winter is easier here than in Winnipeg," Roger observed.

"You have the right of it," said the Count.

Roger brushed his hand over the embossed leather cover of a book printed in Amsterdam almost five hundred years ago. "Do you think you will want to remain here much longer?"

"Perhaps a year or two, until the Center is fully established. It will depend somewhat on the state of the world then; I am not in any particular hurry to return to my homeland, not as things are going now. The government has already seized half the money I left for the university I endowed on the pretext of using it for cultural projects: I would just as soon not provide them more occasions for another raid." He shoved the recliner back, sighing luxuriously as he did so. "These are wonderful inventions."

"So they are," Roger agreed, knowing it was prudent not to press the Count about his plans. "And it is not difficult to conceal your native earth inside them."

"Another advantage," said the Count, and closed his eyes.

❖

"A fifth body!" Solange exclaimed as she stared at her computer screen some twelve days after her second fruitless visit to the Count's house. "Near the University, this time." She shoved back from her workstation and stood so she could see over the top of her cubicle. "Hey, Baxter! You seen this?"

The Night City Editor came over to her, his silk regimental tie loosened and his well-cut hair slightly mussed. "Seen what?"

She pointed to the computer screen. "Another one with a cut throat, blood everywhere, and mutilations. Fair-haired, cut short, above average height, on the plumpish side, between twenty-five and thirty-five years of age—a cookie-cutter victim for this guy." She stamped her foot. "And Hudderston isn't doing anything! Crime Desk—yeah, right!"

"How do you mean?" Baxter asked. "I have his column on the daily report from the police—they say they've doubled patrols, and the crimes are getting top priority. The crime-scene tech is preparing a new report."

"Fisk also says the forensics are inconclusive, even

though there are pools of blood around the victims, the same thing you can get off the Internet, or on the hourly news spots," said Solange. "You saw the report on the confusing DNA results—animal blood mixed with human and both contaminated with chemical additives. Any identification they may make from the analysis of the blood, even though it's accurate, won't hold up under rigorous cross-examination."

"But five women with cut throats, multiple stab wounds in the upper bodies, and perforated uteruses! The public won't stand for much more of this, and arrest—let alone a trial—is a long way off." Baxter sighed. "McKenna has the story on days; if you want to take it on for nights, I won't stop you. I'll clear it with Sung." Louie Sung worked the night Crime Desk, and was known to be territorial about his fiefdom.

Solange tried to contain her excitement. "Sung could say no."

"Not to me," Baxter told her.

"Okay, then. You clear it." Eyes glistening with excitement, Solange picked up her recorder, her camera, and her tote, then reached for her coat. "I'm on it, boss," she vowed, and tapped in her code to block access to her terminal. "I'll call in before one, and I'll report before six."

"Sounds good," said Baxter, and stood aside as Solange swept out of the city room of the Vancouver Print and Media News Corporation, bound for the parking lot and her hybrid hatchback.

✿

At police headquarters, Solange avoided the press office and the front desk where the usual assortment of denizens of the night were gathered with arresting officers; she made straight for the squad room and the desk of Neal Conroy, who shook his head as soon as he caught sight of her. "Barendis, get out of here," he said cordially. "You know I can't talk to you." He was slightly stooped, slightly scruffy: pushing forty, and forty was pushing back.

"Sure you can: here or at your house, Uncle-in-law—you know Aunt Melanie won't keep me out. If you don't tell me what I want to know, she will. And don't tell me you don't talk to her about your cases, because you do," she said, sitting down in the old, straight-backed chair that was intended for visitors and victims of crimes. "The murders. What's happening? And why is the DNA inconclusive? It is identifiable or it isn't."

"You're too nosy for your own good, Barendis," said Conroy.

"That's how I earn my living," she countered, undeterred by the frown he offered.

"Well, use a little good sense for once in your life and keep clear of this one. For your own protection. Melanie would agree with me, if you bother to ask her," Conroy advised her seriously. "This murderer targets women alone, in their late twenties to early thirties, cuts their throats and then chops at the bodies, and adds cows' blood to mess up the crime scene. You know the basics already."

"Chops—with a knife?" Solange asked, pulling out her pen and notebook, saying nothing about her recorder in her tote's outer pocket, already in the *on* position.

"Stop it, Barendis," said Conroy, sounding tired. "I hate it when you fish."

She shook her head, undeterred. "Not a knife, but it cuts throats? For all five women?"

"What can I say—the guy likes blood, lots and lots of it," Conroy told her, deliberately harsh. "Don't put that in your story."

Eyes sparkling, Solange shrugged. "I can't promise anything, but I'll try not to get you into trouble."

"It's not getting *you* into trouble that concerns me," Conroy riposted. "I mean it, Solange. Don't try to make your mark on this one—it won't do you any good, and you could become a target."

"Not a knife, but something that slices—that's for sure," said Solange, paying no attention to Conroy's last statement. "A dagger—*I do* know the difference between a knife and a dagger—or a poniard . . . no."

Conroy took a long, slow breath. "If you will give me your word you won't go after Melanie about any of this, I'll tell you what the medical examiner thinks made the wounds, but you have to keep this out of your story, or you compromise the whole investigation."

Solange sat upright in the chair, and managed to say, "I promise," all the while staring at Conroy.

"It's some kind of curved sword—a saber, a scimitar, a katana—or something like a medieval battle-hammer, with a long, pointed claw at the back of the head—we can't say for sure. There's too much damage." He had lowered his voice and now was paler than he had been.

"That's really—" She stopped before she said something she would regret.

"Appalling," said Conroy.

"God, what grisly stuff," said Solange. "I wish I could use it."

"You try and I'll have your press badge pulled until the perpetrator is caught."

"You know you won't do that. Aunt Melanie would never permit it." She gave him a smug smile.

Conroy sat back. "You're probably right, but that doesn't change anything. Let Fisk and the ME do their jobs, and keep your two cents out of it. You can screw this investigation royally if you don't play by the rules, and that would mean more people getting killed."

"You mean more *women* getting killed," Solange corrected as she got out of the uncomfortable chair. "I'll go along for now, but you had better give me a first call on the story when it breaks."

"Certainly," said Conroy. "You know I'll do that."

"Yes. Or Aunt Melanie won't—"

"—let me hear the end of it," he finished for her.

❖

The restaurant was elegant, the lights low and golden instead of brilliant and white, the upholstery-heavy tapestry to match the draperies, the silverware was sterling, the napery linen, the china Spode, the glassware Riedel. Solange, in her second-best cocktail dress—a designer label, bias-cut, cobalt blue, bat-sleeved sheath—was trying to conceal how impressed she was while reading from the six-page menu. Finally she looked up at her host and asked, "Why did you change your mind, Count?"

"About the interview?" he countered, his demeanor urbane and genial; he was in a tailor-made black silk suit, a very white silk shirt, a burgundy damask tie, with tie-tack and cuff links in white gold with discreet black sapphires for ornamentation.

"Yes," she said, glancing at the approaching waiter. "What are you having?"

"The pleasure of your company, but do not let that deter you in ordering anything you want." He waited for her to ask something more, and when she did not, he went on, "I fear I have a number of . . . allergies, I suppose you could call them. I must constrain my dining, and so, to avoid any unpleasantness, I take my nourishment in private. I am used to having others eat when I do not." He signaled the waiter to take down her order. "And if you have a wine list, I would like to see it."

Solange's eyes lit up. "Then you *drink*—" she began.

"The wine will be for you. I do not drink wine."

She laughed aloud. "You know who says that, don't you?"

With a swift, ironic smile, he answered, "Vampires."

Her laughter increased, and she had to choke back her amusement in order to tell the waiter, "I'd like the cream of wild mushroom soup to start, then the broiled scallops in terrine; for an entree, the duck with cherries and pear onions in port, next the endive salad, and I'll think about dessert when I've finished dinner."

"Very good, ma'am," said the waiter. "I will bring the wine list, Count."

"Thank you, Franco."

"So they know you here." Solange's curiosity was engaged again.

"I have a minor investment in this restaurant, and the hotel across the courtyard." He held out his hand for the wine list as the waiter approached, bringing that and a basket of fresh-baked small loaves of bread and a ramekin of sweet butter.

"You are a man of surprises, Count," said Solange, idly wondering if his investments might be a story worth pursuing at another time.

"Am I?" He opened the wine list, settling on a Côtes Sauvage. "It may not go well with the scallops, but it will complement the soup and the duck."

"For a man who doesn't drink wine, you have a discriminating palate."

He turned his dark eyes on her. "I hope so, Ms. Barendis."

To her astonishment, she felt herself blushing, and she tried to stop the color rising in her face. "I . . . Well, thank you for ordering such an unusual wine." This sounded lame, even to her own ears, so she made another attempt. "I'm very flattered that you're willing to talk to me." That was a little better.

"You're a very persistent young woman, Ms. Barendis; I decided we might as well arrange a discussion, and if we are to discuss difficult questions, we may also be comfortable."

"I wish all my subjects were so reasonable," said Solange archly. She broke one of the small loaves of bread in half and set it down on the bread plate. "It smells wonderful, doesn't it?"

"Yes, it does," he said, rather distantly.

She paused in the act of cutting butter. "Will my eating bother you, considering we will be talking about murder during the meal?"

"No; it is not *my* appetite that could be compromised," he said wryly, and went on, "I realize you are on assignment tonight."

"Yes," she said, as if she had forgotten it. "This is an assignment, and an important one."

"That is why I agreed to the meeting," he said.

"Then I'll thank you for the very civilized way you have of conducting it, even to this public setting, so my reputation wouldn't be damaged. As if gossip can damage a reporter." She took a bite of the bread, feeling somewhat embarrassed for being hungry.

"It may be an unnecessary precaution," he said, "but you are not the only one who could be endangered by the appearance of collusive arrangements."

Her smile was at once worldly-wise and relieved. "You mean that you don't want it said that you are influencing or being influenced by me—it's not worry about people speculating what our relationship might be."

Before he could speak, the waiter brought her soup, promising to return at once with the wine; for the moment all aspects of her story were set aside in favor of the meal.

❖

Midway through the duck, Solange was able to return to the matter that had brought them there. She began to ask the Count questions about the bodies and their ties—if any—to the Blood Center. "Some so-called experts have speculated that the man is close to the investigation, and that is making the police nervous. My aunt's husband is a cop, and he said he feels as if he's under suspicion."

"Do you find your aunt's husband reliable?" the Count inquired. "Some policemen are more so than others."

"Conroy is a model of rectitude," said Solange, and decided the wine was going to her head—she would rarely use the word *rectitude,* especially to describe Neal Conroy; she did her best to soften her meaning. "Dependable, honorable, hardworking, responsible."

"Commendable qualities in any man," the Count approved.

"Yes. He let me know he has questions about the state of the investigation, including similar ones to the reservations expressed by the expert. He's a bit worried about the kind of questions being raised in the press, as well. He wants everything in the case to be above doubt." She was delighted with the meal, in part because it allowed her to spar with the Count while she had this excellent repast.

"Do you recall which expert said the things that bother your aunt's husband—about the killer being close to the investigation?" the Count asked, unperturbed. He studied her face. "Did your aunt's husband have any opinions on the current uncertainty?"

She pondered for several seconds. "Not about the investigation, not directly, no. The expert isn't a cop: I think it was Fisk; the crime-scene tech: he's been talking to the media recently."

"No doubt he has." A suggestion of a frown formed between the Count's brows.

Now Solange was alert. "What do you mean?" She had the uneasy suspicion that the Count—not she—was guiding their conversation, so she prepared a number of lines of inquiry to pursue.

The Count shrugged. "Unlike Fisk, I am no expert, but I find it strange that a man who is so responsible for the quality and preservation of the evidence in this case should call so much of it into question. He has an obligation to keep an open mind, but from what I have read, Fisk is doing more than that." He took the bottle of wine and poured her a third glass.

Much struck, Solange gave this her consideration. "He is only living up to his function, and gathering evidence impartially—evidence is just that: evidence. It has no opinions, only existence."

"That may be, but Dr. Fisk certainly has opinions," said the Count. "He impugns his own work at almost every turn. Had an arrest been made, I would have thought Fisk was a member of the defense."

To give herself a little time to think, Solange took a long sip of the wine, then remarked, "When you put it that way, I see what you mean."

"Is there anything in his past to account for his behavior? Did he give testimony in a trial that was found to be—"

"That could be it!" Solange exclaimed. "He used to work in Moose Jaw, or so he says. I'll check with the cops there."

The Count held up his hand. "I can understand wanting not to appear too much a part of the prosecution instead of an investigator, but this man Fisk has—"

"I know," she interrupted. "Thanks for the observation. You have a point. I'll look into it." Drinking more wine, she had to resist the urge to call Baxter at once; instead she asked one of her queries on her mental list. "Do you think the murder has taken away any of the community benefits the Blood Center promises?"

"For some, no doubt it has," said the Count. "But once the murders are solved and the guilty party brought to justice, then the Center will quickly show its value."

"Aren't you being a bit too optimistic?" She cut a little more duck. "This is very good. I'm sorry you can't enjoy it."

"That's kind of you," said the Count. "No, I don't think my optimism is unrealistic. But time will tell, and time is often the test in these cases."

"Then you're thinking in the long run?" Solange asked.

"For a man in my position, it is the only perspective that makes sense," he told her as she went on with her dinner.

※

Applause burst out in the city room as Solange sauntered in, twenty-six days after her first dinner with the Count. She went to her cubicle, but stood outside it to curtsy three times, smiling proudly. "Thank you, thank you. You're all too kind."

Baxter, who had hung back, now came up to her. "Don't be modest, Barendis," he advised. "Conroy says you were the linchpin in their investigation."

"I'm not being modest," she said. "I know how much luck had to do with catching the guy."

"You put them on the scent, and you kept at the story," Sung said from his office doorway. "You could have followed the rest, hassling the cops for not getting the guy, but you went after Fisk, asking about his reluctance to do anything to break the case. The thing about saying animal blood and human blood could not be separated enough for a valid DNA profile. Very good."

"Thanks," she repeated. "It seemed a good place to begin."

"Did you think it was Fisk?" Hill, who covered building and expansion, made his question sharp.

"I didn't know who it was," said Solange, delighted she had accomplished so much. "I just thought it was odd that Fisk kept running down the evidence he himself was collecting. A crime-scene tech needs to be skeptical, but what Fisk was doing was well beyond skepticism and leaning toward subversion."

"Well, you helped bring him to justice, and you're a credit to the paper," Baxter approved, then went on, "Everyone back to work. You don't want to have to chase the paper tonight."

The celebratory mood vanished at once, and the night staff of the Vancouver Print and Media News Corporation returned to their tasks.

"Management is preparing a bonus for you, Solange," said Baxter, lingering in the opening of her cubicle.

"Thanks," she said.

After a short silence, Baxter said, "So what are you looking at now?"

"I got a lead on a smuggling operation. Not drugs, but high-quality antiques," she told him, unfamiliar hesitation in her response.

"What about the Count—the exile?" Baxter prompted. "The one with so much money in the Blood Center."

Her smile was slow and had a sensuality to it that Baxter had never seen before. "He's a gentleman of the old school—no real story there, except that he still exists."

Baxter pounced on her remark. "Something going on there that I should know about?"

She shook her head. "Only dreams."

"*Those* kind of dreams?" Baxter asked her.

"None of your business, boss," said Solange.

Baxter chuckled. "So long as it doesn't get in the way of your work, dream away."

She contemplated his profile. "It was something the Count said that got me thinking about the smuggling scheme."

"He fed you information?" Baxter seemed surprised.

"No; not even enough to qualify as an unnamed source—he mentioned something a week ago, about trouble his shipping business was having. I decided to ask around, to see if his problems were isolated."

"And I gather they're not," said Baxter and slapped the side of her cubicle. "Well, keep me up to date on your project." He started away from her cubicle.

"You can depend on me, boss," she responded, and began to work on her new story, all the while anticipating the late-night supper she would have with the Count, three hours from now. Grinning inwardly, she promised herself she would have particularly delicious dreams tonight, as a reward for her tenacity, and the result of her rendezvous with the Count.

THE ANNOUNCEMENT

RAMSEY CAMPBELL

"**T**HIS ISN'T ME." As I sprint around the corner of the hotel I shout it louder, but the taxi is already at an intersection. It vanishes along the cross street while I'm sucking in another breath. Three girls find my antics worthy of a titter. I give them an expansive shrug that's meant to be comical, but they've returned to watching half a dozen mute performances by a rock group in the window of a television shop. I'm trudging back to the lobby to ask for directions when a limousine draws up in front of the hotel.

So the taxi could have used that street despite the ban on traffic. Didn't the driver think I merited the exemption? He begrudged me a receipt, as if he didn't believe my journey deserved one or even a taxi. As I scowl at the limousine, a young woman in a severely grey suit climbs out and hurries to open the door for a puffed-up bantam the colour of rust in a T-shirt and jeans. "Mr Rigg won't need you till tomorrow when he's signing," she tells the chauffeur.

I make for her charge as if his name has reeled me in.

"Excuse me, are you Bill Rigg? Are you staying at this hotel?"

His crumpled T-shirt answers my first question. It's printed with the cover of *The Koran Encryption,* his impossibly best-selling novel. He's showing me his mottled face with its mouth pressed as straight as his frown when the limousine cruises away and his minder darts to intervene. "Mr Rigg has finished for today," she informs me. "He'll be reading from his book again tomorrow morning and signing them at Texts."

"I know that." In case I sounded interested I add "I'm a writer. I've been reading at the festival as well."

Rigg unclenches his face to put on a quizzical look, but his features stay too close together. "Should we know you?"

"Joseph Nicholas Brady." Since this earns no recognition, I name my novel. *"The Absolutely True and Indisputably Verifiable Facts about the Universe."*

Rigg scratches his flat shaven pate. "Where'd you get those?"

That's part of the point, as I tried to explain to my audience on the folding chairs in the barely coloured windowless room. The book is a satire on novels that claim to be based on secret history, and all the sources cited in the footnotes derive from my name: Harold Phelan, Jody Lane, Seb Holland, Sally Joiner, Leonard Parr, Neil Boole, Jeannie Charles, Ellen Spencer, Sephirah Hardy, Jess Loman, Phyllis Adler, Joan Bradley, Ned Sloane . . . Someone accused me of cynicism, and because she was clutching a copy of Rigg's wretched thousand-pager I asked whether she would rather believe that all the Islamic elements in art are the code of a conspiracy that's poised to rule the word. By then I'd lost my temper with the voice that had muttered throughout my reading. At first I'd thought it was one of my six listeners, and then I'd grasped that it was seeping through the wall. Now I realise that it sounded like Rigg's voice. Before I can demand where he was performing, the young woman says "Shall we go inside? You don't want to be mobbed by fans this late."

Her advice isn't directed at me, but I won't have them knowing how I've been treated. I'll sit in the bar until they go to their rooms. I'm about to lead the way when Rigg's small eyes peer at me. "Aren't you in the Grand? Sounded like you weren't expecting me to be."

I won't lie in my writing, and I shouldn't even to him, but it costs me an effort to admit "I'm in the Rest."

"The car took us there first by mistake," the young woman laughs, then renders her grin sympathetic. "We're picking up the bill. His publishers."

Mine didn't offer, nor did they provide any copies of my book. "You might want to keep an eye on his publicity this weekend," I tell her, more to display my professionalism than because I care. "I don't think the folk who are running this festival know what publicity means."

While she appreciates my concern or pretends to, Rigg can't be bothered. "Shouldn't need it if you're any good. Sold out tonight and I am tomorrow."

His speech is as perfunctory as his prose. Comparing his carelessness to the pains I take to choose my words makes my head throb. I'm struggling to compose some witticism on the theme of not wanting to sell out when he turns his back. "I'm off to watch myself on telly," he declares, striding at the automatic doors as though he'll butt them if they don't give way to him.

The young woman blinks at me. "Will you be all right now?"

"I don't know where my hotel is from here."

"It isn't far. Shall I call a taxi for you?"

"Just tell me. I'll endeavour not to get mobbed."

She returns her phone to her gilded handbag and hastens to the corner of the building, where she points past the televisions. "Straight along for a few blocks. You'll be ready for bed."

For a moment I indulge in fancying she means this as an invitation, but she's gazing at me to ensure I obey her directions. When I reach the window full of screens I glance back. She hasn't lingered, and I suspect she's bound for Rigg's bed. I stare at the multiplication of yet another prancing rock group in case it's ousted by his image. I wouldn't be able to hear what he says, not that I want to. I almost succeed in thinking that he must be hard up for an audience if he has to watch himself.

As I tramp along the empty street the shopfronts dwindle and grow shabby. After ten minutes, most of them are shuttered with metal if they aren't disused. On the block at the end of which I see a sign stuttering above my hotel, a betting shop nestles against an arcade of fruit machines between *Sensuous Couples,* whose grille has been adorned with a cartoon of an erupting penis, and a wine shop with returns in its doorway, not all of them smashed. Next to my accommodation a second-hand shop is called *Hi Its Fi,* a clump of words that makes me grind my teeth. Has someone left a television switched on behind the shutter? Can that be Rigg's muffled voice? I'm close to resting my ear against the rusty weatherbeaten metal slats when I lurch away in a rage to my hotel.

The sign has lost the bulk of its first syllable. All that flickers whenever it manages to summon up the energy is T ELLER'S REST. The grimy splintered glass of the narrow awning blurs it as I push open the rather less than wholly transparent door, scraping the already ragged brownish carpet of the rudimentary lobby. The stained reception counter is unattended except for a vacuum cleaner slouching beneath the pigeonholes, one of which protrudes a message slip that looks aged yellow by the dim illumination leaking from under the cornices. A placard propped against the extravagantly scratched door of the solitary lift says OUt oF OARdER. So is the slogan, I'd comment if there was anyone to hear. Instead I make for the boxed-in stairs that are partly covered by a trampled blackened carpet and toil up to my room.

Though it's only two floors distant, I'm sweating by the time I reach it. The impressions of landscapes that are presumably intended to relieve the monotony of the sombre corridor look half melted by the central heating that's taking on the August mugginess. When I unlock my door, which is featurelessly pink except for a red 8 dangling from its lower screw, the stark room the colour of old bone seems to have stored up more than its share of the heat. The grubby gamboge curtains have drifted together on their sagging wire. I drag them apart, but the dwarfish double-glazed window opaque with condensation won't budge. I snarl at it and at the room in general, especially the token furniture, which gives me the feeling that it was hurriedly assembled and then crammed into one corner of an attic along with me. I snarl loudest at the midget television perched on a bracket opposite my frayed pillow, because I'm unable to resist switching it on in search of Rigg.

It comes to life with an explosion of noise that makes me desperate to mute it. I poke several buttons on the remote control before I succeed in gagging the set, which is showing a film with dialogue in sentences apparently too short to find space for grammar. The next channel shows a rock group I'm happy to have hushed, and the third brings me Rigg in conversation with a literary critic who surely ought to know better. Perhaps she does. I may never find out, because I can't restore the sound.

I do my best to fancy that his face is red not just with the raw colour but with shame, although his expression is insufferably smug. When I've finished bruising my thumb on the buttons I manage to refrain from flinging the control at him. I extinguish the television and strew the faded bedspread with my clothes on the way to the cupboard that does duty as a toilet and bathroom.

The shower curtain has ripped free of half its hooks.

The water from the clogged shower head keeps faltering and spurting afresh, either much hotter or much colder. As I prance about the narrow bath to avoid the worst excesses of the shower I hear a muffled voice that I have to tell myself isn't commenting on my antics. I flounder out of the bath and grab the single ragged towel from the precariously askew rail beside the cracked sink. As the water finishes giggling in the plughole, I realise that the mutter is in one of the adjoining rooms. While I can't distinguish any of its words, I recognise Rigg's voice.

I'm still wielding the meagre towel as I march into the bedroom. I kneel in the subsiding middle of the bed and press my ear against the damp wall, then squeeze between the wardrobe and the equally shaky dressing-table to listen over there. It must be tiredness that leaves me incapable of deciding which side is playing host to Rigg, unless both are. I stand in the cramped gap between the bed and the dressing-table, one drawer of which protrudes several stubborn inches, and shout "Can you turn that down, please" twice.

At first there's no response. When I halve the request and double my volume, it earns me sleepy protests and thumps on both walls while Rigg's harangue continues as incomprehensibly as ever. I snatch the phone from its hiding-place behind one curtain and poke the zero, which ought to call Reception as well as summing Rigg up. The phone is so dead that I could imagine I'm hearing his voice through the receiver.

I slam it back on the windowsill and struggle into my clammy clothes. Shoving the key on its cumbersome bludgeon into a hip pocket, I dash into the corridor, only for Rigg's voice to disappear as if the thick gloom has engulfed it. I won't be tricked. As soon as I stick my head inside the room I can hear him mumbling on. I bang the door shut and run along the humid corridor to the equally windowless stairs. "Hello?" I shout as I come in sight of the reception counter. "Is someone here, please?"

I'm about to summarise this more loudly when I grasp that Rigg's voice is outside the hotel. Although its words stay indistinct, the timbre makes its source clear, not least because I saw one near the building where I gave my talk. It's a speaker van. What is it saying? Rigg must be broadcasting his presence at the behest of the festival organisers or at least encouraged by them. More to the point, why is the van loitering outside the hotel? How late is it allowed to keep its racket up? I need my sleep. I drag the door over the scraped carpet and pounce out of the hotel.

The van isn't as close as I thought, which is why its message stays unclear. It's beyond a concrete flyover a hundred yards away in the opposite direction from the one that brought me here. As I strain my ears its engine starts with a protracted rasp that sounds insulting, and the voice recedes. I head for the lobby, and then I halt as though I've been grabbed by the shoulders, which hunch up. I'm almost certain that Rigg said my name.

What comment has he recorded about me? Or is he in the vehicle, not watching television after all? Whatever he goes on to say, it's as unintelligible as his previous spiel. I won't be able to sleep while the van could be wandering the streets and undermining any reputation I may have. Perhaps I didn't really hear my name, but I have to know. I step off the patch of light outside the hotel and run to the flyover.

It's four lanes wide and supported by massive concrete pillars. They're sprayed with crude letters that barely form words and with less than words—initials and drawings primitive enough for a cave. Beyond the pillars directly ahead, a street illuminated by fewer lights than there are lamps is packed with dilapidated shops boarded up for the night if not for longer. At the end of the first block I glimpse tail-lights swinging left and trailing Rigg's blurred voice.

As I sprint from beneath the flyover I notice the street

isn't deserted. The shadows between those streetlamps that aren't broken contain women, each of whom murmurs as I pass. I don't need to catch their words to know what they're offering, and I hurry past without responding. I'm nearly at the junction when a less circumspect woman dressed in a small amount of leather steps in front of me. "What are you after, love?"

"Them," I pant, jabbing my hands in front of me. "I'm after them."

She inflates her chest with a taut creak. She must think I had this in mind, because she says "Just these?"

"Not that. None of that," I gasp as I stumble around her. "Him."

"If you're one of that bunch you're up the wrong end."

I gather she's speculating about my sexual tastes, since her colleagues add their ribald thoughts. "I'm not talking about that," I protest. "Can't you hear?"

"We've been hearing you fine. You sound pretty desperate to me."

I haven't time for this, not least because her loose words are obscuring phrases I can almost identify along the street. "What did it say just then?"

"Watch who you're calling an it, love. Show some respect or we'll have to sort you out."

"You're the ones who ought to be showing respect, and a few other people as well." I shouldn't let myself be provoked, because now I'm blotting out the harangue of the van. It couldn't actually have said "He'd send anyone asleep, dopey sod," but what would have sounded like that? I grimace at the women to fend them off as I dash after the van.

It's several hundred yards away and moving just a little faster than I'm able to maintain. At least I can't see anyone ahead to hinder me. All the properties I'm passing are featureless with boards, as far as I can tell by the twitching light of the occasional unvandalised streetlamp. I assume they're shops, although they've shed any names they had. The rear lights of the van blaze between them like a threat of arson, so that I imagine them burning like paper; I could be tempted to dream that they're stacks of copies of Rigg's book. I don't know whether to race after the vehicle in case I can somehow overtake it or to stand still, because the clatter of my footsteps prevents me from distinguishing so much as a syllable. I'm hardly aware of stumbling to a halt as if this may arrest the van. Of course it doesn't, nor does yelling "What did you say?"

"What you say?"

For a moment I think there's an echo, so distorted that it's well-nigh incoherent. Then an object I took to have been abandoned in a bin bag that's sprawled across an un-lit doorway pokes its aggrieved head up. "Not me," I tell it. "Never mind me. What did you just hear?"

"You, you daft bugger. What's the idea waking a man up? You've got no right. You're nobody."

"That's who I am." I'm nearly distracted enough to lean down and bellow this into the unsteady face, because I'm less certain than I want to be that I couldn't have heard Rigg mumble in the distance "Piss on Brady and all his silly slop." Can he be driving the vehicle and broadcasting such stuff? Is he drunk or on drugs or both? The occupant of the doorway struggles to rise but falls back with the clink of a bottle. I've already wasted too much time on him. As I turn my back I realise that the van is nowhere to be seen.

Rigg is all too audible, but I can't be sure of his words. "Here he is"? "See the shabby slob"? I bolt to the end of the shops and glimpse the inflamed lights as they veer around a curve. The street they're following is crowded with houses flush with the pavements, which ought to mean that the ranting of the van will waken some of the householders. I hope it does—they'll want to silence it as much as I do—but as I run past the houses I observe that most of the windows are broken. If I'm not mistaken in the unrelieved darkness, many of the housefronts are blackened by fire. At least if the properties are empty, nobody will hear Rigg's comments about me. I arrive panting at the curve in the road and falter to a standstill. I can't see or hear the van.

"Good riddance," I gasp. It isn't loud—I need to regain my breath—but it prompts a response. "Is that you?"

The whisper is trickling through one or more of several fist-sized holes in the downstairs window of a house as dark as sleep. Since the answer to the question is obviously no, I'm drawing breath to say at least that when the whisperer adds "Don't make such a row. We don't want anybody hearing you."

"You're not the only one who doesn't," I'm stung to retort.

The next whisper is only just discernible. "Is that him?"

A series of thumps and mutters apparently signifies somebody's attempts to reach the window. As I set about stealing away, an eye and the corresponding section of an unkempt head waver up to the lowest hole in the glass. The eye is considerably duller than the glint of a syringe on the littered floor. "No," the owner of the eye decides after the first of several pauses. "That's not him."

For an instant I'm absurdly glad that's settled, and then Rigg's voice revives. It's further blurred by distance, so that I'm uncertain whether he said "Needle Brady." Is he musing—making verbal notes—or issuing instructions? I'm so distracted that I hardly know what I'm saying, let alone to whom. "That's got to bother you as well," I appeal to the silhouette at the window. "Not just me."

"You are, pal."

The response sounds retarded by menace. As I catch sight of the glint again I'm aware what kind of needle I may be in danger from. It's one more reason why I shouldn't linger, but I hope the couple or however many are lurking in the unlit room don't imagine that their hostility has driven me away as I pursue my tormentor's voice.

The next road across the street I'm on is more than twice as wide. Pairs of tall houses intervene their gardens between the pavement and themselves. The left-hand stretch leads into the town centre, towards which the van is receding. Its roof flares orange beneath each concrete streetlamp. Perhaps it's the spaciousness that lets me grasp Rigg's words despite the additional distance. "Prod His Lordship. Enjoy his headache."

Why is nobody except me objecting to him? We must be surrounded by an audience, since the houses are split into flats. "I'll prod you when I get hold of you," I shout and then devote my energy to catching up. I've barely put on speed when a window rattles open at the top of a house ahead. "Stop the noise," a man bellows. "People want to sleep."

"I'm trying to stop it," I roar. "Why don't you help?"

"I'll give you some help all right if you don't shut up."

He must be half asleep to be making so little sense. "Call the police," I urge. "It can't be legal at this time of night."

"What I'll do to you if you don't bugger off won't be for sure. Go home and get yourself some help."

I'm tempted to remain until he admits to hearing Rigg and undertakes to send for the authorities, but I'm too infuriated by Rigg's latest comments. "Brady's been on," he announces. "He's done. I heard him read. Snored all along, I did, me." I dodge into the middle of the road and dash in pursuit of the van, waving my arms as if I'm imitating each reappearance of my shadow and bawling less than words in an attempt to drown out the speaker. "Irony, he says he does," it continues. "All hype. He's a liar. He's a con. He does dire joyless horrid hellish crap."

Rigg's words are beginning to sound like some kind of code. "Posh and oily and sly is all," he adds as windows

overlooking the street emit protests that, grotesquely, seem
to be aimed at me. I'm closer than the vehicle, that's why,
but I'm starting to feel far too much like a scapegoat when
a lone walker appears halfway between me and the van.

She has been exercising her dog in a park at the end of
the houses. I slow down so as not to alarm her while she
ambles towards me, and point beyond her with both hands,
a gesture I don't mean to appear quite so beseeching.
"You've been hearing that, haven't you?" I ask loud
enough for the tenants of the flats to catch.

The hem of the light from a streetlamp slides over her
pale pudgy face and seems to tug her copiously lipsticked
mouth into a smile. "Have you as well? Oh good."

I mustn't let her shrillness deter me. "Did you hear what
it said?"

"Of course," she says and simpers. "Didn't you?"

As she advances, kneeing her long black dress at every
step, I see that she isn't walking a dog but yanking a mis-
shapen bag on a leash. "I believe so," I concentrate on
saying.

"Tell me and I'll tell you if I think you're right."

I clench my fists at Rigg's latest pronouncements and at
forcing myself to repeat them. "He's alone. Poor old
Brady's a horny bachelor and he's all alone. No bride and
no children. Only in his brain."

"Oh, that's sad," the woman says and drags the bag on-
wards, scraping the pavement with a thin brown object that
protrudes from the zip. "Is that you?"

"It's meant to be. He doesn't know anything worth
knowing. Shall I tell you what his last book was? A quiz
book. *How New a Man Are You*, it was called. That's how
opportunistic he is, do you see?"

She looks determined not to give in to bewilderment.
"Just let the ones who care about you talk to you," she ad-
vises. "You only have to find them and then they'll always
be there for you. My gran and grandpa are."

I'm about to enquire why she thinks this relevant to anything I've said when I notice that the gateway through which she emerged leads not to a park but to a graveyard. The scrawny item dangling from her bag must be a withered bunch of flowers, but I'm not anxious to check. For once I'm relieved to hear sounds in the distance, shouts and the smashing of glass. Perhaps the van has encountered a mob. "You'll have to excuse me," I tell the woman and retreat to the opposite pavement to be out of her reach.

More glass shatters as I cross the intersection with the graveyard on the corner. I won't deny hoping that it's a window of the van. Perhaps it's a bottle, since Rigg isn't daunted. Indeed, he sounds enlivened and determined that his message shall be clear. "Please do Brady, lads," he says. "Be physical. Nail him, bloody droner."

An unamplified voice responds, just loud enough for me to hear. "Carry on, boss."

"He's nearby. He's behind. Slippery Joe Brady. He's a real prince, he is. No, he's an arsehole. Bash him, boys. Reshape his head."

For as long as it takes Rigg to say all this I'm unable to move, and then I understand why his voice is growing louder. The van has turned and is coming back towards me. It's surrounded by voices that seem wordless with distance if not brutishness. He's bringing the mob.

I twist around in search of allies. There's no sign of the woman, not that appealing to her would have been much if any use, and all the windows of the flats are shut. I might try making an uproar to goad somebody to call the law, except that the road opposite the graveyard leads to a brighter thoroughfare. That's the business district, and surely where I'm most likely to find police.

I'm too intent on fleeing to observe when the houses give way to larger buildings. They're offices and banks, emblems of prosperity, locked up like safes. They make me feel cast out and ignored, not least because Rigg's monologue is gathering speed towards the junction. "Jab his eyes in. Slash his nose. Bop his ears. Pierce his scalp. Pop his balls. No loss, I'd say. I hope he dies."

I've staggered just a few more gasping paces when it and its attendant shouts spill into the road behind me. Its companions are still doing without language. My shadow is flung flat in the middle of the street like a victim about to be kicked insensible, but a backward glance shows me only the headlamps that have caught me in their spotlight. "I'll shred his papers," Rigg is saying. "I'll sprain his head. He'll yell. He's a jelly. He's a drip. I hope he perishes."

He's repeating himself. He's running out of words. I'd confront him with the limits of his vocabulary if he didn't have his thugs with him—and then his turns of phrase grow clear to me at last. He wouldn't talk like that; I've heard him talk. He's stolen my technique. His messages are built out of the letters of my name.

He'd have no style without me. He'd be nothing, and I swing around to shout it. The lights blind me, but I can hear the gang around them. Perhaps I won't take him on just now after all. To my left I see an alley that leads to a building that looks somehow familiar. Can I have strayed back to the hotel? Even that would be welcome. No sooner do I think it than I've dodged into the alley and am sprinting for the light at the end.

"Hold on, Brady," Rigg booms, and then all I can hear are my breaths trapped between the close walls. I keep nearly falling against the walls as I run. As the dazzle of the headlamps drains from my eyes, the dimness of the alley settles on them. They seem unable to determine how light it is when I stagger out of the alley, but there's no mistaking where I am. Opposite me is the building where I gave my talk, and to my left is a speaker van.

I barely hesitate. Somebody has abandoned a bottle in the doorway of the venue. I wish I had a drink, but I've no time. I glance about the street that looks flat as a stage set under the relentless lights, and then I pull out the hotel key on its heavy club. If other people can break glass, so can I for a purpose. At the very least the van is a refuge. I smash the driver's window with a single blow and pick fragments out of the door, then I unlock it and climb in.

I can no longer hear Rigg and his chosen audience. Ah, silence. The streets are so quiet he might never have been there. It's past time I was heard. Having come this far, I'm sure I'll be able to start the vehicle. Shall I abscond? No chance, as he'd say in idle pride. I can handle any shyness in heroic prose. If we have a shouting match in the street I'll have more to say and better, so long as the speaker operates. I locate the switch and press it, and hear my own breath filling the street. Shall I be horribly acerbic or rely on blarney? Slander idol Bill or deploy balance? Any dross will erode solid personal calibre. Soldier on, Brady. Besides, choice is no hindrance. I'll respond dryly. Nevertheless for an unpleasant moment I'm at a loss for words, and then I know where to start. I tug the microphone closer and say "This isn't me."

THE OUTERMOST BOROUGH

GAHAN WILSON

ONCE AGAIN, WITH a gesture that had turned into a sort of nervous tic during this morning's long waiting, Barstow pressed his face against the dirty glass of his studio's wide central window in order to peer anxiously down the crowded city street below, westward toward Manhattan.

At first his body began to sag in disappointment yet again, but then he suddenly straightened and his sharp little eyes brightened in their darkish sockets at the sight of a shiny black speck making its way smoothly as a shark through the otherwise-dingy traffic.

Barstow clenched his hands into small triumphant fists as he saw the speck draw nearer to the ancient building his loft perched atop, and gleefully observed it shape itself into a long, sleek limousine gliding with regal incongruity amidst graffiti-laden delivery trucks and unwashed second-hand cars scarred with multitudes of dents and dings.

Without any doubt he knew it was the vehicle of Max Ratch, Barstow's longtime associate and the owner of one of New York's most prestigious galleries. He had come as he had promised!

Barstow turned for one last burning survey of the works of art he had spent the whole of last week arranging for Ratch's inspection. He was pleased to see that the thickly textured strokes of oil paint he had spread upon the canvases gave out satisfactorily ominous gleams in the gray light seeping into the studio, and delighted to observe that the portraits and cityscapes, lurking like muggers in the studio's darker corners, created exactly the dangerous and intimidating effect he had striven so carefully to achieve.

Suddenly struck by a disturbing notion, the artist whirled and darted back to the windows just in time to see the large chauffeur open the rear passenger door of the limo and be suddenly diminished by the emergence of Ratch's long, bulky body. The art dealer had barely gotten both feet on the sidewalk when the very much smaller form of his ever-present assistant, Ernestine, darted out after him with the scuttling alacrity of a pet rat.

Barstow peered nervously up and down the street and spat a strangled curse as he spotted Mrs. Fengi and her son, Maurice, swaying rhythmically like inverted pendulums as they waddled unevenly but directly toward his approaching visitors. He could see Mrs. Fengi's enormous, toadlike eyes bulge eagerly while, with considerable difficulty, she accelerated her froggish shuffle.

It was obvious the weird old creature was desperate to buttonhole these exotic strangers to the neighborhood and to gossip with them, and Barstow knew that would never do!

He glared intently down, unbreathing, his teeth clenched, his heart throbbing hurtfully in his chest, and desperately prayed that the dealer and his aide would not turn and observe the approaching duo.

But then a huge wave of grateful relief rushed through his thin body as he saw Ratch and Ernestine purposefully make their way from the limo to the stoop of Barstow's building and glide efficiently up its old worn steps without having made any contact with—or even so much as taken a sideways glance at—the approaching Fengis.

The doorbell rang and Barstow rushed through his studio to push the button releasing the lock downstairs. He shouted instructions to his guests via the entrance intercom as to how they could locate and use the freight elevator, then hurried to the door of his studio and threw it open.

He stood on the landing, rubbing his hands and gloating at the sound of the ancient lift whining and rattling five stories upward, then reached forward so he could haul its squeaking door open the moment it arrived.

Ratch strode majestically out with Ernestine behind him and gazed down at Barstow with his large blue eyes.

"Well, well," he said in his usual reverberating basso. "When you said you'd moved from Manhattan to an outer borough, dear boy, you truly meant an *outer* borough!"

"It's almost as long a trip as that ghastly drive to the Hamptons!" snapped Ernestine behind him.

"I wasn't all that crazy about being this far away from everything myself, at first," Barstow admitted apologetically. "But then I got used to it—really began to see the place— and finally I realized it had turned out to be an inspiration!"

"That is very interesting," Ratch murmured, gazing speculatively at Barstow, and then he turned to his assistant. "Besides, Ernestine, we must not chide poor Barstow for living in such a far-off place. The rents in Manhattan have forced all artists—save for the most outrageously successful—to shelter in odd and obscure locations such as this."

He turned to gaze down benignly at the artist and then bent to firmly grasp both of Barstow's narrow shoulders possessively in his huge gloved hands.

"But let us leave all that aside, shall we? I have a feeling that what we are about to see here will be well worth the ordeal of the journey!"

He increased his stately downward inclination farther until his wide pink face almost touched Barstow, and stared closely at the artist with an odd look of crafty affection.

"Am I right, Kevin?" he whispered. "Do I really smell a breakthrough? Dare I hope that the potential I have always sensed in you has finally started to flower?"

The skin of Barstow's face gave little mouselike quivers under the impact of Ratch's breath and he smiled up at Ratch as a frightened child might smile at a Santa Claus who had actually, terrifyingly, climbed out of the family fireplace.

"I think so!" he whispered back. "I really do!"

Ratch regarded him for a long moment before letting go of the artist and then pointed to the open door of the studio with a flourish.

"Then lead on!" he said.

Without any further discussion, the three of them immediately absorbed themselves in the business at hand, with Barstow gently and unobtrusively guiding Ratch and Ernestine from one work to the next, always moving quietly, always keeping just a glance or two ahead of the art dealer as the large man stepped thoughtfully and elegantly from painting to painting.

Skillfully, like an acolyte, Barstow unobtrusively carried the works to a back wall once they had been observed by Ratch and then gently moved forward the ones he wanted him to look at next.

A clammy—he hoped not very noticeable—sheen of sweat now covered Barstow's face and hands, and occasionally a tremor ran the length of both his arms as he leaned a painting against the leg of an easel or delicately adjusted the positioning of several connected works in a row. It took him an enormous effort to keep his breathing steady and inaudible.

So far he could not determine exactly how positively Ratch was reacting to these new works, but he found himself becoming increasingly hopeful. Though he had made no spoken comment since starting his slow march through Barstow's domain, the artist was encouraged to observe the obvious depth of the dealer's absorption in the paintings.

It was an enormously good sign that Ratch sometimes paused silently before one or another of them for long, thoughtful moments. But when he stripped off his gloves and stuffed them into a pocket of his astrakhan coat so that he could reach upward with his thick but sensitive fingers and tug delicately at the sensuous pout of his full lips, a great beat of triumph throbbed through Barstow, for he knew, from long years of experience, that this was always a foolproof sign of great approval.

After a full hour that seemed to last at least a century, Ratch came to a halt before the grand finale, an enormous painting of a gigantic female nude gazing through what was recognizably the studio's main window at pigeons milling on its sill.

He stood absolutely motionless and expressionless for a very lengthy time and then a satisfied smirk curled his lips and slowly spread into a smile that grew broader and wider and more open until Ratch turned toward Barstow with a full display of his famously fearsome toothiness and violently broke the long silence with an enthusiastic clapping of his hands.

"Bravo, Kevin, bravo!" he cried, spreading his arms like the ringmaster of a three-ring circus and gazing happily at the multitude of paintings about him. Ernestine, who up to now had tagged along behind her employer in quiet watchfulness, vouchsafed the first sure indication that the project would successfully advance by drawing a notebook from her carrying case and from that moment on jotting down in shorthand every word said that might be of historical or legal import.

"Thank you, Max," said Barstow. "Thank you so much!"

"Ah, no, Kevin, ah, no—thank *you*!" said Ratch, waving a huge paw in an elegant sweep around the room. "Not only have you assuredly made both yourself and my gallery a very large amount of money, I am convinced you have guaranteed yourself everlasting fame and glory."

The blood rushed to Barstow's head, and for a moment or two he was terrified that he would actually faint for joy. The art dealer had always been supportive, occasionally even highly encouraging, but this was a level of praise dazzlingly higher than any that had ever been granted before.

In a giddy daze, he watched Ratch almost waltz from one of the paintings to another, gently patting their tops or stroking the sides of their stretchers and sometimes even stopping to inhale the perfume of their paint.

"This is the work you were born to do, my friend," he said. "Everything you have done before has only been a promise of what was to come—merely the tiniest hint!"

He paused at the painting of a hunched, grotesque newsdealer peering out bleakly from the small, dark pit of his shoddy sidewalk stand kiosk, plastered with newspapers, bannered with headlines of war and plague, and tabloid magazines displaying gaudy photos of mutilated freaks and sobbing celebrities and smiled benignly at the way the grotesque creature's fearful, pockmarked face stared out at the viewer with eyes slitted like a lurking crocodile's.

"The totally convincing way you have depicted the reptilian quality of this wretched fellow, the believability of his actually not being altogether human, is simply astounding," he whispered gently while stroking the heads of the tacks that pinned the canvas to its frame.

He stood back and continued to survey the painting.

"Forget Bacon, my dear boy. Forget even Goya."

"Even Goya?" Barstow gasped, then gulped and made his way to a paint-splotched stool lest he indeed fall to the floor. "You say even *Goya*?"

Ratch grinned down at him and, for the first time in his whole long association with this legendary entrepreneur of art, it seemed to Barstow that the broad white curve of his gleaming teeth seemed to have an almost-motherly gentleness.

"Even Goya," whispered Ratch, gently patting the artist on his pale, sweat-bedewed forehead. "And all from within this odd little skull of yours. Ah—the sublime mystery of creative talent!"

He stepped to a painting of extraordinary ominousness depicting a neighborhood butcher-store window filled to bursting with glistening red fragments of dismembered animals artfully displayed in order to promote their consumption and with a sly expression began to archly mimic the speech of a museum guide.

"Here you see that the artist has delicately implied—but somehow not directly revealed—that the meat on display may be even more horribly varied than that put on view in the usual butcher's window. Has this steak with a largish round bone, for instance, come from a lamb's hindquarters or was it chopped from a neighborhood schoolgirl's pale and tender thigh? Eh? *Eh*?"

He chuckled in a sinister, highly theatrical fashion and moved on to a night scene showing a dim and lonely streetlamp only barely illuminating a hunched and frightened old woman in black mourning, making her way along a cracked sidewalk and staring anxiously into the almost-impenetrable darkness of the ancient city street beyond.

"I marvel at the way you've suggested . . . *something* . . . on the glistening tarmac of the narrow street approaching the woman from the direction of the other sidewalk!" whispered Ratch in genuine awe. "It is brilliant how the viewer sometimes reads it this way, sometimes that—it is genuine painterly magic, my dear boy! Wizardry! You can rest assured the critics will never be finished writing competitive essays attempting to explain *that* one."

He then pointed at a painting of a gaping policeman, his gun still drawn, kneeling in hard, bright sunlight over a man he'd clearly just shot and staring in horror, along with a small surrounding crowd, at the thing that was bloodily tearing its way out of the dead man's chest and glaring furiously up at the officer.

"But the true underlying miracle of all these new works is their universal *convincingness!*" he said, patting gently, even lovingly, the glistening face of the entity scrabbling its way out of the corpse. "In spite of myself I find I suspect that this horrible thing may actually exist, that it *may even be alive today* in a hidden chamber of some prison hospital!"

He turned to study Barstow intently and tapped the artist at the exact same spot where the gruesomely productive wound had been painted on the slain man's chest.

"Somehow, Kevin, you have suddenly developed the ability to present fictitious images that are simultaneously entirely fantastic and totally realistic," the art dealer intoned with great solemnity. "Never in my whole career as a dealer have I seen such a world of grotesquely macabre impossibilities more believably presented. I am both frightened and thrilled."

He paused to once again study the gory thing depicted in the painting with undisguised affection and then murmured softly, almost inaudibly, but with enormous pleasure: "We shall become unbelievably rich."

Then, almost reverently, he returned to the largest and most centrally located painting of all: the one of the pale, elephantine female nude staring out through the studio's window. The dead-looking flesh of the huge creature's back was turned to the viewer as she idly observed a crowd of subtly bizarre pigeons milling on the widow's ledge and the fire escape beyond.

"This, as I am sure you are well aware, is the supreme work of the exposition," said Ratch with great solemnity, and then he turned to look at the artist curiously. "Have you given this painting a name?"

Barstow nodded.

"I call it *'Louise,'*" he said.

Ratch nodded sagely.

"As though it was the name of an actual model," he said approvingly. "And so enhanced the ghastly notion it might actually be the depiction of a living monster."

Ernestine, on the other hand, had begun to show signs she had at least momentarily lost something of her customary professional detachment and was regarding the painting with undisguised repulsion.

"My God," she whispered. "Look at the thing's hands! Look at its *claws*!"

Ratch gazed at the unmistakable fear in his assistant's eyes with enormous satisfaction.

"You see?" he crowed. "Even my cool Ernestine is very seriously disturbed by our monster."

A sudden spasm crossed Barstow's face at Ratch's second use of this description.

"I do not think of her as a monster," he said.

Ratch regarded the little artist first with some surprise, and then with dawning understanding.

"Of course you don't," he said, and then he waved in an oddly gentle sort of way at the paintings grouped around them. "Nor do you regard any of the creatures depicted in these other works as monsters. As in the work of Goya, one can tell that they are sympathetically, even affectionately observed. That is the secret of their beauty."

Then, after a thoughtful pause, Ratch turned back to the paintings and began to walk among them as he softly dictated observations and instructions to the now-partially-recovered Ernestine. Barstow stood by and watched them at it until he caught a flickering to his side. He turned and his eyes widened when he saw that a great crowd of pigeons had assembled on the window's outside sills and the old ironwork fire escape beyond.

Quietly, unobtrusively, he made his way over to the windows, and though some of the birds flopped clumsily off at his approach, most of the creatures ignored him.

They were a much more varied group of pigeons than those one would ordinarily observe in, say, Manhattan. Not only were their markings extraordinarily colorful and individual—ranging from playful Matisse-like patterns of stars and spiralings to blurry Monet-style shadings to stern geometric blockings of black and gray and sooty white highly reminiscent of Mondrian's abstractions—their bodies were also quite remarkably unlike one another.

The pigeon pecking at the sill just to Barstow's left, for example, was almost as big as a cat and sported a spectacular hunch on its back; the one next to it was extremely narrow and so thin that the rest of its body seemed an almost snakish extension of its neck; the one next to that appeared to be little more than a feathered pulsating blob with wings and an oddly skewed beak.

Barstow stole a quick look behind him to make sure both Ratch and Ernestine were absorbed in their cataloging and calculations. When he looked back outside, he was alarmed to see that one of the pigeons had wandered off from the sill and begun to march awkwardly but casually up the dirty pane of window with its fat, gummy feet clinging to the dirty glass. Another, after alternately extending and shrinking the length of its body in a series of odd, painful-looking little heaves, was working its way along the underside of the railing of the fire escape, for all the world like a beaked, glittery-eyed worm.

Barstow hastily threw another glance back at his guests to make absolutely certain they still hadn't noticed any of these goings-on and then he executed a series of violent and abrupt gestures that, much to his relief, successfully startled all the pigeons into clumsily flying away from the sills and fire escape and out of sight.

Eventually, after what seemed to be eons of discussion and planning, Ratch and Ernestine and their summoned chauffeur descended in the creaking elevator, along with a very sizable selection of paintings, leaving Barstow with his triumph and a great exhaustion.

He made his way to the stool by his easel and sagged onto it with an enormous sigh. It would be a while before he'd have the energy to stir.

He heard the soft opening of a door behind him and smiled as the studio's floorboards groaned nearer and nearer under Louise's enormous weight. When she leaned over him, Barstow gratefully and deeply breathed in the spicy, slightly moldy air that wafted out from her body.

He felt the hugeness of her breasts resting on his shoulders and shuddered with pleasure when she cooed something not quite words and stroked the top of his head with a sweet tenderness that was truly remarkable, considering the potential brutality of her huge paws.

"He liked them," murmured Barstow, relaxing back against her vast belly. "He'll buy all the work I do from now on. We'll be rich, Louise, you and I. And millions will adore your painting. Millions. And they will see how beautiful you are."

She cooed again, carefully retracted her talons, and began to knead the tension from his narrow shoulders.

DARK DELICACIES OF THE DEAD

RICK PICKMAN

"They're after the place. They don't know why, they just remember . . .
remember that they want to be in here."
—PETER IN GEORGE ROMERO'S *DAWN OF THE DEAD*

"When there's no more room in hell, the dead will rock the earth."
—ELECTRIC FRANKENSTEIN, *DAWN OF ELECTRIC FRANKENSTEIN*

IT WAS REALLY too bad that the biggest signing in the
history of Dark Delicacies had to turn into a terror-filled
nightmare of apocalyptic mayhem.

And it had started so well, too.

The occasion had been set up in honor of the first of the
Dark Delicacies Presents films from New Line Cinema,
starring the store's co-owner Del Howison as "Dark Del," a
Cryptkeeper-ish host with a wry sense of dark humor. In
honor of the release of the film Del and his wife Sue had
assembled an astonishing 49 authors, 24 artists, 4 editors, 6
directors, 10 actors, and 3 people who no one was quite
sure what they did, but they'd sign anything put before
them. By the time all 96 signers had been placed in the
small confines of the store, Sue and Del had realized, to
their chagrin, that there was virtually no room left for customers. Sue had stationed one son—Scott—at the door to
allow one customer in each time the previous customer
left; her other son, Jason, was behind the front counter with
her, handling the phone and questions. The line outside ex-

tended nearly four blocks; hundreds of horror fans clutched their books, posters, and DVDs, waiting with growing impatience. Sue and Del's black canine half-breeds, Morticia and Gomez, watched the whole mess warily from behind the screen that caged them behind the front counter.

Of course, most of the fans were there for only a handful of the guests. Sue and Del had managed to score a few big names for this one. There was Clyde Woofer, the staggeringly handsome British author who had exploded on the horror scene twenty years ago by virtue of being . . . staggeringly handsome; the fact that he was also witty, amiable, and wrote stories with lots of freaky sex hadn't exactly hurt his career, either. There was Richard Grove, a classically trained star of bad B movies who had catapulted to fame with his performance in the first science fiction film adaptation of Shakespeare, *Mechbeth*, and who was now starring in *Dark Delicacies Presents: Screams for Sale*. And there was the legendary Ray Beaumont, who at 112 was still happy to smile up from his seat at his legions of fans and tell them about his boyhood in Illinois. It was too bad—he thought he was actually *currently* living his boyhood in Illinois.

The first sign that Something Was Wrong came at approximately 3:30 that afternoon. It was late September, a clear, bright day, and the sun was still high, beating down on Southern California with 85 degrees of heat. Scott was waiting for the most recent customer to finish up so he could wave another in when a scream sounded outside.

"What now?!" Sue asked, harried behind the register as she rang out a Goth girl with black hair, black nails, black eyeliner, and unbelievable amounts of Daddy's cash.

Scott tried to poke his head out and around the corner of the store. "I dunno. I think somebody just found out they had to *buy* Clyde's book here to get it signed."

The current customer finally finished, and Scott motioned to the next, a man wheeling a small hand truck loaded with boxes of books.

Del looked up from schmoozing with the famed British editor Steve Smith and frowned as he caught sight of the man, an ugly middle-aged guy with bad hair and a smarmy manner. He excused himself and stepped up as the guy started unloading crates. "Barry Craven, right?"

The man turned to him, all unctuous grin and outthrust hand. "Hey, Del, how ya doin'?"

Del didn't take the hand. "You gonna buy anything, Barry?"

Barry lowered the hand and looked abruptly defensive. "C'mon, Del, you know I buy books here all the time—"

The shout came from behind the front counter. "Out!" Sue ordered.

The author who had received Barry's first pile of books, a midlist werewolf writer named Kerry Brattner, started to sign faster. "Del, I bought a copy of Stephen King's book at the last signing he did here—"

"We've never hosted a King signing here, Barry."

Sue's second shout was far shriller. "Out!"

Del turned to wave Scott over. Barry took one look at the approaching bulk and pulled his books right out from under Brattner's pen, repacking frantically. "Okay, okay. I'm gone."

He left without further incident. Scott eyed the next man in line, and saw he also had a small dolly packed with crates. "Should I let him in?"

Del eyed the guy. "Oh, yeah, he's a fan, not a dealer. He'll actually buy something."

Scott stepped back and waved the guy in.

It was forty minutes later when the shit really started to hit the fan. The last customer was about to leave, and Scott suddenly realized there was no one else in line.

"Hey, Del, I guess we've reached the end."

Del, who was now schmoozing the famed genre film-maker Guillermo del Loco, excused himself and walked over to Scott. "There were five hundred people in line twenty minutes ago . . ."

"I know, but—well, look—"

Scott motioned down the short hallway that formed the store's entrance. There was no one there. Del frowned and stepped out to the front door. He opened it and poked his head out, looking in both directions.

The street was empty, as far as he could see in any direction. The stoplights were blinking. There was no sound of traffic, or voices, or aircraft. There was an over-turned car in the nearest intersection. A small fire burned in a parking lot a block away. A newspaper blew up against the building near Del; the headline read THE DEAD WALK.

"Huh!" Del muttered to himself.

He reentered the store, pausing near Scott.

"Are we done?" Scott asked.

"Naw." Del considered, then: "You know how these things come in waves. The second wave'll probably start any minute."

Del walked behind the front counter and leaned down close to Sue. "Was the film company doing any kind of promotion today?"

"Not that I know of. Why?"

Just then a scream erupted from the rear of the store. "Hey, we're out of beer!"

Del and Sue exchanged a look, which ended as Sue exhaled and rolled her eyes. They both knew the voice belonged to Lee Edwards, the reigning king of Extreme Fiction—so called because most of it was Extremely Bad. Del walked out from behind the counter and started pushing his way past bored authors and doodling artists, heading for the 55-gallon trash barrel he'd filled with brewskis less than half an hour ago. He reached it and saw that, sure enough, it now contained nothing but a few inches of water and some tired-looking half-cubes of ice.

"What happened? I just filled this thing!"

Edwards belched loudly, and tilted his chair back to two legs. "So? Fill it again."

Del fixed a steely gaze on Edwards. "There *is* no more. I can't believe you drank it all!"

Edwards slapped his other chair legs down. "I can't believe you didn't fuckin' buy more beer!"

Del was about to respond when Sue shrieked from the front of the store, "WE'RE NOT BUYING MORE BEER!!!"

Suddenly Edwards jumped to his feet. "Fuck it. I'll buy it myself."

He started to weave his way to the front of the store, causing a number of sidelong glances and whispers. Edwards even managed to tread on the toes of Clyde Woofer. "Sorry, dude," he muttered, then continued along.

"Quite alright," Woofer responded amiably. Then, when the short, greasy-looking, and vaguely malodorous Edwards had left the store, Woofer added, "Ugly little bloater. Glad he's gone."

Del, who'd overheard, replied, "He'll be back, Clyde."

"Yes," Clyde responded with a staggeringly handsome grin, "his kind always does."

The half-dozen female authors grouped around Clyde all laughed appropriately, even though they all knew he was very gay. Then, a vampire author on Clyde's left thought moonily, *If I was my Countess Sondra, I'd bite Clyde*; and the vampire author on Clyde's right thought shrewdly, *Maybe I should have my Count St. Francis bite him—I could probably sell another ten thousand copies with a hot gay sex scene right in Chapter One of the next book.*

Just then Dane Ketchuson, a middle-aged master of the genre who these days was likelier to invoke dread in his dinner companions than his readers, stood up and proclaimed, "I'm going out for a smoking break. Anybody want to join me?"

Only the elderly and highly respected Clay John Georgeson stood up and accompanied Dane to the front door. He always did. No one knew why.

Five minutes later Del was schmoozing the soft-core porn actress Glory Osqui when the front door abruptly banged open loudly. Del whirled to see Dane staggering in clutching his left arm. There was blood on his tweed jacket.

"That sonofabitch just tried to bite me!"

Del and Scott ran to Dane. "Who did, Dane?" Del asked.

"That—that stupid kid, the one who's an awful writer . . ."

"Lee Edwards?" Scott asked.

"That's it! He's outside, and he's acting like he's . . . I don't know—"

"Drunk?" Del ventured.

Just then the door flew open again, and Lee Edwards staggered in, looking even worse than usual. His skin had gone several shades more puce, there was blood staining the lower half of his face, and his eyes were, impossibly, both fever-bright and glassy. He staggered forward, making a strange low noise in his throat.

"Did you get the beer?" asked somebody behind Del.

Del saw that there was a six-pack dangling from one of Lee's fingers, but two cans were already missing.

And then Lee was lunging at Dane. The six-pack dropped from his fingers as his arms came up and reached for Dane. The clawing hands clutched at Dane's jacket and the gaping mouth began to move toward the blood on Dane's jacket.

"See? He's doing it again!" screamed Dane.

Scott stepped in and put a restraining hand on Lee's scrawny chest. "C'mon, bro, what are you—?!"

Suddenly Lee turned and snapped at Scott.

Scott jerked back, his eyes wide. "I think he's a zombie! Mom—!"

"Scott, don't be ridiculous," Sue answered. "You may not like his writing, but you can't say that—"

"No, Mom, I'm serious!" Scott danced back to avoid Edwards as he advanced, those strange gray-red eyes now fixed on Scott's neck. "I mean zombie as in walking-dead-cannibal guy!"

"That's it, buddy." Del stepped up. "You're outta here."

He caught Edwards by one arm and spun him around back toward the front doorway. Then he planted one boot firmly in Edwards's chest and heaved. Edwards flew back so hard the front door was hurled open and his body landed on the sidewalk outside with a resounding thunk. As Edwards started to scrabble to his feet again, Del leapt forward and thrust his key into the door's lock. Edwards crashed into the door just as Del locked it.

"Yeah, and your books suck, too!" Del called out at the undead thing that pressed its face up against the glass.

Just then Dane ran up. "What about Clay? He's still out there!"

As if in answer, Clay appeared behind Lee Edwards, staggering, dull-eyed. "Aw, shit," Del muttered softly—he'd always liked the old hippie. "Clay's dead, too."

"No, he's not!" Dane said urgently, "He's just stoned!"

Just then Clay really saw the undead thing pushing against the locked door, and his eyes suddenly popped open in alarm. Without further ado, he turned and high-tailed it down the street.

"Good luck, Clay!" Dane called after him.

Just then the dogs, Morticia and Gomez, began to growl while staring pointedly at Dane. "What is it, girls?" Jason asked, trying to console them.

"I'll tell you what it is!" Scott answered. "He's been bitten, and now he's gonna turn into something just like Lee!"

"That's ridiculous," Dane replied, grimacing as he touched the oozing wound on his arm, "I could never write that badly."

Jack Skatt, one of the famed original "splatterpunks" and coeditor of several renowned anthologies of zombie stories, stepped forward just then. "He's right, Del. Dane's gonna turn."

"Oh, Christ, Skatt! First you wouldn't put me in your books, now this," moaned Dane.

Del ignored Dane and turned to Skatt. "So what do we do?"

"I'm sorry, man, but we gotta stick *him*"—he nodded at Dane—"outside, and then we gotta barricade the doors and that front window."

As if to confirm Skatt's advice, a huge *THUD!* abruptly sounded from the front window.

"Hey, watch it! We can't afford to replace that glass!" Sue yelled at whatever was outside.

Just then another man pushed forward to join the conference. It was Joe Somlumkoontz, current president of the WHO (World Horror Organization). "I'm sorry, Del, but I can't let you throw Dane to the zombies like that. He's an ex-president and a member in good standing of WHO."

An author whose name Del couldn't for the life of him remember but whom he knew was WHO's secretary stepped up and whispered something in Joe's ear. "Okay," Joe corrected, "so he's not currently a member in good standing."

There was another *WHOMP!* against the storefront. Del glanced outside, and—well, quite frankly, nearly shit himself.

The sidewalk in front of the store was crowded with dozens, maybe hundreds of those things. Some had obviously been in the waiting line earlier, and still clutched books in dead fingers. Some drooled. Some already looked like they'd been dead a long time.

"The fans came back!" exclaimed a midlist mystery writer.

Del was already moving. "Jason, get the toolbox in the back room and start breaking down some of the tables—maybe we can nail those up against the window."

"Right!" Jason yelled, already on his way to the back.

Next Del turned to Dane, who was already starting to smell bad. "I'm really sorry, Dane, but you gotta go."

Del moved to the front door, joined by Joe. "WHO's got your back, Del!"

"I don't know. Who does?" Del asked.

"I said WHO does!" Joe responded, irritated.

"WHO's got my back?" Del asked, dimly aware he was repeating an old Abbott and Costello routine.

"Right!" Joe answered.

Del nodded at Joe and then to Scott, while Scott grabbed the protesting Dane. "C'mon, Del, I've made a lot of money for this store—!"

"I'm tellin' ya, Dane, it's nothing personal." With that, Del twisted the key in the lock and wrenched the front door open.

Zombies poured through the doorway.

Joe began battering them with a copy of a huge *Cemetery Dance* lettered edition, while Scott used Dane's body as a bulldozer, shoving him into the crowd of zombies. The zombies began to claw at Dane, and Del took the opportunity to begin pushing with the door. After a second, Skatt and Scott joined him, and together they finally managed to get the door closed and locked again.

Del had barely had time to breathe when Jason showed up lugging a heavy table top, while Lisa Morton, a small-time screenwriter and Dark Delicacies' own Webmistress, appeared behind him with hammer and nails. "Mom and Clyde are working on the front window. We'll get the door."

"Okay," Del panted, stepping back. Outside the zombies moaned and grunted, a sound not unlike the way many of them had sounded before death.

Just then an elderly female voice interrupted (in an affected accent), "I demand to know what's going on here!"

Del sighed and turned to face Jean T. Lebriner, a one-time editor and two-time author whose real claim to fame was her baseless arrogance. "What, Jean?"

"That young man took my table! I don't have anything to sign on right now! This is outrageous!" Jean exclaimed, apparently outraged.

"Well, Jean, we had to use it to board up the storefront against invading zombies," Del explained.

Jean tried to peek past Del at the storefront, where Jason was holding the table while Lisa hammered in the first nail. "That's ridiculous." Jean exclaimed.

"Wanna see?" Del gestured at the door. "Hey, Lisa, let her see."

Lisa stopped hammering, smirking. "Sure."

Lisa nodded at Jason, who obligingly tilted the heavy table far enough to one side that there was a sliver of doorway. Jean stepped forward, bending over to peer out. "I don't really—"

Suddenly Del unlocked the door with one hand while planting his other hand firmly on Jean's back. "Here, Jean, take a closer look."

In an instant, she was gone, and Lisa had locked the door behind her. Del turned around to face those behind him. "Anybody got a problem with that?"

There was a silent beat, broken by a resounding round of applause.

After a moment to let the clapping die down, Joe said, "Just don't get the idea that it's okay to keep feeding them WHO presidents."

"No problem," Del noted, dusting off his hands.

"Hey, they spit her out," Lisa cried out from the front door, before Jason moved the table back into place.

Once the boards were in place, Del turned to face the 92 signers who were left. "Anybody got any ideas?"

"Do we know how widespread this is?" somebody called.

Sue was in the front office, typing at the computer. She stood up, shaking her head. "Power's still on, but the Internet's down. Lisa, can you fix this?"

Lisa stepped behind the computer and went quickly over a few things. "Sorry, Sue—I can't solve a problem with rampaging zombies wiping out the Internet."

"How much food do we have?" another voice asked.

Del and Sue exchanged a quick, worried look. "Not much," Del finally confessed. "Some crackers. Some cookies. Little monster candies that ooze ichor when you bite into 'em."

Skatt noted gloomily, "Nope. Dane ate all of those."

Sue's eyes widened in anger. "Hey, those weren't free!"

Suddenly Harry Palmer, a husky novelist whose werewolf novel had been one of last year's surprise horror hits, asked urgently, "What time is it?"

Del glanced at his watch. "About seven. Sun's probably going down outside. Why, Harry?"

"Well," Harry began, averting his eyes, plainly uncomfortable, "I've got a . . . no, we've *all* got a pretty big problem in just a few minutes. See, there's something you don't know about me, and it's a full moon tonight, and I'll—well, I'll—"

"Harry," Del ventured, "are you trying to tell us you really are a werewolf?"

Harry simply nodded.

"Oh, great!" Del noted sarcastically.

"No, wait a minute, that *is* great!" All eyes turned to Pete Akins, a strapping British screenwriter who was noted for his quick wit and innovative use of barbed wire. "In fact, it's *perfect!*"

"How's that, Pete?" Del asked.

"Harry's a werewolf, right? A ferocious engine of inhuman destruction! The instant he changes, we shove him out into the zombies, and he'll tear 'em apart!"

Del considered, and had to admire the idea. *After all,* he thought, *who better to know about shredding and being shredded than a screenwriter?*

"What do you think, Harry?"

Harry nodded, then grinned. His teeth were already starting to look a trifle pointed. "Sounds doable. In fact, it sounds like party time."

"Okay," Del said, then turned to address the others. "Do we have any other monsters here we should know about?"

After a long pause, one trembling hand went up. The crowd parted to reveal the visiting legend Whimsey Scrampbell, a British author known for the sheer strangeness of his stories. "I'm . . . well, I'm a vampire," he admitted in a trembling voice.

"But Whimsey," Steve Smith exclaimed, "you're always out in the day."

"I'm a vampire like in Stoker's book. The Irish had it right for once: We can go out in sunlight; we're just not very strong."

"But you've never even written a vampire story!" protested Taylor Karn, the vampire writer who had earlier been mooning over Clyde.

"Didn't want to give anything away, y'know," Whimsey muttered in his working-class accent.

Suddenly a young writer who had just sold his first story to the anthology *Incredibly Gross Erotica* shoved his way past the others and fell to his knees before the perplexed Whimsey. "Mr. Scrampbell, I love your work, but this . . .

you gotta bite me. Please, please bite me! I'm having trouble with this vampire story I'm working on, and I just know you could help. . . ."

Whimsey looked down, simultaneously tempted and horrified. "First I have to go out and fight some zombies. Maybe, if I make it back . . ."

The young man was weeping in gratitude now. "Thank you, oh thank you—it would mean so much to me."

Del scanned the rest of the crowd. "Anybody else?"

Another hand shot up. It belonged to Demars Dunise, a pagan who wrote nonfiction books about witchy things. "It's the fall equinox tonight. I could turn the dogs into all-powerful hellhounds."

Sue immediately clutched protectively at the girls. "No, you don't!"

Del shook his head. "Thanks, Demars, but I guess it's a bad idea. Anybody else?"

One last hand was raised. This one was attached to Whitey Striper, whose best-selling series of UFO abduction books were often incorrectly shelved in Fiction. "I've got an anal probe that's also a transceiver. I could call on the aliens to bring the mother ship down and open fire on the zombies."

The ensuing silence was very impressive.

After a few seconds of stunned disbelief, Del waved at Whitey. "Thanks, Whitey, but I think we earthlings can handle this."

Just then Del heard an animal growl behind him, and he spun about, only to see that Harry was starting to transform. His face was already covered in even more fur, and lengthening into a muzzle; his clothes were splitting at the seams. "Quick—we gotta get him to the door."

"No, wait!" Whimsey called, and stepped up. He, too, was transforming, gaining an aura of mystique and sexual magnetism. Even Clyde suddenly found him attractive.

"Let me take him," Whimsey reasoned. "He can't hurt me."

Del acquiesced, and Whimsey grabbed the changing Harry, hustling him toward the front door. Jason and Lisa had already removed the nails from the table, and were sliding it up to allow access to the door. Del ran up, dodging a snapping bite from the lupine Harry, and positioned himself by the door.

"Wait," Whimsey counseled, and Del saw that, indeed, Harry was still changing, his arms contracting into his body to become front paws, his spine curling. "Wait . . . now!"

Del suddenly jerked the door open, and Whimsey stepped out into the zombie mob with the werewolf. "Good luck!" Del called after them, before slamming the door shut.

Almost immediately there came sounds of roaring, flesh-rending, and ripping outside. Del pressed an ear as close to the door as he dared, and he heard the sounds go on for a very long time. They didn't stop, but rather drifted away into the distance, as the vampire and werewolf evidently took down the zombies in an ever-increasing radius.

"Pete, I think we all owe you dinner for that one." Del grinned at the screenwriter.

The rest of the night passed without event. There were no more zombie noises outside. Of course the toilet did overflow once, and several authors demanded that Sue order more copies of their books in the future; but overall the group was surprisingly calm and collected.

At about 7:00 A.M. the next morning, Del awoke from where he'd fallen asleep in his office chair; Sue was shaking him. "What is it, was I snoring?"

"The sun's up outside. I think we should take a look," Sue said.

Del considered, then rubbed the sleep from his eyes, stretched, and rose. "Okay. Seems quiet." He moved to the door and listened for a long time, but heard nothing. He pulled the board partly aside and peeked outside, then looked back at the anxious Sue. "Here goes."

He pushed the door open and stepped out, timidly at first. He took a few more steps, and then they heard him exclaim, "Holy shit! I need a beer."

"What is it?!" cried Sue.

"It's a fuckin' mess out here! It's gonna take us forever to clean this up."

Sue joined him outside, as did a few of the others. There were zombie pieces everywhere—hands in the gutters, legs on the hoods of cars, even a torso across the outstretched arms of the fake Frankenstein monster that beckoned customers into the store. Del picked his way carefully through the chunks of meat and almost stumbled across the naked Harry, snoozing peacefully near what was left of the foliage that had once lined the storefront. Del knelt next to Harry and gently shook a shoulder. "Harry . . . hey, you okay?"

Harry looked up, belched, and went back to sleep.

Del grinned and stepped back. "Yep, he's just fine. Wonder what happened to Whimsey?"

Del jumped a mile as Whimsey called out from behind him, "I'm right here, Del!"

"Christ, Whimsey, don't *do* that!"

Whimsey actually blushed. "Sorry. At least we cleaned out most of this area of the city."

Del nodded. Behind him they were all pouring out onto the sidewalk now. Somebody pointed to a building just beyond Dark Delicacies. "Hey, check this out!"

Del turned to look and saw the name "DANE KETCHU-SON" written in blood on that store's front. "Guess he just had to get in one last signature," somebody noted.

"So, Del," Sue asked her husband, "what are we gonna do now?"

"I don't know," Del admitted. He thought for a second; then, looking around at those others who had survived, he noted, "Hey, we could be the last people left alive on earth, and that wouldn't be so bad, would it? I mean—the horror writers finally get their day!"

There were cheers and applause. There were also more than a few male eyes turned to Glory Osqui, the soft-core actress.

"C'mon"—Del motioned at the group— "I don't know about the rest of you, but I'm starvin'. Let's go see if we can bust into Smart & Final for a shopping spree."

And they did.

DEPOMPA

WILLIAM F. NOLAN

THE YEAR IS 1960.

His name is Terence Rodriguez Antonio DePompa, and he is on his way to death.

He is dressed in casual, wine-colored sports slacks and a white polo shirt. He wears doeskin driving gloves and a black leather cap. A knitted silk scarf, imported from India, whips out behind him like a white flag.

The winding Mexican highway he moves over runs to a dizzy height above the Gulf of California, with the water spreading to the horizon in a rippled sheet of sun-dazzled gold.

The car he drives is an open-cockpit Mercedes-Benz 300 SLR. Its 3-liter, eight-cylinder fuel-injected engine generates nearly 300 horsepower. At 7,000 rpm, this machine is capable of 170 mph. In a near-identical model, the legendary British ace Stirling Moss won the 1955 Mille Miglia, Italy's thousand-mile road race.

Terry had purchased the car directly from the Mercedes factory in Stuttgart after flying to Germany in his private jet. The tooled-leather bucket seat, in fire-engine red, was custom fitted to his five-foot-eight-inch frame (he looked much taller on the screen), and he had the Benz painted in U.S. racing colors: white, with a metallic blue stripe running along the hood and back deck. In the late 1950s, with this car, he'd competed during Speed Week in the Bahamas, winning the Nassau Trophy over a potent trio of Ferraris driven by the prime American racers, Phil Hill, Dan Gurney, and Carroll Shelby. Terry's best friend was killed during this event when a tire blew on the back straight, but the loss was minimal. Best friends were easy to come by.

Following the event, a fat banker from Chicago offered DePompa a million in cash for the Benz. Terry declined politely. That same weekend, over a rum punch in Blackbeard's Tavern, he was offered a factory ride in Europe with Ferrari, which he also declined. A reporter for the *Nassau Blade* asked him why he chose to risk his life in a racing car. Why didn't he just stick to acting?

Terry smiled for the camera (the smile that had fired the hearts of a million young women) and told the reporter: "Well, you see, I'm not sure whether I'm an actor who races or a racer who acts." It was a line he'd often used in the past to explain his passion for motor sport.

Of course, there were many other passions: bullfighting in Spain, bobsledding in Switzerland, big-game hunting in Africa, mountain climbing in Colorado—and beautiful women everywhere. (He'd tried a man once, at a gay bar in Detroit, but that had been a fiasco.)

Margaret, Terry's ex-wife, was working as a top fashion model when they met in New York at a cocktail party for Howard Hughes (who never showed up). She'd been gorgeous, and still retained her slim figure. She also retained their mansion on the Riviera, Terry's custom-designed white Cadillac, their lavishly furnished apartment in Bel Air, three million in diamonds, and their five-bedroom town house on Fifth Avenue. Terry had called her "a greedy bitch" in court, and she had called him "an egotistic bastard."

They understood each other.

DePompa ended up giving Margaret almost everything her lawyers asked for. Since he was now paid over half a million for each of his films, he felt no loss. Keep the bitch happy. Get her (and her lawyers) off his back. At least she was sterile, with no kids to muddy the water.

For Terry DePompa, the Benz is a sheer joy to drive, ballet-gliding the tight curves and devouring the long straights. He savors the raw power of this swift metal beast, all his to control, to dominate (in a way he could never dominate Margaret).

Terry smiles into the flow of heated wind, pressing his booted foot down harder on the gas pedal, feeling the engine surge. Control. Power and control.

He touches the slight scar along his left cheek, remembering the violent fight with Margaret in their Bel Air bedroom last Christmas when she'd raked his face with her sharp nails.

It is nearly dark now, and an approaching truck flashes its headlights at Terry—reminding him of the spotlights shining into his eyes at Grauman's Chinese in Hollywood for the premiere of *Pain World* when he'd placed his hands and shoe prints in the wet square of cement, with the sensual redhead from Vegas pressing her soft, tanned body against his.

He snaps on his high beams, illuminating the chalk white ribbon of cliff road stretching ahead. He enters a mile-long straight with a wickedly sharp U-curve at the end. Terry knows this road, has driven it many times.

His foot jabs harder on the gas pedal and the Benz responds. Roars. Bullet fast. And faster. Eating up the road at 100 . . . 120 . . . 130 . . . 140 . . . 150 . . .

The straight ends. The curve is here.

Terry smiles.

He doesn't slow down.

❖

In his small New York apartment, twenty-five-year-old
Dennie Holmes sits in his frayed pajamas on the faded rose
throw rug in front of the television set. His dark eyes are
intent on the screen as he leans forward to adjust the volume. The voice of newscaster Morley Purvis is now sharp
and clear:

". . . dead at twenty-four in the twisted, charred remains of his fast German sports car. Life had tragically
ended for the young screen idol, cinema's new golden boy,
who was—"

Dennie switches to another channel. This time the
newscaster is a woman:

". . . with the cause of the crash shrouded in mystery.
No tire marks were found on the cliff road, proving that
DePompa did not brake for the deadly hairpin curve. Could
he have suffered a sudden heart attack? His family physi-
cian, Dr. Mark Kalman, claims that DePompa's medical
history shows no evidence of heart disease. However, an
autopsy is not possible, since the actor's body was—"

A third channel.

Margaret DePompa, in her early thirties, is being interviewed at her New York town house. Slim, bottle-blonde,
and cat-featured, she dabs at her eyes with a dainty lace
handkerchief. Her voice is strained: ". . . but our silly little
quarrels meant nothing. Like any couple, we didn't *always*
agree—but we adored each other. Had Terry lived, I'm certain we would have remarried. He was (sobbing) the . . .
the whole world to me."

The interviewer, anchorman Len Lawson, moves the
mike closer to her. "Do you believe that your ex-husband
deliberately drove to his death?"

The reply is fierce and direct: "Never! Terry loved life far too much." And she continues to sob.

Lawson turns to the camera. "The life he loved so much and lived so fully began in poverty for Terence Rodriguez Antonio DePompa . . ."

The scene shifts to a small, squalid Mexican village. The camera moves along the dusty street to enter a crude adobe hut and center on a timeworn old woman. Her head is bowed, as she rocks listlessly back and forth in a wicker chair.

Lawson's voice-over tells us: "Little Terry DePompa grew up here, in this poverty-ridden Mexican village after the boy's father, an Irish-Italian bricklayer, deserted the family when Terry was three. His mother, Maria, mourns her famous son."

The interviewer's voice is soft and gentle: "What was he like, Mrs. DePompa? Can you tell us about your Terry?"

"He . . . don't like play . . . with other boys. He . . . many times run away . . . like burro . . . My Terry . . . he never happy here. Run away to Mexicali for job . . ."

The scene now shifts to DePompa himself, speaking directly into the camera during an earlier interview:

"At fourteen I was working in a coffin maker's shop in Mexicali and spending all my free time at the local movie house, dreaming that someday I might be up there, on that silver screen. Two years later, at sixteen, I got a job on a lemon grove in Chula Vista, on the U.S. side of the border. The owner's wife took what you might call a 'personal interest' in me." A knowing grin for the camera. "She paid my way into Dave Corey's acting class in New York—and that was the start of everything."

The screen features DePompa in class, enacting a scene, fists clenched, eyes blazing.

The documentary now centers on Dave Corey.

"He was a natural," says Corey. "Terry utilized his inner pain as a weapon. Watching him was like being struck by lightning. He shocked you. I knew he'd be great. From the moment he walked into my class, I knew he'd be great."

Lawson's voice-over again, introducing Sidney Shibinson of Universal Pictures.

"Me, I got an instinct for talent," says Shibinson. "When I spotted DePompa doing a scene in Corey's class, I right away knew for a fact that he could be the next Brando. We signed him for Universal that same week and put him into *Drive the Blade Deep*, *The Black-Leather Boys*, and *Restless Rebel*. And bingo!—he becomes famous overnight and makes himself a ton of money."

The voice-over: "Money and instant fame opened many doors for young Terry DePompa, allowing him to experience life on a multitude of exciting levels . . ."

Action photos flash across the screen: Terry on a bucking bronco . . . executing a veronica with a bullfighter's cape . . . speed-jumping a wide ditch on a dirt bike . . . whipping down a vertical ski slope . . . dueling with a masked opponent . . . firing a shotgun from a duck blind . . . mountain climbing in the high Rockies . . . blasting a tennis ball over a net . . . skydiving from a private plane . . . surfing the crest of a massive wave . . . taking the checkered flag in his 300 SLR—always with a beautiful woman in the background.

Lawson once again: "No screen idol since James Dean has ever touched the lives of so many young people . . . "

A nervous teenage girl stands in front of a DePompa poster in the lobby of a movie theater, wearing a T-shirt bearing Terry's smiling face.

Her voice is intense: "My girlfriend and me, we saw *Restless Rebel* fourteen times." She fumbles for words. "Terry was like . . . like a religion to us. . . . He was us!" A tear rolls down her cheek. "Why did he have to die? Why?"

Lawson speaks directly into the camera: "Indeed, there are many unanswered questions regarding the tragic death of Terry DePompa. But one thing is certain: His bright image will continue to burn forever in the hearts of those who—"

Dennie snaps off the TV. He begins to pace the room, hands fisted, his face flushed. "Damn!" he says under his breath. Then, louder: "Damn! Damn! Damn!"

✿

The girl moves back from the table, eyes wide, betraying her fear. She keeps moving away from Dennie as he advances on her.

"Dennie, I—"

"Shut up, bitch! Didn't I tell you to shut your lousy trap?"

"But you lied. You didn't keep your word."

Dennie slaps her hard, across the mouth, bringing tears to her eyes.

"You cheap little tramp," he snarls, "this is the last time you'll ever—"

"Hold it! Hold it!" Dave Corey mounts the raised platform, shaking his head. Several other young men and women, all aspiring actors, are seated in folding wooden chairs, forming a half-circle around the platform.

"What's wrong now?" Dennie demands.

"You're doing him again," Corey declares. "The way you walk, the angle of your head . . . even the way you slapped Susan. All him. All DePompa."

A strained silence.

"True art in acting is never achieved by using borrowed emotions. Each actor must find that individual truth within himself or herself. Imitation is not creation."

Dennie stares at him. "You figure I haven't got it, right?"

"I never said that. You possess genuine talent, but you're

blocking it. You are walking in Terry DePompa's shadow. The trouble is, you won't—"

Dennie cuts in, his voice edged with anger. "The trouble is I've wasted my time listening to you spout a lot of useless crap. I don't need you to tell me what I am—and Terry didn't, either. So I don't happen to fit your mold. Well, Corey, to hell with your mold, and to hell with you!"

And he stalks from the room, slamming the heavy soundproof door behind him.

⬥

Margaret DePompa's town house is alive with a babble of voices, the chiming of cocktail glasses, the tinkle of iced scotch, and the muted cry of a jazz trumpet.

"Some people think that New Orleans jazz is outdated," Margaret tells the mayor of New York, "but I find it liberating."

The rotund little man nods. "It's part of our native culture, and native culture is never out of date."

A servant approaches, hesitant to break into the flow of conversation. Margaret turns to him. "What is it, Jenson?"

"A young gentleman to see you," says Jenson. "He is presently waiting in the foyer."

"And what does this young gentleman wish to see me about?"

"He did not say."

"Name?"

"Dennis Holmes."

She frowns. "Never heard of him."

"He seems quite . . . intense."

She turns back to her guest. "You'll excuse me, Mr. Mayor?"

"Of course, my dear." He glances toward the bar. "I'll just have another glass of your excellent Chablis. Good for the digestion."

And Margaret follows Jenson to the foyer.

✧

"I saw you on television," Terry is saying, "in a newscast about Terry—and I just had to meet you." He hesitates, nervous and uncertain. "I know this is an intrusion, but Terry . . . well, he meant a lot to me."

"Did you know him?" Margaret asks.

"Not personally. I mean, we never actually met. But I've watched all his movies, and I've read everything about him . . . the cover story in *Newsweek* . . . the interview in *Life* . . . I even saw him race once, at the airport in Palm Springs. He's been kind of . . . a role model for me, if you know what I mean."

"Yes, I know. Terry affected many young people that way." She regards him intently. "Your hair . . . you wear it exactly as he did. And that red jacket you're wearing . . ."

"Just like the one he wore in *Restless Rebel*," Dennie says. "I got it from a novelty store in Hollywood. They had it in the window—along with posters from *The Ravaged One*, *Dawn Is for Dying*, and *Fury on Friday*. I got 'em all."

"You're taller than Terry," she says, "but you have his eyes."

Dennie smiles. "Thanks."

". . . and his smile."

He's embarrassed. "Well . . . guess I'd better be going." Dennie extends his right hand. "Been great meeting you, Mrs. DePompa."

Margaret takes his hand, clasping it firmly. Her fingers are warm. "Don't be in such a hurry," she says softly.

✧

After lovemaking, they talk quietly in Margaret's bed, fitted together, flesh to flesh, her naked hip against his leg.

"Tell me about him," says Dennie. "I need to know what

Terry was really like." He hesitates. "Was he . . . a good lover?"

"At first he was overwhelming. It was like making love to a panther. But that didn't last. Everything had to be fresh for Terry, new and fresh. And that included sex. He was never satisfied for long with any one woman, and I was no exception. When he grew bored with our lovemaking, he substituted violence and pain for sex. That's when I knew it was over."

"But didn't you love him? On TV . . . you seemed so broken up over his death."

She smiles. "Quite an act, huh? I was just giving the public what they want." She pauses. "Did I love Terry? Sure, at first, with that smile of his . . . those eyes." She traces a slow finger along Dennie's jaw. "You're incredibly like him—the way he was in the beginning, four years ago."

"Why did . . . I mean, I have to know. Why did he—"

"—kill himself? It was inevitable. Terry was an addictive thrill-seeker, always pushing closer and closer to the limit. When he made *Hell Run*, the film on bobsledding in Switzerland, he broke both ankles when the sled clipped a tree. In Madrid, he was gored by a bull with the horn barely missing a main artery. He'd never let them use a stand-in. Did all the stunts himself. Used to drive the producers crazy. Terry fractured his left shoulder on a dirt bike running a motocross at Indio. Then, just two months ago, his plane crash-landed in the San Bernardino mountains. It burned, but Terry got out in time."

"You're saying he had a death wish?"

"Damn right I am. No question about it. All of the other thrills finally wore off until only death itself remained. He *had* to taste it, savor it, experience it. The ultimate thrill. So he did."

Her fingers ran erotically along Dennie's naked spine. Her voice is soft. "Would you like to see where he died?"

"In Mexico—near the Gulf?"

"Yes. Just above San Felipe, his favorite hideout. Ratty little fishing village. No one ever goes there. When things got too stressed, he'd drive down there from L.A." Her eyes burn into his. "I could take you . . . in Terry's white Cadillac. It's garaged in Beverly Hills. Would you like to go?"

"Oh, yes," says Dennie. "Christ, yes!"

❖

The flight from New York to Los Angeles is smooth. Perfect weather all the way. In Beverly Hills, the white Cadillac is serviced and made ready for the trip into Mexico. Dennie is hyper. For him, this is a dream come true; he can barely contain his excitement.

On the morning of their departure, Margaret appears in a trim white pantsuit, wearing a white straw bonnet to keep off the sun. ("I don't tan, I burn.")

She takes the wheel for the trip down 99 to Calexico. Jokes with the uniformed border guard who waves them through, then takes Dennie to what she terms "the only halfway-decent restaurant in Mexicali."

He doesn't like the noisy border town with its garish purple facades, peeling wooden storefronts, and dirt-blackened neon signs.

"Why are we stopping here?" he asks. "Why can't we eat later, on the road?"

"I thought you'd want to talk to old man Montoya. At his coffin shop."

Dennie brightens. "Where Terry worked when he was fourteen?"

"Right," she says. "If the old bastard's still alive, you can ask him about Terry."

"Terrific!"

❖

They order grilled sea bass with stewed pinto beans, which is served with a large basket of corn tortillas, topped off by two bottles of warm Mexican beer.

Next on the agenda: the coffin maker's shop of Carlos Montoya.

The shop's exterior is painted in funereal black in keeping with the owner's trade.

Lettered on the door: COFFINS MADE TO ORDER

As they enter, Montoya steps forward to greet them. He is toothless, the color of worn leather, needing a shave and a new frame for his taped glasses. He wears ragged coveralls.

"You require the services of Carlos Montoya? A loved one to bury, perhaps?"

"We came to ask you about a boy who once worked here," says Dennie.

"Ah!" The old man chuckles, a dry, rasping sound. "You wish me to speak of Antonio. Many others have come here to ask of him. My fee is fixed. If you pay, I talk."

Margaret hands him money, and he leads them to the rear of the musty shop, past coffins of all sizes, many unfinished. Uncut boards, smelling of sawdust, lean against the walls.

In his dark office Montoya gestures them toward a pair of cane-bottom chairs, seating himself behind a desk cluttered with hammers and saws.

"The world knew him as Terry," says the old man, beginning a speech he has obviously delivered many times, "but I knew him as Antonio. He came to me as a boy of fourteen, eager to learn the trade of a coffin maker."

Montoya opens a desk drawer, removes a photo, and hands it to Dennie. In the photo, Terry DePompa is lying in a coffin, posing as a corpse, eyes closed, hands folded across his chest.

Montoya continues: "I gave him shelter, an honest wage, and shared my knowledge with him. Antonio was quick to learn. I taught him many things."

Margaret cuts in: "You taught him, all right. To lie and

swear and steal. He told me all about you—about your cheating ways and your filth and your foul women." She gestures toward a standing coffin. "You'll soon be in one of these yourself, and when you are, who will come to your funeral, eh? Ask yourself that, old man."

And she herds Dennie from the shop.

Back in the car, the boy is silent. He looks stunned and shaken.

"Well, what did you expect?" asks Margaret.

"I thought . . . that he . . . would be different."

"Different? He's a corrupt old fool. Terry despised him."

Silence. Then Dennie asks: "How long will it take us to reach San Felipe?"

"Four or five hours," she replies. "It's at the edge of the Gulf where the highway dead-ends. We should make it before dark."

With Margaret again at the wheel, threading their way slowly through streets jammed with overloaded fruit and vegetable trucks, bicycles, ancient taxicabs, and sweat-crowded buses, they finally clear the border town and roll onto the long stretch of open highway leading to the Gulf.

Out of Mexicali, they pass the high green arch of the Funeraria Santa Elenaz with its irregular rows of pink-and-blue gravestones. As the sun descends in heated slowness down the western sky the Mexican scenery is spectacular. Rolling hills thrust up like vast brown fists, separated by wide plateaus and dry lakes. Endless sand dunes and spike cactus line the highway to either side. A dead cat lies sprawled on the road shoulder.

A sudden sharp report. Like a gunshot. The white Cad swerves as Margaret fights the wheel, braking to a stop on the gravel verge. "We just blew a tire," she says.

"I thought all the tires were checked before we left."

"Yep, and they were perfect. Obviously we hit something on the road."

They get out with the doors automatically locking behind them. A long sliver of blue bottle glass has penetrated the side wall of a rear tire. Margaret turns to get the keys for the trunk. "Damn!"

"What's wrong?"

"All the doors are locked, and I left the keys in the ignition." She sighs. "But it's okay. I keep a spare set taped inside the front fender."

Crouching, she fumbles for the extra keys, using them to open the driver's door, then retaping them back inside the fender. "In case we ever lock ourselves out again."

She removes a jack and a tire iron from the trunk. "You any good at changing tires?"

Dennie shrugs. "Dunno. I've never had to."

"I'll do it. No big deal."

She jacks up the car, removes the damaged tire, and puts on the spare. Checks her watch. "Close, but I think we can still make it before dark."

Hurriedly, she tosses the jack and tire iron into the rear seat. "And away we go," she says, gunning back onto the highway.

✧

Hours pass as the sun dips lower in the sky. Ahead of them, a jagged rise of black mountains lends a luna texture to the land: raw, alien, hostile.

The Cad is now moving along the winding mountain road above San Felipe.

"There's a long straight about a mile ahead," she tells Dennie. "That's where he sailed off into the blue, at the end of the straight."

Dennie sits rigid, excited, wanting and not wanting to see the spot where Terry died.

They enter the straight. Dennie is silent, tensed, waiting.

"Here's where it happened," says Margaret, stopping the car a few yards short of the tight U-curve. "This is where he went over the edge."

They stand at the lip of the cliff, looking down. "It's a long drop," says Dennie, shivering at the mental image.

"With lots of sharp boulders at the bottom," says Margaret. "When he hit, the gas tank split and his car burned."

"Was he dead when he hit bottom?"

"We'll never know."

They get back in the car and motor on to San Felipe.

The white Cadillac, now gray with dust, reaches the small fishing village—a scatter of rude shacks along a short main street (unpaved), boasting a half-dozen paint-blistered storefronts. The village is nearly deserted. A few local residents lounge in shadowed doorways, staring out at the strangers.

The sun is almost down along the horizon. A dozen small fishing boats ply the red-gold sunset waters, bobbing like corks, their nets out for the evening's catch.

"It's getting dark," says Dennie. "Is there a motel here?"

"One. Just one. But I'm sure they have a vacancy. First, I need a drink."

They leave the locked car, walking to the village cantina located at the end of the street in a weathered two-story building. A rusted Coca-Cola sign is tacked to the front door.

Inside a drift of guitar music reaches them from a cob-webbed ceiling speaker. Three young fishermen are hunched over cards in a far corner of the room. The air is hot and musty, retaining the heat of the day, smelling of sour beer and strong Mexican tobacco.

The owner, a stout little red-faced man in a stained apron, takes their order. Over two Carta Blancas and a plate of stale pretzels, they talk.

"I don't see why Terry would ever come to a dumb place like San Felipe," says Dennie, sipping his beer; it's sour, but cold. "There's nothing here."

"That is exactly what he wanted to find—nothing," says Margaret. "Terry came here to get away from the spotlight."

"It's a hellhole," says Dennie.

"Gotta pee," declares Margaret. "Hold the fort."

As she passes the table where the three young Mexicans are playing cards one of them reaches out to grab her leg. She stops, says something in soft Spanish. The fisherman laughs, lets her go.

Five minutes later she's back with Dennie.

"What was that all about?"

She grins. "Just a friendly pass."

"He had his hand on your leg."

"Yeah, that was nice. He has soft hands."

"You liked it?"

"I didn't mind."

Dennie stares at her.

She smiles. A cat's smile.

§

The motel mattress is thin and lumpy. Coil springs jab sharply into Dennie's back as he sleepily shifts position. He opens his eyes, reaching out to touch Margaret. She's not there. He's alone in the bed. It's 3:00 A.M. by his watch. He gets up to check the bathroom.

Empty. Where is she? Where could she have gone at this time of night in a place like San Felipe?

Dennie slips into a pair of pants, pulls a sweater over his pajama top, and leaves the motel. He pads barefoot through the milky sand. The waters of the Gulf lap softly against the beach, and a gull cries out in the night like a lost child.

Then: rough male voices. Laughter. *Margaret's* laughter. Coming from a nearby tarpaper shack, its lighted window a pale yellow square in the darkness.

Dennie reaches the shack, peering through the glass. Christ! Margaret is inside, in bed with the three fishermen from the cantina. Naked. They are all naked.

She looks up as Dennie appears at the door. Glares. "Go away! Get the hell away!"

The three Mexicans grin at him. One has a gold tooth.

Dennie takes a step toward the bed. "God, but you're rotten."

Her mouth twists in anger. Her eyes are afire. "I *said*, get the hell away!"

Dennie looks agonized. "Why are you doing this to me?"

"To you?" snaps Margaret, scorn in her tone. "That's a laugh. Don't you get it? You walk like him, wear his clothes, even try to make love like him. But it's all a joke. You're not real. You don't exist. You're just a reflected image from a broken mirror."

Her words cut and stab at him. Dennie reels back under her verbal assault, swings around, and stumbles from the shack.

He staggers down the beach, tears clouding his vision. He's numb, directionless, running blindly toward the center of the village. The area is tomb-quiet, dark as spilled ink, with the moon hidden in a clouded sky.

Now Dennie pauses, blinking up at a dusty facade ringed by broken, time-blackened marquee bulbs that long ago spelled out a name: CINEMA JIMINEZ.

Dennie listens. Sounds echo faintly from within the ancient movie house. Someone—or something—lives in the time-haunted interior.

Peeling a loose board from the door, Dennie pushes his way inside, drawn to the sounds. The main auditorium is a shamble of broken seats, discarded trash, and buckled cement.

But the screen is alive:

Dennie gasps as Terry DePompa's head fills the screen. The actor's eyes blaze down at Dennie. Then the mouth gapes wide in a flow of manic laughter. Insane, cacophonous laughter.

Dennie claps both hands to his ears, squeezing his eyes shut against the frightful apparition. When he opens them, seconds later, the cracked, dust-hazed screen is blank and silent.

As if pursued by demons, Dennie runs from the theater, thrusting himself along the main street. He enters a wooden graveyard filled with the decaying corpses of abandoned fishing boats, beached like dead whales, their ruptured hulls black and flaking from wind and sun.

Dennie stumbles forward, falling weakly against the side of *La Ordina*. The boat's interior is gutted, with a rusted engine housing, like a surreal coffin, buried within the rotted hull.

Dennie blinks, staring downward—and now there is an *actual* coffin inside the hull. Fourteen-year-old Terry De-Pompa lies inside, eyes closed, hands folded across his chest—exactly as he appeared in the photo at Montoya's shop.

Then . . . a change. The body of the actor slowly ripple-dissolves into the corpse of the adult DePompa, with half of his face torn away and broken bones protruding obscenely from his charred, crushed body.

Frozen in shock, Dennie continues to stare downward—but the horror has not ended. The corpse-figure changes once again, and it is now Dennie himself who lies in the dank coffin, his body broken and charred.

"Oh, God!" the boy cries out in agony, wheeling away from the boats to stagger up the beach—back to the shack of the three fishermen.

He bolts inside, grabs Margaret by one arm, and drags her, naked and screaming, along the sand to the parked Cadillac.

"I know what you want now," he sobs, "what you brought me down here for. Well, I'm going to give it to you. I'm going to play your sick little game to the end."

He retrieves the spare set of car keys from the fender well, yanks open the passenger door, and pushes Margaret inside. Firing the engine, he roars out of the village onto the mountain highway in a cloud of dust and gravel.

"You're crazy!" shouts Margaret. "Stop the car. Let me out!"

"No, this time *I'm* in charge."

The Cadillac rapidly gains speed, high beams slicing the dark, unraveling the road ahead. The speed is now far too great for Margaret to risk jumping from the passenger seat.

Dennie powers around the serpentine turns, finally reaching the long straight leading to the final curve. He floors the gas pedal—and the car leaps forward . . . 70 . . . 80 . . . 90 . . . 100 . . .

"You want it, and you'll get it." Dennie shouts .

"Want what?" Margaret's voice is frenzied. "*What*?"

"You want to die. You want to share Terry's death, experience it for yourself, share the horror of it, the thrill of it—to end your jaded, empty existence. That's why you brought me here, for *this*!"

They are now almost to the end of the straight, with the white Cadillac bulleting the road, a ghost-rocket heading for destruction.

Margaret twists around to snatch up the tire iron from the backseat, lunging forward to slam it against Dennie's skull. As he slumps sideways, his foot slips from the gas pedal. She jams her foot hard down on the brake, gripping the wheel for control.

The car whips madly across the road as its speed drops to 80 . . . 70 . . . 60 . . . slower, slower. With the U-curve rushing at them, Margaret claws open the passenger door and jumps.

The rolling impact stuns her; road gravel lacerates her bare skin, but she survives, staggering to her feet, bleeding from a dozen cuts. Numbly, she watches the still-moving Cadillac reach the end of the straight and dip over the edge of the cliff road, tumbling down to explode on the rocks below.

Margaret walks slowly to the drop-off point, looking down. Flames illumine the darkness, and smoke swirls around her from the burning machine.

I didn't have the guts, she tells herself. *I wanted to die,*

*just the way Terry did, to achieve what he achieved—the ulti-
mate thrill—but I didn't have the guts. Now I've lost the
chance. And I'll have to live with that . . .* she continues to
stare down at the flaming wreckage . . . *for the rest of my life.*

THE PYRE
AND OTHERS

DAVID J. SCHOW

L EGEND, RUMOR, MYTH had it that the book could
influence dreams. A reader could weather gruesome
adventure, achieve a perverse sexual grail, or drown in a
transport of raw dread. It was even possible that the book
could set you free.

That was what got Franklin started—the elemental
power of hearsay, left to gestate, tended almost as an after-
thought, or lapsed hobby. The way it went was this: You put
the book under your pillow (so it was said), and when you
slept (if you slept), you would be transported into the
dream realm of one of the stories inside the book. Some of
the stories were odd and fanciful, the way you'd like a
quirky dream to be. The catch was that you could not pick
the story that invaded your sleeping mind—libidinous free-
for-all, or a feverish nightmare that just might tip you
over . . . into a padded cell, if you lived. This Russian
roulette proposition, and its obscure proofs through years
of vague documentation, was the central attraction. If more
people had *heard* of the book, its story—its most important

story, the one not part of its table of contents—might have assumed the status of modern urban legend. Nobody Franklin knew had ever heard of the book, which is how he grew to become a zealot about the whole thing.

Franklin Bryant was a faculty member of a midsized liberal arts curriculum, which is to say he earned a paycheck by instructing college students in high school English, while he hacked away at a dissertation objective that might lend him more credibility as a scholar. Academic brownie points. The new semester loomed seven weeks distant, and Franklin did not know whether he had the resolve to stare down another class-load of bright-eyed, entry-level nitwits. Room after room of collegiate-coddled warm bodies with empty heads and a predator's sense of the easy fix. Learning, here, was a social activity, not an intellectual one, and Franklin had let his syllabus decay into rote. Trying to teach college students the finer pleasures of twentieth-century literature was akin to arguing grammar with a beagle. His Lit 106 cannon fodder came trained to memorize (without learning), pass tests (without extrapolating), and trade bored hours for paper validation (without thinking), and he honestly questioned his capacity to withstand another year of that treadmill. The janitors never quite got the dust out of the corners of the molding on the lecterns. Some of that dust was decades old and probably predated his contract. It had solidified into layers of gray permanence; strata you could not chip with a fingernail. It would be there when he resigned, and probably still be there when he died.

The book was called *The Pyre and Others*, by J. Arthur Aldridge. Subtitled *Tales of Disturbance*, it was the writer's only published collection. The short stories comprising its contents were commonly available. Some were even posted online. Others had sifted down through "classic" anthologies and annuals. None were rare. Most were presented semiapologetically, as oddments. Franklin had reread them all many times, and amassed an Aldridge shelf of relevant works—earlier stories, published less significantly as the last gasp of the post–World War II pulps ceded market dominance to a burgeoning of "men's magazines." He scavenged biographical leftovers, including several brief encyclopedia entries, and a copy of the last-known printing of the complete collection, by Royal Ransom Press (London, 1981). Franklin found this last during one of his used-bookstore trolls, used-bookstores themselves teetering on the rim of extinction—a development that always felt ominous, giving Franklin an ever-present sense of impending loss, though he had no idea what to do with the feeling. None of his researches provided any relevant clues to the enigma of the *The Pyre*'s infamy, although the legend itself (such as it was) bore a mention in passing, by the Brit who emceed the book's final republication to date.

This fellow, a former partner in Royal Ransom and earnest champion of the obscure, was named Jonah Siritis, and his introduction to the 1981 reprint attempted to corral the scant scraps of information about J. Arthur Aldridge into one of those arguments why you should read an outdated writer, today. During the late 1950s and early 1960s, Siritis argued, Aldridge's work influenced many writers whose names you'd know (and laboriously did he list them), while Aldridge himself never brushed fame. He had once been married. He had once lived in New Orleans. Photographs were hard to come by since he had been published during a time when pictures of writers were more a luxury than a sales necessity, and worse, the man had no public persona to promote. Similarly, he never wrote editorial ephemera that might divulge something personal; papers, notes, and correspondence were rare, brief, and cryptic. He spoke through his stories, and wrote only short fiction— some thirty known stories in all, with *The Pyre and Others* as his crescendo. He died in 1965 at age thirty-two . . . or in

1963 at age thirty-four . . . or possibly as late as 1967, aged thirty. His career as a writer had basically died by 1961. That was the year he had handed the manuscript copy of *The Pyre* to a small press in Chicago—for free.

Black Rhododendron Press had specialized in the backwaters of "the Eerie and the Weird." Their typesetting was arcane, but usually clean of errors. To the modern eye, the font they employed looked skeletal and basic; probably slugged by hand for whatever web-offset printing was the cheapest in those olden days. The first edition of *The Pyre* was hardbound in thick green cloth boards of an odd trim size—approximately 5¼ by 7½ inches—that made it look like a pocket hymnal. Its pages were rough and clunky; Siritis noted that the book "resisted riffling," and tended "to fall open at unexpected places." Its rudimentary dust jacket hinted at cut-rate deal for paper and the jacket illustration was black-and-white only. It depicted a graveyard, hooded figures, and the swirling flames of the eponymous pyre, all in an embarrassing, amateurish style that suggested a teenager's grasp of Lovecraftian horror. According to Siritis, the book jacket was so unwieldy that it "traveled"—when you opened the book, the jacket fell off; when you shelved the book, the jacket always scooted up, even if you locked the damned thing into a Broadart sleeve.

This, then, was the edition that supposedly invaded your dreams, if you were foolish or curious enough. Black Rhododenron, 1961. Limited to an edition of 500 copies, 20 of which were given to J. Arthur Aldridge as compensation (and presumed destroyed—guess how—upon Aldridge's death by, quote, "a close friend"). Fewer than 200 copies sold. When Black Rhododendron fell apart in 1962 (so said Jonah Siritis), at least another 150 stock copies vanished from whatever basement warehoused them . . . nearly half a century ago. Jonah Siritis actually owned one of these first editions, obtained after much travail in 1995.

Based on some textural differences he had discovered between the original and the reprint, he was presently pushing for a new, revised edition.

As frustrating as the Internet could be for a seeker after Aldridge, the love/hate boon of e-mail permitted Franklin to ask Jonah Siritis the obvious question directly: *So, did you try it?*

Not me, sir, came the reply. *No bravery in that direction, I'm afraid.*

A former librarian, Siritis maintained a continuing interest in posting a definitive online bibliography of Aldridge—if denied a biography—and through contact with him, Franklin began to believe he held the bones of his own dissertation. That was what had kept him going through his previous year at the college. His own warm little niche in the Lit cave, provisioned with a quest, and yes, a mate. Every semester, out of several hundred students, there were always one or two who evinced a sparkle of hope, and if they were female, and not outright beasts, Franklin usually advantaged them so he could have what normal people called a sex life. It was an accepted perk of the educational ladder. He never had to leave them; they always stopped calling when they moved on to other classes, other targets. It was all part of the learning experience.

Serenity—that was really her name—had hauled stakes at the conclusion of the previous term. Of Brazilian extraction, she had possessed a nearly insatiable curiosity coupled with a sexy shyness that could be devastating. Large, liquid brown eyes and a yard of lush dark hair. Cute little round glasses. The curves of classic sculpture, and an ass you could really grab hold of. Spiral notebooks filled with doodles and punishable girly poetry. She had been ripe and willing, a healthy divertissement, until she returned home to São Paulo. Usually it was easy for Franklin to write off his exes, but for some reason he could not codify, Serenity lingered in his memory, as though she had died tragically, instead of hanging around to posit uncomfortable questions about the abuses of love, or departing with no more drama than a sterile handshake. Franklin kept the picture he had taken of her naked, sleeping. Perhaps one day he would allow it to inspire him to write something.

Without Serenity to squander his off-hours, Franklin shifted sights to Aldridge, in a different kind of pursuit. His entree to Siritis—his introduction—had been a no-brainer. You could use genre geeks if you appealed to their vanity and massaged their basic addictions, the quirks that made them self-appointed keepers of the flame. Siritis proved personable and generous (he always answered e-mails within twenty-four hours, and Zeus only knew what he did for an actual living after quitting the library biz—if he had a life, at all). Siritis had subsequently provided Franklin with not only the lowdown on the first edition of *The Pyre,* but a front-to-back photocopy of the whole book, the original.

But photocopies didn't work, where the preternatural was concerned, or the lure of forbidden insight.

Now Franklin could see for himself (as Siritis had claimed) that three of the stories in *The Pyre and Others* were substantially different—and *longer*—than the versions included in the 1981 reprint.

In "The Sacrifice," a woman suffering an unspecified terminal malady speaks to the engagement ring of her dead betrothed, and the ring seems to answer, in intentionally ridiculous rhyming couplets, with *"the voice of some jocular, speaking blossom from a fairy tale."* Laugh all you want—by the close of the story, ten people have died ghastly and point-specific deaths, before the woman's own ticking clock tolls its last.

Aldridge's only obvious rumination on suicide was called "Chekov's Gun"—principally a long interior monologue by possibly the most depressed protagonist on the planet. When the gun finally does its job (with double-ought buckshot, administered orally, no less), the character discovers that the point-blank obliteration of his brain is not the end of his consciousness.

"The Sirens of Westcott," in the original edition, was nearly a third longer. It dealt with the chemical dynamic of sexual attraction, but its theme was bad choices based on physical beauty. Its protagonist, Herman Banks, is a goatish man expert in what Aldridge termed *"the highly unstable hobby of technically proficient intromission."* Hirsute and lumpen, he deludes himself that his goal is love, not lovemaking, but his true satisfaction comes from subjugating the comely women of Westcott Village to his ugliness. Once transported by the erotic rapture of his expertise in bed, the women are summarily discarded by Herman. When several of his victims start comparing notes about *"their greatest sexual experience,"* they band together to entrap him . . . but first, they have to convince the town's most unattainable beauty to act as bait. As Siritis wrote in his summary, "If sex is Hell, then this is a downward plummet with a stop at each agonizing level and circle of damnation."

All three stories had garnered letters of reader complaint to *Esquire* and *Playboy*, where they appeared originally. The first was a shameless manual for murdering your loved ones, it was claimed. The second was an equally bald handbook for suicide. And the third simply did not endorse a happy-go-lucky concept of sex, *at all*. The unexpurgated texts were fairly wince-inducing. Franklin could feel himself flinch at certain passages, and thrilled to the sensation.

He leafed through the unwieldy photocopies, which Siritis had scanned in two-page spreads and Velo-bound on the left side. He refreshed himself on the brooding puzzle-traps of "Shadows Within the Cage." "Wash, Rinse, Repeat" was fairly famous, in that it had been optioned for adaptation by Alfred Hitchcock's production company, Shamley, as an episode of the popular television series—only to remain unproduced. Aldridge did make it into the magazine that bore Hitchcock's name, however, with "The Man Who Blew a Fuse," "The Mortuary Student," and "Box No. 262." The latter fomented more letters of protest that most of the magazine's readership considered long overdue.

An unpublished story, original to *The Pyre*, was "The Narrative of Dr. Shackle and Mr. Lye," apparently an honest attempt at humor by Aldridge, although what the eponymous pair do to their victims was anything but a laff riot. It seesawed between elbow-jabbing one-liners and almost clinically detached slaughter and corpse disposal. It predated quippy slasher movies by two decades, but Franklin found its cumulative effect hard to shake. It was not a wallow in florid adjectives and forensic trivia, gushed off with low-brow, adolescent glee. It was stately. Its impact was that of a literary writer tackling a subject normally deemed taboo for literary writers—well, a "literary writer" who also knew an awful lot about bondage and submission, at any rate. Weird.

Both "Her Idea of Beautiful" and "A Most Necessary Evil" had *also* been censored heavily. Already poisoned at the prestige magazines, Aldridge had trickled down through their imitators, the bargain-basement pretenders, the soon-to-be porn rags. Yet even they had "problems" and "suggestions." It was easy to see why no mainstream publisher would touch Aldridge in the early 1960s. The sex was too honest, exceeding the de facto "frankness" of the time; the narratives were often sacrilegiously profane; the violence was better suited to a world that was—then—over a decade distant, half a war into the future.

You should have written a novel, Franklin thought. *Then they'd be calling you the William S. Burroughs of horror, today.*

Aldridge's envelope pushing encountered no such obstacles at *The Haunt*, a micropress journal published irregularly by a gang of "devotees of the Dark" in Milwaukee.

Most of the editorial column in that issue (#5) was subsumed in fawning gratitude that Mr. Aldridge would even consent to submit "Hugo's Big Blunder." The staff and the readership were familiar with Aldridge's earlier work. When more was solicited eagerly, Aldridge never responded, and the magazine folded two issues later.

That was what writers did, thought Franklin: They pushed envelopes. They knew about submission.

Then there was "The Pyre" itself. Also original to the collection. According to Siritis, Aldridge had submitted *two* versions of the typescript to Black Rhododendron, and apparently—ridiculously—the version used in 1961 never made it into the later printing.

From one of Jonah Siritis' e-mails:

Not much was known about J.A.A., but it doesn't take a genius to conclude that he loved toying with anonymity, and misleading his readers. Maybe he did it to confuse future bibliographers—that whole Imp of the Perverse bent. As you can see from the various encyclopedia entries (cursory, at best), even his birth and death dates have question marks on them. It is a matter of parish record that he married Marie Topaz Severin in November 1953, although by mid-1955 she doesn't seem to be in the picture anymore, and I can find no proof of separation, divorce, or her death. You should also know that shortly after his interment in St. Louis #1, his crypt was plundered by vandals and then knocked down in one of the flash floods common to that area. I checked personally, some ten years ago, during my first trip to the States. J.A.A. is listed in the plot registry, but no evidence of his grave can be seen. I don't think he "went under," or faked his death, however. I interviewed a number of people who attended his funeral, including Stoney Beauchamp, who burned J.A.A.'s personal library

and files, per written instructions (more's the loss!).
Stoney's wife, Lillian, emphasized two things about
J.A.A.: his deep love for his absent Marie Topaz, and
his determined frustration at feeling creatively "hob-
bled," as he put it.

Maybe he murdered her, Franklin wrote back.
I don't think so, replied Siritis. *He loved her too much.*

That was another thing that was "known" about Aldridge:
the sort of detail that would never make it into a reference
book. It was obvious from rereading the guy's fiction:
Aldridge was *very* familiar with women. Cloistered cre-
atives usually doled out hammer-thumbed erotica based
solely on their bovine spouses. Neophytes excreted saccha-
rine, or the sniggering jerk off of boys playing sex mo-chine.
Aldridge wrote like an addict trying to master all he knew of
a ceaselessly mesmerizing alien species. Their form, their
shape, their palette of intimacies. The extrusion of male
through female fascinated him. Women and men, utterly different, fit together just so, in limitless recombination of his
gender with other humans who looked similar, but were not
built the same. Their outsides could lie (one sex, with a bit of
artifice, could pass for its opposite). But the insides told truer
stories; the anatomical insides, followed by the emotional
ones. Aldridge had continually sought some breakthrough
frequency to make his communications more vital.

By some unsuspected agency, thought Franklin, perhaps
the sheer *tone* of the book overwhelmed the susceptible, and
gave rise to the legend about its ability to empower dreams.

Franklin was eager to run this theory past Siritis, who
did not respond for over a week. When he did, it was with a
one-liner, offering apologies and explaining that he had
been *a bit ill of late*.

"The Pyre" was Aldridge's most definitive effort, es-
chewing thematic embroidery to simply state that some

people are driven to kill those they love *because* they love them. It was not about crazy people seeking vengeance, or lunatics nursing romantic fantasies. It was not about wet dreams or misplaced passion. It was about rational, thinking beings, and the palpable doom they generate by courting a magic they do not comprehend, almost as if love itself were a malign god whose notice it was imprudent to rouse. The climactic immolation consumed not only the lovers in the story, but everyone their love had ever touched.

This raised the possibility that Aldridge had submitted *The Pyre*—the book—as his own funeral opera. Franklin's perception was that the entire volume was sequenced as preparation steps toward death. First was the review of a life—its fulfillments, tragedies, conquests, recreations, regrets, and pleasures. Then the weighing of success versus failure. Then, ritual preparations for an end to the suffering.

But to touch such heights, along the way . . . !

Franklin suddenly saw how easily the legend about the book had begun. It was the bibliophile's version of "Gloomy Sunday"—the Hungarian song written in 1933 and credited with a rash of suicides due to the bottomless depression the tune supposedly inspired, especially among jazz fans who heard Billie Holiday's version. Myth had it that the composer, Rezso Seress, penned the song for an ex-girlfriend with whom he believed "he could finally be happy, in death." The girlfriend killed herself, leaving behind a note reading "Gloomy Sunday," and Seress himself committed suicide by jumping from a building in Budapest in 1968—ironically, in despair over his inability to produce another song as famous.

Typically, Franklin knew, people knew the rumor, but could never name any of the individuals responsible for its creation. J. Arthur Aldridge had become a similar lost footnote, lost to history, condemned to deeper oblivion the moment university libraries reshuffled their card catalogs to a computer database. One misstroke of one key was all it took to make a career totally impossible to locate, or referenced wrongly by some crepuscular search engine that guaranteed it would never be found again, let alone corrected, for decades, if ever. Franklin liked to use the analogy of the hand. Draw a human hand, he'd say. Sounds easy. (Hand someone a pencil and ask them to draw a human hand that *looks* like a hand, and no cheating—only kindergarteners outline their real hand on the paper.) It is amazingly difficult, yet everyone thinks they can do it.

The same held true for all those low-wage earners dutifully attempting to retype catalog card entries with no mistakes. Looks easy; misfires all the time. And if you're J. Arthur Aldridge, your existence as a writer is abruptly terminated. All the systems needed time to improve. There was no quick path to knowledge. That was why there was a need for people like Jonah Siritis, and Franklin Bryant.

Impatient, Franklin worked up more notes and dispatched more e-mails to Siritis, on an average of two or three per day. After July bled into August, he received a surprise answer, at last:

Please pardon the impersonal nature of this bulk mailing, but it is my sad obligation to tell you that Jonah Siritis passed away at 7:40 P.M. GST, on Tuesday, 10 August, at Frimley Park Hospital here in Surrey. He was 57 years old. Many of you knew of Jonah's epilepsy. In late July he contracted influenza, running a fever of 104° and vomiting. After an MRI, blood tests, and a lumbar puncture, he was subsequently diagnosed with Acute Viral Encephalitis (AVE) and our neurologist immediately put him on Acyclovir and anticonvulsants. This took over one week, as encephalitis is one of the "most misdiagnosed" afflictions, and Jonah quickly became significantly impaired. Encephalitis is an inflammation of the brain that, in serious cases, rarely offers the op-

tion of full recovery and has a number of physical, behavioral, and cognitive side effects. On 5 August the fever subsided and Jonah experienced seizures and sporadic loss of consciousness. On 6 August he lapsed into coma and remained comatose until he died. A nondenominational service will be held 15 August, in Camberley. Jonah requested cremation.

My name is Kenneth Nuffield and it was my privilege to be Jonah's partner for the past twenty years. I am sending this message to Jonah's e-mail list in the hope of imparting this very sad news to his friends in America and others who may not be able to attend the service. In lieu of flowers, I have a number of organizations (appended below) to which Jonah requested donations be sent.

I trust in your sympathy and love during this bereavement, and shall answer any and all questions in detail or provide further information if you contact me at the address below . . .

Siritis was dead. His brain had burned up.

Mere days now, before the new semester began.

Franklin ventured a couple of delicate messages to Kenneth Nuffield. It was painfully clear that Siritis and Nuffield had been deeply in love. Franklin wondered what that felt like. All the inspiration for his new research seemed to evaporate just as the fact-finding had reached a boil. Concentration became difficult; derailment easy. He scrutinized the stories again—the whole canon of Aldridge's work—but there seemed to be nothing more to unearth between lines. He needed an encouragement, a jump-start over the void left by the loss of Siritis, and exactly one week before classes were to commence, Franklin found what he wanted.

It was a small package from Kenneth Nuffield, festooned with UK postage and a customs slip, half-torn away.

The note from Nuffield read, in part: *Your interest in this Author was a source of great pleasure to Jonah. As he said, "it validated him," and I am certain he would have wanted you to have this.* Wrapped in a tape-sealed inner envelope was Siritis' own copy of *The Pyre and Others*, precisely as described, floppy pages, creeping Broadart and all.

Now Franklin had within his tremulous grasp (he shook, he knew, with barely leashed excitement) the means by which to experiment. He considered the spooky proposition of attempting that which Siritis had never dared, but with a slight modification, a new angle. What if, Franklin thought, one were to open the book to a specific story, and place it beneath the pillow *that* way? Might that countermand the random-dream bliss (or terror) by adding an element of determinism? Or was it all still a mythic crapshoot?

That was what real writers did, thought Franklin: They burned with passion, and sought to solve desire.

Franklin wanted to know what Herman Banks knew about the unquantifiable lure of women. What that fictional character, a projection of some facet of Aldridge, understood, but which was not incorporated into specific lines of text. The unspoken part of "The Pyre." This knowledge, won at great cost, could not only satisfy his academic yearnings, but possibly improve his life.

Love, it seemed, always lurked just beyond the boundaries of perception.

✧

When Franklin was discovered, he resembled a knickknack carved of soapstone, or mahogany, burnished to a deep ebony and curled into a fetal position, because he had been asleep when he burned. No gas leak, no unattended candles, no cigarettes, no suicide. The composed calm on his expression had been captured and rendered durable, as clay fired to luster in a kiln. His bed had cooked down to half-melted toaster coils and the timbers inside the walls had combusted with fantastic, destroying heat, yet Franklin's body was found unblemished by soot, ashes, or char. The temperatures kindled inside his flaming bungalow were so intense that nothing made of paper could have survived.

ALL MY
BLOODY THINGS

A Cal McDonald Crime Story

STEVE NILES

BY THE TIME I came to, fuckhead El Beardo De Psycho was already trying to take a chunk out of my leg with a rusty scalpel. He had my pant leg ripped and my juicy thigh exposed.

The scalpel was pressed right into my flesh when he paused and saw my eyes were open.

He was so fucking dead.

Stupid cannibals.

❖

It all began a couple days ago when I got a call from a guy who talked to a guy who knew this lady who mentioned her brother's family went missing on a lonely stretch of California highway.

I heard about it because the guy—the first guy—got attacked by some weird vampire freak-thing, I saved his ass, and he was calling me to thank me for shooting the beast before it shredded him.

"I still can't believe it happened." He had a high whiny voice that made me want to pop his skull with a hammer.

"Well, believe it!" I said, trying to get off the phone. I wasn't much for follow-up friendships. I save you. Thank you and fuck you. We're done.

"Well, Mr. McDonald, I can't thank you enough for saving me."

"Glad I could help." I went silent. If this conversation was continuing, I wasn't going to be the one keeping it alive. I had shit do to. I had a bag of painkillers just waiting to enter my bloodstream.

"There's something else . . ."

Fuck. Here it comes.

"I have a friend who's dating this lady and she mentioned that her brother's family never showed up driving from Vegas to Los Angeles."

I put my head facedown on the desk blotter. "Call the police. That's missing persons. I only do weird shit."

"The way the lady tells it, it might be . . . weird shit."

I just wanted to get rid of him. "What's this lady's name and number?"

"Um . . . let me see here."

His squealing whine of a voice was shredding my last good nerve.

"Kelly Hughes. She's in Glendale."

He gave me her number, thanked me again. I told him to have a good life and hung up the phone. What a dink.

Ninety percent of what I do is gut feeling. That's why I took the whiny man's lead. People have an inner sense of the strange and supernatural. They tend to believe subconsciously what their conscious minds won't allow them to comprehend.

People always ask me why I'm the only one who sees the freaks and monsters crawling in the dark corners of the world and I tell them it's because I trust my gut. My gut and the fact that I've had my ass smeared across the city by some freak or another enough times to know there's shit out there that just defies logic, plain and simple.

I arrived at Kelly Hughes's house in Glendale. It was one of those Spanish pillbox numbers like I had, but hers was painted and clean, the fence was white picket, and there were flowers planted in window boxes. The whole thing made me sick.

The woman was pleasant enough. She told me how she'd never heard from her brother Andre and his wife Debra and their kid, an eight-year-old boy named Doug, after they were supposed to have arrived a couple days ago. They were driving a 2004 Volvo wagon, silver. Calls had gone unanswered. She tried the police, but they turned up a big doughnut, and frankly, she told me, she thought the worst.

I had nothing to go on but my aforementioned gut, and it told me something was wrong. Families just don't disappear off highways in the middle of the night. I asked her for all the info I'd need, phone numbers, descriptions. All that crap. I figured I'd start by tracing the cell calls and credit-card charges to figure out where they disappeared.

✿

The police are retarded. The last credit-card charge by Andre Hughes was made from a remote spot on Highway 15 between Los Angeles and Las Vegas. What makes the charge interesting is that the amount, some forty bucks, was posted but never charged. Either something happened during the exchange or the merchant decided they didn't want the money. I smelled trouble.

I drove the Nova out that way the same night. I didn't bring Mo'Lock with me because he was meeting with some ghouls who had recently moved from Europe to L.A. In the last few months there had been a large influx of the friendly undead to L.A. It had something to do with me, but frankly, I didn't give a rat's ass as long as they didn't eat anybody.

The drive was long and boring. There were few other cars on the road. It was late and midweek, not the busiest time for Vegas traffic. I popped a few blues to keep sharp, and some codeine to take the edge off, then I put the finishing touches on my buzz with a joint and whiskey pint chaser.

The barb cocktail made my head tingle and the desert night, the hills in the distance, the wide flat of nothing near began to trail brilliant colors until I came up on a small shock of a business next to a run-down gas station with old-fashioned gas pumps straight out of *The Grapes of Wrath*.

There was a silver Volvo station wagon parked around back. It was partially hidden by a wreck of a pickup, but I could see the California plates and luggage still secured to the roof rack.

Follow my gut. Connect the dots. That's what I do that the cops can't seem to. It takes them days to even track leads, people die. It's really a shame.

I parked the car right in front of the place. There was a poorly painted sign that read JUNIORS PULLED MEAT BBQ in crooked red and white letters. Beneath that, in chilly type, it said AIR CONDITIONED.

I entered through a screen door and immediately the smell of blood and BBQ sauce hit my nostrils. There was a counter, old, stained, and disgusting. There were a few tables, just as stained, with broken, rusty chairs. It was dead quiet. I looked toward the counter. Behind the stained Formica I saw a door to the kitchen.

I walked forward. I also removed my gun. All I could smell was blood and all I could hear was the buzz of flies.

I saw two things as I entered; two people, a young boy and an older woman—the Hughes family I assumed—bound to a gas pipe. The other was what was left of the father, Andre

Hughes, naked and tied to a table. He had been stripped of
skin from the chest down to his feet and several large sec-
tions of meat from the buttocks and thigh were cut away.

But worst of all, he was being kept alive. Tubes ran air
to his exposed lungs through his nose, and IVs numbed
him to the pain.

That's what I saw. What I felt as I walked deeper into
the room was a burning pain across the back of my skull.
I'd felt it before. It was probably a wrench being hammered against my head. I reeled forward. The gun fell from
my hand, and I managed to half-turn my head and see a
large man with long blond hair, a mustache, and a Hawaiian print shirt. He had the wrench.

I remember thinking, *My God I'm going to die at the
hands of a giant retard*, and then the wrench came down
again and caught my brow. I hit the floor and fell into a
buzzing pool of total darkness.

✧

That brings us back to the beginning.

I don't know how long I was out cold, but when I started
to come back, my pant leg had been ripped up the leg and
the big guy in the Hawaiian print shirt was making ready to
cut into my thigh. He only stopped because he noticed I
was awake.

My hands were bound behind my back. I was tied on the
pipe about four feet from Momma Hughes and son. Dad
was passed out or dead on the bleeding table.

"What the hell do you think you're doing?" I grunted.

El Beardo looked up. His eyes were yellow; his teeth
were rotten and brown, black along the gum line.

"You didn't stay out long," he commented, almost too
relaxed.

He paused the cutting, but kept the blade pressed to my
leg. If I struggled, he would only cut me. I decided to play
it out.

"So . . . how long you been eating people?"

He seemed taken aback by the question, like nobody had ever asked.

He pulled the blade back slightly. I felt a wave of relief and dizziness. I'd taken way too much shit in the car. I could hardly see straight.

"All my life," he said softly. He had a speech impediment, a sloppy lisp. "My paw taught me how to cook."

When he spoke, the grizzled cannibal looked like a stupid five-year-old, not sure what he was supposed to do. He stared off sadly, then seemed to come back around and looked me in the eyes.

"Eating peoples makes me strong. Eating peoples gives me their soul. That's what Paw said. He ate Maw and said her soul loved me forever inside him."

"No shit?"

The cannibal in the Hawaiian print shirt nodded shyly. I glanced over at the captives. Mom was out cold. She'd probably fainted watching her husband get skinned alive. The kid was awake and aware. His eyes were wide and staring not at his dying father, but at the killer. The kid was staring at him, memorizing him, planning vengeance he might never have.

"Why not let the family go?" I suggested. "You can feast on me. I got enough meat on me to keep you in meat for a month."

He didn't like the idea. The killer shook his head furiously and squeezed the scalpel in his hand. "No, no, no, no, no, no."

I nodded. "You sure?"

"I said no!"

Okay, I needed a new approach. This nut bag was teetering. I had to play my cards right. I had to keep him talking.

"Okay, sorry," I said quietly. "I just never met a guy who sold human-meat sandwiches."

El Beardo had been squatting. He had this round body with no discernible distinction between his upper and lower torso, like a squishy melon with arms and legs, wearing a pineapple print shirt. As he sat down crossing his legs, I saw his sandals and socks were caked with dried blood, dirt, and hair.

He wanted to talk. I wished I wasn't so fucking wasted. On top of the serious concussion I probably suffered, the pills and whiskey didn't mix very friendly-like, and I was feeling beyond screwy.

"I don't sell the people meat."

He spoke very matter-of-factly. His blond hair was thick and wavy, knotted with clots of congealed blood and grease. He had that beach-bum look, the leather-tanned skin, and light facial hair. His hands were like mitts with thick, overworked sausages for fingers. I tried not to think what those hands had done.

"What ya mean you don't *sell* it?" I asked, buying time.

Psycho Beardo shook his head. "People meats for personal use," he said proudly. "Customers get pork and beef BBQ."

"Why is that? People meat too special for customers? They might like it, too, you know?"

"Paw said people meat's for just us, just us special folks who know the truth."

He didn't sound so sure about that last part. He spoke like a parakeet repeating a hard-learned phrase.

My head was spinning. I could barely stay awake. I didn't have a clue what to say to the cannibal. I just wanted to bash his head in with a hammer. Hand out a little payback for the bleeding knots on my head.

While I kept him talking I tried to work a small piece of wire into the cuff lock, but I couldn't get leverage. Behind the killer, Mrs. Hughes had begun to come to. Her eyes were fluttering. The boy, however, still stared wide-eyed, blank. He was in shock. If he didn't get help soon, he'd crack for good.

The killer was slumped, sitting right in front of me on the filthy floor of the backroom slaughterhouse and all of a sudden, despite the blood, he looked like a big-ass baby sitting there. He was even poking at his knee with the scalpel like a pouting child.

"What's the matter, Psycho?" I asked. "You got a hunk of that kid's dad caught in your throat?"

"Nobody never talked to me before," he said with a straight face. "All they ever do is scream."

"Well, maybe that's because you're killing them."

"Yeah, I guess."

I gestured toward Papa Hughes on the table. "You done with that one?"

El Beardo looked over his shoulder at the half-skinless man, then quickly back at me.

"You interrupted me," he said. "Now he's spoiled. I should start on the lady or the kid. Kid's meat's the best if they haven't been fed processed sugar their whole lives. Even with it, they're a better eat than adults."

The killer looked back over his right shoulder, this time at the woman and child. The woman, Debra Hughes, was fully cognizant of her surroundings now. She stared at the bloody, still-breathing body of her husband. His breathing was hard and fast. She was crying and, even though gagged, she still made a lot of noise. Too much noise, I was afraid. The killer kept looking back at them. I had to do something or he'd start hacking them to bits as well.

I looked around the room. My vision was blurred; my teeth were numb. I was in bad shape. What was I thinking, mixing blues, painkillers, and whiskey? I mean, I did it all the time, but it wasn't mixing too well with the massive head injury. I was screwed.

I watched the sloppy killer in the Hawaiian pineapple shirt weigh his choices. He looked from me to the woman to the kid, then back to me. I wasn't sure I was even in the running for the feast, and it was that thought that gave me an idea. A bad one, but an idea nonetheless.

"Hey, Psycho, you got a name?"

He looked at me dumbly. "It's on the front. Can't you read, mister?"

"I can read."

"Says my name on the sign. My paw put it up there right before he passed the business on to me."

I tried to picture the sign out front. I wasn't doing too well. Then it came to me. "Junior?"

The killer smiled a big, wide smile and I saw the inside of his mouth. It was a cave of rotten teeth, a fetid tongue, and rancid meat. There were black spots on his tongue and odd sores around the inside of his lips.

"That's my name," he said, scratched his face, then added, "Me, my paw, and my grandfather was all Juniors."

"You don't say? Was your grampy a people eater, too? Junior smiled. "Uh huh."

Suddenly, Baby Huey got up and walked out of the room. Just like that I was alone with the Hughes family.

I shot a look at Debra Hughes. "Are you okay? Are you hurt?"

She immediately came apart at the seams. "Oh . . . God!" She was screaming.

I shook my head.

She stopped.

I looked at the boy. I saw he had been tied with rope.

"You got any slack in those ropes, son?"

He swallowed. "No."

"Well, work them slowly," I said. "They'll give."

The woman began to shudder. She was gonna blow.

"Keep calm. You've got to lay low. You and the boy," I whispered sharply. "Keep your heads down and eyes closed."

"My . . . my husband . . ."

"Lady, we might be able to see his lungs, but at least they're moving. We have to hope for the best."

I heard El Beardo stomping back our way. I took one last glance at the Hugheses and nodded. They bowed their heads nervously.

Junior came in through the swinging doors and stood there like some sort of Cro-Mag on vacation, looking around the slaughterhouse, bobbing his head. I coughed and made sure I caught his attention.

He looked at me and let out a long, greasy fart. It sounded like popcorn going off in a wet sack. His dull eyes stayed dull, but one corner of his lip rose like an excited dog's leg. I assumed he was grinning.

"What you doing out there?" I asked.

He grunted and walked toward where I was tied on the floor.

"Forgot to lock the door," he said.

"Afraid customers will come in while you're eating somebody?"

He leaned down and slugged me so hard my lip split. Then he just kneeled down and waited for me to recover. When I looked at him like *what the fuck*, he went on.

"I ain't afraid of anybody," he spat. "Anybody comes in here unexpected, dies. Plain and simple. Paw always said nobody can tell if they ain't nobody to tell."

I raised my eyebrows. It was about all I could muster. I'd guess if there was such a thing, right at that point I was peaking on whatever concoction I'd consumed earlier.

"Too bad," I muttered. I didn't really know what I meant.

He seemed to though. He laughed. "Too bad for you, dumb fuck!"

I walked into that one.

While he laughed I worked the cuffs around my wrists. I was fucked up and weak, but I used my numbness to my advantage and pulled hard enough to break my wrists. I hit pay dirt. The pipe moved. Or maybe it was the room. At any rate, something moved.

His laughing turned to a raspy cough, and then he was alternating glances at me and the Hughes woman. But it was the sound from his stomach that worried me most. It was loud, and rumbled. If I had to guess, I'd say the cannibal's stomach was growling hungrily. Not what you want to hear.

And then he licked his lips, catching a string of dripping saliva that slid off his fuzzy yellow tongue.

He was hungry.

I made my move.

"You look like you need some meat, Junior."

He looked at me like I understood.

"I need strength," he said. "I need another soul."

I slurred just a bit. "Then why don't you eat *me*?"

El Beardo went slack-jawed.

"What?"

"I'm the strongest one here. I bet I got a big-ass soul," I reasoned. "Eat me."

Junior picked up the scalpel from the table. I hadn't even noticed he'd placed it down.

"You know a lot about stuff, don't you?" he asked.

"I get around."

The cannibal worked his attention back to my leg. He pulled it straight and ripped the slit a bit extra to show more thigh. He pushed away the material and cleared a large section of my flesh for his handiwork.

He placed the scalpel against the meat of my thigh just below the hipbone and slashed about a quarter inch across and *into* my leg. I closed my eyes and clenched my teeth. When he cut me, I screamed, more like a yelp. It was a stinging pain. Even with all the dope in my system, I felt it.

But that cut was just prep. He placed the scalpel down and wiped the inch-wide, inch-deep gash with a wet rag, already stained with somebody else's blood. Then he reached for what looked like a homemade cheese cutter. It was a length of wire attached between two wooden handles.

God, I thought, *this had better work.*

The cannibal took the cheese cutter by the handles and pulled the thin wire taut. I tensed up, pulling hard on the cuffs until I felt my wrists bleed. I had a pretty good idea what was coming and I couldn't help myself.

It took every ounce of my strength not to lash out and kick the fucker in the face. But I couldn't risk it. I was still cuffed. I might get in a good kick, but he'd have the last laugh. I had to sit and take whatever he dished out.

He took the wire tool to the wound he'd made on my leg and pressed the taut steel under the lip of the cut. I braced. The killer pushed down causing the wire to tuck neatly into the gash. It stung so bad I started to shake.

"Now keep still," the killer said.

And then he yanked!

The wire sliced under the flesh of my thigh fast, like a heated knife through butter, cutting an inch-thick filet of flesh from my leg. It was the most excruciating thing I'd ever felt, but I did my best to stay still.

My eyes and teeth were shut tight, trying to block the searing pain. When I opened my eyes, I saw what I'd been feeling. I saw the killer—Junior—pulling as hard as he could on the handles. He almost had a slab cut off. He was bracing for the final yank.

He pulled one last time and the flap of flesh came loose.

"There!" the killer yelled like he'd achieved something.

I rocked my head. Tears ran in the corners of my eyes. The pain was unbelievable.

Junior tossed aside the bloody tool and carefully handled my strip of flesh. It wobbled and flopped in his hands. It had weight to it. I fought everything I had not to throw up. I was dizzy, nauseous, and my head spun.

In the killer's hands was about a six-inch-by-three-inch wide flap of my leg. There was a matching-shaped, bleeding wound on my thigh that glistened and bled.

I could hardly think. I craned my neck and tried to talk, but I was squeezing my teeth so hard I couldn't part them.

Then I got it out; "Now what, Junior?"

"Gonna cook and eat this-here people steak," he said, staring at the flesh jiggling in his hands.

"Cook it?" I spat. "You some kind of sissy?"

This upset Junior. He almost dropped the bloody slab on the dirty floor.

"What d' you mean?" he asked, raising his chin defiantly.

"I mean, everybody knows when you cook people you lose all the goodness." I could hardly speak.

All I wanted to do was scream. All I wanted to do was scream at the top of my lungs and break Junior's skull open. I pictured myself beating him with a pipe, choking him with my hands, strangling the life out of him. I could almost feel his throat in my hands.

The cannibal was looking at his meat, my skin. He looked as though he was genuinely concerned with what I told him.

"Really?" he asked.

"That's what I heard."

Junior grabbed a plate from a shelf and slapped the slab of bloody flesh onto it for further examination. Behind him was a gas stove that he glanced at, in between looking at me and once or twice at the Hugheses, who listened to me and continued to play possum even when they heard me yell.

Between the concussion, the bleeding wound, and the near-overdose, I was hanging on by a thread and I began to doubt my plan would even work. And to boot, it looked like the crazy motherfucker wasn't going to play along.

Junior poked at the hairy, bloody slab. "You sure? Cuz Paw always taught me to cook what I eat."

I nodded, trying in vain to hide the pain. "The heat makes the soul leave the meat."

"Really?"

"Really." I had no clue.

Junior thought about it for half a second, then placed the dish down and walked to a drawer. He opened it and took out, to my relief, a fork and knife. It was time to eat and time to see if I'd save the day or become the day's special.

I didn't want to, but I watched as he sliced a piece of my flesh from the jiggling chunk of thigh. He pinned the edge with the fork and sawed with the knife until he had a small, relatively hairless piece of people meat to taste. It wobbled on the fork as he lifted it to his mouth and shoved it inside.

He chewed on me for a good minute, rolled me in his mouth and then, finally, swallowed with a big, loud gulp. I could almost hear the last of me sliding down his gullet.

He looked around the room in that food-taster sort of manner, then went back to the place for the next slice.

"How am I?" I asked, as sarcastic as I could summon. I was hurting, dizzy.

"Meat's good," he said smacking his lips. "Chewy."

I felt sick. When I looked down, the fish-shaped, oval wound on my leg was bleeding so badly, my leg was drenched and dripping hot gore.

Junior decided he liked me, I guess, because he started slicing up the filet of McDonald on the plate into evenly cut, easy-to-chew strips. I watched him closely as he ate one strip, chewed, then moved on to the next. Each one he chewed, hair, blood, and all, and swallowed without showing any effects.

I glanced at the Hughes boy. His head was down, but I could see movement around his arms. *Good boy,* I thought, *he's working those ropes.*

Junior finished the last of the meat and then licked the plate. I watched him, looking for any signs. He seemed to be acting exactly as he had before . . . until he didn't. I saw his eyes flutter, and he sort of swayed as he rubbed his face.

Junior smiled and turned and, as soon as he did, I saw my

incredibly stupid plan had worked. I might have the tolerance
built up to take a handful of painkillers, pot, and whiskey and
live to tell about it, but Junior the cannibal obviously did not.

He was wasted.

Eating me had wasted him.

I was toxic.

Junior stumbled forward, rubbing his face, and laughed.
He looked like a big freak. He just wasn't close enough yet,
but it was most definitely kicking time.

"How's it going there, Junior?" I asked. "Ready for another serving?"

El Beardo Boy laughed again and looked at me like I
was his best friend in the whole wide world. I tried to look
pleasant, but I was holding on to consciousness like a red-
neck gripping a greased pig. I was gonna slip any second. I
had to egg him on.

"Come on, big boy," I said. "You can eat more than just
one little piece of me!"

Junior laughed and then picked up the fork and knife.
He was swaying erratically now, and his eyes were wet and
half-closed and appeared to be getting worse by the second. He even tried to rub his face again and almost stabbed
himself in the eye.

I laid there until he got close. When he did, I opened my
eyes wide and stared him down before delivering my right,
uneaten leg so hard into his testicles that I actually heard
an audible crunching sound. He doubled over, dropping
the knife and fork. The knife slashed my open leg wound
as it fell.

Hurt. So bad.

Junior hit the floor in front of me. He was balled up and
vomiting foam. I looked at the Hughes boy. His head and his
mother's were up. The kid had gotten one hand free and he
was working on the other. I gave him a wink.

"You two might want to close your eyes again." I said

raising my leg into the air above Junior's head on the ground.

"Don't!"

I stopped. Looked up.

The Hughes boy had freed himself. He was frantically pulling the last of the rope off himself. I put my leg down.

I watched as the Hughes boy walked across the slaughterhouse to his father on the slab and put his head barely above the draining table. Nothing can describe the pain in the boy's eyes as he discovered his dad had finally passed. His exposed lungs were no longer moving.

The kid's expression changed from sorrow to pissed in less time than I'd ever seen, and I'd seen it plenty. He glared at the killer rolling on the floor, then at the assortment of tools.

He chose a small hammer-ax combo deal that looked like something for cutting bone, and then walked over and stood over Junior, who was unaware of everything going down around him, except he was fucked up and his balls were crushed. Within minutes, Junior's head would be added to the *crushed* list, too.

"Hey, kid," I muttered.

The boy looked at me. His eyes were blank rage. "Yeah?"

"You sure you want to do that?" I said. "I can take care of it if you don't want to."

The kid slammed the blunt end of the tool down onto Junior's skull so hard, his sandals and bloody feet kicked up.

The kid said, "I'm sure."

Even if I could have, I don't think I would have stopped the kid. He was working out what would've turned into a lifetime of rage right there on the scene.

It took about a dozen equally hard whacks until the cannibal stopped moving. His head was pulp and hair. The Hughes kid just let the tool fall from his hand. He was done. He had his vengeance.

The boy's eyes cooled and he came over to me. He saw the cuff, then without asking checked the dead killer's pockets and came out with the keys. He unlocked the cuffs. My hands came free.

I didn't—or rather couldn't—get up right away, so I sat there waiting for the feeling to come back in my hands while the boy untied his mother.

✿

And that was that. Case fucking closed.

I stuck around long enough to make sure the remains of the Hughes family were okay. I covered the father's body and walked them out front where they wouldn't have to look at the bodies.

Then I cleared the cash register for my pay. I made forty-six dollars and twenty-seven cents. It would barely cover gas.

I didn't stick around for the cops. What good would it do? The freak was dead. The only remaining question was how the fuck did this psycho family exist off the main highway all these years without getting checked out?

Like I said, cops are retarded. They don't see what's right in front of them because they don't want to believe how bad things can get.

It's a big, dark, scary world out there as it is. Can you imagine what it would be like if they believed in monsters? You'd think they would know. Some of the worst are human.

THE DIVING GIRL

RICHARD LAYMON

I NEVER WOULD'VE known she was there, but last night I found myself unable to sleep and I had a story deadline coming up. So at about midnight, I walked through the darkness from my house to my brand-new garage, unlocked its side door, turned on a light, and climbed the stairs to my office.

The office, though large, was nearly airtight. Open or shut the door, and a small suction of air disturbs window blinds twenty-five feet away. Being so well sealed, it was also uncommonly quiet.

So the moment I opened my office door, I knew something wasn't right. The air didn't have the proper tightness or silence. Apparently I'd forgotten to shut a window.

For the past couple of weeks, I'd been opening all my office windows during the day to let the mild summer breezes drift through. At the end of each workday, I would shut and lock them. In Los Angeles, even on the west side, one can't be too careful.

But one sometimes does make mistakes, become distracted and neglect a detail. I'd apparently shut all the windows except one.

From where I stood just inside the door, I knew exactly which window was open. While the rest of the office remained silent, sounds were coming from the direction of the back wall: leaves rubbing together in the breeze, cars and trucks on nearby streets, a helicopter somewhere far away—sounds of the outside world pouring in like water through one gaping hole in an otherwise tightly sealed boat.

In daylight hours, I might've welcomed it and opened the rest of the windows. But not at this hour of the night. I needed to be sealed in, snug and safe.

The window had to be shut.

Leaving the office lights off, I walked toward it. The horizontal blinds were not quite closed, so moonlight squeezed through spaces and painted faint gray stripes across the carpet, showing me the way.

The window was a sideways slider. I would've done better installing vertical blinds. If I'd had verticals, I might've simply reached through the slats and pulled the window shut. Horizontals, however, needed to be raised.

Standing at the window, I reached forward and tried to find the pull cord. I couldn't see it at all, but I was fairly sure of its location. As I fingered the darkness—

Buh-whoom!

The sound came from somewhere outside my open window. Though it seemed familiar, I couldn't place it.

Then came a heavy splash.

My fingers brushed a dangling cord. I grabbed it and pulled and the blinds skittered up to the top of the window. Suddenly I faced the L.A. night with its usual array of buildings and billboards and trees and lights and distant hills.

But there was also an area of light where I'd never noticed it before—off to the right, very nearby and very bright. It appeared to come from the backyard of a house directly behind my next-door neighbor's property.

From my second-story window, I was high above the fence that enclosed the stranger's yard. However, my angle was bad. Also, trees blocked much of the view. As a result, I could only see small segments of the house and none of the swimming pool at all.

There had to be a pool; I'd not only heard the sounds, but I could see the diving board.

The entire length of the springboard, the shiny chrome handrails at the top of the ladder, the upper reaches of the ladder itself were well lighted and nicely framed by the leafy branches of the very trees that blocked so much of my view.

I was only mildly surprised to find a swimming pool in such close proximity, this being Los Angeles. While pools aren't as prevalent in my neighborhood as they are in wealthier areas such as Bel Air or in ungodly hot areas as the Valley, pools are hardly a rarity.

But I hadn't known of this one.

It was not behind *my* house, after all, but behind the house and lawn and garage and fence of my next-door neighbor, with numerous bushes and trees and still another fence in the way. Also, my own house was only one story high. The pool might've existed for years without my knowledge. It might've *remained* unknown to me if I hadn't come up to my new two-story garage to do some late-night work, and if I hadn't neglected to shut the only window offering a view of it, and if I hadn't been alerted by the sounds of someone diving.

Obviously, I'd looked out this window before.

Not often, however. And never before at such a late hour of the night. The times I had looked out, the high dive beyond the gap in the trees had escaped my notice.

It's right there, I thought. How could I have missed it?

What is it, thirty feet away? Forty?

A pair of hands entered the view, reaching up and grabbing the ladder's side rails. Then came bare arms, followed by a head with wet straw-colored hair.

A girl. A young woman.

Her hair was short and matted down. It stopped at the nape of her neck. Her shoulders were bare. Her back, too, was bare, except for the tied strings of her white bikini top.

She was slender, softly tanned, and shiny wet.

The way her arms were raised, I had a side view of her right breast in its thin pouch of bikini and how it went up and down with the motions of her climbing.

Her right hip was bare except for the tied strings of her bikini pants. Her right buttock was a glossy slope. Her legs were long and sleek.

Atop the high dive, she grabbed the curved rails and swung herself forward. Without a pause, she walked out on the springboard. It wobbled up and down. At the end of the board, she halted.

Waiting for the board to settle down, she took a deep breath. She reached back with one hand and plucked at the seat of her bikini pants. She adjusted her top. Then she lowered her arms to her sides, seemed to stiffen and arch her entire body, took a deep breath, let it out, and leaped forward. She came straight down, both feet hitting the board.

Buh-whoom!

Tossed by the board, she seemed to spring toward the sky, reaching high, gliding away . . . and disappearing behind the leaves and branches framing my view.

Moments later came the sound of her splash. Though I couldn't see her with my eyes, my mind watched her plunge deep into the water of a large, well-lighted swimming pool. Near the bottom, she curved upward and kicked silently to the surface.

I listened for the sounds of her swimming toward a side of the pool, but the drone of an airliner ruined any chance of that.

No problem, I thought. Soon she'll be up on the board again.

I stared at the high dive.

Any moment, the girl's reaching hands would appear at the lowest place visible on the ladder and she would climb up into full view.

Seconds passed. Minutes passed.

Perhaps she had decided to swim some laps before returning to the board. Or maybe she was taking a little rest by the pool.

Give her a few more minutes, I thought, and she'll be back up the ladder.

I gave her more than a few minutes.

Had I looked out my office window just in time to witness her very last dive of the night?

I considered quitting my watch and trying to do the work for which I'd come up to my office. A story needed to be written. I had no prayer of concentrating on it, however, with my mind full of the diving girl.

Beside, I knew better than to turn on any lights. No matter how well I might close the blinds, light would leak out between the slats and around the edges. If the girl should happen to climb the high dive again and notice my lights, she would certainly realize that the window offered a view of her.

And that might ruin it all.

I watched for a while longer. At last, I gave up. Though I left the window open, I slowly and silently shut the blinds before returning to my house and going to bed.

✧

The next morning, back in my office, I opened the blinds very slightly and peered out between a couple of slats at the high dive. Nobody was on it. Nor did any sounds come from that direction.

I watched for a few minutes longer, then opened all the other windows and sat at my desk and tried to work. For a while, I found myself unable to concentrate. I kept looking toward the window, imagining the girl, and frequently hurrying to the window to make sure I wasn't missing her. Each time, the high dive stood deserted in its framework of branches.

She probably doesn't dive during the day, I told myself.

Though my office was fairly new, I'd been working in it daily for more than a month ... often with the windows open. If anyone had been using the pool, I would've heard the splashes, voices, *something* long before last night.

The girl probably works during the day, I thought.

There was no reason at all to think she might appear during my own work hours. With that in mind, I put her out of my mind and set to work with nearly as much concentration as usual. At least for brief periods of time.

Every so often, I went to the window and peered out.

No sign of her. Of course not.

In spite of the interruptions, I managed to finish writing the short story before returning to the house for lunch. After lunch, things didn't go nearly so well. I struggled with my novel, but couldn't focus on it for more than a few minutes before my mind wandered off to dwell on the girl.

I kept going to the window and peering out.

I fully understood that I was being ridiculous.

✧

Down in my house, I had a cocktail, and then cooked up a lasagna dinner in the microwave. I watched the news on television while I ate. Then I tried to read a mystery, but my mind kept wandering.

I took a shower.

Afterward, I tried to find other ways to pass the time. It wasn't even dark yet.

Maybe she would be earlier tonight.

What if I'm missing her?

Binoculars hanging from my neck, I hurried out to the garage. I let myself in, locked the door behind me, and hurried upstairs to my office.

At the back window, I peered through the slats of my horizontal blinds. Not very far away, framed by the leafy branches, was the top of the high dive. I watched it for a while. Nobody appeared. Nor did I hear any sounds from the swimming pool. At length, I went over to my desk. I reclined on my swivel chair to wait.

I considered taking care of some e-mail, but had no interest in it. I had no interest in accomplishing anything. I simply sat there, thinking about the girl and staring across my office. Darkness slowly came. I welcomed it as I had never before welcomed nightfall.

Afraid I might miss the girl's first dive, I didn't wait to be alerted by sounds. I crossed my dark office to the window, raised the blinds, and looked out.

Where there had been such bright light last night, there was only darkness. I couldn't see the diving board at all.

It's still early, I told myself. Wait. Just wait. She'll come.

So I waited. And waited. The minutes crept by.

Though the hour was still early, I began to doubt whether she would show up at all. Perhaps she had other plans for tonight. After all, this was Friday. Such a lovely young woman might very well have a boyfriend, a lover. Maybe she'd gone away to be with him.

Worse, perhaps last night had been a complete fluke— the one and only time all summer that she had used the pool, or would.

For that matter, maybe she'd only been at the house for a visit. Perhaps she lives in another city, even in another state. Last night when she used the pool, she was staying with a relative or an old friend—*for one night only*.

No, I thought. It can't be that. I *have* to see her again. One more time, at least. Please, please.

She *has* to come, I thought. I'd hardly seen her at all last night. A mere glimpse as she prepared for her final dive. It just wouldn't be fair to be allowed such brief moments with her, and then have her taken away forever.

Not fair at all, but since when did fairness apply?

Never count on fairness. Count only on irony.

More often than not, it seems that God is a joker with a mean streak.

I'll never see her again, I thought.

And then the pool lights came on.

Yes! Yes! Yes!

I raised the blinds. Then I rested my elbows on the windowsill and put the binoculars to my eyes. Fingering the little wheel, I brought into focus the gleaming chrome handrails at the top of the high dive. They came in sharply.

I might've been standing only six feet away when the girl climbed into view.

She stole my breath away. I trembled.

She hadn't yet been in the water. As she climbed off the ladder and stood up straight on the board, the breeze ruffled her short blond hair. Her skin looked dusky and smooth. She wore what appeared to be the same white bikini as last night. Dry, it wasn't clinging to her body and seemed loose.

She stepped to the end of the board and halted.

My view was so fine that I might've been standing on the board with her.

Now if you'll just turn around. Show me your face. Show me your front all the way up and down.

She didn't.

She jumped, came down, and sprang upward. *Buhwhoom!* She vanished, hidden by the branches. Moments later came the splash.

I waited.

Let's not have it like last night, I thought. Let's have this be the first of many dives. Please.

What's taking her so long?

Maybe she dives only every once in a while. Goes off the board, spends some time swimming around, and maybe rests on a lounge before making another trip up the high dive.

Be patient, I told myself. It takes time to climb out of the pool, walk back to the ladder. . . .

She climbed into sight. Now, she was wet. Hair matted to her scalp. Skin shiny. Bikini clinging. With binoculars, I could see water dripping off the lobe of her right ear, dribbles sliding down her back and right side and down the backs of her legs.

She walked to the end of the board, stopped, and turned around.

Yes!

More often than not, women who look wonderful from behind are best seen only from the rear. Their faces don't measure up. Their faces ruin it all.

Not this time.

Oh, not this time at all. My diver's face was the sort that you hope to see, but almost never do, when someone so spectacular from behind turns around.

That's not true. It was *better* than you hope for.

It made my heart thud fast. It took my breath away. It gave me a thick feeling in my throat.

As she took a deep breath, getting ready for the dive, I looked through the binoculars at her long, slender neck, her smooth chest, and how her breasts filled the small, flimsy pouches of her bikini top. Her nipples were stiff and I could see their darkness through the white of the fabric.

Lower, her belly was smooth and flat.

Lower still, the front of her bikini pants was a meager white triangle held in place by strings that were tied at her hips.

I moaned.

As my gaze roamed upward again, I wondered why she continued to stand there. Could she be nervous about doing a backward dive? Maybe reconsidering?

Take all the time you want, I told her in my mind. Stand like this all night.

I lingered for a few more seconds on her breasts, then

eased my view higher, relishing the smoothness of her upper chest, the curves of her collarbones, the dip at the base of her throat, her slender neck, her soft chin, her lips and her nose and her astonishing blue eyes. . . .

Blue eyes aimed at me.

My heart slammed. No! She just happens to be looking in this direction! She doesn't see *me!* Impossible. I was behind the window of a completely dark room, so she couldn't possibly . . .

She smiled, raised a hand, and waved.

At me?

"Oh, my God!" I muttered and jerked the binoculars down below the windowsill.

A little late for that, I thought. She's already seen me spying on her like a pervert.

Doesn't seem angry, though. Not at all.

She almost seemed glad to see me.

Can't be, I thought.

She turned her hand, showing me the back of it, and beckoned me to come.

Me?

I looked over my shoulder, idiotically making sure her signal wasn't meant for someone behind me in my office. When I looked at the girl again, she was mouthing words in my direction. Even without binoculars, I could read her lips: *Come on over.*

She can't possibly mean it, I thought.

I stared out at her, stunned and amazed and wondering . . . Prufrock and a mermaid.

They do not sing to me.

This one does.

Impossible.

Frowning slightly but also looking amused, she called out, "Hey! You in the window! Come on over! The water's fine!"

I murmured again, "Oh, my God."

✿

I took the direct route: down the stairs and out the garage door, then straight to my back fence. I climbed over it and dropped to the other side, then made my way to the right through a narrow wilderness of bushes and trees. It was tough going. A little scary, too: no telling what might be lurking in this dark, strange region between the properties.

But I could hear the girl diving.

Buh-whoom!

Splash!

She was still there, diving while she waited for me.

I could hardly believe that I was going to her. Or that she had invited me. Such things just don't happen. Not to me.

Too good to be real.

If it's too good to be real, they say, it usually is.

I wasn't dreaming, though. (I'm almost positive of that.) She'd caught me spying on her with binoculars and she'd asked me to come over.

Doesn't make sense!

Oh, yes it does, I thought as I struggled closer to the last fence. Makes perfect sense.

She wants to get back at me. Wants revenge.

Maybe she has someone with her—a tough guy all set to beat the crap out of me the minute I show up.

It must be something like that, I thought. Something sinister. Nothing else makes sense.

Unless she's just lonely.

Fat chance.

I stopped at the redwood fence. Through the cracks between its boards, I could see the lights of the swimming pool.

Buh-whoom!

Splash.

I was close enough to hear the water sprinkle down after the splash. Close enough to hear the girl swimming. Close enough to smell the chlorine of the pool.

This side of the fence had support posts and cross-beams. They would make the climb fairly easy.

Don't do it, I thought. She's probably got a nasty surprise waiting on the other side. Just go home and forget the whole thing.

Sure.

Well, at least take a look around before you jump.

That's what I'll do.

When I reached the top of the fence, however, it was too precarious to spend any time scouting the area. I couldn't even spot the girl before making my off-kilter leap. My sneakers smacked the concrete. I stumbled forward, fighting to stay up, and managed to stop myself just short of the pool.

Then I stood up straight and looked around.

The pool was brightly lighted, clean and blue and shimmering. The girl didn't seem to be in it. Nor was anybody else in sight. Here and there, I saw wet places on the concrete apron—probably where the girl had climbed out after her dives. Across the pool, the patio lights were on. The ranch-style house, mostly glass facing the pool, looked dark inside.

"I'm glad you came."

I jerked my head toward the voice and found the girl high to the left, striding out on the diving board.

"Thanks for asking me," I said. My heart was thundering.

She halted near the end of the board. "Do you enjoy watching me dive?" she asked.

"I couldn't really see much from where I was."

"This should be better for you."

"Much better. Thank you."

"Thank *you* for coming over."

I smiled and shrugged, amazed by her friendliness.

"Do you mind if I take this off?" she asked, reaching behind her back with both hands.

I almost choked. "Whatever . . . you want."

Her hands were busy behind her back for a few seconds. Then behind her neck. After giving her bikini top a swing by one of its neck strings, she sent it flying out over the pool. It made it to the shallow end, where it splashed softly and drifted toward the bottom.

The skimpy pants of her bikini flew not quite so far as the top.

This cannot be happening, I thought. I am dreaming. I've gotta be.

But it was just one of those things you tell yourself when something happens that is just too wonderful or too horrible to believe. Sometimes you actually do wake up and find that you've been dreaming. I knew I was awake, though. Or at least I knew it with as much certainty as anyone ever has in matters of consciousness or reality.

"Ready?" the girl asked.

I stared at her up there. She stood straight and naked at the end of the diving board, arms against her sides. Illuminated from below by the underwater lights, tremors and ripples seemed to be climbing her body.

"Ready when you are." My voice came out husky.

She leaped straight up and came straight down. Both feet hit the board. She bent her knees as the board bowed beneath her. Flinging her arms high, she jumped again as the board hurled her upward.

She bounced again and again, going higher each time like a girl on a trampoline, her short hair leaping around her head, her breasts lurching and jerking. Finally, she went so high that she soared above the reach of the lights. Up there, a pale wonderful form against the summer sky, she leaned forward and spread her arms and glided out over the pool like some unknown and wonderful human bird. Then she suddenly tucked her knees up close to her chest and tumbled downward, somersault after somersault so fast I couldn't count them until at the last instant she somehow unbent herself. Arms straight out over her head, back arched, buttocks gleaming, legs tight together and straight above her, toes pointing at the stars, she lanced into the pool with hardly a splash.

Down deep, she curved away from the bottom and glided underwater to the shallow end. There, she stood up. Wiping water from her face, she turned to me.

"Was it okay?" she asked.

"Okay? It was . . . great."

"Thank you."

"I've never seen such a beautiful dive. Or diver."

Her smile spread. "That's very nice of you. Wouldn't you like to come in for a swim?"

"Oh, I don't know."

"Sure you would."

"I don't have a bathing suit."

"Do *I*?"

The two parts of her bikini were barely visible against the pale blue tiles of the pool bottom. "Well," I said, "You have one."

"But I'm not wearing it."

"I noticed."

She laughed softly. "There's no reason to be shy around me."

I shrugged.

"But you are, aren't you?"

"A little, I guess."

So then she waded through the waist-high water, waded straight toward me and climbed out of the pool. Water spilling off her body, splashing the concrete around her feet, she stepped up to me.

"I'll help," she said.

"I don't—"

"Sure you do." Her fingers worked at the buttons of my shirt. I stood motionless, stunned, embarrassed, excited, more than a little disoriented.

This cannot be happening. Not to me.

After my shirt was off, she began with my belt. I took hold of her wrists and shook my head.

"You *are* shy."

"It's just—"

"This?" She reached lower and pressed a hand against the bulging front of my pants. "Feels lovely," she said. "Why would you want to keep it hidden?"

"I don't know."

"Allow me."

"All right."

She removed all the rest of my clothes and then we made love on the concrete beside the pool, me on top, my knees hurting, my mouth kissing her all the way down beginning with her eyes, lingering a long time with her open urgent mouth, moving downward to her wonderful soft firm breasts with their stiff nipples, then down and down, down to the slippery cleft between her wide-open thighs, kissing and tonguing her there while she writhed and flinched and moaned, then working my way back upward with my mouth and sliding my penis into her.

For a while after we'd finished, I sat on the edge of the pool and watched her dive. She was magnificent, soaring high, twirling, folding in half to touch her toes, somersaulting, arching gracefully and slicing her way into the water.

As wonderful as the dives were, I found as much joy in watching her climb all sleek and dripping out of the pool and stride away, making tracks on the smooth, dusky concrete, and climb the high ladder to the springboard.

After a particularly exciting dive in which she descended from the sky facing me all the way down, she remained submerged and glided over to me. My legs were dangling in the water. Not surfacing for air, she parted my knees. Then she came up between them and took me into her mouth.

When we were done, she climbed out of the pool and sat beside me. We held hands.

"Would you like to try diving?" she asked.

"It's awfully high," I said.

"That's what makes it so exciting."

"Anyway, I'd rather watch you. I've never seen anyone who can dive like you. Have you ever competed?"

She shook her head. "I do it only for myself. And for you."

"I sure appreciate it."

"I know you do." Smiling she turned and kissed me on the mouth and I felt a nipple rub the side of my arm. I put my hand gently on her other breast. When she took her mouth away, she asked, "Will you come back again after tonight?"

"Are you kidding?"

Smiling, she kissed me again.

"When do you want me?" I asked.

She whispered, "Always." Then: "Now."

I eased her backward and we made love on the concrete by the side of the pool. This time, I was on my back. Straddling me, she seemed to suck my rigid flesh up into her. She was snug and juicy.

Braced above me, she glided up and down, squirming and moaning, her breasts hovering over my face. I caressed them, fingered her nipples, and she eased downward to let my mouth reach them.

When it was over, she lay on top of me. We were both breathless, sweaty, worn out. I remember wrapping my arms around her wet back and squeezing her hard against me. I remember her giving my chin a playful nibble.

I was still buried inside her when I fell asleep.

✧

I woke up on my back on the concrete beside the pool. The girl was no longer on top of me. I sat up and looked around for her.

The pool and the patio lights had been turned off, and the house was dark.

The girl seemed to be gone.

I turned my gaze to the high dive. It was illuminated only by the dim glow of distant streetlights, but there was enough light to see the girl if she'd been there.

She wasn't.

I opened my mouth to call out. And realized I'd never asked her name.

I called toward the house, *"Hello?"*

It gave me the creeps, shouting like that at such an hour of the night.

No answer came.

Well, I thought, I'll see her tomorrow.

I put on my clothes, climbed the back fence, and returned to my house by the same route I'd used earlier that night.

✧

Today I couldn't wait to see her again.

Couldn't wait for dark.

In the afternoon, I visited a flower shop and bought a bright, beautiful bouquet in a vase decorated with seashells. Home again, I showered, shaved, and dressed like a guy getting ready for his first date with the love of his life . . . and maybe I was.

My plan was to present her with the flowers, and then take her out to a nice restaurant.

If she's home.

Please let her be home.

Carrying the vase of flowers, I left my house by the front door, went to the sidewalk, and headed for the corner. Though I'd rarely paid attention to the houses on the other side of my block, I had a fairly good idea about the location of the diving girl's house: the fourth from the corner.

Walking there, I grew more nervous and excited with every stride.

I came to the fourth house and halted, shocked, sinking inside.

FOR SALE.

No!

I only met her last night! She *can't* be moving away. It isn't fair!

Fair?

Sick inside, I crossed the lawn and walked straight up to the bay window and stared in. Carpet. Walls. No furniture at all. Not even draperies across the wall of glass at the back of the house.

I could see all the way to the pool.

And gasped, *"Huh?"*

I dropped the vase and ran. The gate by the side of the house was locked. I climbed over it, dropped to the other side, stumbled and fell, and scampered up and ran some more.

And halted and stared.

I wanted to believe I had the wrong house, but the high dive was there. So was the pool. It was all there.

The concrete apron around the pool looked like an old, abandoned street, weeds growing out of the countless cracks, it's pavement littered with debris: twigs and leaves, a few old newspaper pages and food wrappers and hundreds of other odds and ends that had probably been brought there by the wind.

The chrome of the high dive's ladder, so shiny last night, was dull and mottled with rust. The springboard was tilted crooked as if broken and ready to fall.

As for the pool itself, you could climb in, walk down to its murky water from the shallow end and your feet would stay dry until you were almost below the broken springboard. The lingering water was green, afloat with moss and litter.

I went to the shallow end and climbed down its rusty ladder. Leaves and other matter crunching under my shoes, I walked carefully down the sloping bottom. I stopped twice to bend down and pick up parts of a skimpy garment.

I brushed them off.

They felt slightly damp. They were white and smelled faintly of chlorine.

I took them home with me.

❖

I spent the rest of the afternoon and evening writing these pages, telling my story of the diving girl.

I'm almost done now.

Darkness has fallen. In a couple of minutes, I'll shut off my computer, turn off my office lights, open the blinds of the back window, and begin my wait.

Do I know what's going on?

No.

Not at all.

I know only one thing for sure.

If the pool lights come on tonight and she climbs the high dive, I will go to her.

Whatever she is.

HAECKEL'S TALE

CLIVE BARKER

PURRUCKER DIED LAST week, after a long illness. I never much liked the man, but the news of his passing still saddened me. With him gone I am now the last of our little group; there's no one left with whom to talk over the old times. Not that I ever did; at least not with him. We followed such different paths, after Hamburg. He became a physicist, and lived mostly, I think, in Paris. I stayed here in Germany, and worked with Herman Helmholtz, mainly working in the area of mathematics, but occasionally offering my contribution to other disciplines. I do not think I will be remembered when I go. Herman was touched by greatness; I never was. But I found comfort in the cool shadow of his theories. He had a clear mind, a precise mind. He refused to let sentiment or superstition into his view of the world. I learned a good deal from that.

And yet now, as I think back over my life to my early twenties (I'm two years younger than the century, which turns in a month), it is not the times of intellectual triumph that I find myself remembering; it is not Helmholtz's analytical skills, or his gentle detachment.

In truth, it is little more than the slip of a story that's on my mind right now. But it refuses to go away, so I am setting it down here, as a way of clearing it from my mind.

✿

In 1822, I was—along with Purrucker and another eight or so bright young men—a member of an informal club of aspirant intellectuals in Hamburg. We were all of us in that circle learning to be scientists, and being young had great ambition, both for ourselves and for the future of scientific endeavor. Every Sunday we gathered at a coffeehouse on the Reeperbahn, and in a back room that we hired for the purpose, fell to debate on any subject that suited us, as long as we felt the exchanges in some manner advanced our comprehension of the world. We were pompous, no doubt, and very full of ourselves; but our ardor was quite genuine. It was an exciting time. Every week, it seemed, one of us would come to a meeting with some new idea.

It was an evening during the summer—which was, that year, oppressively hot, even at night—when Ernst Haeckel told us all the story I am about to relate. I remember the circumstances well. At least I think I do. Memory is less exact than it believes itself to be, yes? Well, it scarcely matters. What I remember may as well *be* the truth. After all, there's nobody left to disprove it. What happened was this: toward the end of the evening, when everyone had drunk enough beer to float the German fleet, and the keen edge of intellectual debate had been dulled somewhat (to be honest we were descending into gossip, as we inevitably did after midnight), Eisentrout, who later became a great surgeon, made casual mention of a man called Montesquino. The fellow's name was familiar to us all, though none of us had met him. He had come into the city a month before, and attracted a good deal of attention in society, because he claimed to be a necromancer. He could speak with and even raise the dead, he claimed, and was holding seances in the houses of the rich. He was charging the ladies of the city a small fortune for his services.

The mention of Montesquino's name brought a chorus of slurred opinions from around the room, every one of them unflattering. He was a contemptuous cheat and a sham. He should be sent back to France—from whence he'd come—but not before the skin had been flogged off his back for his impertinence.

The only voice in the room that was not raised against him was that of Ernst Haeckel, who in my opinion was the finest mind amongst us. He sat by the open window—hoping perhaps for some stir of a breeze off the Elbe on this smothering night—with his chin laid against his hand.

"What do you think of all this, Ernst?" I asked him.

"You don't want to know," he said softly.

"Yes we do. Of course we do."

Haeckel looked back at us. "Very well then," he said. "I'll tell you."

His face looked sickly in the candlelight, and I remember thinking—distinctly thinking—that I'd never seen such a look in his eyes as he had at that moment. Whatever thoughts had ventured into his head, they had muddied the clarity of his gaze. He looked fretful.

"Here's what I think," he said. "That we should be careful when we talk about necromancers."

"Careful?" said Purrucker, who was an argumentative man at the best of times, and even more volatile when drunk. "Why should we be *careful* of a little French prick who preys on our women? Good Lord, he's practically stealing from their purses!"

"How so?"

"Because he's telling them he can raise the dead!" Purrucker yelled, banging the table for emphasis.

"And how do we know he cannot?"

"Oh now Haeckel," I said, "you don't believe—"

"I believe the evidence of my eyes, Theodor," Haeckel said to me. "And I saw—once in my life—what I take to be proof that such crafts as this Montesquino professes are real."

The room erupted with laughter and protests. Haeckel sat them out, unmoving. At last, when all our din had subsided, he said: "Do you want to hear what I have to say or don't you?"

"Of *course* we want to hear," said Julius Linneman, who doted on Haeckel; almost girlishly, we used to think.

"Then listen," Haeckel said. "What I'm about to tell you is absolutely true, though by the time I get to the end of it you may not welcome me back into this room, because you may think I am a little crazy. More than a little perhaps."

The softness of his voice, and the haunted look in his eyes, had quieted everyone, even the volatile Purrucker. We all took seats, or lounged against the mantelpiece, and listened. After a moment of introspection, Haeckel began to tell his tale. And as best I remember it, this is what he told us.

"Ten years ago I was at Wittenberg, studying philosophy under Wilhem Hauser. He was a metaphysician, of course; monkish in his ways. He didn't care for the physical world; it didn't touch him, really. And he urged his students to live with the same asceticism as he himself practices. This was of course hard for us. We were very young, and full of appetite. But while I was in Wittenberg, and under his watchful eye, I really tried to live as close to his precepts as I could.

"In the spring of my second year under Hauser, I got

word that my father—who lived in Luneburg—was seriously ill, and I had to leave my studies and return home. I
was a student. I'd spent all my money on books and bread.
I couldn't afford the carriage fare. So I had to walk. It was
several days' journey, of course, across the empty heath,
but I had my meditations to accompany, and I was happy
enough. At least for the first half of the journey. Then, out
of nowhere there came a terrible rainstorm. I was soaked to
the skin, and despite my valiant attempts to put my concern
for physical comfort out of my mind, I could not. I was
cold and unhappy, and the rarifications of the metaphysical
life were very far from my mind.

"On the fourth or fifth evening, sniffling and cursing, I
gathered some twigs and made a fire against a little stone
wall, hoping to dry myself out before I slept. While I was
gathering moss to make a pillow for my head an old man,
his face the very portrait of melancholy, appeared out of
the gloom, and spoke to me like a prophet.

" 'It would not be wise for you to sleep here tonight,' he
said to me.

"I was in no mood to debate the issue with him. I was
too fed up. 'I'm not going to move an inch,' I told him.
'This is an open road. I have every right to sleep here if I
wish to.'

" 'Of course you do,' the old man said to me. 'I didn't
say the right was not yours. I simply said it wasn't wise.'

"I was a little ashamed of my sharpness, to be honest.
'I'm sorry,' I said to him. 'I'm cold and I'm tired and I'm
hungry. I meant no insult.'

"The old man said that none was taken. His name, he
said, was Walter Wolfram.

"I told him my name, and my situation. He listened,
then offered to bring me back to his house, which he said
was close by. There I might enjoy a proper fire and some
hot potato soup. I did not refuse him, of course. But I did

ask him, when I'd risen, why he thought it was unwise for
me to sleep in that place.

"He gave me such a sorrowful look. A heartbreaking
look, the meaning of which I did not comprehend. Then he
said: 'You are a young man, and no doubt you do not fear
the workings of the world. But please believe me when I
tell you there are nights when it's not good to sleep next to
a place where the dead are laid.'

"'The dead?' I replied, and looked back. In my exhausted state I had not seen what lay on the other side of
the stone wall. Now, with the rain clouds cleared and the
moon climbing, I could see a large number of graves there,
old and new intermingled. Usually such a sight would not
have much disturbed me. Hauser had taught us to look
coldly on death. It should not, he said, move a man more
than the prospect of sunrise, for it is just as certain, and just
as unremarkable. It was good advice when heard on a
warm afternoon in a classroom in Wittenberg. But here—
out in the middle of nowhere, with an old man murmuring
his superstitions at my side—I was not so certain it made
sense.

"Anyway, Wolfram took me home to his little house,
which lay no more than half a mile from the necropolis.
There was the fire, as he'd promised. And the soup, as he'd
promised. But there also, much to my surprise and delight,
his wife, Elise.

"She could not have been more than twenty-two, and
easily the most beautiful woman I had ever seen. Wittenberg had its share of beauties, of course. But I don't believe
its streets ever boasted a woman as perfect as this. Chestnut
hair, all the way down to her tiny waist. Full lips, full hips,
full breasts. And such eyes! When they met mine they
seemed to consume me.

"I did my best, for decency's sake, to conceal my ad-
miration, but it was hard to do. I wanted to fall down on

my knees and declare my undying devotion to her, there and then.

"If Walter noticed any of this, he made no sign. He was anxious about something, I began to realize. He constantly glanced up at the clock on the mantel, and looked toward the door.

"I was glad of his distraction, in truth. It allowed me to talk to Elise, who—though she was reticent at first—grew more animated as the evening proceeded. She kept plying me with wine, and I kept drinking it, until sometime before midnight I fell asleep, right there amongst the dishes I'd eaten from."

At this juncture, somebody in our little assembly—I think it may have been Purrucker—remarked that he hoped this wasn't going to be a story about disappointed love, because he really wasn't in the mood. To which Haeckel replied that the story had absolutely nothing to do with love in any shape or form. It was a simple enough reply, but it did the job: it silenced the man who'd interrupted, and it deepened our sense of foreboding.

The noise from the café had by now died almost completely; as had the sounds from the street outside. Hamburg had retired to bed. But we were held there, by the story, and by the look in Ernst Haeckel's eyes.

"I awoke a little while later," he went on, "but I was so weary and so heavy with wine, I barely opened my eyes. The door was ajar, and on the threshold stood a man in a dark cloak. He was having a whispered conversation with Walter. There was, I thought, an exchange of money; though I couldn't see clearly. Then the man departed. I got only the merest glimpse of his face, by the light thrown from the fire. It was not the face of a man I would like to quarrel with, I thought. Nor indeed even meet. Narrow eyes, sunk deep in fretful flesh. I was glad he was gone. As Walter closed the door I lay my head back down and almost closed my eyes, preferring that he not know I was awake. I can't tell you exactly why. I just knew that something was going on I was better not becoming involved with.

"Then, as I lay there, listening, I heard a baby crying. Walter called for Elise, instructing her to calm the infant down. I didn't hear her response. Rather, I heard it, I just couldn't make any sense of it. Her voice, which had been soft and sweet when I'd talked with her, now sounded strange. Through the slits of my eyes I could see that she'd gone to the window, and was staring out, her palms pressed flat against the glass.

"Again, Walter told her to attend to the child. Again, she gave him some guttural reply. This time she turned to him, and I saw that she was by no means the same woman as I'd conversed with. She seemed to be in the early stages of some kind of fit. Her color was high, her eyes wild, her lips drawn back from her teeth.

"So much that had seemed, earlier, evidence of her beauty and vitality now looked more like a glimpse of the sickness that was consuming her. She'd glowed too brightly; like someone consumed by a fever, who in that hour when all is at risk seems to burn with a terrible vividness.

"One of her hands went down between her legs and she began to rub herself there, in a most disturbing manner. If you've ever been to a madhouse you've maybe seen some of the kind of behavior she was exhibiting.

"'Patience,' Walter said to her, 'everything's being taken care of. Now go and look after the child.'

"Finally she conceded to his request, and off she went into the next room. Until I'd heard the infant crying I hadn't even realized they had a child, and it seemed odd to me that Elise had not made mention of it. Lying there, feigning sleep, I tried to work out what I should do next. Should I perhaps pretend to wake, and announce to my host that I would not after all be accepting his hospitality? I decided against this course. I would stay where I was. As long as they thought I was asleep they'd ignore me. Or so I hoped.

"The baby's crying had now subsided. Elise's presence had soothed it.

" 'Make sure he's had enough before you put him down,' I heard Walter say to her. 'I don't want him waking and crying for you when you're gone.'

"From this I gathered that she was breast-feeding the child; which fact explained the lovely generosity of her breasts. They were plump with milk. And I must admit, even after the way Elise had looked when she was at the window, I felt a little spasm of envy for the child, suckling at those lovely breasts.

"Then I returned my thoughts to the business of trying to understand what was happening here. Who was the man who'd come to the front door? Elise's lover, perhaps? If so, why was Walter *paying* him? Was it possible that the old man had hired this fellow to satisfy his wife, because he was incapable of doing the job himself? Was Elise's twitching at the window simply erotic anticipation?

"At last, she came out of the infant's room, and very carefully closed the door. There was a whispered exchange between the husband and wife, which I caught no part of, but which set off a new round of questions in my head. Suppose they were conspiring to kill me? I will tell you, my neck felt very naked at that moment . . .

"But I needn't have worried. After a minute they finished their whispering and Elise left the house. Walter, for his part, went to sit by the fire. I heard him pour himself a drink, and down it noisily; then pour himself another. Plainly he was drowning his sorrows; or doing his best. He kept drinking, and muttering to himself while he drank. Presently, the muttering became tearful. Soon he was sobbing.

"I couldn't bear this any longer. I raised my head off the table, and I turned to him.

" 'Herr Wolfram,' I said, 'what's going on here?'

"He had tears pouring down his face, running into his beard.

" 'Oh my friend,' he said, shaking his head, 'I could not begin to explain. This is a night of unutterable sadness.'

" 'Would you prefer that I left you to your tears?' I asked him.

" '*No*,' he said. 'No, I don't want you to go out there right now.'

"I wanted to know why, of course. Was there something he was afraid I'd see?

"I had risen from the table, and now went to him. 'The man who came to the door—'

"Walter's lip curled at my mention of him. 'Who is he?' I asked.

" 'His name is Doctor Skal. He's an Englishman of my acquaintance.'

"I waited for further explanation. But when none was forthcoming, I said: 'And a friend of your wife's.'

" 'No,' Walter said. 'It's not what you think it is.' He poured himself some more brandy, and drank again. 'You're supposing they're lovers. But they're not. Elise has not the slightest interest in the company of Doctor Skal, believe me. Nor indeed in any visitor to this house.'

"I assumed this remark was a little barb directed at me, and I began to defend myself, but Walter waved my protestations away.

" 'Don't concern yourself,' he said, 'I took no offense at the looks you gave my wife. How could you not? She's a very beautiful woman, and I'd be surprised if a young man such as yourself *didn't* try to seduce her. At least in his heart. But let me tell you, my friend: you could never satisfy her.' He let this remark lie for a moment. Then he added: 'Neither, of course, could I. When I married her I was already too old to be a husband to her in the truest sense.'

" 'But you have a baby,' I said to him.

" 'The boy isn't mine,' Walter replied.

" 'So you're raising this infant, even though he isn't yours?'

" 'Yes.'

" 'Where's the father?'

" 'I'm afraid he's dead.'

" 'Ah.' This all began to seem very tragic. Elise pregnant, the father dead, and Walter coming to the rescue, saving her from dishonor. That was the story constructed in my head. The only part I could not yet fit into this neat scheme was Doctor Skal, whose cloaked presence at the door had so unsettled me.

" 'I know none of this is my business—,' I said to Walter.

" 'And better keep it that way,' he replied.

" 'But I have one more question.'

" 'Ask it.'

" 'What kind of doctor is this man Skal?'

" 'Ah.' Walter set his glass down, and stared into the fire. It had not been fed in a while, and now was little more than a heap of glowing embers. 'The esteemed Doctor Skal is a necromancer. He deals in a science which I do not profess to understand.' He leaned a little closer to the fire, as though talking of the mysterious man had chilled him to the marrow. I felt something similar. I knew very little about the work of a necromancer, but I knew that they dealt with the dead.

"I thought of the graveyard, and of Walter's first words to me:

" *'It would not be wise for you to sleep here tonight.'*

"Suddenly, I understood. I got to my feet, my barely sobered head throbbing. 'I know what's going on here,' I announced. 'You paid Skal so that Elise could speak to the dead! To the man who fathered her baby.' Walter continued to stare into the fire. I came close to him. 'That's

it, isn't it? And now Skal's going to play some miserable
trick on poor Elise to make her believe she's talking to a
spirit.'

" 'It's *not* a trick,' Walter said. For the first time during
this grim exchange he looked up at me. 'What Skal does is
real, I'm afraid to say. Which is why you should stay in
here until it's over and done with. It's nothing you need
ever—'

"He broke off at that moment, his thought unfinished,
because we heard Elise's voice. It wasn't a word she ut-
tered, it was a sob; and then another, and another, I knew
whence they came, of course. Elise was at the graveyard
with Skal. In the stillness of the night her voice carried
easily.

" 'Listen to her,' I said.

" 'Better not,' Walter said.

"I ignored him, and went to the door, driven by a kind of
morbid fascination. I didn't for a moment believe what
Walter had said about the necromancer. Though much else
that Hauser had taught me had become hard to believe tonight, I still believed in his teachings on the matter of life
and death. The soul, he'd taught us, was certainly immor-
tal. But once it was released from the constraints of flesh
and blood, the body had no more significance than a piece
of rotted meat. The man or woman who had animated it
was gone, to be with those who had already left this life.
There was, he insisted, no way to call that spirit back. And
nor therefore—though Hauser had never extrapolated this
far—was there any validity in the claims of those who said
that they could commune with the dead.

"In short, Doctor Skal was a fake: this was my certain
belief. And poor distracted Elise was his dupe. God knows
what demands he was making of her, to have her sobbing
that way! My imagination—having first dwelt on the
woman's charms shamelessly, and then decided she was

mad—now reinvented her a third time, as Skal's hapless victim. I knew from stories I'd heard in Hamburg what power charlatans like this wielded over vulnerable women. I'd heard of some necromancers who demanded that their seances be held with everyone as naked as Adam, for purity's sake! Others who had so battered the tender hearts of their victims with their ghoulishness that the women had swooned, and been violated in their swoon. I pictured all this happening to Elise. And the louder her sobs and cries became the more certain I was that my worst imaginings were true.

"At last I couldn't bear it any longer, and I stepped out into the darkness to get her.

"Herr Wolfram came after me, and caught hold of my arm. 'Come back into the house!' he demanded. 'For pity's sake, leave this alone *and come back into the house!*'

"Elise was shrieking now. I couldn't have gone back in if my life had depended upon it. I shook myself free of Wolfram's grip and started out for the graveyard. At first I thought he was going to leave me alone, but when I glanced back I saw that though he'd returned into the house he was now emerging again, cradling a musket in his arms. I thought at first he intended to threaten me with it, but instead he said:

" 'Take it!' offering the weapon to me.

" 'I don't intend to kill anybody!' I said, feeling very heroic and self-righteous now that I was on my way. 'I just want to get Elise out of this damn Englishman's hands.'

" 'She won't come, believe me,' Walter said. 'Please take the musket! You're a good fellow. I don't want to see any harm come to you.'

"I ignored him and strode on. Though Walter's age made him wheeze, he did his best to keep up with me. He even managed to talk, though what he said—between my agitated state and his panting—wasn't always easy to grasp.

" 'She has a sickness . . . she's had it all her life . . . what did I know? . . . I loved her . . . wanted her to be happy . . .'

" 'She doesn't sound very happy right now,' I remarked.

" 'It's not what you think . . . it is and it isn't . . . oh God, please come back to the house!'

" 'I said no! I don't want her being molested by that man!'

" 'You don't understand. We couldn't begin to please her. Neither of us.'

" 'So you hire Skal to service her, Jesus!'

"I turned and pushed him hard in the chest, then I picked up my pace. Any last doubts I might have entertained about what was going on in the graveyard were forgotten. All this talk of necromancy was just a morbid veil drawn over the filthy truth of the matter. Poor Elise! Stuck with a broken-down husband, who knew no better way to please than to give her over to an Englishman for an occasional pleasuring. Of all things, an Englishman! As if the English knew anything about making love.

"As I ran, I envisaged what I'd do when I reached the graveyard. I imagined myself hopping over the wall and with a shout racing at Skal, and plucking him off my poor Elise. Then I'd beat him senseless. And when he was laid low, and I'd proved just how heroic a fellow I was, I'd go to the girl, take her in my arms, and show her what a good German does when he wants to make a woman happy.

"Oh, my head was spinning with ideas, right up until the moment that I emerged from the corner of the trees and came in sight of the necropolis . . ."

Here, after several minutes of headlong narration, Haeckel ceased speaking. It was not for dramatic effect, I think. He was simply preparing himself, mentally, for the final stretch of his story. I'm sure that none of us in that room doubted that what lay ahead would not be pleasant. From the beginning this had been a tale overshadowed by

the prospect of some horror. None of us spoke; that I do remember. We sat there, in thrall to the persuasions of
Haeckel's tale, waiting for him to begin again. We were
like children.

After a minute or so, during which time he stared out of
the window at the night sky (though seeing, I think, nothing of its beauty) he turned back to us and rewarded our
patience.

"The moon was full and white," he said. "It showed me
every detail. There were no great, noble tombs in this
place, such as you'd see at the Ohlsdorf Cemetery; just
coarsely carved headstones and wooden crosses. And in
their midst, a kind of ceremony was going on. There were
candles set in the grass, their flames steady in the still air. I
suppose they made some kind of circle—perhaps ten feet
across—in which the necromancer had performed his rituals. Now, however, with his work done, he had retired some
distance from this place. He was sitting on a tombstone,
smoking a long, Turkish pipe, and watching.

"The subject of his study, of course, was Elise. When I
had first laid eyes on her I had guiltily imagined what she
would look like stripped of her clothes. Now I had my answer. There she was, lit by the gold of the candle flames
and the silver of the moon. Available to my eyes in all her
glory.

"But oh God! What she was doing turned every single
drop of pleasure I might have taken in her beauty to the bit-
terest gall.

"Those cries I'd heard—those sobs that had made my
heart go out to her—they weren't provoked by the paw-
ings of Doctor Skal, but by the touch of the dead. The
dead, raised out of their dirt to pleasure her! She was
squatting, and there between her legs was a face, pushed
up out of the earth. A man recently buried, to judge by
his condition, the flesh still moist on the bone, and the

tongue—Jesus, the tongue!—still flicking between his bared teeth.

"If this had been all it would have been enough. But it was not all. The same grotesque genius that had inspired the cadaver between her legs into this resemblance of life had also brought forth a crop of smaller parts—pieces of the whole, which had wormed their way out of the grave by some means or other. Bony pieces, held together with leathery sinew. A rib cage, crawling around on its elbows; a head, propelled by a whiplash length of stripped spine; several hands, with some fleshless lengths of bone attached. There was a morbid bestiary of these things. And they were all upon her, or waiting their turn to be upon her.

"Nor did she for a moment protest their attentions. Quite the contrary. Having climbed off the corpse that was pleasuring her from below, she rolled over onto her back and invited a dozen of these pieces upon her, like a whore in a fever, and they came, oh God they came, as though they might have out of her the juices that would return them to wholesomeness.

"Walter, by now, had caught up with me.

" 'I warned you,' he said.

" 'You knew this was happening?'

" 'Of course I knew. I'm afraid it's the only way she's satisfied.'

" 'What is she?' I said to him.

" 'A woman,' Walter replied.

" 'No natural woman would endure *that*,' I said. 'Jesus! Jesus!'

"The sight before me was getting worse by the moment. Elise was up on her knees in the grave dirt now, and a second corpse—stripped of whatever garments he had been buried in—was coupling with her, his motion vigorous, his pleasure intense, to judge by the way he threw back his putrefying head. As for Elise, she was kneading her full tits, directing arcs of milk into the air so that it rained down on the vile menagerie cavorting before her. Her lovers were in ecstasy. They clattered and scampered around in the torrents, as though they were being blessed.

"I took the musket from Walter.

" 'Don't hurt her!' he begged. 'She's not to blame.'

"I ignored him, and made my way toward the yard, calling to the necromancer as I did so.

" 'Skal! *Skal!'*

"He looked up from his meditations, whatever they were, and seeing the musket I was brandishing, immediately began to protest his innocence. His German wasn't good, but I didn't have any difficulty catching his general drift. He was just doing what he'd been paid to do, he said. He wasn't to blame.

"I clambered over the wall and approached him through the graves, instructing him to get to his feet. He got up, his hands raised in surrender. Plainly he was terrified that I was going to shoot him. But that wasn't my intention. I just wanted to stop this obscenity.

" 'Whatever you did to start this, *undo it!'* I told him.

"He shook his head, his eyes wild. I thought perhaps he didn't understand so I repeated the instruction.

"Again, he shook his head. All his composure was gone. He looked like a shabby little cutpurse who'd just been caught in the act. I was right in front of him, and I jabbed the musket in his belly. If he didn't stop this, I told him, I'd shoot him.

"I might have done it too, but for Herr Wolfram, who had clambered over the wall and was approaching his wife, calling her name.

" 'Elise . . . please, Elise . . . you should come home.'

"I've never in my life heard anything as absurd or as sad as that man calling to his wife. *'You should come home . . .'*

"Of course she didn't listen to him. Didn't *hear* him,

probably, in the heat of what she was doing, and what was being done to her.

"But her *lovers* heard. One of the men who'd been raised up whole, and was waiting his turn at the woman, started shambling toward Walter, waving him away. It was a curious thing to see. The corpse trying to shoo the old man off. But Walter wouldn't go. He kept calling to Elise, the tears pouring down his face. Calling to her, calling to her—

"I yelled to him to stay away. He didn't listen to me. I suppose he thought if he got close enough he could maybe catch hold of her arm. But the corpse came at him, still waving its hands, still shooing, and when Walter wouldn't be shooed the thing simply knocked him down. I saw him flail for a moment, and then try to get back up. But the dead—or pieces of the dead—were everywhere in the grass around his feet. And once he was down, they were upon him.

"I told the Englishman to come with me, and I started off across the yard to help Walter. There was only one ball in the musket, so I didn't want to waste it firing from a distance, and maybe missing my target. Besides I wasn't sure what I was going to fire at. The closer I got to the circle in which Elise was crawling around—still being clawed and petted—the more of Skal's unholy handiwork I saw. Whatever spells he'd cast here, they seemed to have raised every last dead thing in the place. The ground was crawling with bits of this and that; fingers, pieces of dried up flesh with locks of hair attached; wormy fragments that were beyond recognition.

"By the time we reached Walter, he'd already lost the fight. The horrors he'd paid to have resurrected— ungrateful things—had torn him open in a hundred places. One of his eyes had been thumbed out, there was a gaping hole in his chest.

"His murderers were still working on him. I batted a few limbs off him with the musket, but there were so many it was only a matter of time, I knew, before they came after me. I turned around to Skal, intending to order him again to bring this abomination to a halt, but he was springing off between the graves. In a sudden surge of rage, I raised the musket and I fired. The felon went down, howling in the grass. I went to him. He was badly wounded, and in great pain, but I was in no mood to help him. He was responsible for all this. Wolfram dead, and Elise still crouching amongst her rotted admirers; all of this was Skal's fault. I had no sympathy for the man.

" 'What does it take to make this stop?' I asked him. *'What are the words?'*

"His teeth were chattering. It was hard to make out what he was saying. Finally I understood.

" 'When . . . the . . . sun . . . comes up . . . ,' he said to me.

" 'You can't stop it any other way?'

" 'No,' he said. 'No . . . other . . . way . . .'

"Then he died. You can imagine my despair. I could do nothing. There was no way to get to Elise without suffering the same fate as Walter. And anyway, she wouldn't have come. It was an hour from dawn, at least. All I could do was what I did: climb over the wall, and wait. The sounds were horrible. In some ways, worse than the sight. She must have been exhausted by now, but she kept going. Sighing sometimes, sobbing sometimes, moaning sometimes. Not—let me make it perfectly clear—the despairing moan of a woman who understands that she is in the grip of the dead. This was the moan of a deeply pleasured woman; a woman in bliss.

"Just a few minutes before dawn, the sounds subsided. Only when they had died away completely did I look back over the wall. Elise had gone. Her lovers lay around in the ground, exhausted as perhaps only the dead can be. The clouds were lightening in the East. I suppose resurrected flesh has a fear of the light, because as the last stars crept away so did the dead. They crawled back into the earth, and covered themselves with the dirt that had been shoveled down upon their coffins . . ."

Haeckel's voice had become a whisper in these last minutes, and now it trailed away completely. We sat around not looking at one another, each of us deep in thought. If any of us had entertained the notion that Haeckel's tale was some invention, the force of his telling—the whiteness of his skin, the tears that had now and then appeared in his eyes—had thrust such doubts from us, at least for now.

It was Purrucker who spoke first, inevitably. "So you killed a man," he said. "I'm impressed."

Haeckel looked up at him. "I haven't finished my story," he said.

"Jesus . . . ," I murmured, ". . . what else is there to tell?"

"If you remember, I'd left all my books, and some gifts I'd brought from Wittenberg for my father, at Herr Wolfram's house. So I made my way back there. I was in a kind of terrified trance, my mind still barely able to grasp what I'd seen.

"When I got to the house I heard somebody singing. A sweet lilting voice it was. I went to the door. My belongings were sitting there on the table where I'd left them. The room was empty. Praying that I'd go unheard, I entered. As I picked up my philosophy books and my father's gift the singing stopped.

"I retreated to the door but before I could reach the threshold Elise appeared, with her infant in her arms. The woman looked the worse for her philanderings, no question about that. There were scratches all over her face, and her arms, and on the plump breast at which the baby now sucked. But marked as she was, there was nothing but happiness in her eyes. She was sweetly content with her life at that moment.

"I thought perhaps she had no memory of what had happened to her. Maybe the necromancer had put her into some kind of trance, I reasoned; and now she'd woken from it the past was all forgotten.

"I started to explain to her. 'Walter . . . ,' I said.

" 'Yes, I know—,' she replied. 'He's dead.' She smiled at me; a May morning smile. 'He was old,' she said, matter-of-factly. 'But he was always kind to me. Old men are the best husbands. As long as you don't want children.'

"My gaze must have gone from her radiant face to the baby at her nipple, because she said:

" 'Oh, this isn't Walter's boy.'

"As she spoke she tenderly teased the infant from her breast, and it looked my way. There it was: life-in-death, perfected. Its face was shiny pink, and its limbs fat from its mother's milk, but its sockets were deep as the grave, and its mouth wide, so that its teeth, which were not an infant's teeth, were bared in a perpetual grimace.

"The dead, it seemed, had given her more than pleasure.

"I dropped the books and the gift for my father there on the doorstep. I stumbled back out into the daylight, and I ran—oh God in Heaven, I ran!—afraid to the very depths of my soul. I kept on running until I reached the road. Though I had no desire to venture past the graveyard again, I had no choice: it was the only route I knew, and I did not want to get lost, I wanted to be home. I wanted a church, an altar, piety, prayers.

"It was not a busy thoroughfare by any means, and if anyone had passed along it since daybreak they'd decided to leave the necromancer's body where it lay beside the wall. But the crows were at his face, and foxes at his hands and feet. I crept by without disturbing their feast."

Again, Haeckel halted. This time, he expelled a long,

long sigh. "And that, gentlemen, is why I advise you to be careful in your judgments of this man Montesquino."

He rose as he spoke, and went to the door. Of course we all had questions, but none of us spoke then, not then. We let him go. And for my part, gladly. I'd enough of these horrors for one night.

✧

Make of all this what you will. I don't know to this day whether I believe the story or not (though I can't see any reason why Haeckel would have *invented* it. Just as he'd predicted, he was treated very differently after that night; kept at arm's length). The point is that the thing still haunts me; in part, I suppose, *because* I never made up my mind whether I thought it was a falsehood or not. I've sometimes wondered what part it played in the shaping of my life: if perhaps my cleaving to empiricism—my devotion to Helmholtz's methodologies—was not in some way the consequence of this hour spent in the company of Haeckel's account.

Nor do I think I was alone in my preoccupation with what I heard. Though I saw less and less of the other members of the group as the years went by, on those occasions when we did meet up the conversation would often drift round to that story, and our voices would drop to near-whispers, as though we were embarrassed to be confessing that we even remembered what Haeckel had said.

A couple of members of the group went to some lengths to pluck holes in what they'd heard, I remember; to expose it as nonsense. I think Eisentrout actually claimed he'd re-traced Haeckel's journey from Wittenberg to Luneburg, and claimed there was no necropolis along the route. As for Haeckel himself, he treated these attacks upon his veracity with indifference. We had asked him to tell us what he thought of necromancers, and he'd told us. There was nothing more to say on the matter.

And in a way he was right. It was just a story told on a hot night, long ago, when I was still dreaming of what I would become.

And yet now, sitting here at the window, knowing I will never again be strong enough to step outside, and that soon I must join Purrucker and the others in the earth, I find the terror coming back to me; the terror of some convulsive place where death has a beautiful woman in its teeth, and she gives voice to bliss. I have, if you will, fled Haeckel's story over the years; hidden my head under the covers of reason. But here, at the end, I see that there is no asylum to be had from it; or rather, from the terrible suspicion that it contains a clue to the ruling principle of the world.

BEFORE YOU LEAVE

DEL HOWISON

THERE HAVE BEEN two schools of thought regarding tales of darkness and dread. One was that the theater of the macabre was for young people who liked sensationalized stories of the shadowlands they had yet to experience. They would grow out of their obsessions in time. So horror was marketed to teens. The other thought was that legends and tales of the supernatural occupied a basement room filled with folklore or campfire tales or (more recently) urban legends to teach a lesson. But beyond their moralistic teachings, tales of horror and the supernatural didn't count for much when compared to "real writing."

Horror has always been the blues of literature. However, like the blues in music, everything in literature can be traced back to its roots. It's unavoidable. Whether it is *Beowulf*, *The Iliad*, and *The Odyssey*, or Shakespeare's *Midsummer Night's Dream*, there have always been imps and monsters, supernatural events and psychological terror. There was horror in an eclipse and horror in religion.

Nowadays there is horror in politics and horror in your daily newspaper. There has always been horror, and there will always be horror. Sometimes, in an effort to be current with the times, there have been efforts by people in the field to legitimize horror by claiming it's not a genre. They try to put other names on it to mask what we all know is true. It's not Dark Fantasy. It's not a Thriller. It's not even an alternate state of mind. Because horror is involved in every other genre, they want to say it is not a genre itself. All I can say is hogwash. Face the truth. Sure, there are horror mysteries, horror westerns, horror thrillers, supernatural horror, etc. Everybody in this book knows what horror is. They are all wearing different masks but they have all come to the same party. For that I thank them sincerely and hope to see them back at my next party.

❖

But horror is horror. Putting a little mystery in a story does not make that story a mystery, but it doesn't eliminate mysteries from being their own genre. Watch a film or read a book. If it's horror, you know it, and nobody, no matter how learned, can tell you different. You're scared. You're disturbed. You're repelled as the worm turns within your own brain and sensibilities and it touches you in that deep, dark personal spot in your stomach. Horror has a smell, a taste, and a touch all its own. You know what that is. In fact, you've just read it. It makes you smile and shiver at the same time. You, like Jeff Gelb and myself, love it and embrace it. That's why we're all here together. Like the roller coaster at the park, you want to ride again. You want to "blow it out."

❖

You're still holding this book. Go ahead.

✧

Or you can just roll over and go to sleep.

✧

Fat chance.

CONTRIBUTOR BIOGRAPHIES

CLIVE BARKER—The bestselling author of twenty books, including the *New York Times* bestseller *Abarat*, Clive Barker is also an acclaimed artist, film producer, and director. Mr. Barker lives in California with his partner, the photographer David Armstrong, and their daughter, Nicole. They share their house with five dogs, sixty fish, nine rats, innumerable wild geckos, five cockatiels, an African gray parrot called Smokey, and a yellow-headed Amazon parrot called Malingo.

RAY BRADBURY—The author of more than thirty books, Ray Bradbury is one of the most celebrated writers of our time. Among his best-known works are *Fahrenheit 451*, *The Martian Chronicles*, *The Illustrated Man*, *Dandelion Wine*, and *Something Wicked This Way Comes*. He has written for the theater and the cinema, including the screenplay for John Huston's classic film adaptation of *Moby Dick*, and was nominated for an Academy Award. He adapted sixty-five of his stories for television's *The Ray Bradbury Theater* and won an Emmy for his teleplay of *The Halloween Tree*. In

2000, Ray Bradbury was honored by the National Book Foundation with a medal for Distinguished Contribution to American letters. Among his most recent books are *Let's All Kill Constance* and *From the Dust Returned*, which was selected as one of the Best Books of the Year by the *Los Angeles Times*. HarperCollins published *Bradbury Stories*, a new collection of one hundred of his short stories, in September 2003, and a short story collection, *The Cat's Pajamas*, in 2004. He lives in Los Angeles.

RAMSEY CAMPBELL—*The Oxford Companion to English Literature* describes Ramsey Campbell as "Britain's most respected living horror writer." He has been given more awards than any other writer in the field, including the Grand Master Award of the World Horror Convention and the Lifetime Achievement Award of the Horror Writers Association. Among his novels (most from Tor) are *The Face That Must Die, Incarnate, Midnight Sun, The Count of Eleven, Silent Children, The Darkest Part of the Woods*, and *The Overnight*. Forthcoming are *Secret Stories* and *Spanked by Nuns*. His collections include *Waking Nightmares, Alone with the Horrors, Ghosts and Grisly Things*, and *Told by the Dead*, and his nonfiction is collected as *Ramsey Campbell, Probably*. His novels *The Nameless* and *Pact of the Fathers* have been filmed in Spain. Ramsey Campbell lives on Merseyside with his wife, Jenny. He reviews films and DVDs weekly for BBC Radio Merseyside. His pleasures include classical music, good food and wine, and whatever's in that pipe. His Web site is at www .ramseycampbell.com.

JOHN FARRIS—The 2002 Horror Writer's Association Lifetime Achievement Award winner, Farris is the author of numerous bestsellers including *The Fury, Shatter*, and *Son of the Endless Night*. His most recent novel is *Phantom Nights* (February 2005). He lives in Marietta, Georgia, where he spends five days a week writing and the other two days just staring into space thinking about stuff.

JEFF GELB—*Dark Delicacies* is Gelb's twentieth anthology as editor or coeditor. He cocreated the ongoing, internationally published Hot Blood series with Michael Garrett, and coedited the Flesh & Blood anthologies with Max Allan Collins. He has also edited several Shock Rock editions, and *Fear Itself*. Gelb's one novel is *Specters*, and he also has one comic book writing credit: *Bettie Page Comics*, done with Dave Stevens. Gelb lives in Southern California with his wife, Terry Gladstone, and their son, Levi.

NANCY HOLDER—The *Los Angeles Times* bestseller is the author of sixty-eight books, and over two hundred short stories, essays, and articles. She has received three Bram Stoker Awards for her short fiction, and an additional Stoker for Best Novel for *Dead in the Water*. She was a charter member and former trustee of the Horror Writers Association. She has written and/or cowritten approximately four dozen Buffy the Vampire Slayer and Angel works, including the first two volumes of the *Buffy the Vampire Slayer Watcher's Guide* and *Angel: Casefiles, Volume One*. Her recent works include *Outsiders: An Anthology of Misfits*, coedited with Nancy Kilpatrick, a young adult horror novel, *Pretty Little Devils*, and *Buffy the Vampire Slayer: Queen of the Slayers*. She teaches "Writing the Horror Story" through UC San Diego Extension. Her Web site is www.nancyholder.com.

DEL HOWISON—Along with his wife, Sue, Howison created America's only all-horror book and gift store, Dark Delicacies, as fans and for fans, and they remain among horror's biggest aficionados. They, and the store, have been featured on many television documentaries concerning horror and the nature of evil. As a former photojournalist, Del has written articles for a variety of publications, including *Rue Morgue* and *Gauntlet* magazines, along with a foreword for the Wildside Press edition of *Varney the Vampyre*. His short stories have appeared in a variety of anthologies. This is his first editing stint.

ROBERTA LANNES—Lannes's first love was writing. In 1985, she took a course in writing genre fiction at UCLA, where she met horror writer Dennis Etchison. In 1986, he published her first horror story, "Goodbye, Dark Love," in his acclaimed *Cutting Edge* anthology. Since then, her sixty-plus short stories have been published in three genres and over a dozen languages, and a movie was made from her work by Ian Kerkhof (*Ten Monologues from the Lives of the Serial Killers*). Her premier story collection, *The Mirror of Night*, came out in 1997. Her most recent stories are found in *Taverns of the Dead* and *Don't Turn Out the Lights*. Roberta Lannes is a Southern California native whose day job is fine arts and digital design teacher at a high school. She lives with her husband, poet-author-editor Mark Sealey.

RICHARD LAYMON—Laymon was author of over thirty extreme horror novels and over sixty short stories before his untimely death in 2001. He is still immensely popular, here and overseas. Among his best-known works are *The Cellar*, *After Midnight*, *Bite*, and *The Woods Are Dark*. Of Laymon, Stephen King wrote, "If you've missed Laymon, you've missed a treat."

BRIAN LUMLEY—With *Harry Keogh: Necroscope and Other Weird Heroes!* Lumley has recently completed his epic Necroscope saga in fourteen volumes. Brian's list of titles now runs to fifty and counting. A prolific if not compulsive writer, the bulk of his work has seen print in the last twenty-three years, this following a full span of twenty-two years of military service. Although he retired from the Army in December 1980, Lumley's first work—short stories, and eventually two collections—had been published many years earlier by the then dean of macabre publishers, August Derleth, at Arkham House in Wisconsin. Thus, though he had long been an acknowledged master of the "Cthulhu Mythos" subgenre inspired by H. P. Lovecraft's fiction, it wasn't until 1986, with his military career behind him, that the UK saw first publication of Brian's dead-waking, ground-breaking horror novel

344 | CONTRIBUTOR BIOGRAPHIES

Necroscope, featuring Harry Keogh, the man who talks to dead people. The-not-quite-instant success of *Necroscope* resulted in four more books in the original series: *Wamphyri!*, *The Source*, *Deadspeak*, and *Deadspawn*. This success spawned Lumley's massive Vampire World Trilogy: *Blood Brothers*, *The Last Aerie*, and *Bloodwars*, and almost seven years after the first publication of *Necroscope* in paperback, such was its continuing impact that it was reissued in hardcover. Since then, all of the first five have appeared in hardcover. Thirteen countries (and counting) have now published or are in the process of publishing these books, which in the U.S. alone have sold well over two million copies. In addition, *Necroscope* comic books, graphic novels, a role-playing game, and quality figurines have been created from themes and characters in the books. Other books to Lumley's credit are: *The House of Doors* and the sequel *Maze of Worlds*, *Demogorgon*, six novels in the Titus Crow series, four in the Dreams series, the Psychomech Trilogy, several other one-off novels, and over one hundred short stories—one of which won a British Fantasy Award in 1989. Also, recently, *The Brian Lumley Companion* has been released. One of his short stories was adapted for Ridley Scott's "The Hunger" series on the Showtime Television Network, and other tales from Brian's short fiction list have often been selected for various "Year's Best Horror" anthologies. At the World Horror Convention in Phoenix, Arizona, 1998, Lumley received the genre's much coveted Grand Master Award in recognition of his work. When not traveling, Brian and his American wife, Barbara Ann ("Silky"), keep house in Devon, England.

RICHARD MATHESON—Matheson is the celebrated author of *Somewhere in Time* and *What Dreams May Come*, along with *Incredible Shrinking Man*, *I Am Legend*, *Legend of Hell House*, and other classic novels of horror and fantasy. The prolific Matheson has written well over one hundred short stories, many of which became memorable *Twilight Zone* episodes that Matheson himself penned. As a screenwriter, he is responsible for the early Spielberg classic *Duel*, as well as *House of Usher, Raven, The Pit and the Pendulum*, and many others. Matheson has won numerable prestigious awards, including the World Fantasy Convention's Life Achievement Award, the Bram Stoker Award for Life Achievement, the Hugo Award, the Edgar Allan Poe Award, the Golden Spur Award, and the Writer's Guild Award.

LISA MORTON—Lisa Morton's fiction has appeared in numerous books and magazines, including *The Mammoth Book of Frankenstein, White of the Moon, After Shocks, Shelf Life: Fantastic Stories Celebrating Bookstores, Midnight Premiere*, and the award-winning anthologies *The Museum of Horrors, Dark Terrors 6*, and *Horrors! 365 Scary Stories*. Her screenplay credits include *Meet the Hollowheads, Tornado Warning, Thralls, Blue Demon*, and *The Glass Trap*, and she is the author of two nonfiction books, *The Cinema of Tsui Hark* and *The Halloween Encyclopedia*.

STEVE NILES—Currently the *hot* name in comic book horror fiction, Niles is responsible for the graphic novel *30 Days of Night*, soon to be filmed by Sam Raimi's production company. Several of Niles's other projects have also been optioned by Hollywood, including his Cal MacDonald horror detective novels and comic book miniseries.

WILLIAM F. NOLAN—With more than eighty books to his credit, Nolan has seen his work selected for some three hundred anthologies and textbooks around the world. Among many honors, he is twice winner of the Edgar Allan Poe Special Award, has been cited for excellence by the American Library Association, and was voted a "Living Legend in Dark Fantasy" by the International Horror Guild. Author of more than one hundred short stories, Nolan has also written extensively for films and TV. He's best known for his Logan series (*Logan's Run, Logan's World, Logan's Search, Logan's Return*), the first of which was also an MGM film and CBS television series. *Logan's Run* is now in preproduction as a megabudget remake at Warner Bros. to be directed by Bryan Singer (of *X-Men* fame).

RICK PICKMAN—Pickman is a graphic designer who has designed theatre posters and programs, Web sites, and Flash animations (including an easter egg for the DVD of *The Haunted World of Edward D. Wood, Jr.*). As a photographer, his work has appeared in newspapers including the *Los Angeles Times* and *Daily News*, and *Fangoria* magazine. He has also provided illustrations for *Conjuring Dark Delicacies*, *The Altruistic Alphabet*, and Lisa Morton's *The Free Way*. "Dark Delicacies of the Dead" is Rick's first published piece of fiction. When not drawing or writing, his interests include collecting antique Halloween noisemakers and studying the written Chinese language. Oh, and he *really* likes zombie movies.

ROBERT STEVEN RHINE—Rhine has published fiction in over one hundred magazines and a dozen anthologies. His first book, *My Brain Escapes Me*, was heralded by *Publishers Weekly* as a "successful mix of humor and horror." In 1997, Rhine received the prestigious Herman M. Swafford Award for Fiction. His "humorrific" comic books, *Selected Reading from Satan's Powder Room*, *Chicken Soup for Satan*, and *Satan Gone Wild* led to the graphic novel *Satan's 3 Ring Circus of Hell*. Rhine wrote, produced, and starred in the filmed pilot, *Vinnie & Angela's Beauty Salon and Funeral Parlor*, grand prize winner at the Australian International Film Festival and Worldfest Houston. The film sold to Universal's Hypnotic Films and premiered on HBO in Canada. Rhine also wrote, produced, directed, and starred in the epic/cult/satire *Road Lawyers and Other Briefs*, winner at the Chicago, New York, Houston, and Australian film fests. The comedy was distributed by A.I.P. Rhine's animated pilot, Sickcom, is touring the world with *Spike & Mike's Sick and Twisted Festival of Animation*. In 2005, Robert won the fiction contest at the World Horror Convention. His Web site is www.RobertRhine.com.

DAVID J. SCHOW—Schow is a short story writer, novelist, screenwriter (teleplays and features), columnist, essayist, editor, photographer, and winner of the World Fantasy and International Horror Guild awards (for short fiction and nonfiction, respectively). Peripherally he has written everything from CD liner notes to book introductions to catalogue copy for monster toys. As expert witness, he appears in many genre-related documentaries, has traveled from New Zealand to Shanghai to Mexico City for the same, and recently turned to producing/writing/directing DVD supplements. He lives in a house on a hill in Los Angeles. His Web site is www.davidjschow.com.

D. LYNN SMITH—D. Lynn has spent the last fifteen years writing and producing such television shows as *The Trials of Rosie O'Neill*; *Murder, She Wrote*; *Dr. Quinn, Medicine Woman*; *Promised Land*; and *Touched by an Angel*. In addition to her television credits, Debbie has published nonfiction articles in the *Dark Shadows Almanac* and *Fangoria*, and has a short story slated for publication in *PanGaia*. She is currently working on a science fiction novel, *The Shaman's Gene*.

WHITLEY STRIEBER—Strieber is the author of many best-selling novels and works of nonfiction, and has had four movies based on his books. Among his best-known novels are *The Wolfen*, which was made into a film with Albert Finney and Gregory Hines, and *The Hunger*, which was made into a film with David Bowie, Susan Sarandon, and Catherine Deneuve. His chronicle of strange personal experiences, *Communion*, became a film starring Christopher Walken. Most recently, *The Coming Global Superstorm*, which he wrote with radio host Art Bell, became the basis for the 2004 film *The Day After Tomorrow*. He is the author of the Caldecott Award–winning children's book *Wolf of Shadows*, and two works of speculative fiction with James Kunetka, *Warday* and *Nature's End*. Strieber is best known for his nonfiction works about a series of unexplained personal experiences that appeared to some to involve alien contact. These books are

Communion, *Transformation*, *Breakthrough*, *The Secret School*, and *Confirmation*. In 2001, Strieber returned to the writing of fiction with *The Last Vampire* and *Lilith's Dream*. The two books are the basis of a miniseries in development at the Science Fiction Channel. His Web site, www.Unknown country.com, is the most popular edge science Web site in the world, with over a million monthly visitors generating fifty million-plus hits.

F. PAUL WILSON—F. Paul Wilson is the author of more than thirty books. His six science fiction novels include *Healer*, *Wheels Within Wheels*, and *An Enemy of the State*. He has also written eight horror novels, including *The Keep* (which became a movie directed by Michael Mann), *The Tomb*, *Reborn*, and *Sibs*. His three contemporary thrillers are *The Select*, *Implant*, and *Deep as the Marrow*. He has also collaborated on a number of novels. He has written seven novels chronicling the adventures of Repairman Jack (now optioned by Paramount Studios), including *Gateways* and *Crisscross*, and his newest novel is *Midnight Mass* (Tor). In 2005, Paul received the Grand Master Award at the World Horror Convention.

GAHAN WILSON—Gahan Wilson is an internationally famous *Playboy* cartoonist of the macabre, with dozens of collections of his cartoons in print. He is also a well-known and popular horror and mystery novelist. His many works include *Eddie Deco's Last Caper*, *Everybody's Favorite Duck*, and *Gravedigger's Party*.

CHELSEA QUINN YARBRO—A professional writer for more than thirty-five years, Yarbro has sold over seventy books and more than eighty works of short fiction and essays. She lives in her hometown—Berkeley, California—with three autocratic cats. In 2003, the World Horror Association presented her with a Grand Master Award.

COPYRIGHTS